"You are no gentleman!

"For, if you were, you would know emphatically I am not the kind of female to invite or enjoy a man's…"

Victoria's words dwindled. It really was rather tricky to phrase her thoughts and not be…crude.

"A man's…" Logan prompted, raising one dark eyebrow.

She met his speculative gaze and detected an abundance of silent laughter. She wanted to hurl the heavy book she cradled at him, but there was the matter of the ax.

"A man's physical attentions," she said through gritted teeth. "I may be the first one you've ever met, but let me assure you I am a lady."

"Well, then…"

"Well, then, *what*?" she fairly snarled at him.

"Who would have guessed ladies could be so hot-blooded?"

She flinched. "If my blood is hot, it's because you have the capacity to make me angrier than anyone I've ever met…!"

Dear Reader,

Beloved Outcast by Pat Tracy is a dramatic Western about an Eastern spinster who is hired by a man with a notorious reputation to tutor his adopted daughter. And those of you who have read Pat Tracy would probably agree with *Affaire de Coeur* when they recently labeled Pat as "one author definitely worth watching." This talented author just keeps getting better and better.

Whether writing atmospheric Medievals or sexy Regencies, Deborah Simmons continues to delight readers with her romantic stories. In this month's *Maiden Bride*, the sequel to *The Devil's Lady*, Nicholas de Laci transfers his blood lust to his enemy's niece, Gillian, his future wife by royal decree. Don't miss this wonderful tale.

Fans of *Romantic Times* Career Achievement Award winner Veronica Sattler will be thrilled to see this month's reissue of her Worldwide Library release, *Jesse's Lady*. We hope you'll enjoy this exciting story of a young heiress and her handsome guardian. And our fourth book this month is *The Wager* by Sally Cheney, the story of a young Englishwoman who reluctantly falls in love with a man who won her in a game of cards.

We hope you'll keep a lookout for all four titles wherever Harlequin Historicals are sold.

Sincerely,

Tracy Farrell
Senior Editor

PAT TRACY

Beloved OUTCAST

Harlequin Books

TORONTO • NEW YORK • LONDON
AMSTERDAM • PARIS • SYDNEY • HAMBURG
STOCKHOLM • ATHENS • TOKYO • MILAN
MADRID • WARSAW • BUDAPEST • AUCKLAND

ISBN 0-373-28933-2

BELOVED OUTCAST

This edition published by arrangement with Harlequin Books S.A.

® and TM are trademarks of the publisher. Trademarks indicated with ® are registered in the United States Patent and Trademark Office, the Canadian Trade Marks Office and in other countries.

Printed in U.S.A.

Books by Pat Tracy

Harlequin Historicals

The Flaming #121
Winter Fire #188
Saddle the Wind #273
Beloved Outcast #333

PAT TRACY

lives in a farming community outside of Idaho Falls. Pat's love of historical romance began when she was thirteen and read *Gone with the Wind*. After reading Rhett and Scarlett's story, Pat immediately penned a hasty sequel wherein the couple lived happily ever after. According to Pat, there is a magic to be found in historical romances that can be found nowhere else, and she enjoys reading the many popular and talented writers who share that magic with their readers. You can write to the author at the following address:

P.O. Box 17
Ucon, Idaho 83454

This book is dedicated to Sheriann Tracy, my youngest daughter, who is funny, smart, brave, strong-willed, independent, athletic, artistic and beautiful. Sweetheart, you're definitely heroine material.

Mother's Note: A couple of months after this dedication was written, Sheriann was killed in an automobile accident. She was fourteen. Darling, you have my heart—always. Love, Mom

* * * * * *

Acknowledgments:

I would like to thank Sherry Roseberry, Vicki Scaggs and Martha Tew, gifted writers and true friends. Without your generous editing efforts, I would look sooo foolish. (I'm thinking particularly of my hero being "within" instead of "without.") And thank you, Patti McAllister, for your last-minute read of the final version. Thank you. Thank you. Thank you.

Chapter One

Idaho Territory, 1868

"Sit down, Youngblood."

Logan Youngblood stared at the army-issue revolver pointed at his chest. "Somehow this isn't quite the welcome I expected, Colonel Windham."

The mustached cavalry officer gestured with the Remington's barrel toward the chair that faced his desk. "By your own account, you rode for two days and a night to warn us about the fort being attacked. Surely you could do with a rest."

The only outward evidence of the colonel's displeasure, other than the drawn weapon, was reflected in his cold blue eyes.

Logan glanced at the other three uniformed men present. They were young lieutenants, dressed in pristine dark blue uniforms trimmed with enough newly minted gold braid to make a dead man stand up and salute. From their uneasy expressions, though, he could tell they were baffled by their commanding officer's behavior.

Logan moved toward the waiting chair. Until he found out what was going on, he would accept Windham's not-so-gracious hospitality. Unexpectedly, Logan's thoughts turned to Madison, and what would happen to her, should the gun barrel he was staring down serve its intended purpose.

But then, Madison's tumultuous arrival in his life seemed to herald the beginning of a series of complications, not the least of which was the necessity of securing a qualified woman to educate the twelve-year-old girl.

"Wait a minute," the colonel ordered tersely. "Take his gun, Lawson."

"Sir?" the young soldier queried, as if he weren't sure he understood the order.

"You heard me."

Logan stood perfectly still as the Colt .44 he'd taken to wearing since coming west was extracted from his holster. He didn't know what Windham was up to, but he was fairly certain the officer wouldn't shoot him in front of three witnesses.

Logan claimed the proffered chair.

"Tie him up," came the next tight-lipped command.

Logan shot to his feet. "Enough is enough, Windham. I came here to warn you that several tribes are planning to attack. Now that I've done that, I'm going to ride out of here and—"

The ominous click of a service revolver being cocked interrupted Logan. His attention again focused on the drawn gun.

"I don't like Indian-lovers, Youngblood. As far as I'm concerned I'd be doing the entire territory a favor by killing you where you stand. Unfortunately, because I am civilized, I have to obey the law. So, by the letter of that law, I'm placing you under military arrest for abetting murderous redskins. Now sit the hell down!"

The revolver's nine-inch barrel remained steady. With four armed soldiers against one unarmed civilian, the odds weren't exactly in his favor. Still, having survived countless Civil War battles and his first few hazardous months in the Idaho Territory, Logan felt reasonably calm. He couldn't see his life ending in this room. He was grateful, however, as he eased onto the chair, that he hadn't put off seeing to Madison's future. Thank God his good friend and associate Martin Pritchert had already made arrangements to bring a tutor from the East to instruct the uneducated girl. Since she was now legally Logan's ward, she would be cared for no matter what happened to him. For the time being, Martin's wife was watching over Madison.

It took all the self-discipline Logan possessed for him to submit to having his hands tied behind the back of the chair while another length of rope was secured around his ankles.

"Your time has run out, Youngblood." Windham pushed his face an inch from Logan's. "I want to know where those murdering savages are camped, and I want to know now."

Logan stared into Windham's unyielding features. Somehow, even though he suspected the military man was beyond reasoning with, Logan had to convince him that not all Indians were "murdering savages."

"Night Wolf's people are at peace," he pointed out flatly. "They had nothing to do with attacking the families on that wagon train, and they won't have any part of assaulting the fort."

Windham turned his back to Logan and, with careful deliberateness, laid his gleaming revolver upon the desk. Then, without warning, the officer spun around and plowed his fist into Logan's jaw.

The chair he'd been tied to scraped stridently against the wood-planked floor. Logan's head shot back, but the pain was tolerable. Windham didn't pack much of a punch, which was true of most small men wrapped in gold-spangled uniforms.

"That was the wrong answer, Youngblood."

Through a dull haze of pain, Logan noticed a loop of spittle hanging from the colonel's curled upper lip. The frozen image of a mad dog Logan had seen once as a boy in Scotland danced briefly in his thoughts. Yet Windham's manner remained eerily calm.

"It's the only answer I've got." Logan's gaze went to the three other men in Windham's office. Each soldier wore a look of distaste. Logan didn't know whether their grim expressions were a result of their commanding officer's violent behavior or Logan's refusal to provide them with directions to Night Wolf's camp.

"Leave me alone with the prisoner," Windham ordered abruptly. Open contempt radiated from his pale blue eyes.

"Sir, do you think that's a good idea?" one of the young lieutenants questioned, his voice notched with uncertainty.

"He's tied up, Lawson," Windham answered with heavy sarcasm. "There's no danger of him getting free and doing me any harm."

"Uh, sir—he did bring the warning about the Blackfeet and other tribes going on the warpath."

"He won't tell us where to find them," Windham snarled. "I want to wipe out every heathen man, woman and child infesting the Idaho Territory."

"But this is Mr. Youngblood here," Lawson pointed out, his tone placating. "He's the president of the Territorial Bank."

"Are you questioning a direct order, soldier?"

Lawson's cherub cheeks reddened as he snapped to attention. "No, Sir!"

The two other cavalrymen present were already filing from the room. It didn't take the young lieutenant long to rethink his tenuous position with his commanding officer and follow them.

When the door shut behind the departing soldiers, an oppressive silence filled the commandant's office.

"Well, Youngblood, it's just you and me now."

"Under the circumstances," Logan drawled, his gaze lowering to his bound arms, "I'm sure you'll excuse me for not shaking your hand."

"Always the clever retort." Windham retrieved his gun from his desk. "You cut quite the figure with the ladies, don't you?"

"What?" Obviously he hadn't heard the officer correctly.

"'Passion's Pirate,' that's what they call you," Windham continued, his neatly trimmed mustache tilting to one side as he made the sneering observation.

"*What?*" Logan repeated. This time he knew he couldn't have heard the cavalryman correctly. *Passion's Pirate?* What the hell was the man babbling about? Logan had never been to sea, and—

"You didn't know?" Windham's tone was skeptical. "That's what the few good women of Trinity Falls call you when they're gossiping about your bedroom exploits with the town's bad women."

Logan knew his mouth was hanging open. He felt as if he'd stepped from the orderly, rational world of his daily existence into a bizarre nightmare. What interest could this pompous, Indian-hating cavalry officer have in his love life?

"Athena is one of them."

A sense of doom gripped Logan. "Athena?"

"My wife," Windham responded softly. "My beautiful, *faithless* wife. You remember her. After all, it's hardly been a week since you bedded her."

The accusation brought sudden clarity to the strange episode. Unfortunately, it also brought the unsettling memory of the woman...groping him when her husband's back was turned.

"That's what this is all about," Logan said warily. "You think I've been with your wife."

"Don't deny it. Your guilty expression says it all. I saw how you looked at her. Every man looks at her that way. Every man wants her, but until you came along, she was loyal to me."

"You've lost your senses. I haven't touched your wife. Damnation, I've only seen her three times. You were with her on every occasion."

That much was true. Except for the minor detail of Mrs. Windham damn near giving him a heart attack when she bumped against him and her fingertips rested momentarily against the front closure of his trousers. Logan had been so stunned by the unexpected contact he almost yelped.

Another memory knifed through Logan. He shifted against the ropes binding him. Six years ago, the protestations of the older brother he loved and admired had rung in Logan's ears. Burke had denied seducing Logan's fiancée. The difference between then and now was that Burke had lied, and Logan spoke the truth.

The officer laughed bitterly. "Am I supposed to believe the denials of 'Passion's Pirate'?"

"I can't be held accountable for the gossip frustrated women spin."

"Athena isn't frustrated!"

"I don't give a tinker's damn about the details of your married life, Colonel. I came to the fort to warn you that an Indian attack is imminent. Night Wolf's band has been beaten down to a few old men and some women and children. They are not a threat to you, but you'd better start making plans about how you're going to fight off the Shoshones and the Blackfeet tribes who *are* on the warpath."

Windham's head snapped back as if he'd been struck. "Don't presume to give me orders, Youngblood."

"Think of them as suggestions," Logan answered grimly. "Are you ready to untie me?"

"Untie you?" The man's mouth curved mockingly. "You must be insane to think I'd do that now."

Logan knew one of them was insane. Unfortunately for him, it was the man with the Remington.

Chapter Two

Victoria Amory wrapped her fingers around the wide leather reins and tugged with all her might. The oxen pulling her covered wagon came to a belligerent stop. She craned her head, looking in all directions, but saw no evidence of human habitation in the lush wilderness known as the Idaho Territory. Nor was there any sign of the fort she'd been told was nearby. After four days alone on the trail, she calculated that she was still sixty miles or so from the town of Trinity Falls, where her new employer and her new life awaited her.

Victoria rose to better survey her primitive surroundings. There was no way she could have been more alone—if she didn't count the birds trilling to each other and periodically bursting skyward in clusters of raucous mayhem. The entire forest was in a state of continuous animation as squirrels and other small animals scurried through the fertile underbrush.

"Can anybody hear me?" she called.

In response, there was only the endless shifting of pungent pine boughs and fluttering of the coin-size green leaves that graced the narrow, white-trunked aspen trees dotting meadows of mountain grass. It was foolish to expect a reply, yet she was still disappointed. She'd had such high hopes when she accepted Martin Pritchert's letter offering her employment as a live-in tutor for his employer's ward.

A new beginning had sounded so appealing. Her purpose in leaving Boston outweighed the little pricks of doubt that occasionally pierced her resolve. With her reputation in shreds, her continued presence at home had become an embarrassment she refused to inflict upon her family.

Not wishing to dwell on that sad truth, Victoria consoled herself with the hope that, since she was now out of the picture, her sister, Annalee, would be free to accept one of the numerous marriage proposals she'd received. No amount of arguing from Victoria had managed to convince her parents that their younger daughter should be allowed to wed before their elder one.

Victoria sighed. She was twenty-four years old and she had yet to meet a man she wanted to call husband. Still, because of her parents' old-fashioned beliefs, the second item of business she needed to accomplish in Trinity Falls was to find herself a spouse. It seemed the least she could do for Annalee, who was the kindest, most loving sister anyone could wish for.

The wheels of Victoria's mind turned with the same steady rhythm as those of the lumbering wagon. Perhaps she really didn't need to marry before Annalee. Maybe it would satisfy her parents' archaic code of propriety if she was *engaged* to be wed. Now that she was almost a thousand miles from home, she would be free to do a little...creative letter-writing. Naturally, an outright falsehood was beyond her, but she could exaggerate—

The right front wheel struck a deep rut, and the wagon lurched violently as Victoria was bucked upward, then slammed against the wooden seat. Just that quickly, her thoughts jerked back to her immediate circumstances.

Her great Western adventure was falling far short of her expectations. Who would have supposed that the wagon train would continue without her because she was unable to keep up? It had shocked her that the wagon master couldn't comprehend that, even if she was slowing down the group, she simply couldn't abandon her precious cargo along the trail.

Victoria harbored no ill feelings toward the man. He and the others didn't understand that her treasured volumes, some of them first editions of Jane Austen and James Fenimore Cooper, were impossible for her to part with.

Initially, she hadn't been all that alarmed at being left behind. The overland trail was wide, and clearly marked by the hundreds of wagons that had preceded her west. She had plenty of food, and the obliging nearness of the Ruby River provided all the fresh drinking water she and her team needed. Also, the wagon master had assured her that a fort was nearby. Once she reached the fort she'd arrange for a party of soldiers to escort her to Trinity Falls.

But the loneliness had begun to wear upon her nerves, and there was the matter of the fearsome Indian warriors she'd heard so much about. It would have been somewhat reassuring to have a firearm for protection. Unfortunately, she'd had a slight mishap with her rifle the fifth day on the trail, and the wagon master had confiscated the weapon from her on the grounds that she was a menace to both herself and the rest of them with a loaded gun in her possession.

Victoria frowned. Goodness, she could hardly be faulted for shooting Mr. Hyrum Dodson in the foot. The man *had* been prowling around her wagon in the wee hours of the morning. And he very well could have been the bear she'd mistaken him for. As far as she was concerned, it was an understandable error on her part.

Neither the wagon master nor Mr. Dodson, however, had been inclined to be understanding.

Which brought Victoria to her third reason for going west. It seemed that people in general were disinclined to be tolerant of life's little mishaps. For instance, take the innocent incident when one of her sister's suitors had been caught with his pants at half-mast in Victoria's bedchamber. Had anyone been interested in hearing that the hapless man had scaled the outside trellis and was delivering a rose to Annalee?

Not that she wouldn't be the first to admit that his romantic gesture was the stuff of foolishness. But, foolish though it might have been, the cavalier act had been conceived and executed in innocence. It had been the merest accident that he chose the wrong bedchamber.

Unfortunately, at the instant of his arrival, Victoria had been changing and had been in her chemise and drawers. She wasn't sure which of them had been more startled when they laid shocked gazes upon each other. Before he could depart her chamber, however, a crazed bumblebee had emerged from the bedraggled rose, circled Mr. Threadgill twice and then flown up the inside of his pant leg.

Victoria had acted without forethought, tugging down the man's britches and landing several energetic whacks upon the trapped but clearly homicidal bee with her hairbrush.

If only Threadgill hadn't screamed . . .

Her mother's afternoon guests, the Reverend Golly's wife among them, had heard Horace's distressed cries and come charging upstairs. It had been the most mortifying occasion of Victoria's life to be caught in a state of undress on her knees in front of the hysterical, half-clad man.

No one had been interested in explanations that day. The scandalized women had departed from her parents' home and spread the most outrageous gossip about the entirely innocent episode. In a single afternoon, Victoria's reputation had been hopelessly tarnished. Poor Mr. Threadgill had vacated his Boston abode. The last she'd heard, he'd decided to visit the Continent.

No doubt he'd been afraid that he would be obligated to redeem her reputation with a proposal of marriage. Clearly, the man had no intention of making such a drastic act of restitution on the basis of one demented bee and her honor.

She still couldn't get over the fact that an entire lifetime of prudent and circumspect behavior could be overturned by one unfortunate occurrence. The very idea that anyone could think she would try to divest a man of his britches, against his will, and assert her runaway passions upon him was ludicrous.

She shook the reins.

"Ha!"

The oxen stayed put. Perhaps they were as weary as she was and needed a good rest. She would have loved to accommodate them, but she knew they had to keep moving. Determinedly she reached for the unwieldy bullwhip and cracked it over their broad backs.

"I said, *Ha!*" This time they moved toward the horizon where high-peaked mountains towered. Victoria laid aside the whip and used her sleeve to wipe the perspiration from her face.

The twisting river caused the flattened thoroughfare that ran alongside it to wind around yet another bend. When she rounded the curve, a large edifice several hundred yards away greeted Victoria. She blinked several times, lest it somehow disappear into nothingness. The building remained.

She'd finally made it to human habitation. Victoria strained to discern what the distant structure might be. Then she laughed at herself. Even if it wasn't the fort, it didn't matter. In her present mood, even a saloon would be welcome.

People lived there.

That was the only thing that mattered.

As she drew closer, the large building miraculously revealed itself to indeed be a military outpost. Relief swept through her. She was safe. For as long as she remained at...

Victoria squinted, trying to make out the name that had been crudely burned into a wide plank of wood suspended horizontally above the great open gate.

Fort Brockton.

Seeing the giant log poles less than twenty yards ahead filled Victoria with an overwhelming sense of euphoria. One by one, the tense muscles in her neck and shoulders relaxed.

A gust of wind came up. With it came a lonely, mournful cry that made the fine hairs at the nape of her neck rise.

Despite the reality of the immense log structure, Victoria was struck by the eerie impression that she was the last woman on earth. The jangle of leather harnesses and the plodding of her team's hooves joined the whispering screech of air rushing through and around the fort's timbers.

Her stomach knotted, and she tried to talk herself out of the nebulous fears that scurried through the corners of her mind. Only a few feet now separated her from the wide log doors, which gaped open with a kind of drunken clumsiness.

She halted. No uniformed man stared down from the fort's watchtowers. No concerned soldier surged forward to draw her wagon inside protective walls. No sound of occupation reached her. Tingles of alarm scraped her skin. Simultaneously, a fierce blast of wind battered her sunbonnet. Victoria flinched at the almost physical assault and peeled back the tendrils of hair the disturbance had plastered to her cheek and mouth.

"Hello?"

The uncertain greeting was plucked from her lips and swallowed up by the wind that rollicked around her.

"Ha!"

Her voice was stronger, and she again urged the oxen forward. The sinister sense of danger permeating the trembling pines and aspen trees drove her to seek the tangible security of the empty fortress. No matter how bizarre the circumstances, surely being *inside* was safer than being out.

Victoria studied the fort's deserted inner courtyard. Compact buildings that were a mixture of military offices and personal dwellings shared common walls, so that it appeared she was looking at a small town enclosed by high ramparts.

Every door hung ajar.

"Hello!" she called again.

Silence answered her. She was simply unable to grasp that a fortress this size, one obviously designed to hold several hundred people, could actually have been abandoned.

Victoria climbed from the wagon, forcing back the uneasiness that continued to grow within her. The oxen were restless. She assumed they smelled the water inside the low rock cisterns that stood beside the empty corrals. Her mind balked at the realization that the huge animals would have to be unhitched in order to drink.

She was so blasted tired she was all but staggering.

And yet there was only her and the oxen. If they were going to be watered, it was up to her to do it. Their survival was in her hands. Blinking back tears of weariness, she went to the lead oxen's giant halter. Simple wishing wouldn't get the arduous task done. As she slid the leather harnesses through fist-size coupling rings, Victoria reflected that beginning a new life on the Western frontier was a far tougher endeavor than she'd imagined when she contemplated the contract Mr. Pritchert had sent her. Of course, she'd signed the document in the comfort of her family's cozy parlor. How far away that parlor seemed at this moment.

When she had finally freed the animals to drink, Victoria proceeded to search every building that lined the fort's interior. Each office and residence showed signs of urgent flight. Drawers were left open, their varied contents spilled onto the floor in wild heaps of clutter. Beds and blankets were in a state of upheaval.

In the largest office, it appeared that a whirlwind had come charging through. Papers and maps were tossed about. A chair was tipped over, and several lengths of rope lay on the floor.

No matter how exhausted she was, she had to *think*. What terrible menace could have caused the commanding officer to evacuate his troops?

The incredible, numbing silence of the deserted military facility heightened her already taut nerves. For the first time in her life, she didn't know what to do next.

It seemed madness to stay in a place that an armed militia had fled. Her shoulders sagged as she turned from the doorway and retraced her steps across the military yard. Returning to the unhitched wagon, she scarcely registered the presence of a squat log stockade. She was tired and hungry—a poor set of circumstances under which to make anything but a bad decision. Perhaps things wouldn't seem quite so bleak if she took care of the gnawing emptiness in her stomach. Who knew, if her legs ceased to tremble and she didn't feel quite so light-headed, she might be able to make sense of her macabre surroundings?

Within minutes, Victoria had set up a campsite in the middle of the military yard. Early in her exodus west, she'd learned the subtle nuances of building a vigorous fire.

To prepare the biscuits, all she needed was some coarse brown flour, salt, water and a bit of grease. It took no time at all to knead the dough into egg-size lumps and drop them into the bubbling grease that lined the thick frying skillet. The simple action gave her a sense of being in control.

Dusk fell across the buildings silhouetted by her fire. The frying dough sent a pleasant aroma through the cooling air. She reached across the rocks she'd interspersed with pieces of wood and used a long-handled fork to spear and flip the biscuits.

"Who the hell are you?"

The husky male voice leaped from the encroaching darkness and vibrated in the very air Victoria drew into her lungs. She jumped back from the campfire, dropping her fork. She scoured the deepening shadows for a clue as to where the intruder lurked.

"I asked you..." There was a pause, as if the man were catching his breath "...a question." The gritty voice tugged at her nerves with the same raspy irritation as the gravelly rocks that shifted beneath the soles of her shoes. "Did Windham send you to let me out?"

Out?

Her gaze pivoted to the small stockade just ten feet from where she'd built her campfire. With stomach-tightening dread, she realized she wasn't alone after all.

The smell of frying dough drew her attention to the biscuits. They were about to burn; she refused to let that happen. With a well-aimed kick, the toe of her shoe dislodged the long-handled fork from where it had landed. The hem of her petticoats served as a pot holder as she wielded the rod to salvage the biscuits.

"Who's out there?" came the low voice again.

Victoria thought she detected both wariness and anger in the deep, masculine voice. After she retrieved the last biscuit and set it on a china plate to cool, she approached the stockade. She wiped her palms against her skirts and took comfort in the sight of the metal beam lodged between two iron posts that guaranteed the prison door wouldn't come flying open. Surely only the most hardened, most vile, of villains would have been locked inside such a horrible, crude cell.

Ah, but to be abandoned to a slow and painful death by starvation . . .

Every soft and feminine instinct she possessed urged her to set him free. What crime could have been so heinous as to warrant such cruel punishment?

Murder, came the immediate answer. A murderer might be left to such an awful fate.

Victoria continued to stare in horrified fascination at the simple but effective bar laid across the stockade's entry.

It struck her suddenly that she was responsible not only for the oxen under her care, but also for the nameless prisoner on the other side of the rough wooden door. Unless the cavalry suddenly returned, it would be up to her whether or not this man lived or died.

"Answer me, dammit! Who are you?"

Victoria looked from the door to her shaking hands. Even though she might pity the stranger for being left to die this way, she would be a fool to let him out before discovering the crime he'd committed. She would also be a fool to let him know he was talking to a woman, she thought, reasoning that men credited other men with more intelligence than they did the weaker sex.

She coughed twice and lowered her voice as best she could.

"The question, sir, is who are you, and what did you do to land in such an awful situation?"

Chapter Three

Logan strained to hear the muffled question. Battered and hurting from the beating Windham had ordered, he'd lost track of how much time had passed since he'd been locked inside the stockade. He'd drunk the last of his water a few hours back.

"Sir, I asked you who you are," came that suspicious sounding voice again.

Logan shook his head to clear it. He must have been unconscious for most of the day. It had been the glorious aroma of cooking food that nudged him to full alertness. He could have sworn someone had pitched camp outside his cell door.

Saliva pooled in his mouth, and his tongue seemed twice its normal size. Hot food. His stomach shuddered in sweet anticipation.

"The name's Logan," he growled, relieved the newcomer's arrival hadn't been a hallucination. "Logan Youngblood. How about letting me out of here and sharing some of that food? While you're at it, I'd appreciate a drink of water."

The only response to his request was more silence. Frustration, and the possibility that he was going to pass out again and never come to, snapped Logan's patience.

"What are you waiting for? Open the damned door!"

"I don't think that would be a good idea. The soldiers who put you in there must have had a good reason."

Outraged, Logan couldn't believe he'd heard the newcomer right. "You mean you're going to leave me in here to die?"

There was another silence.

"That would make you a murderer," Logan pressed, anger gnawing holes in his control.

"I—I wasn't the one who put you in there."

"When they locked me up, they took away my gun," he pointed out, just in case the nature of his plight wasn't clear. "I'm unarmed and ready to pass out."

More silence.

"Even if you're alone, you've got to be carrying a rifle or a shotgun or a pistol," Logan persisted. "How can I be a threat?"

Silence.

He ground his teeth, which made his head hurt all the worse. "Say something, damn you."

"You swear too much."

"Say something relevant."

"I'm not letting you out until—"

"Hell freezes over?" he said savagely.

"Are you wounded?"

The words seemed closer. For the first time, Logan thought he detected a note of concern in the stranger's tone. His hopes rose about the time his legs gave out.

"Some cracked ribs, and a headache that's strong enough to split my skull in two," he admitted hoarsely.

"I'm sorry."

"Then let me out."

"What did you do?"

Even though the question was reasonable, Logan's control unraveled further. "What does it matter? I told you, I'm too weak to cause you any trouble."

"You could be lying. Perhaps you have a…club. If I were to open the door, you could attack me," came the husky voice.

"So shoot me."

More silence. An incredible notion struck him.

"Don't tell me you don't have a gun!"

Silence.

Logan swore feelingly. "What kind of fool comes poking around Idaho Territory without a gun?"

"Fortunately, there happens to be a cannon nearby," came the snippy answer.

Logan suddenly was struck by a mental flash of what the unexpected visitor might look like.

A *boy*.

That would explain the odd fluctuations he heard in the low voice from time to time. It would also explain why the lad had such tender ears, and why he was afraid to let Logan out of the stockade. It all fit. A wave of reluctant sympathy tugged at Logan. A lot of young men had shown up in Trinity Falls, hoping to fill their pockets with gold. To them, every stranger was a potential enemy.

"You don't have to raise the bolt to feed me, kid. Just shove some of that food you've been cooking through the small opening at the bottom of the door. I'll pass you my canteen, and you can fill it at the well."

"Why did you call me kid?" came the definitely edgy query.

"Hit the nail on the head, didn't I?"

"I'm no child."

"I'm sure you've traveled far and faced your share of hardships," he conceded. "Now how about that food and water?"

The metal grate came up abruptly. No light flooded through the puny opening. Logan realized night had fallen. He fumbled in the darkness for his empty canteen and pushed it through the open grate. Then he waited.

"Here," came the gruff voice.

Logan cupped his hand beneath the slot. A fragrant, warm lump fell into his palm. When he took his first bite of the biscuit, his taste buds wept more saliva. Considering the exacting standards he expected from the hotel chef at the Prairie Rose, his starvation must be at an advanced level for him to take delight in such humble fare. Of course, when he lived with the Shoshone, he'd learned to appreciate simply cooked foods.

Moments later, his canteen rolled to his feet. He sat on the ground with his back against the log wall and tipped his head, letting the life-sustaining liquid trickle down his dry throat. Nothing had ever tasted so good, except for—

"Do you have any whiskey you'd like to share, kid?"

"Certainly not! And stop calling me kid."

"Don't tell me," Logan said. "Your folks don't approve of a man enjoying liquor now and again."

"That's right!"

Somehow he wasn't surprised. "I finished my biscuit. Do you have any more?"

The grate came up, and Logan held out his hand expectantly. *Three* more biscuits filled his palm. If he was a religious man, he might have burst into hallelujahs.

"You're a good cook, kid," Logan said around a mouthful of filling bread. "Do you do it for a living?" In between sips of water, Logan savored his third biscuit. "What's your name?"

A hesitation followed his question. *What else was new?*

"Amory."

Despite his desperate circumstances, Logan discovered, he could still smile. "That a first or a last name?"

"Last."

"Got a first initial you'd like to share, or do you want me calling you Amory?"

Silence.

"You don't talk much." A feeling of welcome fullness coupled with incredible fatigue washed over Logan. "That's fine with me, Amory."

Silence.

Logan's eyelids drifted shut.

"V.!"

The strident shout fairly rocked the stockade door. Logan chuckled. His ribs made their presence known. Grimacing, he sank onto a pallet. That he could find anything amusing in his present predicament suggested that he might live after all.

"V.A. it is." Logan was going to have to tell him that each time he lost his temper, his youthful voice went up several notches.

Now that he had some food in his stomach, Logan's exhaustion caught up with him. He told himself he'd rest a bit before trying to convince the youth to release him.

Victoria looked down for several moments at the small, square hole into which she'd shoved the prisoner's food and water. Then she pushed shut the metal grate and stepped from the cell.

She bit her lip, trying not to feel guilty about keeping the wretched man inside the stockade. Yet the plain and simple truth was, she did feel sorry for Mr. Logan Youngblood. Not sorry enough, however, to risk her life by setting the foul-spoken criminal free. At least not until she'd discovered what he'd done to warrant such harsh punishment. Only a simpleton would ignore the fact that he'd been abandoned to certain death. It stood to reason that Logan Youngblood's sins must be black indeed.

Victoria set about tidying the campsite. The familiar ritual brought a measure of peace. Later, she stretched out upon the blankets she'd spread beneath the wagon. For once, because of the smoothness of the military yard, no sharp sticks or rocks poked through her bedding and into her skin.

Even though the fort was filled with available beds, Victoria wasn't tempted to spend the night in any of them. Too fresh in her memory was the eerie sensation of standing in empty rooms and feeling the ghostly presence of their former occupants.

"Amory, get your butt over here!"

The surly command jerked Victoria from the few minutes of extra sleep she'd tried to steal from the brightening dawn. She sat up and promptly rammed her forehead against the wagon's underbelly. A disorienting wave of pain shot through her skull. Simultaneously, her back muscles protested the sudden movement. She pressed her eyelids shut and waited for the shocks to her body to lessen before crawling from beneath the wagon.

"Move it, Amory. We've got to get out of here!"

Victoria glared balefully at the stockade.

"I was asleep," she said, her voice groggy.

"Kid, if you don't haul your butt over here and let me out, we're both going to be meat for the buzzards."

In the morning light, the stockade was a small, crude building that looked both forbidding and forlorn. She steeled herself against any further sympathy for Mr. Youngblood, locked inside its dark interior. Again, she reminded herself that the man must be an evildoer of the blackest sort, and therefore was suffering only what he deserved.

Her jaw tightened. "Relax, Mr. Youngblood. No buzzard is going to get you while you're inside your cell."

As she waited for the prisoner's response, Victoria's stomach rolled over. She'd forgotten to disguise her voice as that of a man! Apprehensive, she awaited Logan's next words.

"Kid, just how old are you?"

Victoria couldn't tear her gaze from the small log building. She coughed once, then cleared her throat and tried to speak from the region of her toes. "Old enough."

"Ten? Twelve?"

"None of your business."

"I'm going to make this simple. Any time now, several bands of Indians are going to ride down upon this fort. If the United States Army didn't care to hang around for the outcome, don't you think you should reconsider setting up a camp here?"

At the open scorn coating the prisoner's question, Victoria winced. She looked toward the fort's gaping entrance. Perhaps she should have closed the gate behind her.

"Look, kid—" The man broke off. "*Amory,* the Indians plan on burning Fort Brockton to the ground. They don't intend on taking any prisoners. Unless you want a burning arrow through the gut, I suggest we get the hell out of here."

"How do you know they're coming?" Victoria asked, her throat muscles tight.

"That doesn't matter. What's important is that we—"

"What do you mean, *we?*" she demanded, hating the new fear Logan Youngblood's words had unleashed within her. "I told you, I'm not letting you out until you tell me what your crime was."

"Do you honestly think you have a choice?"

"Yes, I think just that."

"Dammit, you need all the help you can get. One snot-nosed kid isn't going to hold off a band of revenge-minded Indians."

"I told you, I'm not—"

"I've got ears, Amory. You sound about ten to me. I don't know what in blazes you're doing running around the Idaho Territory on your own. But I do know that, if you intend to see eleven, you better haul yourself over here and unbolt this door."

"Why didn't you tell me this last night?" Victoria asked, wondering if Logan Youngblood was making up this new threat to scare her into freeing him.

"I was only thinking about the hole in my stomach that needed filling," came the clearly grudging admission. "I must have passed out afterward."

"And this morning you came to with the sudden recollection that this fort was about to be attacked?"

"That's right, boy. We need to get to Trinity Falls."

Trinity Falls—exactly where she wanted to be.

"Why did they lock you up, Mr. Youngblood?" she repeated, wondering if she could believe anything he told her. Obviously, it served his best interests to lie.

There was a distinct pause.

"I brought the warning of the attack."

"And they put you in the stockade for that?" Victoria couldn't suppress her disappointment that he would prevaricate in this dire situation.

"Not exactly."

"Well, what was it *exactly*, Mr. Youngblood?"

"They wanted to know how I knew the Indians' plans."

"A most sensible question," she pointed out.

"I told them Night Wolf had warned me."

"Night Wolf?"

"He's an . . . acquaintance of mine."

"Really?" Victoria asked, intrigued that anyone should count an Indian among his circle of acquaintances. "How did you meet?"

"That's hardly important."

"I suppose not." Still, she was curious about such an odd circumstance. "Why did Night Wolf warn you about the attack?"

"He realizes that more bloodshed will only make it harder for his people to coexist peacefully with the white man."

"I see."

Victoria knew she was in the minority in sympathizing with the primitives. To her, they seemed like beautiful and free people who were rapidly losing their home in a land that had sheltered them for generations. If only there could be an end to the violence that raged between the settlers and the Indians, and a place could be preserved for the country's native inhabitants.

"You still haven't told me why they locked you up."

"I refused to lead Colonel Windham to Night Wolf's camp."

"Why on earth would you object to doing that?"

"I told you, Night's Wolf's people are at peace."

"Then they have nothing to worry about."

"Boy, you can't be green enough to believe that."

Victoria's teeth clicked together. "I'm smart enough to stay out of jail."

"But foolish enough to land in the middle of Indian country during a war."

"Mr. Youngblood?"

"Yes?"

"Are you comfortable in your cell?"

"Not really."

"That's unfortunate, because at this rate you're going to remain there."

"Amory, we're running out of time." A pounding blow sent a flurry of dust motes flying from the stockade door.

She jumped back. "Stop that!"

"Listen to me, you stubborn brat—the Indians *are* coming."

"So you said."

"And you don't believe me?" he asked, his tone furious. "Where the hell do you think everybody went? To a barn raising?"

Victoria stood before the barred entry and eyed the heavy beam holding it closed. For the first time, she was tempted to unlatch it. If the man was telling the truth about having brought news of an attack, he didn't deserve to die.

The sun's rays bore down. She closed her eyes and sent a hasty prayer heavenward, asking for divine guidance.

"Kid?"

The deep voice was relentless.

No answer came to her prayer, at least not in the form of words. But as she stared at the stockade, a sense of inevitability washed over her. The plain and simple truth was that she was incapable of leaving Mr. Youngblood to rot inside his log prison.

"I'm going to open the door."

"When?"

She struggled to lift the heavy bar lodged tightly between the metal posts. "Now."

"Smart move, Amory," came the approving voice. "We'll ride hard and fast for Trinity Falls."

"And, once we're there, we'll be safe?"

"Since the last gold strike, the town's swollen to more than five thousand miners," he informed her. "It's in no danger of being attacked. Do you have a good horse?"

"No." A splinter stabbed her index finger. "I've got a team of oxen."

"Well, hell, what kind of time do you think we're going to make with oxen?"

"They may not be fast, but they're steady. And they've had time to rest. They'll pull my wagon just fine."

Victoria gave up trying to raise the bar with her bare hands and went to fetch her cooking fork. She was sure it was sturdy enough to dislodge the metal beam.

"You've got a wagon?"

Her efforts began to noticeably budge the crossbar. "That's right."

"I don't like the idea of using a wagon."

The heavy iron arm finally came free and toppled to the ground. The stockade door swung outward, revealing a sinister black hole.

The prisoner stepped toward the light. "Wheel tracks are too easy to follow."

Without the barrier of the log portal between them, the deep voice sounded alarmingly close.

"We're going to need the wagon. I refuse to leave my precious cargo behind."

Mr. Youngblood emerged from the shadowed doorway, blinking against the sudden onslaught of sunlight.

"Precious cargo—?" He broke off abruptly. She saw his dark eyes narrow at the sight of her. "Well, hell . . ."

The observation was his, the sentiment hers.

Chapter Four

The man before Victoria was unlike any she'd ever seen. He filled her entire field of vision and, with every foot he drew closer, seemed to grow in stature. Her mouth went dry, and she took a stumbling step back.

The morning breeze ruffled the tattered remnants of a white shirt that, despite its torn state, managed to adhere to his muscular shoulders. She had never seen an uncovered male chest before, and thus was unprepared for the shocking sight of the lush pelt of black hair that grazed his bared flesh. Goodness, surely no American Indian roaming the western plains could appear more awesomely proportioned than Logan Youngblood.

Or more distressingly primitive.

"Where's the kid?"

The gruff question jerked her gaze from his almost naked torso to a dark pair of glittering eyes. She swallowed. The man looked as if he'd been pummeled by an angry mob. His blackened right eye was almost swollen shut. He also sported a bruised, whiskered jaw and a split bottom lip.

The single thought that danced in her head was that, if she hadn't released the devil himself from the stockade, she'd surely freed one of his henchmen to murder, plunder and pillage.

"The—the kid?" she repeated stupidly.

He took another step forward. She tipped her head back to keep his daunting visage in view.

"The one I've been talking to since last night."

"I *told* you I wasn't a child," she answered, hearing the wobble in her voice and regretting it.

His savage gaze shriveled to a blistering slit. "You mean all this time I've been talking to *you? A female?*"

The derisive way he pronounced "female" caused a hot flush to singe her cheeks. She stood taller, digging for a measure of her normal pluck. "I should think that would be obvious to anyone of reasonable intelligence."

Usually she didn't approve of cutting remarks designed to wound another's sensibilities. But in Mr. Youngblood's case, she felt justified in making an exception. Clearly the criminal possessed no sensibilities with which to concern herself.

His glare was of sufficient scorching intensity to fry a buckwheat biscuit without benefit of fire.

"I don't believe it."

"It's true." Had his confinement addled his senses, making him incapable of grasping that she had only pretended to be of the male gender? "I can assure you I am traveling alone. There is no one with me, least of all a child."

She couldn't make her explanation any simpler.

His good eye, the one that wasn't fiercely swollen, studied her balefully. "Why?"

"Why what?" She assessed the challenge of getting the confused man to Trinity Falls. Of course, there was a positive side to his apparent simplemindedness. It was possible that he was mistaken about the Indians being on the warpath. "Are you wondering why I wanted you to think you were talking to a man?"

He shook his head, then winced. "I don't give a damn about your theatrics. I want to know why you're alone."

"Oh, that." She glanced from his ruthless stare. She hated admitting to this disreputable stranger that she'd been banished from the wagon train. She attempted a reassuring smile. "I don't have the plague, if that's worrying you."

A grave expression settled over his battered features. "Were you attacked?"

Victoria's thoughts immediately went to her late-night mishap with Hyrum Dodson, the unfortunate discharge of her rifle, and his piercing howl as he'd hopped about on one foot while trying to ascertain the damage to his other one. "I wouldn't call it an 'attack' so much as a misunderstanding."

Mr. Youngblood's good eye narrowed. "Misunderstanding?"

"You see, I thought a bear was invading my wagon."

Confusion seemed to sweep his countenance. "A bear?"

The man really was limited in his reasoning abilities. She regretted her earlier cutting remark about anyone of reasonable intelligence being able to comprehend her explanations.

But she hadn't known that Logan Youngblood was blighted by limited mental prowess. Her gaze made a quick foray across his virile physique. What a pity that his physical endowments were not matched by an equally keen intellect. Had his lack of mental fortitude led to an association with unsavory men who'd introduced him to a life of crime?

"Of course, as it turned out, there really wasn't a bear." She carefully enunciated each word so that he could grasp what had happened. "But I had no way of knowing that at the time, did I?"

His cracked lips parted, but he didn't speak. Instead, he seemed to regard her with a kind of morbid fascination.

Since leaving Boston, Victoria had become familiar with that look. As usual in her encounters with Western men, she was mystified as to why he had difficulty understanding her.

"The point is, I didn't mean to hurt Mr. Dodson. He just happened to be in the wrong place at the wrong time."

"How did you . . . hurt him?"

She sighed. "I shot him."

Mr. Youngblood retreated a step. "You *what?*"

"I heard something outside my wagon in the wee hours of the morning. The day before, one of the men mentioned seeing a black bear in the vicinity. He warned us to be on the lookout."

"Couldn't you tell the difference between a man and a bear?"

"It was dark."

Mr. Youngblood's good eye blinked spasmodically. "Lady, you're the one who should be locked up."

At the reminder of how she'd found the battered Logan Youngblood, Victoria's gaze drifted to the stockade. "I didn't mortally wound Mr. Dodson. I just winged him."

"Where?"

"Does it really matter?"

"I'm sure it did to him," Youngblood countered.

"His foot."

"What were you aiming for?"

She licked her lips, not at all liking the feeling that she'd lost control of their conversation. If anyone ought to be answering questions, it was him. He was the one who'd been incarcerated.

Strictly speaking, even if he wasn't behind bars, he was still a prisoner. To be more specific, he was *her* prisoner. And, as she saw it, she was duty-bound to escort him to Trinity Falls to answer for his ill deeds.

"Everything happened so quickly, I didn't really have time to aim at anything in particular." She straightened. "But we seem to have strayed from the central topic."

"So they kicked you off the wagon train for shooting one of its members?" he asked grimly, ignoring her efforts to get their discussion on track.

"Oh, no, they just took away my rifle for that."

The nervous tic quickened. "Then what happened? I mean, other than the wagon train being attacked and everyone but you being killed, I can't think of a single reason for you to have been separated from the others."

"Of course you can't," she conceded, striving for the patience one used when dealing with a child. The trouble was, she hadn't been around that many children.

"Let me guess," he interjected softly. "They tossed you off the train because you drove them crazy with your damned riddles."

She'd heard head injuries caused confusion. Was that why he seemed incapable of understanding the simplest of concepts? "How many blows to the head did you receive?"

Logan bit back an oath. Swearing at the contrary female who'd released him from the stockade would do no earthly good. He raked a hand through his hair. The subsequent flash of pain made him suck in his breath.

He looked toward the morning sun. Time was running out for them. They needed to leave the fort. "Look, lady, I—"

"My name is *Miss Amory*," she told him in that dainty, haughty voice of hers.

"Which will make no difference to an Indian with justice on his mind."

Her greenish eyes widened. "Justice?"

"The red man's kind of justice. It's swift and hard."

She looked over her shoulder, as if expecting an arrow to come flying at her. Framed by a splash of yellow sunlight, she appeared achingly vulnerable. A slim woman, with reddish hair that was in the process of escaping its anchoring pins.

There was little logic to it, but he felt compelled to protect the foolish creature.

"We need to be on our way," he repeated.

"I wasn't the one asking all the questions."

He scowled. Irritating female.

He would find out later how she'd become separated from the wagon train. He was sure that when he did, he'd learn she was responsible for her predicament. As his gaze dropped to the pert curve of her breasts and the slight fullness of her hips, outlined by her dusty dark green dress, there was something else he was sure of. Mr. Dodson with the shot foot had been prowling around Miss Amory's wagon with mischief on his mind.

The kind of mischief that had been going on since Eve had plucked that forbidden apple from its branch and offered it to Adam. The kind of mischief that would probably shock this red-haired Eastern woman to the soles of her sensible little black walking shoes.

Again he was struck by how vulnerable she appeared in her makeshift campsite in the middle of the abandoned fort. He turned again to the six placid oxen munching on the loose hay scattered around them. "I'll hitch the wagon."

"I've been responsible for my team since leaving Independence, and I'm fully capable of attending to them now."

Miss Amory's raised voice halted him in his tracks. He turned on his heel and glared at the contrary woman. "Are you turning down my help?"

"No, but I don't need a felon ordering me about. While we're on the subject, there's something else we need to clear up."

Her casual use of the word *felon* made Logan yearn to shake her. Instead, he swallowed his anger. He didn't have time to trade insults with Miss Amory, not with warring tribes of Blackfeet and Shoshones on the verge of attacking.

Later, he promised himself, he would delight in making this overbearing woman take back every insult she'd heaped upon him.

"Do you want to live or die, Miss Amory?"

Her slender hand shot to the bodice of her simple dress. "Are—are you threatening me?"

"Hell no, but we're in a tough spot and need to move."

"So you keep telling me."

He closed the eye that wasn't swollen shut and prayed for patience. "They're still out there."

"I'm aware of that. But surely we have enough time to establish our...er...chain of command, as I believe it's called."

Feeling not one iota of increased patience, Logan opened his eye. He felt downright mean and put-upon. He'd ridden to the fort to deliver Night Wolf's warning. His reward for leaving the safety of Trinity Falls had been a nasty showdown with Windham, a brutal beating, and being left to die.

Almost miraculously, he'd been freed. But, evidently, fate still wasn't done having a laugh at his expense, because his rescuer was the craziest female he'd ever had the misfortune to meet. And something about her well-bred, faintly censorious voice grated on his already savaged nerves.

His gaze narrowed. A shot of pain radiated from his right eye. "Where are you from, Miss Amory?"

"I hardly think that's relevant."

"Boston, right?"

"Not that it matters, but yes, that is my hometown."

He flinched. He should have known. Few good things had happened to him in Boston, which was why he'd left. As far as he was concerned, it was the hypocrisy capital of America, a place where men and women cared too much about appearances and not enough about integrity. It was where trust and loyalty fell before expediency and selfish desire.

"From your dour expression, I gather Boston is not one of your favorite places," Miss Amory observed.

Nothing like a bit of understatement. "You might say that."

"But where I come from hasn't really anything to do with our present situation."

She was speaking slowly again, as if she thought he were having trouble understanding her. Which he was, of course. But his lack of understanding had nothing to do with how fast or slowly she spoke. It was her confusing habit of talking in circles that made his head throb with more than the pain of the beating he'd survived.

Logan's glance flicked to the stockade. He felt nostalgic about his internment there. While inside its dark interior, he hadn't been forced to deal with a flame-haired harpy.

He rubbed the back of his neck. "Stop."

She licked her damnably soft lips. "What is it, precisely, that you wish for me to stop doing?"

"Addressing me as if I were some kind of half-wit."

Her already rosy cheeks flushed a brighter shade of pink. Was that it? Did she really think he was dim-witted?

Indignation tore through Logan. That this capricious female considered herself superior to him was the last straw. Her words kept darting off in a dozen different directions. Trying to speak with her was like carrying on a conversation with a bundle of colorful butterflies.

"There's no need to be sensitive about it." Her Boston accent was crisp and officious. "Not everyone can boast a keen intellect."

Astonishment popped the bubble of anger that had built within Logan. He couldn't remember the last time he'd been so soundly offended. Not even Windham, with his ridiculous claim about Logan bedding his wife, had struck such a deep blow.

Logan found he disliked having his intelligence insulted more than he disliked having his honor-impugned. A man could redeem his honor in a fair fight. There was no quick and final way, however, to convince this green-eyed witch that he was her intellectual equal. He told himself it didn't matter what she thought.

"Now, about who's in charge here," she continued, as if she hadn't just mortally insulted him. "As it's my wagon, and my team, and you are now in my custody, I should be the one to decide who does what."

"All right," he managed to say through his clenched jaw, not wanting to waste time arguing.

She smiled. "Why don't you go ahead and load the wagon, then, and I'll..."

He said nothing, contenting himself with images of her being bound and gagged and tossed into the back of her wagon.

She gestured toward a row of privies. "Well, you know..."

He maintained his stoic silence.

Only after she left did Logan let out the breath he'd been holding. He stalked toward the team, each step making his ribs ache. Little Miss Boston Accent didn't know it, but marauding Blackfeet were the least of her troubles. She would be damned lucky if she made it to Trinity Falls without him throttling her.

A short while later, with the climbing sun raising a bead of sweat on his skin after his exertions in harnessing the team, Logan looked into the back of Miss Amory's covered wagon.

At first he didn't believe what he saw.

When it finally dawned on him that he wasn't imagining things, a heartfelt oath escaped his cracked lips.

"Well, hell, that's why they left her."

He lofted himself into the wagon, ignoring a stab of pain from his bruised ribs. He would demonstrate to Miss Amory that the West had its own code of survival. It was a lesson he'd learned, and he would see that she damn well learned it, too.

For both their sakes.

After performing her morning ablutions, Victoria felt revived as she walked back toward the wagon. She'd overcome her aversion to entering the abandoned domiciles and scrubbed her face and hands in a floral ceramic washbowl she'd found in one of the eerily silent bedchambers. She'd also borrowed a comb and refashioned her hair into a semblance of order.

Gazing into the mirror above the washstand, she'd studied her features. The freckles scattered across the bridge of her nose and cheeks were more prominent than ever. The Western sun was responsible for that, no doubt. There was one good thing about her profusion of freckles, Victoria had decided as she refastened her cuffs. Men did not find freckled women attractive, which meant that even a disreputable sort like Logan Youngblood wouldn't direct any unseemly attentions to her.

As Victoria crossed the gravel yard, she said a hasty prayer on behalf of those who'd fled the fort. She included her own welfare on the list of those needing Divine assistance. When she added Logan Youngblood's name to the silent litany, however, she felt that her prisoner needed a series of independently voiced prayers pronounced on behalf of his felonious soul, as well as his physical well-being.

He had already hitched the oxen and loaded up the campsite, and was hunched over, reaching into the back of the wagon. When he emerged, two things registered. The first was that he'd found a blue military shirt to replace the tattered white one that had been falling off his powerfully sculpted shoulders. Thank goodness for that.

Her sense of relief was short-lived, though, when she realized he held several of her treasured books in his broad hands.

She raced forward. "What are you doing?"

He looked up from the volumes, a narrow-lipped frown making his already pummeled features even more menacing. "I'm lightening the load so we can make better time."

Victoria recoiled. He couldn't have hurt her more if he'd shot her. "You will return those books to where they belong."

"They belong in Boston."

She shook her head. "They are my possessions and will come with me."

"I think not, Miss Amory."

She straightened and leveled her most chiding glare at the obtuse man. "We've already established that I'm the one who gives the orders, and I say my precious cargo goes with me to Trinity Falls."

Not looking at all chastised, Youngblood's good eye narrowed to pinpoint fury. "*This* is your precious cargo?"

"That's right, and I've no intention of leaving it."

"Lady, they're not loved ones, they're books," he said flatly, tossing her beloved copy of *The Last of the Mohicans* into the dust. "And they're certainly not worth dying for."

At his callous gesture, outrage filled Victoria. She bent instinctively to gather Cooper's epic to her bosom.

"How dare you!"

He startled her by kneeling across from her. "Lady, there's lots more copies of this book around. When we get to Trinity Falls, you can order another one—of it and all the others."

"This is a first edition!"

With an absent flick of his wrist, he discarded Louisa May Alcott's new volume, *Little Women*. Victoria's indignation grew. She hadn't even had a chance to read it yet!

"The wagon master may have been willing to ride off without you, Miss Amory. He probably figured you'd come to your senses and lighten your load. He made a mistake I'm not willing to. The books stay. We go."

Victoria stared into Mr. Youngblood's unwavering gaze and knew intuitively that he would not yield to any pleas to spare her beloved volumes. Yet a spark of defiance still burned within her.

Inspiration struck. "It would take half the morning to unload the wagon. Don't you think we should leave now?"

She forced a determined smile onto her stiff lips. Oh, there was a rational part of her that knew it was foolish to risk her life over inanimate objects. But there was another part that was convinced she could keep both her scalp and the works of Cooper, Hardy and Brontë. After all, man did not live by bread alone.

Youngblood rose to his full height. A look of frustrated resignation stamped his rugged features. Victoria held her breath as she silently counted off the passage of seconds. She truly had no idea what the barbaric man might do.

Abruptly he turned his broad back to her.

"Get into the wagon," he ordered brusquely.

She scooped Alcott's book from the ground, shook the dust from it, then hurried up onto the wagon's high bench seat. She supposed she shouldn't have been surprised that her surly companion was there ahead of her, already taking his place behind the reins.

She swallowed back her protest, counting herself fortunate that he'd agreed that there wasn't time to unload all the volumes she'd spent days meticulously organizing and arranging in the corners and crannies of her wagon's interior.

Victoria had scarcely clambered beside Youngblood before he released the hand brake and reached for the bullwhip. In a careless gesture, he uncurled it above the animals' backs.

A loud crack sounded, cutting through the fort's stillness. As one, the team lurched forward toward the open gate.

With a start, Victoria realized she'd linked her hopes for survival to a total stranger. She couldn't help wondering whether she'd just made the worst mistake of her life.

Chapter Five

From the corner of her eye, Victoria sneaked covert glances at the man sitting beside her. They had been following this fairly wide stretch of wagon-rutted roadway for close to an hour, and he had yet to address one word to her. His profile was harsh and unrelenting. As luck would have it, his swollen eye faced her. Whenever a wheel struck a particularly deep rut, the jostling provoked a tight-lipped grimace from him.

At this evidence of his pain, her feelings toward him might have softened, had he offered a friendly word or two. His continued silence, however, grated on her nerves. It seemed unfair that fate should shackle her to a companion who was no more inclined to conversation than her plodding oxen. At least the animals had never glowered at her disapprovingly.

The wilderness continued to roll by, mile after mile of lush greenery. The air was redolent with the unrestrained scent of pine. Nearby, the Ruby River splashed across granite boulders.

The sun climbed higher in the cloudless blue sky. It didn't take long for the warming rays to intensify to an uncomfortable degree. She shifted on the wooden seat, convinced she could feel new freckles popping out on her skin. By the time they reached Trinity Falls, she would probably have a hundred more of the unattractive little devils spotting her face.

She tried to think where she'd left her sunbonnet, recalling that she'd worn it the day before. She remembered removing the bonnet when she crawled beneath the wagon to sleep. With a pang, she realized she'd left the wide-brimmed covering on her makeshift bed when Youngblood's voice jerked her awake. Had he thought to include the bonnet when he packed up her campsite?

She turned to peek into the wagon's interior. One of their wheels slammed into another deep rut. Caught off balance, she steadied herself by clutching at the closest thing of substance, which turned out to be Youngblood.

She let out a startled yelp. At the same time, Youngblood's powerful arm curved around her, anchoring her to his side. Several impressions struck her. First and foremost, she was aware of the muscular strength in the arm that bound her to Logan Youngblood. Secondly, she sensed that same latent power leashed in the rest of the strong body she was pressed tightly against.

The rough fabric of his blue shirt scraped the tip of her nose. His male scent inexorably wove itself into the very air she breathed. While not unpleasant, the earthy aroma seemed shockingly invasive. Goodness, she'd never been as close to, or as aware of, any man in her entire life. Not even seeing Horace Threadgill with his trousers around his ankles in her bedchamber had seemed as intimate as being trapped in this scoundrel's embrace.

"What in the blazes are you trying to do?"

His husky voice vibrated in her eardrum, causing a strange tingle to skip across her forearms. Her palms came up to push herself free. "I'm trying to right myself."

He gave her a look of disgust. "You could have fooled me."

"You may release me now."

His mauled countenance hovered a scant inch from her upturned face. She looked into his good eye. It was the darkest shade of brown, almost black. It was also penetratingly intent. She felt as if she were caught in a beam of lantern light shining from a lighthouse on a fogbound night—which made no sense, because his glare was as dark and forbidding as a moonless sky.

"Are you ready to sit still?"

It was the kind of question one would address to an unruly child, and she resented it.

"I was trying to fetch my sunbonnet," she informed him loftily as she struggled to extricate herself from his embrace. She didn't want to trigger an all-out tug-of-war that would make him aware of how indelicately he held her.

Her instincts warned it was essential she keep a safe distance from a man as unapologetically primitive as Youngblood.

He eased his grip. "You should have warned me."

"I'll remember to do so next time." She sank back to her side of the seat.

He pulled back on the reins. The oxen came to a dusty halt.

"Thank you for stopping," she said briskly, turning again to look inside the wagon's interior. "Do you happen to remember picking up my sunbonnet?"

She leaned more fully inside, scanning her dust-covered possessions for the green calico fabric. Her companion made no comment. Irritation nipped at her fragilely held patience.

She glanced at him from her ungainly position of being half in and half out of her wagon. "I asked you if—"

She broke off, disconcerted by how Mr. Youngblood's gaze seemed affixed to that portion of her anatomy stuck outside the canvas opening. The indecorous upward thrust of her bottom was mere inches from that interested regard.

What a rude rascal he was, not to avert his glance. She scooted onto the seat, trying to regain a more orthodox pose. She blew back the strands of hair that had fallen into her eyes.

"Did you think to retrieve my bonnet as you loaded the wagon?" She refused to comment upon his impertinent inspection of her lower person. There was little point in trying to teach manners to a man who frequented military stockades.

"I rolled it up in one of your blankets."

She let out a sigh of relief. "Thank goodness. I was afraid you had left it. Just give me a minute, and I'll get it."

"Be quick about it."

Such a gracious fellow. She turned and entered the inside of her wagon feetfirst. It was still an awkward movement, but at least she wasn't sticking out in all the wrong places for Mr. Youngblood's entertainment.

She found the blanket she'd used last night and located the sadly bedraggled hat. Before returning to her seat, she took the opportunity to carefully tuck away the books she'd reclaimed before boarding the wagon.

"I'm all set now," she announced as she climbed back next to him, shaking the winkles and dust from the much-abused bonnet.

He said nothing, nor did he make any move to proceed.

"Well, just don't sit there and stare at me," she muttered dourly. "According to you, time is of the essence."

"Are you going to put that thing on?"

She looked at him in surprise. "Of course."

"Then do it."

"You know, Mr. Youngblood, you're a downright irritating fellow." She sought to untangle the snarled ribbon ties. "I wouldn't be the least surprised to discover that's why you were locked up—for being generally obnoxious."

"I'm waiting for you to put on your damned hat so we can get going without you tumbling onto your sweetly shaped behind."

He *had* been sneaking peeks at her posterior! A hot flush bathed her cheeks. Good grief, he *was* a barbarian.

Naturally, she was somewhat mollified to learn that he approved of what he'd seen. Still, the man needed the most basic of lessons on how to conduct himself with a lady. But then, criminals of his sort probably didn't often associate with ladies, not even ones with her own somewhat maligned reputation.

"I think I can manage to put my bonnet on and remain seated," she said sharply. "Provided, of course, that you can manage to avoid the larger holes pocking this charming road we're obliged to follow."

"We're not staying on the main road."

She stopped fiddling with the knot she'd been trying to unravel. He had her full attention now. "Why on earth not?"

"It's sixty miles to Trinity Falls on this route. That's a six-day journey, with a fully loaded wagon pulled by oxen."

"So?"

"That's six days on flat terrain that will leave us exposed to attack from any roaming Indians."

"Which isn't a good situation to be in," she mused aloud.

"A better choice for us would be to leave the main road and detour through those mountains."

Victoria looked toward the mountains in question. They loomed large and inhospitable—great granite crags stretching skyward. Caps of snow from the previous winter still covered the upper reaches. Even the tenacious pines and cedars hadn't trespassed to those higher realms.

"You *are* simpleminded to think my team and wagon can scale those rugged cliffs."

It wasn't until the words popped out of her mouth that Victoria realized she'd spoken plainly enough for even a simpleton to realize he'd been insulted. She kept her gaze pinned resolutely on the jagged outcroppings.

"Do you plan to insult me all the way to Trinity Falls?"

There was no ignoring his tone's stony timbre.

She decided only a coward would refuse to look at him when she answered his question. Until this very moment, Victoria hadn't realized she had a cowardly bone in her body. She drew in a breath and ceased her futile struggles with her ribbon ties. Turning slowly, she confronted her offended companion.

"I apologize, Mr. Youngblood, for hurting your feelings."

He stared at her hard enough with that cyclopean eye of his to raise goose bumps on her skin.

"And," she continued gamely, "in the future, I will endeavor to control my tongue."

At her words, his harsh gaze swooped to her lips. Her goose bumps multiplied a hundredfold.

His mouth curved. On someone else the gesture would have resembled a smile. On him, the action had a kind of carnivorous aspect. She suspected that the Big Bad Wolf had sized up Little Red Riding Hood in that exact predatory fashion.

"It's at this point that you're supposed to accept my apology," she instructed.

"If it will get that damned bonnet on your head any quicker, I'll accept your most humble apologies."

She bit back her objections to his profanity, his reference to her "most humble" apologies and his entirely offensive manner. Instead she concentrated on unknotting the damned snarl that had—

Victoria winced. Goodness, the crude man was already proving to have a corrupting effect upon her moral character. She *never* swore. Not when being falsely accused of misconduct with her sister's beau, not when an unsympathetic wagon master refused to wait for her, not when dealing with unrepentant criminals.

She governed her life by a high set of principles. And it was especially important now that she adhere to that superior code of conduct. After all, when she reached Trinity Falls, she would be instructing a young woman in the elements of being a proper lady, as well as handling the girl's general education. It wouldn't do at all for Victoria to show up in her new environment contaminated by her association with Logan Youngblood.

It was she who needed to exert a positive influence upon him. Surely, with a diligent effort upon her part, he could be dissuaded from his wayward ways.

The knot finally loosened enough for her to free the ribbons. She wasted no time in securing the hat to her head.

"We're not going *over* the mountains," Youngblood said. "There are trails and passes I'm hoping to get this wagon through. Once we're shielded by the forest, I'll feel better."

"I suppose it does make sense for us to make ourselves less conspicuous," she conceded reluctantly. The thought of entering the mysterious denseness of the wooded wilderness, however, was daunting to a city girl like herself. It seemed that it would be very easy to become lost among those pines that grew so astonishingly close to each other. It looked as if even the sunlight had to struggle to penetrate the tightly packed clusters of trees. "Are you sure you know the way to Trinity Falls?"

It was clear to Logan that Victoria Amory did not have the slightest confidence in his abilities to get her safely to civilization. He probably shouldn't have been surprised by her lack of trust. She had the lowest opinion of him of anyone he'd ever met, and that probably included Colonel Windham.

She sat next to him with that pitiful scrap of mangled fabric on her head and still managed to appear as composed as a schoolmistress about to call her class to order. He supposed she was just naturally bossy.

He limited himself to answering, "I've lived in the West for a while now."

"In these hills?" she asked, obviously still needing reassurance.

He raised the whip to get the team moving again. "No, I've lived in town."

No doubt dividing his time between saloons and the city jail, Victoria thought.

Logan maneuvered the wagon off the road, taking an upward strip of flattened grass that wound northward through the pines. Sharp-needled branches scraped their canvas-covered canopy. The ride became rougher. Miss Amory latched on to the side of her seat like a limpet stuck to a ship's hull.

"I'm not so sure this is a good idea," she said, her voice a virtual squeak. "I don't have a map we can refer to."

"I don't need a map."

"Forgive me for not having more confidence in you," she began, using that snippy tone of hers. "But I was warned most forcibly by the wagon master to remain on the main road."

"You can bet that if he was in our situation, he would try to make himself invisible to the Indians, too."

The wagon took another sharp lurch. Victoria almost bounced off her seat. He reached out and pulled her to him.

"What do you think you're doing?"

"Keeping you from breaking your neck," he answered grimly. She felt so small and fragile next to him. Again a strong sense of protectiveness surged within him. It wasn't a feeling he welcomed, but he seemed unable to fight it. "If we were going at a slower pace, I'd let you walk. It would mean less wear and tear on your...body. But for the rest of the day, at least, we need to put as much distance between us and the fort as we can."

She stopped struggling. One of her palms curled around his arm. Her other hand gripped his shoulder. "If we leave the river, how will we find water for the oxen?"

"There's quite a few streams that feed into the Ruby. Don't worry, water won't be a problem."

"But how will you know where to—"

"Look, Miss Amory, this isn't the time or place to have a discussion. I've got to concentrate on keeping these animals on a path that's no bigger than a cat's behind. We'll talk later."

He ducked, pulling her down with him, when a low-hanging branch threatened to take their heads off. Dust and dead pine needles flew as the limb smacked the top of the lurching wagon.

She buried her face in his sleeve. When she came up for air, she was coughing. "As long as you realize I'm in charge."

Little gasps kept time with each bump they experienced. He didn't know whether to laugh or swear at the stubborn female. She had the most one-track mind of any woman he'd ever met.

"Oh, yeah," he growled, feeling the jarring in his tender ribs. "You're definitely in charge."

He would let her think that all the way to Trinity Falls.

It seemed to Victoria that her entire twenty-four years had shrunk to this jerky passage through the Idaho wilderness. They had been traveling for hours now. And there was no outward sign from Youngblood that he meant to stop anytime soon. Because the thickly timbered landscape blocked most of the sun's rays, it was difficult to gauge the time of day. From her stomach's not-so-discreet rumblings, though, she assumed it was well past noon.

The grim-faced man beside her hadn't spoken for the longest time. But then, their violent progress discouraged conversation. She had to admit he was good with her team. She doubted she could have bullied them along this wild stretch.

Victoria marveled that he managed to keep to the narrow trail. There were instances when she thought they'd taken a blind alley and would have to turn around, but despite numerous twists and turns, Youngblood always moved forward.

They came to a relatively smooth section of the path, and the sounds of the wagon's creaking protests softened. She heard the excited chatter of darting squirrels and the lively calls of birds.

"I can't believe how close the trees are to each other," she remarked, feeling disoriented by the thousands upon thousands of thin-trunked pines around them. Only inches separated the tall narrow-beamed trees from one another.

Her taciturn companion looked from the trail and gazed into the immense forest that embraced them on all sides as far as the eye could see. "Lodgepole pines grow that way."

"It's really quite beautiful, isn't it?" she asked, succumbing to a need to share her appreciation of the untamed splendor in which she found herself.

He turned toward her. At the sight of his rawly bruised face, just inches from hers, she flinched. His facial injuries spoke of unchecked violence and the often brutal nature of men.

"Beautiful and deadly."

His matter-of-factness chilled her. It was as if he was deliberately trying to frighten her. His intent stare made her wonder again if she'd delivered herself into the hands of the devil. Was he waiting for the right place, away from any signs of civilization, to do away with her and steal her wagon?

She fortified herself with a gulp of pine-scented air. "Deadly because of the Indians?"

He nodded. "There's that. But there's also bears, rattlers, wolves and mountain lions."

Her stomach flipped. She wished he hadn't bothered itemizing the various menacing creatures shielded by the forest.

Before Victoria could comment, the smooth stretch they were traversing became steeper and more uneven. She held on tighter to the wagon's side panel and gritted her teeth to keep from biting her tongue.

Harness leather groaned as the oxen lowered their heads and plodded onward. The wild ride continued for several yards, and then Youngblood pulled back on the reins.

"Whoa!" came his clearly exasperated shout.

Three lodgepole pines had fallen across the faint trail. Youngblood handed her the reins. "It looks like we're going to be here for a while." He stepped down from the high bench seat, his face turned toward her. A look of pain flashed across his grimly set features. "I hope you've got an ax tucked away somewhere among all those books."

"It's lashed to the side of the wagon. Are you going to try and chop a path through those trees?"

He shot her an impatient glance. "I'm not going to *try*. I'm going to do it."

In light of his arrogance, her sympathy for the injured man diminished. "While you're doing that, I'd like to stretch my legs." She tossed the reins to him and scooted into position to descend. "If we're going to be here for a while, I'll build us a fire and fry us up some pan biscuits."

"There aren't going to be any fires."

His harsh voice was surprisingly close. She stopped midway to the ground and glanced over her shoulder. She found herself looking into the pinpoint focus of Youngblood's cyclopean eyeball. She blinked, feeling strangely bound by his unexpected proximity. She swallowed; any words she'd been about to utter were forgotten.

His strong hands came around her waist, and he lowered her to the pine-needled carpet that covered the forest floor. There was a buzzing in her ears. It took her a moment to realize that a fat black deerfly was responsible for the distracting hum.

"We can't afford to reveal our presence by building a fire," he continued, his large palms still engulfing her. "Not for at least another day, anyway."

Victoria had nowhere to go. With Youngblood pressed up behind her and the wagon in front, she was his prisoner.

"I still need to stretch my legs," she told him. To her own ears, her voice sounded hoarse. She stepped to her right, assuming he would let her twist free. The next couple of seconds were the longest of her life. But when she pushed against his constraining hold, he moved back and released her.

"I'll get the ax."

It was the kind of statement that needed no response. She walked a few feet from the wagon and inhaled the rich mountain air. A strong hint of wild mint laced the cooling afternoon breeze.

Victoria noticed several clusters of purplish berries growing in heaps of green foliage. She recognized them as a variety of wild chokecherries and decided to gather some. When she returned to the wagon to retrieve a pail, the sound of the falling ax echoed through their secluded stopping place.

In response to the discordant *thwack* of the ax, raucous birds took to the sky in noisy protest. Pail in hand, Victoria circled the wagon. Youngblood stood in a shaft of pooling sunlight that managed to find its way through the cover of pine boughs. He had removed his shirt for his physical exertions, and he swung the long-handled blade with an economy of motion. Each strike of sharp metal bit deeply into the wood. Bits of bark and needles billowed from the steady blows.

Standing less than ten feet from him, she read the agony on his face. His labors were obviously taking a toll on his battered body. Sympathy tugged at her. He'd voiced no complaint about seeing to the arduous task. Instead, he'd applied himself to what had to be done.

The muscles that shaped his back contracted and relaxed with each upward and downward arc of the ax. Every rhythmic slice into the bark seemed an extension of his bunched arm and shoulder muscles. Already one narrow trunk had been severed.

Victoria shrugged off the strange sense of lethargy that came over her as she watched Youngblood clear their path. She gripped the pail tighter and turned to the tiny harvest of berries that beckoned in the tangled underbrush.

It was a puny harvest indeed, only a couple of dozen bits of the plump morsels. Still, they would taste delicious, Victoria decided as she returned to the wagon.

Youngblood was drinking deeply from a canteen when she joined him. His head was tipped back, and his Adam's apple moved with each swallow he took. A faint gleam of perspiration covered his naked torso. She knew she ought to look away, to give him a degree of privacy. Had their positions been reversed, she certainly would have wanted him to avert his gaze.

Without speaking, he finished drinking and capped the canteen. He reached for his shirt and carelessly rubbed the blue material across the back of his neck. Victoria couldn't have been more fascinated by his actions had she been visiting a Boston zoological exhibit. For in truth, Logan Youngblood was a mysteriously exotic creature to her.

He was a man.

Without the civilized trappings of his clothing, he seemed unlike any gentleman with whom she'd previously dealt. Horace Threadgill and the male members of the wagon train had been as citified as she was, and her association with them hadn't been the least bit as intriguing as watching Logan Youngblood. He shook the wrinkles from the shirt and shrugged it on. Again she was aware of the flashes of pain that crossed his features.

He glanced from the button he was fastening. "What have you got there?"

Self-consciously she looked at her insignificant offering. "Some wild berries."

His mouth curved. Had his bottom lip not been swollen, she would have called the gesture a genuine smile.

"Good for you."

A compliment, coming from him? It was ridiculous, but she experienced a surge of pleasure.

"I wasn't able to find that many," she felt compelled to confess, lest he get his expectations up.

"At least you didn't sit around doing nothing, waiting for me to finish cutting us a path through those trees."

"That would have been pretty silly," she returned, some of the glow from his praise fading.

"I've observed that, in general, women tend to be silly."
He held out his hand. "I'll take that."

Chafing at his condescending manner, she gripped the
handle tighter. "Why should I give you the pail?"

His dark eyebrows converged over his nose. "Do you always have to be so damned suspicious?"

"Why should I give them to you?"

He leaned forward and pried her fingers loose from the
metal handle. "Because, Miss Amory, you'll need both your
hands to climb into the wagon."

"Oh." Surrendering the berries, she turned away from
him. With as much regal disdain as she could muster, she
marched to her side of the wagon. As she climbed to her
side of the seat, she had to admit that she did feel somewhat ... silly.

Chapter Six

They ate the berries as they traveled. Sweetly tart, the juicy bits of fruit didn't last long, yet they quenched Victoria's thirst and temporarily took the edge off her hunger.

She smiled ruefully, recalling the wonderful meals her family's cook had prepared. In the face of her present travails, it was remarkable that she'd taken those perfectly prepared repasts for granted, except, of course, during the horrific civil conflict that was only three years past.

At her country's most vulnerable hour, Victoria had often thought about the Northern and Southern soldiers subjected to countless deprivations, including meager rations. Both she and Annalee had done their part to contribute to the welfare of their "boys," by rolling bandages, sewing uniforms and donating their personal allowances to the cause. She remembered how good it had felt to be needed, to be of service.

She sighed, her glance straying to the silent man beside her. In battered profile, he was more than a little frightening. He had eaten the berries in what she was coming to view as his customary attitude of withdrawal. Because of his superior size, she'd assumed he would claim a greater portion of the plump morsels. That had not been the case, however, as he'd helped himself to only a few of the berries.

She was left to conclude one of three things: He didn't care for the taste of the fruit; he wasn't hungry; or he was demonstrating an unexpected degree of chivalry in allowing her to have the larger portion. None of those possibilities seemed likely.

Without warning, he turned to her. "Are my lips blue?"

"What?"

"The way you keep staring at me, I'm wondering if those berries turned my lips blue."

A hot flush stole up her throat. He was right. She had been staring. She returned her gaze to the oxen's swaying rumps. "Actually, your lips are a reddish color—due, no doubt, to their bloodied condition. It is your eye, however, that is the most remarkable array of hues, ranging from blue to black to purple."

He surprised her by chuckling. "I must look like hell. That's how I feel, anyway."

She frowned, uncomfortable with the thought that he was in pain. "Do your injuries hurt terribly?"

From the corner of her eye, she could see that he was still looking at her. She kept her attention on the animals pulling their wagon. She was reluctant to meet his stare. Something about it disturbed her. She might tell herself that his pummeled features repulsed her, but she didn't altogether believe that.

"Now and then I feel a twinge."

He was being brave; she was sure of it. When she performed volunteer work at the military hospital, nursing wounded soldiers, they'd acted the same way, dismissing the severity of their injuries, even when they'd lost a limb.

She remembered the lines of agony gripping his face as he'd swung the ax. "I should have been the one to cut the trees."

"And why is that?"

She heard the skepticism in his voice and suppressed a sigh. She was used to men undervaluing the contributions of women. Her father was a prime example of a male holding women in benign contempt. "Obviously, I could have spared you further suffering."

"That's quite a generous offer. Considering."

"Considering what?" she couldn't keep from asking.

"Considering that I'm your prisoner and you think you're taking me to Trinity Falls to stand some kind of trial."

She'd momentarily forgotten about that. "I don't *think* I'm taking you there for that reason. I know I am." Forgetting her earlier reservations about talking to the man eye-to-eye, she turned to him. "It's very important to accept responsibility for your actions. When you do something wrong, you must pay your debt to society. Otherwise, our country would be in anarchy."

His stare was as intense as she recalled, but she didn't glance away. He looked as if he had something important to say. Was he about to confess to his crimes? She prepared herself to hear anything. She promised herself that, no matter how depraved or violent his misdeeds, she would remain calm.

"You don't believe any of the things I've told you, do you?"

"That you were falsely imprisoned after carrying a warning to the fort and not revealing the whereabouts of a tribe of friendly Indians?" she said dubiously.

His features tightened into a scowl. "It's pointless for me to keep protesting my innocence, isn't it?"

"I can't believe soldiers of the United States Army would do anything as reprehensible as imprisoning an innocent man."

He returned his attention to the trail. "There's something you should think about."

She didn't trust the subtle deepening of his already husky voice. "What's that?"

"If I'm such a terrible miscreant, why are you still alive?"

Her throat muscles constricted. "Wh-what?"

"If I'm as bad as you think, I would have had my way with your delectable body, hacked you up with your own ax, roasted you over a vigorous fire and made a hot meal of your tender flesh.''

Her heart pounded. That he could envision such deviltry proved he was dangerous. All her sympathetic thoughts about him rose to reproach her. She'd been a fool to release him from the stockade. And a greater fool not to arm herself with a knife.

Logan flicked a quick glance at his traveling companion. Damnation, she was as white as a ghost. It infuriated him that his careless words, words intended to reassure her, could actually terrify her. He didn't know who he was angrier at, himself for uttering such hogwash or her for being so gullible.

I should have been the one to cut the trees....

Her gentle comment cut through his thoughts. She'd been concerned about him. And he'd repaid her generosity with a nasty remark about raping, dismembering and cannibalizing her!

''You can start breathing again. I won't hurt you.''

''I don't need you to tell me to breathe.''

Her bravado sparked a tug of admiration. The woman might be scared, but she wasn't going to let him know it. The best way to deal with her so that she didn't run screaming into the forest was to establish a rapport with her. Which meant he would have to learn more about her. He had to foster a degree of trust in this Eastern woman, because both their lives might come down to her obeying his orders without question. But he knew she wasn't ready to hear that he was the temporary mayor of Trinity Falls and owned a bank. She'd think he was lying and become even more difficult to deal with.

''Why are you traveling alone?''

''You don't recall?''

Her vivid green eyes looked...bewildered and, he thought with repugnance, filled with pity. Hell, she was back to treating him like a half-wit.

''Recall what?''

"I—I already explained that the wagon master was unwilling to slow his pace... And remember my books? The ones you wanted to leave behind at the fort—that large wooden structure with the big gate?"

He gritted his teeth so hard that his already aching jaw shot new waves of pain through his skull. "I meant, why were you alone in the first place? Most women travel west with their parents or husbands." He couldn't resist adding, "Parents are the people who give birth and raise you. A husband is a man a woman marries when she's ready to start a family. A family—"

"I get your message." Flags of scarlet decorated her cheeks.

Satisfaction warmed him. It was time Miss Amory understood how it felt to be treated like a simpleton.

"And?" he prompted.

"And what?" she snapped.

Logan realized he wasn't making much headway in establishing a bond of trust between them, but at least she didn't look as if she were in imminent danger of fainting.

"Why are you traveling alone?"

"It didn't start out that way." Her vibrant green eyes looked into the distance. "I was to make the trip with another family. Their oldest son was going to manage the team. At the last moment, however, their plans changed."

Her explanation told him little. "Why did you decide to leave your home in the first place?"

Victoria's already flushed face turned a brighter shade of pink. Logan sensed his question had struck a deep chord.

She was lying. That caught him off guard. She didn't look like the kind of woman to prevaricate about anything. "And your parents let you go?"

"They... accepted my decision."

There were a lot of things she *wasn't* telling him. He sensed that leaving home had been painful for her.

"And your husband?" He was baiting her now, and he knew it.

She puffed up like a furious little red-feathered bird.

"I do not have a husband."

"Fiancé?"

"That is hardly any of your business, Mr. Youngblood."

"Call me Logan," he commanded softly. "I intend to call you Victoria. It's only fair I allow you the same privilege."

She blinked at him. She'd done that before when something he said surprised her. The very feminine gesture appeared to be her way of getting her bearings.

"How do you know my first name?"

"You must have written it in every book you own."

"Oh." She studied him gravely. "Under the circumstances, I suppose it would be foolish not to be on a first-name basis."

Such a well-bred, reluctant concession.

He liked the way her lips shaped her words—so precisely, so daintily. They were inviting lips—shaped with delicate fullness. Despite her mouth's soft beauty, she didn't look like the kind of woman to invite a kiss. Instead, she projected a directness that dared a man to cross the boundaries she'd set.

He pulled his gaze from hers before he did something totally asinine, like find out how those delectable lips tasted.

"Well, Victoria, what's your answer?"

"My—my answer?"

"Are you engaged, married or widowed?"

Has any man been able to break through that formidable facade of yours?

"Mr. Young—"

"Logan," he corrected firmly.

"Logan, ours is strictly a temporary association, and as I stated before, there's no reason for you to know whether or not there's someone . . . special in my life."

"When this is over, suppose a man shows up, claiming you belong to him, and he demands to know what happened between us?"

"First of all, no such person exists." Exasperation laced her cultured voice. "Second, the *only* thing that's going to happen is that we're going to reach Trinity Falls alive."

It was hard to accept that the woman next to him was bound to no man. It was obvious from her independent manner that she felt no need to justify her single state. He tried to guess her age, which was no easy accomplishment.

A frown scrunched her lips. Her delicately proportioned chin was thrust at a disapproving angle. Her lashes were a golden red, reflecting the same tawny highlights that burnished her bound hair. She might have been eighteen, but her bearing was that of someone older, maybe twenty-four or twenty-six.

He scowled. She had no business being on her own, in the Idaho Territory or anywhere else. She was too attractive not to have a father, brother or husband watching over her. She was also too headstrong to be left to her own devices. Her present situation proved that. Good Lord, what if Windham had left a real hardened criminal locked up in the stockade? Victoria would have freed him and then been at the brute's mercy.

His scowl deepened. For her own good, she needed to learn that a lone woman couldn't go traipsing across the country as she pleased. Logan realized his sense of outraged possessiveness was illogical. Yet he couldn't seem to help himself.

It had been this same sense of heretofore-unacknowledged protectiveness that resulted in his accepting Madison Earley as his ward. When a prospector showed up at the bank with the story that a white girl was living with the Shoshones, Logan had taken it upon himself to ride to Night Wolf's camp and retrieve her. It had turned out that Madison's mother had died a long time ago, and the child had been raised by her father, who'd been working a small gold claim.

Bushwhackers had murdered the man for his small cache of gold dust. Night Wolf's tribe had sheltered Madison for a while, but clearly her place was with her own people. Logan could easily have sent her to an orphanage in the East, yet something within him had balked at casting her adrift in the world.

He shook his head. It was hard to believe he'd lived thirty years without knowing he had this lamentable streak of sentimentality coursing through his veins. It had been this same latent sense of caring, no doubt, that sent him to the fort to deliver Night Wolf's warning about the attack.

And now he was saddled with a woman who cherished her collection of rare books more than she valued her own life. She was wrong if she thought he'd yielded to her insistence to keep them. Tonight, when she was asleep, he meant to lighten the load the oxen were struggling with to get over the next small rise. By the time they reached Trinity Falls, she would be lucky to have one book left.

He leveled a hard glance at her. All right, maybe he would be selective. He'd let her keep Cooper's ridiculously romantic yarn about the Mohicans. Louisa May Alcott was going to go, though. *Little Women* was a new novel and could be purchased at any bookshop.

His dark mood was appeased by the knowledge that the domineering woman would ultimately be put in her place. Logan visualized their arrival in town. He could see Victoria marching him off to the sheriff's office, all self-righteous and determined to have him get his just punishments. It would be a pleasure to watch the entirely too smug woman discover that her *prisoner* was none other than the acting mayor and the president of Trinity Falls's largest bank, along with a dozen other financial institutions.

He decided watching her eat crow would be the most satisfying thing he'd done in a long time. When the oxen seemed to hesitate cresting the next pine-covered slope, Logan reached for the whip to offer them a little encouragement.

His thoughts turned from Victoria to their immediate destination, a small tributary feeding into the Ruby River.

They should reach it before dark. Once there, he might believe they had a chance of making it to town alive. They would be in Night Wolf's domain, and that much closer to keeping their scalps.

She's not a complainer...

Logan's mind again filled itself with thoughts about Victoria Amory. One way or another, he decided, he'd find out why she'd left Boston and what she planned to do in Trinity Falls.

Everything about her manner bespoke Eastern refinement.

There wasn't a single reason for her to be running loose in the Idaho Territory. He knew one thing for sure; she wouldn't be looking for work at Jubilee Joe's or any of the other saloons dotting Main Street.

A grin caught him by surprise as he visualized the prim and proper Victoria Amory serving drinks at a local saloon. She'd probably present each glass of whiskey with a linen napkin and a severe warning about the moral dangers of intemperance.

The image of Victoria in a spangled red gown rose fully blown in Logan's mind. The dress was low-cut, and short enough to show her knees. Her perky little breasts would be all but spilling out of the tight-fitting bodice and her ankles would be trim and well shaped. There would be a scattering of golden freckles across her creamy flesh, he was certain. Surely those impudent little spots wouldn't stop at the high collar of her conservative green dress.

Logan swallowed, trying to curb his runaway imaginings. He couldn't believe he was sitting next to this prissy-mannered female, seeing her in a flashy outfit that she'd probably rather be shot in than be seen wearing. It was the time he'd spent in the stockade, he assured himself, that was making his mind play tricks on him. That, and the fact that it had been a while since he'd been able to keep company with one of Trinity Falls's cheerfully irreverent fancy women. Ever since Madison had become part of his life several months ago, he'd been reluctant to pursue his usual nighttime encounters with Cherry, Jasmine, or any of the other gals who didn't demand a wedding ring in exchange for their favors.

That was definitely going to change when he returned to town. He would find a way to pick up the threads of his former life without tarnishing Madison's world. Either that, or he was going to become a menace to decent women, because, like it or not, all he could do was think carnal thoughts about Victoria's sensuously shaped mouth and her tidy little breasts and her gently flared hips and—

Lord, he *was* losing his mind. There was nothing the least bit appealing about the prudish woman. And he was going to keep repeating that small lie to himself all the way home.

Chapter Seven

Slashes of twilight stalked the day's waning brightness. Restless shadows scuttled beyond the ever-shrinking horizon, disappearing into gaping holes of blackness. Unpredictable crosscurrents of chilling breezes cut through Victoria's clothing. She shivered, glancing uneasily about.

When Logan finally brought their team to a halt, night's rapid descent had transformed the mood of the dense pine woods to one of danger.

"Well, we're here."

"Wh-where's here?" That the question came out in a dazed squeak didn't surprise her.

It required a spurt of determination for her not to scoot across the seat and draw closer to Logan. She was startled by the need to seek comfort from a near stranger, especially this intimidating one. Her self-sufficiency was a trait she'd always taken pride in. Yet tonight, in this alien landscape, she battled the urge to reach out and touch Logan's sleeve, to reassure herself that she wasn't alone in this isolated stretch of timberland.

Valiantly she subdued the treacherous weakness. He might not be the despicable criminal she'd originally thought, but it wouldn't be wise to become too familiar with him. It had been drilled into her since girlhood that distinct barriers must be maintained between herself and any member of the opposite sex.

The one occasion when she'd violated that stricture had been when she tried to aid Horace Threadgill in his battle against a homicidal bee. Look where that innocent act had landed her! In the middle of a wilderness, in the company of a man who'd entered her life under the most suspect circumstances!

Logan stepped down from the wagon. "This is where we will spend the night."

She squinted into the thickening darkness. Just beyond the oxen's shifting feet, she made out the outline of a narrow stream cutting across the nearly invisible trail they'd been following.

"I'll unhitch the team so they can drink," he went on to say. "We'll be on the move again at first light."

He was back to issuing orders. Victoria was too sore and tired, though, to make an issue of that fact. All she wanted was to stretch out on a blanket under the wagon.

She climbed down, painfully aware of the numbed but tender portion of her anatomy that had endured the jarring slap of the lurching wagon seat for their seemingly endless day of travel. Her thigh muscles trembled, and for a moment she wasn't sure her legs would support her. It was because of the relentless pace he'd set and the rough terrain they'd covered that she was feeling so battered.

She stood beside a broad-spoked wheel, shivering as the rising mountain wind buffeted her. She knew she ought to do something useful, like find the extra pan biscuits she'd made the night before, at the fort. Her mind seemed incapable of provoking her body to movement, however.

"Victoria?"

She started. Had Logan already finished freeing the oxen so that they could drink? Surely she hadn't been idle that long.

"What?"

She raised her head and tried to focus her blurred vision on the towering figure that had materialized before her.

"You look dead on your feet."

She was too tired to take offense at his blunt remark. How could one argue with the truth?

"I'll be all right. Just give me a minute."

The mumbled request floated from her lips while she continued to stand in a stupor, knowing she should be doing something, but lacking the energy to decide what that something was.

A pair of strong hands settled on her weary shoulders. "I know I pushed us hard today, Victoria."

She wanted to shrug off the unexpected gentleness of his tone, just as she wanted to shrug off the weight of his firm touch. She was incapable of doing either. The concern that laced his deep voice pierced a vulnerable spot within her. A sting of moisture filled her eyes. His hands massaged her sore shoulder muscles in slow, steady circles.

She tried to stand straight. She'd come this far alone. She was a resilient woman who didn't need the respect of her parents, the loyalty of her sister or the association of friends. And she certainly didn't need this man to offer comfort.

To Victoria's horror, she felt the burning sensation of tears that would not be denied. The hot wetness welled up in her eyes and spilled down her cheeks in emotional rivers of release. Somehow her face became pressed against Logan's shirt.

She hated breaking down. She wanted to be strong. Besides, he was her prisoner. If anyone should be weeping, it was him. The more she struggled to subdue her tears, however, the freer they fell. His palms stroked her back. She felt as if she'd found shelter from a fierce mountain storm within the arms of this menacing stranger.

Which wouldn't do at all, the logical side of her mind pointed out. As the flow of tears ebbed, that inner voice grew louder. She sought to extricate herself from his surprisingly tender embrace. That was what her mind instructed her to do, anyway. Her body seemed to have ideas of its own, however, and she couldn't quite seem to pull free.

He held her with more than the indisputable strength of his arms. He held her with the silent solace another human being could transmit to another. The powerful cadence of his heartbeat kept time with a mysterious rhythm that soothed her ragged sense of control. His earthy, manly scent permeated her senses.

The feeling that she was close to experiencing something rare, something meaningful, momentarily drifted through her numbed thoughts before dissipating into the night air.

With a final, and this time successful, lunge for selfmastery, Victoria eased herself from Logan's hold. As before, when he'd assisted her from the wagon, she thought she detected the smallest hesitation on his part before he released her.

"I'm sorry. I can't think what came over me."

Glaringly aware that Logan's shirtfront had been drenched by her tearful assault, she braced herself for the words that would reveal his male superiority at her deplorable weakness.

In a like circumstance, her father would have been coldly contemptuous of her feminine frailty. Though, when she was growing up, she'd never known for certain whether her father's disdainful attitude toward any form of human weakness was because he was a judge and therefore immune to sentiment, or because it went against his nature to view with patience any female shortcoming.

"It's my fault," Logan shocked her by saying. "I drove us pretty hard. What you need is food and a good night's sleep."

"Those chokecherries didn't go very far." She took a surreptitious swipe at her eyes, striving to compose herself.

A huge yawn came from nowhere, overwhelming her. She pushed back the hair that had fallen into her eyes. Her fingers brushed her sunbonnet's wide brim, and she reached up to jerk it off. "Did you think to bring the extra pan biscuits from last night?"

His arm came around her waist, and he guided her forward. "I not only brought the biscuits, but I made a quick search of the fort and found some jerked beef and tins of peaches. I didn't want to take the time to dig them out earlier. Just because tonight's a cold camp, that doesn't mean we're going to starve."

Victoria yawned again, thinking that whatever Logan Youngblood's moral flaws, he did boast some favorable qualities. Like kindness and an enterprising attitude.

He went to the unhitched wagon and entered it. It wasn't long before he emerged with several blankets. He spread them beneath the high-wheeled conveyance, then raised his head from his crouched position. "Come here."

She staggered forward, feeling as if she'd exhausted the last particle of her energy. As she knelt to slip beneath the wagon, every muscle she possessed cried out in distress. Again Logan's hands came to the rescue. He absorbed most of her weary weight and drew her the rest of the way onto the blankets.

It felt so wonderful to stretch out. She closed her eyes, even as she felt Logan lay another blanket over her.

"Thank you."

"You're welcome," came his low, disembodied voice. "I'm going to unhook your walking shoes. I noticed you slept in them last night. If we don't get them off for a few hours, your feet are going to swell."

"That's nice. . . ."

She thought she heard him chuckle. "You're really tuckered out, aren't you, little deputy?"

"Little deputy?"

"Since I don't think you're planning on earning a reward by turning me in to the sheriff when we get to Trinity Falls, I won't insult you by calling you a bounty hunter."

His words made little sense. But his tone was unusually warm, she thought. Even though she couldn't see his battered features with her eyes shut, she suspected he might be smiling.

The blanket shifted, and a cool breeze rustled over her as he fumbled with the fastenings on her shoes. The sensation of being taken care of brought a tightness to her chest. A few unshed tears, the last of the torrent she'd released in his arms, trickled down her cheeks. His touch reminded her of her mother's ministrations when Victoria was a child.

"Rest for a few minutes."

As if she needed him to tell her to...

Victoria surrendered gratefully to the cloud of sleepiness that descended over her. She had no idea how much time had passed before she felt Logan shake her shoulder. She closed her eyelids tighter and willed him to leave her in peace.

"You need to eat before you fall completely asleep."

Too late, she thought rolling to her side. "Go away."

He continued to shake her. How could she have thought him kind? He was the cruelest creature alive to try and waken her.

"Here, at least have a biscuit."

She opened her eyes. He was hunched over her, proffering the leftover food. She frowned, raising herself to her elbows.

He was little more than a shadow. She opened her mouth to explain that she didn't want anything to eat. Evidently he could see her better than she could see him, because he pressed the hard flour lump to her lips.

"Eat this," came the gruff order. "We'll save the peaches for the morning, when you can enjoy them."

She bit down on the biscuit and chewed. It was flavorless, but she had to admit, several bites later, that it was filling. Such was her fatigue that the act of swallowing the dry mouthfuls increased her weariness.

"Drink this." She felt the edge of the canteen pressed against her lips. She tipped her head and drank deeply.

"Thank you," she said again when her thirst was quenched.

"Such a polite little deputy..."

His gritty observation danced through her disoriented thoughts. He lowered her to the pallet of blankets.

"Such a considerate big bad villain."

As she dozed on the brink of oblivion, she felt his firm touch upon her stockinged feet. It was to the wondrously pleasurable sensation of him massaging her aching arches that she lost her last grasp of coherent reflection.

Something solid cradled Victoria. She snuggled closer to the center of her secure haven. She was dreaming, and in the way of many dreams, she had an awareness that what was happening wasn't real. Because she knew, of course, that she wasn't a red-feathered bird, weaving a nest high atop a lodgepole pine.

Yet it was gloriously inspiring to view the forest from a swaying pine bower, and she savored the mind's magic that made it possible. She was close enough to the sun to warm her feathers against its golden heat. The clouds floating beneath her reminded her of the white, billowing sails that dotted Boston Harbor.

She felt invincible! As soon as she finished fussing with the last of the twigs she'd brought to her pine paradise, she would have a nest to rival those of any of her winged neighbors.

A shadow flitted across her sanctuary. Victoria looked upward. The proud, powerful descent of a great black-winged eagle caught her attention. She held her breath, waiting for the predatory bird to alter his course, but he didn't deviate from his path. He boldly invaded her perfect little nest.

Anger pricked Victoria. There wasn't room in the cozy nest for both of them. He didn't belong here. He was trespassing . . . but his beak *was* most impressive, however.

"Victoria, stop it."

A man's chiding voice came from the eagle's curved beak.

"You must go," she told the intrusive bird. "There isn't room for you."

"There was plenty of room last night."

Victoria's eyelids slammed open. Logan Youngblood's somewhat blurred countenance appeared at the tip of her nose.

She gasped. The self-serving brute had invaded her bed while she slept. Her head rested against his shoulder, and one of her arms was draped around his waist. Their legs were intertwined, and her skirts were hiked up almost to her knees. As these appalling circumstances penetrated her sleep-fogged brain, Victoria sprang into movement.

She tried to twist from him, but her loosened hair conspired to foil her efforts to obtain her freedom. The unanchored strands were trapped under his unyielding shoulder.

"Let me go, you—you blackguard!"

Instead of retreating, he rolled forward so that he sprawled across her, pinning her beneath his heavy body. His fierce gaze bored into her. Their faces were so close, their eyelashes almost collided. She swallowed. In the morning light, his beleaguered countenance was sporting even more bruised colors.

"Good morning, Victoria."

The benign greeting was so at odds with his threatening expression and her struggles to wrest herself from his possession that she was taken aback.

She licked her lips, struggling for composure, struggling to control her heart's desperate pounding. The direction of his morose glare lowered to her lips. This certainly wasn't the first time she'd felt his stare on her mouth. But Logan was closer than he'd ever been before. His substantial body seemed to touch her *everywhere.*

His masculine scent was impossible to ignore, somehow reinforcing his rock-hard invasion. A reaction that was not simple fear made Victoria shiver. Primitive awareness trembled to life within her. A desire, previously unawakened, stirred.

She felt the rigid length of him lodged bluntly against her bunched-up skirts. His raspy breathing gusted gently across her upturned face. An increased harshness sharpened his already severely stamped features.

She held her breath as a new, elemental knowledge pumped through her. She'd never puzzled it out logically before. But now, with this hard-edged invader draped across her, she understood intuitively how man was fashioned to couple with woman. She blinked, wondering how she could have lived so long without putting all the pieces together.

This must be the passionate act Rochester had contemplated experiencing with dear, sweet Jane Eyre. What Lancelot and Guinevere had done to betray King Arthur. What Mr. Darcy expected from the sensible Miss Elizabeth Bennet once they were wed. What her own father had surely done once or twice with her mother, though she found that last thought somewhat farfetched.

Victoria supposed that, since she'd never been called upon before to utilize this knowledge, it had lain dormant within her, awaiting that moment when she would be called upon to deliver her innocence. Surely this wasn't that moment!

Slowly she released the breath she'd been holding. She knew he could feel the warm exhalation of air upon his face, just as she felt his breath upon her skin.

What an incredibly intimate act. To share the same air.

Logan's head lowered. She knew without asking that he was going to kiss her. *Stop him!* warned a cautionary inner voice that saw to such things as survival. It was the same voice that would have advised her to flee a burning building or—

He didn't close his eyes.

His smooth lips brushed against her closed mouth.

She couldn't tear her gaze from his. Her breath came in jerky, shallow pants that provided little air and somehow intensified the incredible tension between herself and the man whose broad chest rested against her breasts.

Her lips tingled. There was a strange unraveling sensation throughout her body. She felt the touch of his firm mouth in a myriad of forbidden places, places that pulsed with tremulous urgency. A deep shudder coursed through her. *Enough!* her mind warned. *Not nearly enough,* countered an awakening part of her that wanted to prolong the fiercely pleasurable closeness.

He raised his head.

She couldn't speak. Instead, she shifted restlessly beneath him.

Something hot and powerful flickered in his already heated gaze. "Hold still, Victoria."

"I will not!"

She heard the raw desperation in her voice. It jarred her as much as her vulnerable position beneath Logan Youngblood.

He had the nerve to smile at her. And it wasn't even the nasty, smug kind of smile that she could have worked up some resentment toward. Instead, a hint of tenderness tinged his expression, shaking her determination to fight him to the last breath in her body to preserve her honor.

"If you keep wiggling, Victoria, something is going to happen between us I'm sure you'd rather avoid."

Her gaze narrowed. She'd been right about him. He was a pillager and a plunderer!

"I'll die before I let you have your way with me."

Without warning, his mouth swooped down on hers. This kiss was very different from the first. It was hard and swift and showed not one iota of tenderness.

It didn't take him long to finish his dastardly assault. When he raised his dark head above her again, she felt as if she'd been branded by his quietly savage possession.

Barely restrained violence simmered in eyes that had moments before been unexpectedly gentle. "If I decided to take you, your puny resistance wouldn't be enough to stop me."

She wanted to hurl his threat back in his face, but he'd demonstrated quite effectively that her objections to his physical conquest meant nothing to him.

"Please..."

She loathed pleading, but she had no intention of being used by this ruffian. She promised herself that the moment she gained her freedom, she was going to get a knife and cut his black heart from the broad chest that was presently squishing the air from her lungs. Her hands fisted around the material of his shirt. Maybe she'd speed things up a bit and use the ax.

Satisfaction simmered in his gaze.

She decided upon the ax.

"I wasn't trying to, as you so melodramatically put it, 'have my way with you,'" he began curtly. "I slept *next* to you last night, not *with* you. You were the one who rolled to my side of the bedding. You were the one who invaded my territory. You were the one who draped yourself across me."

"I did no such thing!" she protested, but she had the sinking feeling that he told the truth. When they were small and shared the same bed, her sister, Annalee, always had claimed Victoria took more than her fair portion of the mattress.

"Another thing," he said through gritted teeth. "I haven't had the ... pleasure of being with a woman for several months now."

Victoria's cheeks burned with mortification. She knew what he was telling her, knew with a vengeance, now that she'd sorted out how men and women ... fit together. How could he reveal such a private matter to her?

"That's hardly any of my business," she gasped, deeply offended by his directness.

Twin flames smoldered in his darkened gaze. "For as long as we're together, it definitely is your business."

She swallowed. A powerful force she'd heretofore been oblivious of ignited his gaze. She sensed that Logan Youngblood was deadly serious, and that she'd better pay heed to his remarks.

"All right," she conceded shakily.

"All right, what?" he growled hoarsely.

She blinked at him. She honestly didn't know what she'd just agreed to.

"I have no idea." She didn't bother to hide her bewilderment. She didn't understand how things had spun so quickly out of control, but she blamed Logan for the entire fiasco.

"Then I'll spell it out for you."

He could spell?

An incipient giggle trembled behind Victoria's pursed lips. She guessed she was on the verge of giving way to hysterical laughter. She'd only done so once or twice in her whole life. It didn't seem to matter that this was a perfectly awful moment to surrender to irreverent amusement.

She wasn't really amused, after all. She was just a bit...unhinged. This was the first time she'd ever carried on a conversation with a man spread across her reclining body.

"Keep your distance, and nothing of a ... personal nature will happen between us."

She took immediate exception to his arrogant manner *and* his implication that this episode was in some way her fault. "Then I suggest we have this discussion in a vertical position." She shoved hard against his unyielding chest. *"Get off!"*

"Yeah, that's exactly what I should do," he agreed, his eyes gleaming with slumberous heat.

Instead of removing himself from atop her, however, he shifted slightly. His maleness rubbed against the juncture of her thighs. How could anything so improper feel so...nice?

His eyelids lowered briefly. When he raised them, his gaze radiated a steely determination that alarmed her. She felt totally dominated by his masculine invasion.

"Well?" she demanded. Her own breathless tone disheartened her. Now certainly wasn't the time to dissolve into something of the consistency of freshly mixed bread dough. She needed to be strong, to put this incorrigible ruffian in his place. And his place was surely *not* on top of her!

"Well, what?"

Was that laughter lurking in his dark gaze? How dare this cur find anything amusing in his trespass upon her person!

Again she shoved against him. Harder than before. A grimace tightened his features. She didn't feel even a smidgen of sympathy. Men like Logan Youngblood brought their own misfortune upon themselves with their intemperate behavior.

"I'm moving," he told her. His voice sounded strangely strangled. "Just give me a minute."

She bit her lip. He really did appear to be in pain. Perhaps she'd pushed against him with a tad too much force. She kept forgetting about his bruised ribs.

Using his powerful forearms, he levered himself from her. His action momentarily increased the pressure of his groin against her hips. Despite the barrier of their clothing, the subtle friction caused a pulsing tremor to squeeze something inside her that had never before made its presence known. It was all she could do not to reach out and draw Logan back to her. Deeply embarrassed by her reaction to the felon, Victoria tried to shut out the powerful sensations flooding through her.

When Logan finally rolled from beneath the covered wagon, she lay there for several dazed moments, trying to collect her scattered senses. How strange that the simple act of putting two bodies in close proximity could incite such alarming pleasure. Had he, too, felt that fluttering sensation deep inside him?

"Come on, Victoria, it's time we were on our way."

As she crawled into the morning sunlight, she tried to put what had happened out of her mind. Because, when one got right down to it, nothing had happened. She'd just strayed to his side of the bedding. He'd rolled on top of her. And they'd kissed. A simple, straightforward series of incidents. Surely there had been nothing magical about the encounter.

Of course, she'd never been kissed before. That must be what had indelibly imprinted the experience on her mind.

Just because she felt profoundly shaken, that didn't mean she would remember this event for the rest of her life, remember the musky male scent of Logan Youngblood, remember the lazy hunger glinting in his eyes, remember the purposeful brush of his lips against hers.

After trying to smooth the wrinkles from her dress, she looked up and found him staring at her. Her breath caught in her throat. Goodness, he looked like a ferocious man-eating dragon this morning. His mauled features accounted for a major portion of the impression, that and the fire burning in his gaze.

Her mouth went dry. "What is it now, Mr. Youngblood?"

"Logan," he fairly snarled.

"Logan," she returned, striving for briskness while curling her toes into the pine-needled ground.

With a start, she remembered him taking off her walking half boots last night and massaging her tired feet. A hot blush crept across her cheeks. She must have been exhausted beyond sanity to permit such intimate contact.

"Stop staring at me as if you want to eat me," she blustered at him. "If you have something to say, say it."

Her words seemed to spark a flash fire in his already smoldering gaze.

"Lady, you really do need a keeper. Don't ever tell a man he looks like he wants to eat you."

She blinked in surprise. What a peculiar thing to say. She almost found herself reassessing Logan's level of intelligence. But they'd come too far for that. She knew he wasn't limited in his reasoning abilities. He was just a darned strange man.

"All right." Surely it was best to humor him when he got this way.

If anything, his frown intensified. "Don't ask me why."

"I hadn't intended to."

He opened his mouth, as if he had something more to say on the subject, then seemed to think better of the matter.

"Now that I reflect upon the issue, however," she continued, "I can't think of any reason why I shouldn't make such an observation—providing, of course, that I don't meet up with a cannibal."

She thought her attempt at humor might bring a softening to his rigid countenance. It didn't. She glanced around uneasily. Could it be that there *were* cannibals in the Idaho Territory?

He ran a hand through his longish hair. For no reason, her stomach turned over. This time, it was Victoria who frowned. She really needed to gain control of her chaotic senses.

"We'll have those peaches this morning," he advised her sharply. "Then I'll hitch the team."

The change of topic was abrupt but welcome.

"All right."

"We won't be pushing so hard today. You can walk."

That was a relief. There would be no jarring, bruising wagon seat to contend with.

"About what happened..." His words trailed off, and his glance shot to the tangled pallets beneath the wagon.

Her gaze followed his. Not trusting anything he might have to say on the subject, she decided to get her piece in first. "It's all right. There's no need to dissect what occurred between us. I suspect you were telling the truth about me moving to your side of the bedding. My sister says I have a habit of doing that."

Victoria realized she was wringing her hands, and stopped. "It was wrong of me to accuse you of trying to have your way with me. And, if we take into account your prolonged lack of female companionship—" her gaze encountered his stockinged feet and remained there "—we have an adequate explanation."

"All nice and tidy," he agreed.

She thought she detected a sarcastic edge to his tone. Her head jerked up. It dismayed her that her first and only kiss thus far in life had come from this disreputable example of the male population. Good grief, *anyone* would have been preferable to this criminal!

"I don't think it's fair for you to hold me entirely responsible for the kiss," she felt compelled to point out.

A shuttered expression settled over his rugged features. "What makes you think I do?"

"You said that I should be the one to keep my distance from you," she reminded him.

"That's right."

"Well, don't you see?" she demanded in exasperation. "That makes it appear I'm the one at fault. If you're going to be fair about this, then you must accept your portion of responsibility for what happened and keep your distance from me."

She thought she'd expressed herself very well, and was pleased with her logic. Surely he had to agree with her.

The contrary man shook his head.

"There's a couple of things you're overlooking."

"Such as?"

"Life isn't fair."

She always hated it when people felt the need to tell her that. Life *should* be fair!

"And," he went on, "the reason I said you should keep away from me is because I'm a man and you're a woman."

She rolled her eyes. "Oh, really, sir, surely you're not going to drag out that tired bit of reasoning, that I'm to blame solely because I'm a female."

He took a step toward her. She held her ground and raised her chin. She was fed up with men, like her father, always falling back on a woman's supposed weakness to justify blaming them for any and all problems that arose between the sexes.

"I guess I'm going to have to be blunt."

His roughly voiced announcement raised faint tingles of uneasiness. "When have you *not* been blunt?"

Something hot and predatory glinted in his eyes. She had the uneasy sensation that her attempt to put him in his place had somehow given him permission to cross an invisible line that might have existed for her own protection.

His hand dropped to the front of his trousers. "Men have needs."

Her gaze innocently followed his action. Her eyes widened in mortification as she watched him adjust the clothing covering his lower person. *Blunt?* Oh, he was crude beyond redemption.

"We grow hard and hurting when it's been a long time without female…comfort. When that happens, and we find ourselves getting too close to a woman, we stop thinking with our heads, and—" He broke off.

Victoria held her breath. She feared what he might say next, but found herself fascinated by his explanation. In the space of a few minutes, she'd discovered more about life in general and men in particular than she'd learned in all her twenty-four years. It had been an embarrassing education, but she was hopelessly ensnared by her unlikely tutor.

If anyone knew anything about a man's baser instincts, surely it was Logan Youngblood.

"You're too damned pretty and innocent for your own good."

The compliment came as a shock to her.

He thought she was pretty? She regretted the warmth that flowed through her, but she couldn't suppress it. As for her naiveté, good grief, if he just continued talking for another five minutes, she would consider herself an expert on male needs.

"A man will reach out and grab what he wants when it's within touching distance. A woman has more restraint. That's why I suggested you keep your distance."

"I see." He really had more confidence in women than she thought was warranted, for she remembered the moment when she'd almost pulled him to her. If that wasn't grabbing, she didn't know what was. "Uh, you know, I might be able to help you, Logan."

A look of absolute astonishment swept his features. *"What?"*

"You needn't act so surprised," she grumbled, irritated that he didn't seem to think she was capable of solving his dilemma. "As you stated, I am a woman, and therefore I am the perfect one to solve your little problem."

He took another step toward her. *"Little?"*

"As I see it, your main difficulty is that you've been deprived of feminine companionship."

He raised his hand and ran his fingertips across her cheek. She shivered at the contact.

"You're just full of surprises, Victoria."

Another compliment . . . She found herself smiling at this not-so-complex man.

"It's really very simple, Logan. All we have to do is reform you. We'll change your wayward ways, and while we're at it, we'll mend your deplorable lack of manners."

He dropped his hand as if he'd been burned. "Will you?"

She nodded, pleased at her inspired suggestion. "It's the perfect solution," she continued enthusiastically. "I can teach you how to be...civilized. That way, you'll be able to find a good, decent woman who won't reject you. Then you won't be lonely any longer. And, once we've reformed you, you won't be locked up in any more abandoned forts.

"Of course, you will have to marry the object of your affections," she pointed out, warming up to her subject. "But once you do, you'll have a constant supply of... I believe you called it 'female comfort.'"

She looked at him expectantly, waiting for him to thank her for her highly generous offer.

"Hell."

Chapter Eight

Victoria tramped alongside the lumbering wagon and fumed at Logan's pigheadedness. It must be clear to anyone with a grain of intelligence that he needed all the help he could get. No doubt it was his pride that kept him from accepting her offer of assistance.

She swatted at the pesky deerfly that circled her head. When she returned from her morning's call of nature, she'd found Logan trying to wrap his own ribs with a length of sheeting. Even though she was exasperated with him and his rude rejection, she'd swallowed her wounded feelings and volunteered to help with the bindings.

He'd announced that he was capable of tending to his own needs. Well, the foolish man obviously had no idea how to take care of himself, or he wouldn't be residing in abandoned prison cells.

Suspecting it would be a waste of time to point out that his obstinacy was only hurting him, she'd sat on a stump, eating from the tin of peaches he'd opened. Periodically she'd glanced in his direction as he awkwardly secured the strip of cloth around his muscular torso.

Naturally, she'd been obliged to notice his darkly furred chest. Again. It was a puzzling development, this preoccupation with the man's magnificent...er, adequately formed chest. It was hard to believe she'd cradled her cheek upon it last night. She frowned, wishing she hadn't slept through the experience.

Without warning, Victoria's toe caught on a narrow protruding root in the trail's loosely packed soil. Abruptly she and her wayward thoughts went flying across the uneven ground. She came to rest upon her hands and knees, nose to nose with a terrified squirrel clutching a tiny pinecone. Within the blink of an eye, the small creature darted away.

She stood, brushing swirls of dust and dried pine needles from her dress. The wagon continued up the path, its wheels spitting more dust and pine needles behind it. Shafts of shifting sunlight highlighted columns of dancing motes trapped like fireflies in the luminescent ribbons of brightness.

Obviously, she needed to keep her mind on what she was doing, instead of dreaming about Logan's chest. Little the worse for wear, Victoria started walking again. Except for the narrow strip of flattened ground beyond which the wagon had already proceeded, breathtaking mountain scenery surrounded her.

She swallowed a disgruntled sigh. Evidently, if she didn't keep up with Logan, he would go on without her. He probably wouldn't miss her until dark. Were all Western men so impatient?

Her earlier sympathy toward him evaporated.

She'd found the books, the ones he'd thrown away, no doubt thinking she wouldn't discover his foul deed until they reached Trinity Falls. But she'd found her precious volumes of William Shakespeare, and when Logan wasn't looking, she'd returned them to the wagon.

The man was a barbarian. As far as she was concerned, he'd demonstrated that he was capable of anything. He would probably defile a holy shrine if it stood between him and his objectives.

Plus, there was the matter of his sneakiness, the way he'd succeeded in slipping past her tired defenses and lulled her into a false sense of security. Again, she vividly recalled the previous night and his comforting tenderness. He'd fed her, given her something to drink and virtually tucked her into bed. He'd even massaged her feet! No one had ever done that for her. She was still astonished that his humble act had felt so... splendid. If she were a cat, she surely would have purred. Reflecting back on it, he'd done everything but tell her a bedtime story.

He'd only known her two days, and she'd almost destroyed him. Logan knew his body would never be the same after he'd held Victoria in his arms until he was ready to explode and then had to release her. No man was meant to take that kind of punishment.

Victoria Amory was a menace to herself and to everyone with whom she came into contact. He'd wager that the wagon master who had ridden ahead without her and Dodson with the shot foot had both counted themselves lucky they'd survived their association with the infuriating woman.

He thought back to last night, when he'd played the role of Good Samaritan. She'd been so worn out she wasn't able to string two coherent sentences together. For reasons that baffled him, her vulnerability had touched him. Suddenly it had seemed the most important thing in the world to care for her, to make sure she didn't go to sleep on an empty stomach.

He'd done everything but sing her a lullaby.

Logan scowled. When he went to bed, his intentions had been honorable—to get a good night's rest. He'd lain several feet from her under the wagon. The muffled sound of her breathing had almost lulled him to sleep.

He'd been awake, though, when she rolled in his direction, and he'd noticed things like her scent; it was elementally female. He'd also noticed how her lips were slightly parted; he'd had to strain to see that in the moonlit darkness. And he'd noticed how she looked as if she would fit perfectly in his arms, if she would turn just one more time.

He must have lain awake another hour, waiting to see if she would close the infinitesimal distance between them. And then she had. He hadn't suffered a pang of guilt when he gathered her to him. It amazed him how much satisfaction he'd derived from simply holding her. Her mind might be full of hairpin twists and turns, but her feminine shape was soft and inviting.

He hadn't taken advantage of her. Exactly. Only a bastard would resort to such unfair tactics. But he had allowed his hands the furtive pleasure of making a fleeting sweep across her when he settled her more comfortably against him.

Lord, she did fit.

Her head had rested on his shoulder. Her palm had lain against his chest. Her legs had slid between his. To hold a desirable woman in his arms and proceed no further was slow torture, more painful than anything a white man or an Indian could devise. His body had protested the drought of his prolonged abstinence.

The kiss had been unplanned. But he'd been hard and hurting for so long that when he rolled on top of her, he'd gone momentarily crazy. There was something in those green eyes of hers, something that hinted at passion untapped.

It had been a damn fool thing to do, to kiss her. But if a man was going to make a fool of himself, he ought to have the foresight to do a thorough job. He should have taken opportunity where he found it and acquainted himself with the taste and texture of the inside of her mouth. He would gamble all the money in the bank's vault that, despite her tart manner, she was a sweet-tasting woman.

He didn't delude himself about her innocence. It was that innocence that made her pure trouble. She'd actually offered to bind his ribs, which showed just how naive she was. After the hot kiss they'd shared, did she really think he could stand to have her nimble fingers brushing against his bare flesh and *not* take things further than they'd already gone?

It was as obvious as the golden freckles dusting her nose that Victoria Amory had no knowledge of a man's passionate inner workings. Nor did she have any idea of the narrow escape she'd had this morning. Even if it killed him, he intended to deliver her to Trinity Falls in that untouched condition.

Which was really ironic, when he considered that she thought him lower than river scum. But it didn't matter how she viewed him. He had his own code of ethics, and that code didn't include seducing Bostonian bluestockings in search of... What had she called it? Oh yeah, a Western adventure. Logan grimaced at the overly romantic phrase. His mood turned darker when he realized he never was going to find out how she tasted.

A cooling breeze swirled around him. Curious about the lateness of the hour, he reached for his timepiece. It took a moment to realize it was gone. He'd noticed it was missing when he came to in the stockade. No doubt one of the soldiers had helped himself to the gold watch. He studied the lowering angle of the sun and gauged that it was close to dusk. A twinge of guilt pricked him. He'd stopped only once to allow Victoria to rest.

"Whoa!" he called. The oxen halted. He put the hand brake in place. Rising, he made a quick study of their location. Another couple of miles would bring them to where he planned on making camp. They were now deep in Night Wolf's territory. It would be safe to have a fire. He climbed down from the wagon and waited for her to close the ten yards that separated them.

She walked with her head down, her gaze trained on the trail. He took in the weary droop of her shoulders, the lopsided slant of her limp bonnet and the torn right sleeve of her green dress. His guilt intensified. The woman looked as if she'd battled a mountain lion and lost.

"What happened to you?" The anger he heard in his voice was directed at himself.

At his abrupt question, her head snapped up. Her green eyes flashed fire every bit as spectacular as the northern lights. He wanted to grin, but checked the impulse. She would probably take offense, thinking he was amused by her sorry state. The truth was, he was impressed that there was enough fire left in her to prevail over any obstacle.

"Nothing happened." She stopped. "I'm having a grand time, strolling through this park you call the Idaho Territory." She waved her arm to encompass the pine scenery that bordered them. "I'm just getting my second wind. So why don't you hop back on the wagon, and we'll walk another hundred miles before sunset?"

From her flushed cheeks and narrowed gaze, Logan concluded she'd been pushed to the limits of her endurance. Her smile presented a lot of dainty white teeth. He wouldn't have been surprised to hear her growl.

He sighed. She had every right to be upset.

The rip at her shoulder seam held his attention. He reached out and touched the soft, slightly sunburned strip of flesh the tear revealed. When his fingers brushed against her pinkened skin, he expected her to flinch or pull away. She surprised him by remaining still and looking at him with somber eyes.

"Did you fall?"

She nodded mutely.

His body tightened at the contact of his fingertips resting against her shoulder. No scrape marred the finely boned joint. He found himself fascinated by her delicacy.

"You should have called out. I'd have stopped for you, honey."

The endearment sprang of its own accord from his lips. He mentally counted off the seconds before she took issue with the overly personal term. He got to three.

"Don't call me honey." Her slightly slanted green eyes glinted militantly. "I'm capable of keeping up with you."

"You tore your dress." It was a trivial observation. He was having trouble getting his fingers to stop caressing her. No. He wouldn't lie to himself. He *was* caressing her.

"It's old." She stepped back. "The seam just gave way."

He turned, trying to think of something other than her sweetly curved body.

"It's only a couple of more miles to where we're going to camp for the night, Victoria. The trail ahead is relatively even. You won't get too jostled riding in the wagon."

"I can walk another couple of miles."

"Suit yourself."

Victoria sat on a fallen log, staring into the low-burning campfire she'd built while Logan caught their dinner in a nearby stream. She'd fried the mountain trout, along with a pan of buckwheat biscuits, over the fire, and they'd topped off their meal with more canned peaches.

As darkness closed around them and the stars multiplied in the night sky, Victoria felt full and content. The red-and-gold flames had died down, and she suspected that they would soon burn out. Still, the fiery tendrils had enough life in them to produce a hypnotic effect.

"I wonder what makes fire so fascinating?" she asked idly, pulling her attention from the flickering glow to Logan.

Cast in a shadowy silhouette that seemed to merge with the night fabric that had begun to enfold them, he sat on the other side of the campfire.

"That's like asking why grass is green or the sky is blue."

There were times when logic was irritating, she thought. "I remember when I was a little girl, I used to stare for hours into our fireplace. Sometimes I would see dragons like those that knights of olden times fought. Other times I would see castles or stormy seas or herds of racing cattle. What do you see when you look into the flames?"

A distinct pause greeted her question. She wondered if Logan was incapable of using his imagination. There were people like that, she knew. Her father was one of them.

"Actually, it's not a good idea to stare into the flames."

"Why not? Is there some Western rule against it?"

"You might say that."

"Well, by all means, share it," she said, not understanding why his practical attitude vexed her.

"It's a matter of survival. If you look into a fire for any length of time, it causes a kind of night blindness. If something unexpected happens—say a cougar or, for that matter, a two-legged intruder shows up—and you need to use your gun in a hurry, you won't be able to shoot accurately because all you'll see is a lingering image of flames."

Victoria shivered. When Logan referred to a two-legged intruder, she was certain he referred to a lawman who'd once been on his trail with the specific mission of arresting Logan. What a horrible way to live, always expecting trouble from respectable society. Had he ever known any other kind of life?

"You're a strange man, Logan Youngblood."

"How many times do you suppose you've insulted me since we met, Victoria?"

There was a wry quality to his question that made her flush.

"I wasn't trying to be insulting."

"That makes it worse," he said, unperturbed. "Because your opinion of me is so low, you don't even have to try to find something rude to say."

She stiffened. "I don't have a rude bone in my body."

"I think we're better off not bringing your body into this."

What did he mean by that? Didn't he approve of her body?

"When I said you were a strange man," she said through gritted teeth, determined to make him understand that her observation hadn't been mean-spirited, "I meant that you were peculiar."

"Well, that's makes all the difference," he muttered dourly.

"Would you just shut up and listen?"

When Victoria realized what she'd said, she slapped her hand over her mouth. She'd never told anyone in her entire life to shut up. Which just went to prove how maddening Logan was. Why, he could drive a nun to profanity!

A pool of deepening silence shrouded the small campsite. It dawned on Victoria that Logan was obeying her tactless command.

"What's peculiar is that when we started our trip, you said you'd spent most of your time in Trinity Falls, not in these mountains. Yet you seem to know where every stream is, which turns to take on this tiny trail, how to catch fish without a fishing pole, *and* the fine points of campfire etiquette. That's what I find unusual."

She paused to catch her breath, wondering if she'd placated the touchy man. Then she wondered why it mattered that she'd offended him in the first place.

"I used your cooking fork to spear our dinner," he said, choosing the most irrelevant of her questions to answer.

"There you go," she snapped. "That's not only peculiar, it's amazing."

"Maybe for a white man."

"Logan, you *are* a white man."

"But I've spent time with the Indians."

The Last of the Mohicans was one of her most beloved books. To think that the man sitting across the fire from her had actually lived among the primitives and had learned their noble secrets stirred her imagination. She was curious to know everything about his adventure.

"Was this Night Wolf person one of the Indians you spent time with?"

"I lived with his tribe for a while."

Victoria leaned forward. She wished getting information from Logan wasn't so wretchedly difficult. "Did you become blood brothers? Is that why he brought the warning to you about the fort being attacked?"

"We became friends."

Victoria refused to be disappointed. She was certain something exciting had happened to Logan when he lived with the Indians. All she had to do was get him to impart the details of his adventure. Who knew? Perhaps Logan's life had the necessary elements of derring-do to make up a novel like the one James Fenimore Cooper had penned. She closed her eyes, imagining the title. *The Chronicles of Logan Youngblood among the Primitives.* Didn't that have a marvelous ring to it?

"How did you meet?"

She pictured Logan or Night Wolf saving the other's life, perhaps from a wild bear or a band of renegades. There would have been bursts of gunfire and galloping steeds.

"The first time I saw Night Wolf, he was trading for supplies at Gealy's General Mercantile."

"Oh."

"You sound disappointed. Did you think I'd saved him from a lynching?"

His question was so close to the mark that she shifted uncomfortably.

"No, wait," he continued, not giving her the opportunity to respond. "In any sequence of events you cooked up, I would have been the one with the rope around his neck."

Feeling that anything she said would surely be used against her, she kept her thoughts to herself.

"No comment?" Logan pressed, clearly not content to allow her the luxury of silence.

She limited herself to saying, "So you first met Night Wolf in a general store. What happened next?"

"Are you sure you really want to hear this?"

"Very much," she assured him.

"I don't get it," he muttered.

"Get what?"

"Why you're interested in learning about me and Night Wolf."

"It's not so difficult to understand. I've never met an Indian, and I'm curious. Besides, I want to find out how you seem to know where every rock, tree and boulder is on the path we've been following. When you were looking at the sun earlier, I'll bet you knew exactly what time it was."

"Not exactly," he said blandly. "Not to the minute, anyway. And if I still had my timepiece, you can bet I would have consulted it."

"Did you lose it?" she asked sympathetically, knowing how costly such items were. They also had sentimental value.

"One of the soldiers must have taken it when I was unconscious."

"Why, that's disgraceful! He should be reported to his commanding officer and severely reprimanded. And he should be forced to give it back to you."

Logan chuckled softly. "That can be your next assignment, after you turn me in."

He would bring up that unpleasant subject, just when they were getting along so well. "Please tell me about you and Night Wolf."

"Why would you believe anything I told you?"

His question stunned her. Had she made her suspicions about him that obvious? Another hot flush crawled across her cheeks. She had made it abundantly clear from the beginning that she mistrusted him profoundly. Of course, discovering him locked up in that stockade and abandoned by the soldiers had more or less sealed her opinion of the man's character. Yet she didn't think of him as a liar. Oh, perhaps a murderer or a thief...

Her faulty reasoning reproached her. She tried and failed to come to terms with her ambivalent feelings about Logan Youngblood. The truth was, he was a mystery to her. His motivations were locked in obscurity. He seemed to have the ability to confound her on every level—from the way his gaze sometimes trapped her in its unfathomable depths, to his unexplained acts of kindness, to his gruff manner. He had the power to keep her off balance, to make her want to trust him and then make her fearful of where such trust might lead.

The one irrefutable fact she knew about him was that he'd committed an act so heinous it demanded a death sentence.

Yet she also knew she would be predisposed to believe most anything he told her—provided it wasn't too far-fetched, of course. She was an intelligent woman, after all.

"You're taking a long time to answer my question."

"I'm not certain I would believe *everything* you told me," she stated honestly. "But, even though it makes little sense, I am inclined to trust your account of your time with Night Wolf."

"I should count myself lucky you're in such a generous mood."

"Have I told you that you have an annoying tendency to be sarcastic?"

"Chalk it up to just one more grievance you can lay at my door."

"So you met Night Wolf at the general store," she repeated obstinately, determined that he would share his Indian adventure with her, even if they had to stay up all night.

"Damn, you're a stubborn female."

"Just chalk it up to another grievance you can lay at my door," she said with feigned sweetness.

"And you have the nerve to call me sarcastic?" He shook his head. "Lady, you could give lessons on cutting people down to size."

You're exactly the right size. Big and awe-inspiring. That inappropriate observation waltzed through her thoughts like a tardy dancer searching for a partner after the music had begun.

"Logan, what happened in the general store?" she demanded.

Abruptly she wondered if perhaps he'd been there to rob it. Was that why he was hesitant to discuss the incident?

"No, Victoria," he said, his tone resigned.

"No, what?"

"No, I wasn't at Gealy's with the intent of robbing the place."

Good grief! When had he mastered the alarming skill of reading her mind?

Chapter Nine

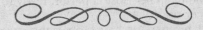

Logan stared across the campfire at Victoria, battling the urge to either shake or kiss her. As much as he might want to deny it, he found her enthusiasm oddly captivating. There was nothing jaded or hypocritical about the woman. She came across as the most direct and straightforward person he'd ever met. Whatever was on her mind, she said it, which suited him just fine, because he'd never been one to mince words. Although he had to admit he would find her honesty more agreeable if she had a higher opinion of him.

He leaned forward and picked up a stick with which to prod the fire. His ribs were healing; he didn't experience the flash of pain he'd braced himself for. He was tender, but on the mend.

"I stopped by the store to *buy* some tobacco." He put emphasis on the word *buy*.

"I didn't know you smoked."

Her Boston accent laced her words with a snooty scorn that rippled across his tranquillity like a silken leash. Damned if he didn't find even that appealing.

He was in trouble, if he found himself remotely charmed by this woman's prissy way of speaking. But he *was* charmed, he admitted reluctantly.

"I like a good cheroot from time to time." He tried not to sound defensive. There were some privileges a man shouldn't have to apologize for enjoying.

She rose and smoothed the lines of her skirts. He almost grinned at the contrast between her aristocratic bearing and her bedraggled state. Her hair was undone and flying wildly around her shoulders. It resembled a reddish cloud burnished gold by the setting sun. That bare patch of skin peeped from the ripped material at her shoulder, and her cheek boasted a smudge. Yet, from her manner, she could have been standing in her Boston parlor, ready to receive the cream of proper society.

He guessed his parents had been right; good breeding showed. They had carried that edict to the extreme, however, when they expected him to marry Robeena Stockard to preserve their family's prestige within their rarefied circle of acquaintances. It had been of little consequence that his fiancée had slept with his brother. Her betrayal had been secondary to keeping any hint of scandal from the Youngblood name. They were respected bankers, after all. A tawdry public washing of their soiled family linen might negatively effect business. And, of course, that could not be tolerated. So they had taken Burke's side, claiming that Logan had misunderstood what he saw with his own eyes.

"Well, thank goodness you haven't picked up the repulsive habit of chewing tobacco," Victoria mused, moving away from a curling column of smoke.

"Not yet," he said, jerking his thoughts from the past with a vengeance.

"Goodness, Logan, you've enough bad habits to overcome as it is. You don't want to start adding new ones."

Victoria rounded the fire and strolled toward him. Without an invitation, she gracefully sank next to him on the blanket that he'd spread as far away from her as he could get while still sharing the same campsite. He'd learned his lesson yesterday morning, even though she obviously hadn't. Getting too close was dangerous for both of them, as well as painful to his body.

Despite his admonition, she stared into the fire. Glimmers of firelight danced over her high cheekbones. Her profile was utterly feminine, utterly appealing. He shifted on the blanket, promising himself a cold bath in the nearby stream after she retired for the night. Fed by frigid mountain lakes, the water should be the right temperature to cool the heat Victoria generated whenever she was within touching distance, and she was within touching distance as she arranged her skirts on his blanket.

He ought to address the barb with which she'd jabbed him. He didn't have any more bad habits than the next man. Instead, his thoughts swung to undressing. Both herself and him.

"It's nice to know you have my interests at heart."

She turned and regarded him with earnest eyes. His stomach clenched. Stunned that she could have such an effect on him, he poked at the fire. He'd been too long without a woman. That was why Victoria was getting under his skin.

"Please tell me how you and Night Wolf came to be friends," she said, placing her fingertips against his sleeve.

She'd said *please*. For some reason, that word, coming from her soft lips, made his skin tighten. His glance fell to where she was touching his arm. Such a small, fragile hand. Perfectly shaped. He couldn't help wondering how it would feel against his heated skin without his shirt's fabric as a barrier.

Talking about Night Wolf might break the spell she was weaving over him. He ordered himself to withdraw his arm from Victoria's obviously innocent, yet nevertheless provocative, contact. The arm stayed put.

"It was February." Logan's voice sounded gritty to his own ears. He remembered the snow had laid heavily upon the land. It had been his first winter away from home, his first February in the territory. "Night Wolf was trading gold nuggets for supplies." Logan recalled how the Shoshone chief had stood with quiet dignity at the counter. "There was a time when his people would have had enough buffalo meat to feed them through the winter."

"I've heard about the great slaughters the railroads are sponsoring," Victoria said. "What a terrible waste."

Her awareness of the problem and her opinion of it surprised Logan.

"It's worse than wasteful. When the last of the buffalo are gone, the Indians are going to be left in desperate straits."

"Do you think all the herds will be wiped out?"

"They're on their way to extinction now. In a few years, the rails will be laid across the country. With them will come farmers, ranchers and towns. There won't be room for buffalo, or for Night Wolf's people and the other tribes."

"Perhaps the Indians could become farmers or ranchers."

"After living with Night Wolf's people, I don't think many of them would settle down to anything as regimented as farming or ranching. They seem to resent keeping schedules. They also think of the land differently than we do."

"What do you mean?"

He wasn't sure he could put the alien philosophy into words. "It's as if they don't feel the land should be used the way white men use it. They seem to hold it in some kind of trust for the next generation. I think it's kind of a religion to them."

"From what I've read, they do worship nature—the sun, the moon, the earth, the water, the buffalo...."

"Well, one thing's for certain, they don't seek to amass great fortunes. They live simply, putting their families' immediate needs first."

"It sounds like a very satisfying way to live, doesn't it?"

Logan smiled. "Before you decide to embrace the Indian way of life, you should know their womenfolk put in long days, making beaded deerskin clothing, moccasins, and blankets from buffalo hides. They tan leather, chew it to make it supple, and cook all their food over open fires. They never seem to be in a hurry, but they work from sunup to sundown."

"Some white women work just as hard," Victoria pointed out. "Homesteaders' wives might not chew buffalo hides, but they haul water, make soap, wash mountains of laundry, cook, clean and help with farm chores. Why, I'll wager their days are longer than their husbands', because when the men come in from their chores at night, their day's work is done. With the convenience of lanterns, women work long past sundown. They might not make beaded garments, but they sew their clothes and decorate them with embroidery. And they bake bread and—"

"Whoa! You've convinced me. Some white women work every bit as hard as Indian women."

"Getting back to Night Wolf..." She drew her knees up and encircled them with her clasped arms. "Did he get his supplies?"

"Eventually."

"What does that mean? Honestly, Logan, this story is going to take all night if you don't speed it up."

Victoria's eagerness sharpened Logan's awareness of her sitting too damn close to him. He wondered if she would bring that same fervency to bed with her when she made love. This time it was Logan who shifted his position.

"It was a rare sight back then to see an Indian in town. Night Wolf's appearance at the store drew a crowd of onlookers. It's hard to know whether people were more curious about him or about the gold nuggets he began taking out of a rawhide pouch."

"He was alone?"

Logan nodded. "He must have traded for a wagon and team before he showed up at Gealy's. It was clear he intended taking a full load of supplies back to his village."

"And was he able to?"

"After a fashion. Gealy was cheating Night Wolf, charging four times as much for the goods as they were worth."

"How awful! Someone should have put a stop to it."

"In a way, Night Wolf did. He conducted himself with such dignity that I think he shamed Sam Gealy into being more fair."

"Good for Night Wolf."

"But there are people who haven't got a conscience that can be shamed," Logan observed. "The sight of gold can have a potent effect, and the size and purity of the nuggets Night Wolf traded was enough to stir gold fever in those watching."

"Surely they couldn't rob him while he was in the store."

"The fever doesn't work that way, Victoria."

"I don't understand."

"From what I've seen, when it gets hold of a man, his first instinct is to look at everyone else as a potential enemy. Each of the men watching the proceedings was plotting to follow Night Wolf out of town, hoping to get the Indian alone."

"But all the gold would have been at Gealy's store. Night Wolf would have had just the supplies."

"And the knowledge of where he'd found the gold. A claim like that could turn a pauper into a rich man."

"Did Night Wolf realize he was in danger?"

Logan remembered his gaze drifting across the crowded mercantile to the Shoshone chief. In that split second, a silent communication had flashed between them. The Indian had known he was in trouble, but his people's plight was so desperate he'd taken the risk of coming to Trinity Falls on their behalf.

"He knew."

"What happened next?"

"He loaded up the wagon and headed out of town. I decided to follow him."

"Oh, Logan. Not you, too."

His thoughts were so fixed on the past that it took a moment for Victoria's disappointed observation to register. He stiffened, swearing that if she insulted his honor or his intelligence just one more time, he would throttle her.

"Me, too, *what*, Victoria?" he asked pointedly.

She hesitated, staring at her hands, joined around her drawn up knees. "Well, I don't wish to be unkind, but from everything you've told me about this gold fever, it sounds as if..."

"As if?" he prodded coldly.

She raised her gaze and considered him from beneath her knitted brow. "Never mind. It wasn't important."

"You're sure?"

She nodded jerkily. "Go on with your story. What happened next?"

"I wasn't the only one to ride out. At least a dozen other men, most of them lone riders, had a sudden desire to leave town. And they rode after the supply wagon."

"Why did *you* ride out after him?"

For some reason, with night closing over them, the fire burning down to ashes and a cold breeze blowing across them, Logan felt Victoria would believe what he told her. His eyes narrowed. He usually wasn't one for self-delusion.

"I couldn't turn my back on a man with enough guts to lay his life on the line for those too weak to take care of themselves. Too many good men went to their graves in the war."

"You fought in the war?"

Logan nodded. He'd shut his war experiences behind a locked door, knowing one supreme truth—wars, no matter how nobly envisioned, chewed up men, bones, blood and souls. Those who survived were often maimed in spirit, as well as in body.

"Anyway, despite each man's individual greed that February afternoon, they were united in one goal—to make Night Wolf show them where he'd found those nuggets."

Logan saw Victoria shiver. He didn't know whether it was his story or the rising wind that caused her to tremble. To keep from reaching out and drawing her into his arms, his hand fisted around the stick he still held.

"Night Wolf drove his team at a steady trot for the first few miles. Gradually he pressed the horses harder. The men following him picked up the faster pace. There came a point when everyone was pushing their mounts full bore. The men from town were closing the distance. The wagon crested a low hill and dropped out of sight.

"The shelter of the forest was only a couple hundred yards away, but there was no way Night Wolf could make it there before being surrounded. And even if he'd made it to the trees, he'd have had to leave the wagon behind to avoid capture."

"Then his entire trip would have been wasted."

"As it turned out, he was smarter than those chasing him."

"How did he get away?"

"He'd planned a little surprise for anyone who decided to pursue him. When the men charged down the other side of that hill, they were greeted by twenty or so Shoshone braves. The subsequent fight was very short and very final."

Silence briefly settled over their shared blanket.

"It's sad that anyone had to die, but I'm glad Night Wolf was able to get the supplies to his people."

Logan didn't regret the deaths of the cowardly thieves who'd tried to waylay the chief. But he was a man, and he knew men tended to look at things more practically than women.

"Since I was trailing behind the group that had been pursuing the wagon, I heard the gunfire before I reached the rise. I reined in my horse, without seeing what had happened. As far as I knew, Night Wolf had been attacked and killed. But that didn't make any sense, because with him dead, there was no way they would discover where he'd found the gold."

"Don't keep me in suspense. What happened next?"

"I headed to the top of the slope. Before I reached it, though, Night Wolf rode over it toward me."

"He must have thought you were after gold, too."

"The same thought occurred to me," Logan admitted. "There was a strong chance my life would end on the snow-covered plateau. Night Wolf sized me up with those black, penetrating eyes of his and asked why I'd followed him."

"What did you tell him?"

"The truth—that I didn't like the odds between him and those who'd followed him."

"And he believed you?"

"I'm still alive, so he must have."

"But what made him accept the word of a white man, when he and his people had just killed a dozen who'd tried to hunt him down as if he were some kind of wild animal?"

"I doubt I'll ever know the answer to that. But I can tell you this, there's something about his eyes that makes a person think he might be able to read a man's thoughts."

"Goodness, Logan, that's a most amazing story. Why, I'd wager you could write a book about your Western experiences and thousands of people would want to read it."

"Trust you to think of something like that."

"Don't dismiss the idea out of hand." Her fingers tightened their fragile pressure upon his sleeve. "My acquaintances back east are fascinated by tales of the West. You could become as famous as Hawkeye, the intrepid frontiersman created by James Fenimore Cooper."

Two thoughts struck Logan. First, if Victoria's palm stayed on his arm one moment longer, he was going to do something reckless—like press her down upon the blanket and have another sampling of her lips. Only this time he was going to make damned sure he found out what she tasted like.

His second came in the form of a question. How had the woman come by her peculiar fascination with books? He decided it was safer to investigate the latter puzzle, rather than discover what a real openmouthed kiss would feel like.

"Is that why you came west? Because of all the stories you've read in those books of yours?"

She gave him an incredulous look.

Why wasn't he surprised that logical reasoning proved useless when trying to understand Victoria? There was nothing logical about her or her cometlike entry into his world. In that way, she reminded him of Madison. The tomboyish girl had also swept into his life with the spectacular flourish of a shooting star streaking across the night sky.

"What a fanciful idea, Logan."

That she reminded him of a shooting star? With her flashing green eyes and fiery red hair, she sparkled brightly enough to be compared to such a heavenly creation.

"I came west for the most practical of reasons. I was offered employment."

"Doing what?"

Again the image of Victoria in a red spangled dress sneaked into Logan's mind. It was a ridiculous picture. The Bostonian miss sitting next to him would probably prefer death by hanging to donning a dancehall gal's glittery rigging.

"Martin Pritchert hired me to tutor a young woman by the name of Madison Earley."

Logan stopped breathing. He heard a strange pounding in his ears. It was a familiar sound. It had always preceded that deathless moment just before the bugle sounded the charge into battle. In those cataclysmic seconds prior to chaos, Logan had always thought he felt fate breathing down his neck.

That was how he felt now, as if there had been a subtle shifting in the universe and fate was directing its ominous attention to Logan Youngblood.

"I know Pritchert." The words didn't come easily.

Of all the qualified women in the country, had his friend hired someone from *Boston?* Logan's lips thinned. Martin knew better than anyone how much Logan loathed his hometown and the kind of rigid adherence to rules it forced upon its residents.

There was nothing rigid about Victoria Amory, some deviant part of his brain insisted on pointing out. Her body was as soft and supple as a sleek cat's.

"Then perhaps you know Mr. Pritchert's employer, the one whose ward I'm going to instruct."

"What's his name?" Logan asked, realizing that for some reason Martin had not disclosed it to Victoria. If he had, she would have recognized it when Logan told her who he was in the stockade.

"It's the oddest thing, but now that I reflect upon it, Mr. Pritchert failed to mention it to me. I can't imagine why."

Logan could. The name Logan Youngblood was a tainted one in proper Boston society. Obviously, if Martin planned on hiring a member of the town's elite circles, he wouldn't have informed the applicant that her would-be employer was the same man who'd left his fiancée standing at the altar on his wedding day.

For the first time since the morning he'd ridden out of Boston, Logan felt a twinge of guilt at the way he'd broken off with Robeena. But he'd been so furious by her betrayal that he exacted his revenge and salvaged his pride in the most primitively satisfactory way he could find. Since then, he had made it a rule never to casually discuss his family, his brother or any of the happenings in Boston with Martin. And up until he'd employed Victoria, his friend had honored Logan's avoidance of anything to do with his hometown. Logan had always supposed that, with him out of the picture, Burke and Robeena had married.

"I guess it isn't important," Victoria said. "I'll find out soon enough who he is when we arrive in Trinity Falls."

"That you will."

Tell her, it's you....

He slid her a penetrating glance. She was gazing into the distance. He followed the direction of her stare. A shooting star fell from the heavens, leaving a trail of shimmering shards scattered across the night firmament.

Victoria gasped. "Did you see that?"

"Yeah."

"I don't think I've ever seen anything as beautiful."

His attention was no longer focused on the distant distraction. "Neither have I."

"It's amazing how many more stars you can see out west. Goodness, at home I don't remember the sky being as crowded."

He'd noticed the same thing when he first arrived in Trinity Falls. They drifted into a companionable silence.

He wasn't going to tell her who he was.

Victoria hadn't connected the name Logan Youngblood with her hometown because she was unaware of any connection between him and Boston.

She already thought he was a common felon. She would be more than ready to believe he was also the kind of man who would abandon his bride at the altar. Of course, he *was* exactly that kind of man, but Robeena had gotten what she deserved.

What was the harm of enjoying Victoria's company for a few more days without providing her with new reasons to look down her aristocratic nose at him? Those days would give him the opportunity to decide whether she was competent to instruct Madison.

He knew damned well *that* was a lie.

Victoria Amory had already proven her mettle. She had character, intelligence, and spirit. She was a lady down to her little black walking boots. Martin had done a hell of a job in hiring the indomitable Miss Amory. Even if she was from Boston.

"The fire's almost out," she said, smothering a yawn.

She was right. Only a few smoldering bits of wood still burned. The wind had picked up, and she'd moved even closer to him, no doubt in search of warmth.

"I wish it wasn't so windy."

He fought the temptation to put his arm around her and draw her even closer. "Why is that?"

"I was waiting for it to get dark so I could wash off in the river," she said shyly.

Logan thought of Victoria wet and naked. His body immediately hardened.

"You'd freeze out there tonight." His voice was as gritty as if he'd swallowed a mouthful of gravelly sand from the river bottom.

She got to her feet. He immediately missed the contact of her palm upon his sleeve.

"The first thing I'm going to do when we reach Trinity Falls is take a long hot bath."

He pictured her in a big porcelain tub and no longer noticed the chilling breeze.

"We might as well call it a night," he said, trying to rid his mind of the image of Victoria's sleek little body sitting in a tub full of scented bubbles. Damned if those bubbles didn't slide off her pink-tipped breasts. Even though it was only his imagination that was fueling his forbidden thoughts, Logan had a hard time scrambling to his feet.

Sometimes a man's imagination was more invigorating than the real thing. Only, with Victoria, Logan was sure that wasn't true. Not when he found himself aroused by just thinking about the soft curves he'd already held against him.

"Do you think it's going to rain?"

Victoria's question had him looking at the sky again. The stars were disappearing under a covering of thick black clouds that the wind chased overhead.

"It might. We better get our bedding laid out under the wagon."

For the next few minutes, they worked together, securing their campsite. The wind continued to gain momentum, and by the time they were in their pallets beneath the wagon, it felt as if a major storm was brewing.

He heard Victoria's teeth chattering next to him. He knew it was dangerous to even contemplate drawing her into his arms to warm her up.

"Come here," he said roughly, raising the edge of his blanket. "You'll freeze if you stay where you are."

You're a fool, came the inner voice he recognized as his conscience. *You're not going to be able to get a wink of sleep if this woman shares your bed again.*

Victoria scooted to him and slipped beneath his blanket. He let out the breath he hadn't realized he was holding. Her cold, trembling body lay stiffly next to him. He bit down an oath and pulled her the rest of the way into his embrace. She continued to shake. He found himself stroking her back.

"Relax," he ordered gruffly. "You're not afraid of a piddly little storm, are you?"

"Nooo..."

Maybe you should be afraid of me....

Even though it might have an element of truth, he disliked the thought. He wanted Victoria to start trusting him before she found out anything more about him. And, just maybe, he wanted to start trusting himself again.

Logan made a vow. For once, he was going to consider someone else's needs before his own. When he deserted Robeena, it had been a selfish act designed to salvage his pride.

But the woman in his arms had done no wrong. In fact, she'd saved his life. His gut-wrenching attraction to her was something he had to fight. Because, Victoria was the one woman in the territory he could not seduce or allow himself to be innocently seduced by, even though her subtle femininity was the most seductive lure he'd ever tried to steel himself against.

Not that he'd often been required to exercise restraint where an available woman was involved. Until this juncture, the only woman he'd been drawn to this strongly was Robeena Stockard. That attraction had demolished his reasoning ability to such an extent that he asked the amoral woman to marry him.

Since that unmitigated disaster, he'd scrupulously avoided any involvement with the feminine sex that might result in a similar derailment of his common sense. He held in his arms a woman who tempted him to violate the cold-blooded promise he'd made to himself six years ago to enjoy only the most superficial alliance with any female—to be more specific, a *carnal* alliance.

But Victoria had come west to instruct Madison. A peculiar set of circumstances had brought the young girl under his protection, and it was up to him to see that she was shielded from any taint of scandal. He didn't know where this heretofore-unrecognized streak of protectiveness had come from. But, even as he resented the unfamiliar need to safeguard Madison, he could not fight it. She had endured a life of hardships up until this point, and Logan would be damned if he caused her any further trials.

When Victoria Amory arrived in Trinity Falls, she would do so with a spotless reputation. Which, even if he continued to resist his attraction to her, would be no easy feat. Because of his own less-than-sterling behavior with the town's fancy women, there were bound to be gossips titillated that he and Victoria had spent days and nights alone on the trail. Martin's wife would be one of them.

Logan might be sophisticated enough to act as if nothing of an intimate nature had happened between himself and Victoria, but her wholesome features would broadcast to the world that he'd broken down the barriers of her innocence, barriers like the one that allowed her to blithely snuggle into his embrace, as if they were children rather than passionate adults.

No, if he was to yield to the temptation to make love to her, afterward she would no doubt blush and stammer and demand marriage to right the horrible wrong he'd inflicted upon her.

A particularly violent gust of wind rocked the wagon, and she squirmed more closely against him. Sweat beaded his brow. At the moment, marriage didn't sound nearly as painful as the frustrated state that gripped him.

His hands moved slowly over her. When he reached the outline of her buttocks, covered by her dress, he squeezed softly.

"Logan!"

His chin rested against the crown of her head. He felt her outraged gasp against his throat.

He smiled. "Hmm?"

"Wh-what do you think you're doing?"

"Just trying to keep you warm."

"I—I'm warm enough. There's no need to... to pinch me."

"It was hardly a pinch. I would call it more of a squeeze."

"Well, whatever you call it, don't do it again."

He didn't answer. It occurred to him that he'd taken for granted her sweet compliance if he should weaken and pass the bounds of propriety.

As he continued to hold her, he reflected that Victoria might not be his simply for the taking. She had a stubborn resolve that suggested a man would have to woo her mind and her heart if he was going to successfully avail himself of her sweetly formed body.

He thought he might be just the one to succeed where others had failed.

But was he willing to pay the price?

Chapter Ten

Victoria's trembling had little to do with the winds that whipped across her and Logan. Goodness, she still couldn't believe how shockingly pleasant it had felt to have his large palms cup her bottom and gently squeeze her. Whatever had he been thinking, to take such a bold liberty?

Her cheek was plastered against his chest, and she heard the steady beating of his heart in her ear. Last night, she'd been so exhausted she slept through the remarkable intimacy of lying against him. Tonight, sleep was the last thing on her mind.

It amazed her how much heat Logan generated. She felt as if she were anchored against a hot furnace. His broad hands were draped respectably against the middle of her back. She was turned into him, with her palm resting against his belt buckle. One of her legs lay cradled between his, just as one of his strong limbs had insinuated itself between her skirts.

She'd never felt more protected, or more rawly exposed. Wherever her body rubbed against his—and there were so many places of contact—his hard heat pressed through her clothing.

Her heart pounded as if she just run a great distance. His masculine scent carried with it traces of leather, camp smoke, and an earthy muskiness that made her surprisingly conscious of her femininity. She felt soft everywhere he wasn't.

She burrowed the tip of her nose into the fabric of his shirt. She wanted to fix his unique smell in her memory, so that, years from now, she would be able to recall it with absolute clarity. The foolishness of the act was not lost upon her. She decided, this once, to be foolish.

"What are you doing, Victoria?"

Memorizing you...

"My nose had an itch. I was just scratching it."

Goodness, she did feel as if she had a terrible itch. And it seemed to cover her entire body. She hadn't felt this squirmy since she'd been eight and infected with the chicken pox.

She sighed. "Do you think it's going to rain?"

"Probably."

She twisted again, trying to accomplish the impossible—to get comfortable, and get closer to him, too. "If it does rain, will the stream overflow?"

"We're camped on high ground. If it starts to flood, the water will fall off on the downhill side."

She wriggled again. "You're very smart, Logan."

"I never thought I'd hear you say that to me," came his droll voice from the darkness.

She flushed and raised her hand from its resting place on his belt buckle. Her nervous fingers strolled up his shirt-front. "Did you learn about these mountains from the Indians?"

One of Logan's hands gripped her wandering fingertips.

"Don't do that," he instructed in a virtual growl.

"I'm sorry. Are your ribs still tender?"

There was a marked hesitation before he answered. "Yeah."

"You didn't answer my question," she reminded him when another moment passed without him speaking.

"I learned everything I know about this forest during the time I lived with Night Wolf's people."

"How did that come about? When did you meet him again?"

"Victoria, we need to rest. We're going to be up early."

He sounded so much like a chiding parent that she smiled.

"How can anyone sleep with the wind howling like a demented wolf?" *And with you holding me so closely that it's hard to know where I end and you begin?*

"Just close your eyes and try."

She lowered her eyelids and waited. Nothing happened. "When I was little and unable to drift off to sleep, our housekeeper would give me warm milk to drink."

"We're fresh out of cold or warm milk, Victoria."

Again his autocratic manner made her feel about ten.

She shifted against him, stretching the leg that lay between both of his. "There's no need to be rude."

"Dammit, Victoria. Hold still."

She bit her lip. It was ridiculous to allow his testiness to hurt her feelings. Obviously, he wasn't experiencing the suppressed excitement she felt in sharing his bed. His callused palm still gripped her free hand. She tried to jerk it loose.

"If you would let go of me, maybe I'd be able to get comfortable."

He finally released her. "Whatever it takes for you to settle down, do it."

No longer sounding parentlike, his tone was as rough and mean as if she'd done him a grievous wrong. Drawing her leg from its sandwiched position, she rolled onto her other side. With her back pressed firmly against him, she rested her cheek against her curved arm. The position was hardly comfortable, but at least she wasn't draped all over him. She felt him turn, also, putting his back to her. Their bottoms bumped.

He uttered another low-voiced oath as he switched to his other side and succeeded in taking the entire blanket with him, leaving Victoria exposed to the biting wind. She refused to complain, and scrunched into a tight, protective ball.

He shifted again, spreading the blanket while he curled around her. Now her bottom was pushed into his groin. His arms came around her, linked just below her breasts. Surely the position had to be uncomfortable for him.

She felt disoriented and oddly dissatisfied, but there was no way she could manage even the tiniest wiggle. Her backside was pressed so tightly against Logan that there was no free space in which to maneuver. And she was still awake enough to recite every poem she'd ever memorized.

"This isn't going to work, Logan," she said, after several excruciating moments of enforced paralysis.

"What isn't?"

"Us sleeping together."

"And why is that?" he inquired in a lazy drawl that made her stomach flutter.

"Because you're squeezing me so tightly I can't breathe."

The pressure of his embrace eased marginally, and his hands massaged her midriff. "I'm barely touching you."

At his alarming caress, her insides trembled. "Stop that."

At least he didn't ask her what it was she wanted him to cease doing. Instead, he continued to idly rest his palms just beneath her bosom. Goodness, if he raised his hands a fraction of an inch, they would—

"Try counting sheep," came his rough-edged suggestion. "That's what I'm doing."

"Is it working?"

Another furious blast of wind roared over and beneath the wagon. "Not exactly."

"As long as we're both awake, I don't understand why we can't talk about your experiences with Night Wolf."

"Has anyone ever told you that you're stubborn, Victoria?"

"Just my mother and my father," she mused idly. "Oh, and my sister, along with a few close friends. My grandparents might have alluded to it a time or two, I suppose. The

Reverend Golly made reference to it on several occasions, and my teachers at finishing school were inclined to lecture upon the subject, but other than that, no one has really dwelled upon the point.''

"I see.''

"Besides, I would rather think of it as determination rather than simple stubbornness.''

"The difference being?''

"There's an enormous difference,'' she felt compelled to explain. "Stubbornness is a failure to listen to reason. Determination is a sign of character. It's what drove Columbus to persevere in crossing the ocean and enabled George Washington to lead his men to victory against the tyranny of King George. It's what enabled Abraham Lincoln to save the Union.''

"Determination?'' Logan repeated dryly.

"Exactly!'' she agreed with satisfaction.

Needing something to occupy her hands, she began to idly brush her fingertips against the backs of his wrists, which lay joined across her midriff. The springy texture of the hair dusting his skin felt oddly compelling. "Oh, some people might call it fortitude or even pluck. But, whatever it is, it's certainly more than simple stubbornness.''

"I doubt there's anything simple about you, Victoria.''

She warmed to what she viewed as a compliment. "Thank you.''

"You're welcome,'' he responded gravely.

She missed hearing the sound of his heartbeat, but it was pleasant to have his deeply pitched voice rumble through her.

"So, when did you meet Night Wolf the second time?''

Logan's laughter embraced her. It made no sense, but she found herself smiling again.

"What's so funny?'' she asked.

"Nothing. Everything.''

"Oh, well, that's clear enough.''

"As clear as anything else in our crazy lives," he said with a sigh.

"What does that mean?"

"It means that I'm a grown man, and you're a grown woman, but it sounds as if you want me to tell you a bedtime story."

Her smile deepened. She couldn't imagine anything more incongruous than Logan Youngblood reciting a bedtime story.

Picturing the rugged man with a toddler nestled upon his lap was beyond her ability to imagine. And yet there was something sweetly poignant about the thought of this tough Westerner subjecting himself to a young child's needs.

"Since there's no warm milk," she teased lightly, "I very well might need a story if I'm to fall asleep."

He tucked the corners of the blanket more snugly around her. The casual movement made her stop running her fingertips across his arms. When his hands returned to their former resting place, they seemed higher than before. Without a tape measure, she had no way of knowing for sure, of course. But it seemed that a smaller distance now separated his hands from the underside of her breasts. Her fingers resumed their restless stroking.

"Anything to settle you down," came his husky voice.

Anything? Of course, a kiss would hardly settle her down, but she found herself thinking about it. Had it been only this morning that he brushed his mouth against her startled lips? It seemed a lifetime ago. She firmly put all thoughts of the kiss from her mind. Or, at any rate, she tried to.

"The second time I ran into Night Wolf was the next spring. News reached us of a wagon train that had been attacked by Indians. The men in town rode out to investigate."

"Isn't that something the military would handle?"

"The fort hadn't been built yet. It was the assault on the wagon train that led to the cavalry being dispatched to this part of the territory and Fort Brockton being constructed."

"Were there survivors?"

"Quite a few. It turned out that only a small band of renegades took part in the ambush."

"I wonder when peace will finally come," Victoria mused. "Imagine what it would be like if everyone could get along."

"It must be what the preachers call heaven. It's going to be interesting how the Almighty works everything out behind those pearly gates of his so the angels get along."

"Goodness, Logan, what a peculiar thing to say."

"Do you suppose the Indian angels will beat tom-toms instead of strumming harps?" Logan inquired, amusement lacing his tone.

A startled giggle escaped Victoria. It sprang from visualizing angels with exotic headdresses and beaded moccasins. But the more she contemplated the image, the more she liked it.

"There's no way to know what heaven is going to be like until we get there," she pointed out.

"And you're thinking I'll never find out."

"Thank goodness, mere mortals don't decide who gets in and who doesn't."

"Such a diplomatic answer."

There was no way of mistaking the sarcasm that edged his words.

"Please continue with your story about your second encounter with Night Wolf," she instructed for her own peace of mind.

"I like it when you say please."

The husky timbre of Logan's tone so shook Victoria that she felt it in her toes and her stomach. "I'll endeavor to say it more often, then."

He drew her closer. She felt the hardened bulge of his masculinity and wondered if that was a natural occurrence for him every time he assumed a reclining position.

Perhaps all men's bodies behaved in a like fashion. She sighed, wishing she wasn't so ignorant about the ins and outs of male anatomy. What a pity that women didn't have the opportunity to discover such facts about men from books, where one wouldn't be unduly influenced by the powerful currents of awareness that a close proximity with the masculine form seemed to induce.

"I was a greenhorn when I came west."

"Where did you come from?" she asked curiously. It seemed that everything he told her had a way of spawning more questions.

"The East," he said vaguely. "That afternoon, a group of us were following tracks left by the renegades. When we reached the hills, we separated. It wasn't far from here that I stopped to refill my canteen at this stream. When I turned around, I was facing Night Wolf. He was on horseback, I was on foot. My rifle was secured on my horse and I hadn't taken to wearing my Colt yet."

"You must have been terrified," she said sympathetically.

"Victoria, men are never terrified," he corrected firmly. "That's something that happens only to women."

"Don't be silly. All humans are subject to trepidation, and that certainly includes men. Go on with your story."

"Not before we clear this up, honey."

She sucked in a breath. He'd called her "honey" again. Somehow, with the wind and darkness roiling about them, the endearment wasn't repugnant. "Logan, it's all right to admit you were frightened when you faced an Indian without a weapon to defend yourself. Even Hawkeye was afraid from time to time."

"Who the devil is this Hawkeye person you keep mentioning?"

"Oh, you know, the brave scout who protected Cora and her sister Alice from Magua."

"How can you call him brave and frightened at the same time?"

, avoid certain words like the plague.''

"Pray enlighten me," she instructed loftily.

"Why are you talking like my grandmother all of the sudden?"

She twisted in his arms. "You have a grandmother?"

"Two of them," his answered forbiddingly.

His eyebrows were drawn together in a fierce scowl. She hadn't the vaguest notion why he was upset.

"What are they like?" she inquired curiously, again fascinated by any tidbit of information she could glean about Logan.

"That does it." He shocked her by rolling on top of her.

"Do get off me. I can't breathe, Logan."

"Try harder," he said unhelpfully, even as he raised to his elbows to provide her with sufficient room to draw air into her lungs. "We're going to get a few things straight, Miss Amory."

"All—all right," she whispered solemnly, staring up into his battle-bruised features with a tinge of awe. Good grief, the man looked like a fearsome warrior, spoiling for an opponent to demolish. She couldn't imagine what had set him

"He passed out," Logan clarified softly.

"You mean it's a matter of semantics?"

"It's a matter of accuracy," he stately firmly. "Men pass out. Women faint or succumb to the vapors. Women become terrified. Men become...cautious."

"So you were feeling cautious with Night Wolf?"

"Exactly."

"Logan," she said, struggling to control the mirth his explanation triggered, "do you honestly believe that?"

"I honestly believe you're driving me crazy, Victoria."

Her humorous mood evaporated. "How am I doing that?"

"Every time we have a conversation, you go off on a dozen different tangents. One minute we're discussing Indians, and the next you're asking me about my grandmother. I find that *taxing*."

"You would prefer I stay on one topic at a time?" His was a complaint she'd heard more than once. It was just that when she became excited about something, she sort of lost her focus.

He shifted against her, insinuating himself more deeply between her parted legs. A wave of heat stung her cheeks.

"As I stated before, the terror would come upon him occasionally, when he feared an imminent attack from Magua."

"That's the second time you've mentioned Magua. Who is he?"

"He was the villainous savage who wanted revenge against General Munro."

"You're talking about characters from one of those books of yours, aren't you?"

"Of course."

"Of course," he repeated in a tone of disgust. "Well, real men don't behave like characters in books."

"Some do," she protested, not willing to hear him disparage her heroes.

"*Real* men," he continued, clearly unaffected by her defense, "avoid certain words like the plague."

"Pray enlighten me," she instructed loftily.

"Why are you talking like my grandmother all of the sudden?"

She twisted in his arms. "You have a grandmother?"

"Two of them," his answered forbiddingly.

His eyebrows were drawn together in a fierce scowl. She hadn't the vaguest notion why he was upset.

"What are they like?" she inquired curiously, again fascinated by any tidbit of information she could glean about Logan.

"That does it." He shocked her by rolling on top of her.

"Do get off me. I can't breathe, Logan."

"Try harder," he said unhelpfully, even as he raised to his elbows to provide her with sufficient room to draw air into her lungs. "We're going to get a few things straight, Miss Amory."

"All—all right," she whispered solemnly, staring up into his battle-bruised features with a tinge of awe. Good grief, the man looked like a fearsome warrior, spoiling for an opponent to demolish. She couldn't imagine what had set him off. From her point of view, they had been conversing most satisfactorily.

"First, running into Night Wolf without a gun in my hand didn't terrify me. Men don't get terrified, just like they don't get the vapors or faint. Got that?"

She nodded. "Uh, Logan, I should tell you, though, that Hyrum Dodson was a man, and he fainted."

"Let me guess. It was when you shot him?"

She nodded again. "He didn't faint right away. At first he hopped around a bit. Then he saw the blood. And then he . . ."

Her explanation trailed off under Logan's ominous scowl.

"He did not faint," he corrected succinctly.

"But you weren't even there," she felt obliged to point out.

"He passed out," Logan clarified softly.

"You mean it's a matter of semantics?"

"It's a matter of accuracy," he stately firmly. "Men pass out. Women faint or succumb to the vapors. Women become terrified. Men become . . . cautious."

"So you were feeling cautious with Night Wolf?"

"Exactly."

"Logan," she said, struggling to control the mirth his explanation triggered, "do you honestly believe that?"

"I honestly believe you're driving me crazy, Victoria."

Her humorous mood evaporated. "How am I doing that?"

"Every time we have a conversation, you go off on a dozen different tangents. One minute we're discussing Indians, and the next you're asking me about my grandmother. I find that *taxing.*"

"You would prefer I stay on one topic at a time?" His was a complaint she'd heard more than once. It was just that when she became excited about something, she sort of lost her focus.

He shifted against her, insinuating himself more deeply between her parted legs. A wave of heat stung her cheeks.

"Haven't you noticed how hard I am?"

His hoarse question shattered the remnants of her composure.

"Wh-what?"

"See how distracting it is when someone suddenly changes the subject?"

"Yes."

"Yes, what?"

Yes to everything! "I can see how confusing changing one's topic of discussion can be," she breathed. "And, yes, I've noticed that you are...er...that is to say...somewhat firm."

He closed his eyes. In the moonlit darkness, his frowning features looked as if they'd been chiseled from granite by a sculptor in a bad mood.

"We've got a lot of night left," he murmured starkly. "Something's got to give."

"I don't know what you mean."

And she really didn't want to know, either. There was something about his hungry gaze that made her think it not be prudent to gaze directly into it. Perhaps Logan's warning about the dangers of staring into campfires should apply to him, also. At the moment, he appeared very much like a two-legged predator, and she wasn't at all prepared to deal with him.

"Do you have any idea how good you feel to me?"

The gruff question melted a significant portion of her insides. She tried to think of an appropriate answer for the darkly intimate query, but her mind seemed to have shut down.

What if he weren't a criminal on the run? What if he were instead a respected member of society? What if he were her legally wedded husband? Then she would be free to stroke his roughly bearded jaw. She would be free to trace the outline of his lips with her tongue. She would be free to wriggle her lower person against him and feel the delightful tingles and tremors any direct contact with him provoked.

But, because Logan Youngblood was not a man she could ever call husband, he was utterly forbidden to her, as forbidden as the shocking yearnings he stirred within her racing heart.

"You really must get off me."

His head lowered, blocking the meager moonlight. No longer did she hear the mournful cry of the wind.

His taut countenance hovered above her. "You're right."

"Then back away, Logan. Please."

At the final word, something hot and elemental sprang to life in his eyes. Her stomach rolled over.

"You do please me, Victoria."

"But I can't. This isn't right."

"I know."

"Then, surely, you must—"

"No more talking."

A flash of white-hot light erupted around them. It momentarily transfused the cramped space under the wagon with a burst of dazzling brightness that revealed with numbing starkness the harshly etched lines of Logan's tensely held features. Seconds later, a blast of thunder rocked the clearing. The patter of raindrops striking the canvas-topped wagon followed.

"I just want to know what you taste like," he breathed. "I won't hurt you."

Surely there could be no harm in a kiss. Besides, she wanted to discover how he tasted, too.

Even though an intimate knowledge of this man was forbidden to her, she would savor what her conscience permitted. A few heated kisses. Perhaps a caress or two. No one would ever know. After Logan disappeared from her life, she would have these treasured memories to warm her during long winter nights. "Then do it," she whispered. "The waiting is killing me."

There was another flash of lightning. Another overwhelming glimpse of Logan's savagely carved features. Her toes curled. Her insides turned to bubbling molasses.

With the cannonlike blast of thunder raging in her ears, she felt Logan's mouth upon hers. Ravenous need seemed to drive him. She encircled his corded neck, drawing him closer. His lips were hot, searing. His tongue was... persistent. She felt the tip of it probe her sealed mouth. It seemed he wanted inside. The novel thought scarcely registered before that was exactly where he was. Inside. With his hot, flicking tongue.

Startled, but not repulsed, she accepted his unexpected invasion. He'd been serious about tasting her.

She realized she was making faint moaning sounds as the kiss spiraled to new heights. She realized, also, that his hands were charting their own bold course across her body. They were on her breasts, fondling, lightly squeezing, restlessly stroking. Her hips rotated against his, and she rubbed his arms.

And the kiss... It had a life of its own. Logan's fingers moved to her bodice. She pretended she didn't notice what they were doing, so that she wouldn't have to call a halt to their... It was called *lovemaking*. There wasn't another word for it.

Then his callused palms touched her bared breasts. Rough skin against her naked flesh. He pulled his mouth from hers and trailed steaming kisses along her throat.

"Ah, Victoria, you feel better than I imagined. And you taste..." He took the tip of a breast into his mouth. Victoria bucked helplessly.

What was he doing to her? She knew she had to make him stop, but, dear God, stopping was the last thing on her mind. Wherever this tempestuous passion led, she wanted to follow.

His tongue moved slickly over a tight, tingling nipple.

"Damn the darkness," he said hoarsely. "I want to see you."

Hot flickers of fire shot from the tips of her breasts and careened through the rest of her.

"Oh, Logan..." His name was a breathless rush of air.

"Yeah, honey, that's it. Say my name just like that."

His large hands bunched up her skirts. She felt his fingers on her thighs. A tingling contraction gripped her womb. She was aware of a surge of indescribable warmth, his heavy breathing, and her own runaway heartbeat. Nothing else existed. Nothing else mattered.

His fingers moved higher. She gasped again, and clutched at his arms. She sensed him adjusting the front of his trousers.

"I'll make it right," he said, his mouth moving to her other breast. "Don't worry. I'll take care of you."

She thought he meant he'd make the painful ache that held her in its pitiless thrall go away. Before he could do so, however, a huge fist seemed to shake the wagon.

"What the hell?"

He raised and looked around. Another wood-groaning shudder seized the overhead structure, causing it to lurch. Logan peered out between the tall wheels.

Victoria concentrated on not shattering into a million pieces. The interruption, whatever its origin—earthquake, volcanic eruption, typhoon—had permitted her overheated flesh to cool and allowed her brain to function again. She couldn't believe what had almost happened between herself and this man.

None of it made sense. They had nothing in common, no abiding affection, no marital contract. . . . How was it that whenever they got close, sparks seemed to fly off his body to hers?

Her fingers went to the buttons on her bodice.

"Damn, it's the oxen," Logan muttered.

There was a momentary lull in the thunderous tumult raging around them. In that fleeting pool of quiet, a spine-tingling shriek rebounded through the night.

Victoria shuddered. "Good Lord, what was that?"

"A mountain lion," Logan answered succinctly. "It and the storm are spooking the animals."

The feral cry rang out again, triggering an instinctive fear of a bloodthirsty predator on the prowl.

Another rocking blow struck the wagon. Logan scrambled from their shelter into the driving rain. Victoria pulled down her skirts and shook off her paralyzing dread of the mountain cat.

She assured the Almighty that she recognized a miracle when she saw one and vowed never to place herself in a situation where she needed a miracle of this magnitude—surely rampaging oxen and a ferocious cougar constituted a monumental miracle—to deliver her from moral destruction.

From this moment on, she promised, trying desperately to compose her fevered, swirling thoughts, she would avoid Logan Youngblood like the plague. She would render herself immune to being intrigued by his Indian stories or fascinated by his unquestionably superb masculine form. She would feel no sympathy for him. Nor would she try to reform his severely flawed character.

In short, she would regard him as she'd regarded the grizzled, foul-smelling, loud-voiced wagon master.

Logan was simply a means to an end.

And that end was getting safely to Trinity Falls. With her dignity intact. And the rest of her, too!

In the meantime, she thought grimly as she crawled from beneath the wagon, she was his equal partner in this joint venture of getting to civilization alive. Surrendering herself to the wet and tumultuous assault of the mountain storm, she blinked her rain-soaked lashes, trying to make out Logan's silhouette in the darkness. She had no trouble finding the oxen; they were pressed up against the wagon and bellowing.

"You're getting drenched!" came Logan's wind-tossed yell.

Victoria turned in the direction of his shout. He was shoving against a two-ton ox, trying to deflect it from the wagon.

She threaded her way toward him. "I want to help!"

The rain had slicked his hair to his scalp, making his features even more harshly defined.

"You're too small to be of any use!" he yelled back.

Drenched to her goosefleshed skin, Victoria took immediate offense. "You need all the help you can get!" *And I'm going to provide it, you bullheaded lummox.*

She only slipped once as she traversed the muddy terrain, and she was grateful that she and Logan hadn't removed their shoes while caught in the throes of their unrestrained passion. If she had, she would have had to brave the distance in her stocking feet.

When she finally reached him, she shoved against the stubborn oxen. As she pressed her palms against the water-slicked hide, it occurred to her that Logan and the dumb beast had a lot in common. They were both great hulking examples of unyielding mass.

Oh, perhaps Logan wasn't quite as hairy or foul-smelling, but as far as she was concerned, the similarities far outweighed the differences.

Chapter Eleven

Victoria sat on a log, unfastening one of her walking half boots. Because they were caked with mud and pine needles, it was difficult to work the laces through the anchoring hooks. She glanced up. A thick gray mist clung to the wetly gleaming pine trees that towered above their campsite. The dense, encroaching fog made their temporary resting place seem like an inadequate haven against the eerie shroud.

Logan was nowhere to be seen. There was no breeze, but she shivered anyway. Her clothes were clammy and damp, and her hair hung in cold, stringy clumps against her neck and shoulders.

After an interminable struggle, she and Logan had managed to return the oxen to the holding area he'd established by the river. It was then that they'd discovered one of the animals had wandered off. Logan had instructed her to wait at camp while he hunted the lost beast. Naturally, she'd ignored his order and begun her own search of the dense forest. Her efforts had produced sightings of beavers, otters and ferrets—all washed from their homes by the ferocity of the summer storm.

Victoria had just given up finding the missing animal when she bumped into its hindquarters. At the time, her attention had been focused on the waterlogged skunk she was backing away from. Fortunately, the drenched creature had been in too much of a hurry to direct any of its nasty spray at her.

She'd shooed the ox to camp, but Logan hadn't been there when she arrived. She'd called to him that she'd succeeded in her quest. Evidently, he was too far away to hear her. How ironic it would be if he'd become lost in the sprawling timberlands.

Victoria realized her teeth were chattering. While waiting for Logan's return, the most sensible thing to do would be to make a fire. Frowning, she surveyed their rain-soaked surroundings, wondering if anything would burn in the dripping forest.

Her glance returned to her feet. She had one shoe on and the other off. Sighing, she went to work on the muddy laces.

The crack of a twig snapping broke the hushed stillness of Victoria's fogbound world. She stood and backed toward the wagon while she scanned the clearing's outer perimeter. She needed a weapon, she decided, wishing for the dozenth time that her rifle hadn't been confiscated by the wagon master. Even a nice sturdy rock would have been appreciated at the moment. Her desperate gaze, however, fell only upon scattered pinecones, trampled mountain grass and a few slender, moss-covered twigs.

She inched across the spongy ground. When she judged she was close to the wagon, she turned and leaped behind it. Unfortunately, the ax Logan had used the night before to chop firewood was nowhere in sight. This was just one more example of the man's untrustworthy nature. How difficult could it be to return a tool to its proper place?

She slid her hand beneath the wagon's canvas covering and groped about. Her fingers curled around a comfortingly thick book. It wasn't much of a weapon, but it was better than nothing.

More rustling movements broke the morning stillness. She peeked around the corner of the wagon. Damp gray fog continued to weave itself through and around the encircling pines. She raised the book, which she absently noted was an early edition of *The Decline and Fall of the Roman Empire.*

Should she call out a warning? She bit her lip. Weighty though this intellectual tome might be, it was hardly as menacing as a loaded rifle. A warning would be wasted.

She waited, supporting the heavy volume with her straining wrist, wishing Logan was here to bolster her courage. Surely, one look at his cruelly swollen features would make anyone bent on mischief rethink his course. But then, maybe it was a wild creature that was stalking through the underbrush and drawing ever closer.

As Victoria watched, the otherworldly gray mist parted. Through it, the dark silhouette of a man took shape. Not a wild beast, then. Her heart still took up residence in her throat. Was she about to come face-to-face with a fearsome Indian?

The figure moved boldly forward.

As if delivered by an icy fingertip, a shiver trickled down her spine.

Then a shaft of sunlight touched the emerging silhouette. From the clinging, insubstantial vapors stepped Logan. Instead of slowing, her heartbeat raced faster. She had the unsettling feeling that this moment would be forever trapped in her memory—Logan striding from the swirling currents of fog.

Where the lingering mist yielded, he materialized—broadshouldered, lean-hipped, supremely masculine. His dark eyes glittered with forbidding intensity. He gripped the missing ax.

In that moment, he seemed more a savage intruder than the man who'd driven her to the edge of sanity with his burning kisses and urgent caresses. He'd bared her bosom, she recalled in dazed wonder. He'd flicked the slick rasp of his tongue across her exposed breasts, tasting them as if they were exotic fruit. A hot flush stung her cheeks. He'd also slipped his hand beneath her skirts and ran his callused fingertips up her legs, stroking the sensitive skin of her inner thighs.

That searing memory made her knees tremble.

As Logan stalked toward her, she thought what an odd pair they were—she ready to use a book to wage war, he with an ax at his disposal. It was hardly an even match. She lowered her arm. She didn't delude herself that it was the sharp-edged weapon he carried that gave Logan the advantage.

No, the traitorous weakness he inspired within her to yield to him was the most devastating weapon of all. What made it so frighteningly effective was that even now, even knowing how close she'd come to disaster, she still savored the splendid chaos he'd wreaked within her, still savored the remembered texture of his tongue and lips, still savored his close heat.

She swallowed. Logan didn't stop until he stood a foot away. She watched his measuring gaze move over her. And, Lord help her, she felt it, too.

He cocked his head. "Don't tell me—a sudden, uncontrollable urge to read overwhelmed you."

The lightly mocking observation induced a reluctant smile. She found herself noticing stray details about the man. His hair was an unruly pelt of gleaming black. The bruises and swelling that had distorted his face had begun to subside. No longer did he look meanly mauled. It came to her with a ripple of shock that Logan Youngblood could actually be called…handsome. It was difficult to know for sure, however, because a black beard had begun to obscure his features.

"I heard a noise." She tried not to let her gaze linger on his unbuttoned shirt and the muscular, hair-roughened expanse of chest exposed for all the world to see. She hefted the book self-consciously, knowing she was about to look the fool. "I couldn't find the ax," she explained, glancing significantly at the lethal object dangling from his right hand. "I thought—"

She broke off. Was she really about to tell him that she'd intended to defend herself with a recounting of Rome's demise?

"You thought you would bore to death anyone who invaded our campsite?"

She debated hurling the book, to show how powerful the written word could be. "I admit it isn't much of a weapon, but it's better than nothing."

An unnatural stillness seemed to arrest Logan's expression. Gone was his earlier light manner. She found his intense gaze both enigmatic and disturbing.

"Do you realize this is the third day I've known you?" An edge overrode his mild tone.

Had it only been three days? There didn't seem to have been a time when Logan wasn't a part of her life. And to think that she'd almost given herself to him in a moment of heedless passion... She felt faintly ill at the thought. It was terrifying to realize that he'd insinuated himself so profoundly into her emotions in so short a time. Truly, he was a force with which to be reckoned. Just like the wild storm that had lashed out at them the night before.

She clutched the book to her. "I haven't counted the days."

"I have," Logan said, in that same quiet, yet ominous, tone.

"To what purpose?"

"To keep myself in line," he answered. "To remind myself you don't belong to me, and I need to keep my hands off you." *His hands? What about the rest of him?* "I remind myself of other things," he continued thoughtfully, slowly swinging the ax in a gentle, rhythmic motion. "I remind myself there are two kinds of women in Trinity Falls."

She angled her chin upward, in anticipation of him dispensing knowledge she had no wish to discover. "Indeed?"

He nodded.

"Pray, enlighten me." She infused the invitation with as much disdain as she could summon.

Fire flickered in Logan's eyes. Victoria winced. She had the feeling she'd issued a challenge to the vexing man. She hadn't meant to. There was something about his disagreeable nature, however, that spurred her to prod him. He was too blasted smug for her peace of mind. And how dare he act so superior, when he was nothing more than a common criminal? With a criminal's perfidious mind and heart, she told herself self-righteously.

And he had no desire to better his abysmal state!

That was his most damning shortcoming. She'd been taught since birth that it was each person's duty to improve his mind and his place in the world. Naturally, because she was a woman, her improvement would entail finding a worthy mate. It would be his responsibility to provide her and future children with financial stability and a respected place in the community.

The plan was straightforward. Except, of course, for the part about finding a worthy man. That took a bit of doing.

Logan leaned forward. "I'll be glad to enlighten you about the women of Trinity Falls. And I'll try not to offend your delicate sensibilities while doing it, but the truth is, Victoria, you need educating in the worst way."

"Well, that certainly qualifies you for the job."

His gaze flashed hotter. She gripped the book more tightly.

"In Trinity Falls, you have your good women on one side, though there aren't that many of them in a boomtown like Trinity. Mostly they're married, or widowed, or too young to be called women. You'll probably be the only single female in town who might be termed one of the 'good' ones."

"*Might?*" she demanded, deeply affronted.

His narrow lips curved into a mocking smile. "Now, the other women, whom some call the 'bad' ones, are really the fun gals. They know how to kick up their heels and have a good time."

"I'll just bet they do."

She disliked intensely the "fun gals" Logan described. He had no business consorting with such creatures. She had a fair notion of what his idea of a "good time" would be. Alcohol would play a major role in his depraved activities. And gambling would no doubt also constitute a significant element of his dissolute partying. And dancing the waltz in squalid drinking establishments. Kissing would surely be involved. And...more!

Then he would probably finish off his evening of base indulgence with a fat, foul-smelling cigar. Oh, yes, the man would have an affinity for a varied number of vices.

"You don't approve?" Logan inquired dryly.

"Certainly not!"

"Good women usually don't," he said mildly. "They fume and fuss over a man's amusements."

"Amusements, or wicked diversions?"

"I think it's because the prim and proper women of the world want to eliminate all the bachelors. They just can't abide the thought of any man being footloose and fancy-free."

"If you intend to drink the milk, Logan, you must purchase the cow," she told him sharply, falling back on one of her grandmother Celeste's favorite adages.

"Well, now, I happen to have a powerful craving for milk."

It suddenly struck Victoria what it was she and Logan were discussing in this remote clearing. Until recently, she'd thought her grandmother's saying referred to indiscriminately given kisses. Now that she'd reasoned things out, however, it occurred to her what the elderly woman meant by unchaste behavior—physical coupling without the sanction of marriage.

New heat crawled up Victoria's throat and spread across her cheeks. They shouldn't be having this conversation. It was far too personal. Far too...titillating.

"Uh, Logan..."

"So the question I want answered is, what kind of woman are *you?*"

He had to ask? Why, that was downright insulting! Her earlier misgivings about discussing this delicate topic forgotten, she straightened. "For someone who doesn't like insults, you certainly know how to deliver them."

"Thank you."

"You're not welcome!"

Logan seemed to receive as much satisfaction from provoking her as she derived from prodding him. Surely that made for a dangerous combination.

"At first I assumed you were one of the good ones," he said, ignoring her outburst. "With your prim collar and long sleeves and those snug little cuffs, you're packaged up as neat and tidy as a ham wrapped in butcher paper and tied with string."

A ham? Her mouth fell open. She didn't think she'd ever been so horribly described. "Now see here—"

"But whenever we get close, you heat up like a firecracker on the Fourth of July."

That she much preferred being called a firecracker to being described as a ham said little for her character, she supposed. "I think you've already expressed yourself sufficiently on that subject."

"So I'm wondering," he persisted, paying no heed to her protest. "Do you or don't you?"

She blinked at him. Could he actually be asking what she thought? He deserved the dressing-down she was about to deliver.

"I should tell you to take yourself to Hades rather than discuss something of such a personal nature, something that is clearly none of your business," she told him in precise and clipped syllables. "That you would even ask such a thing proves you're no gentleman. For, if you were, you would know emphatically that I am *not* the kind of female to invite or enjoy a man's..."

Her words dwindled. It really was rather tricky to phrase her thoughts and not be . . . crude.

He raised one dark eyebrow. "A man's . . ."

She met Logan's speculative gaze and detected an abundance of silent laughter therein. She wanted to hurl the heavy book she cradled at him, but there was still the matter of the ax.

"A man's physical attentions. I may be the first one you've ever met, but let me assure you, I am a lady."

"Well, then . . ."

"Well, then, *what?*" she fairly snarled.

"Who would have guessed ladies could be so hot-blooded?"

She flinched. "If my blood is hot, it's because you have the capacity to make me angrier than anyone I've ever met."

"So you kissed me in . . . anger?"

"You kissed *me!*"

"I couldn't help myself," he admitted, without any indication of remorse. "And that's why *you* kissed me back, isn't it? Because you couldn't help yourself, either?"

The way he phrased his question, and the subtle sobering of his features, suggested Logan had tired of the game he'd played with her and was now deadly earnest.

"You don't have to answer," he said when she remained silent. "The way you come alive in my arms, the way you open your mouth for my tongue, the way you offer your breasts to me—"

"Oh, stop!"

"We have to get this out in the open, Victoria."

"No, we don't. We can just forget what happened, and—"

"We didn't get any sleep after the storm hit. We're standing here, exhausted, in wet clothes. We need to build another fire, strip down to our skin and spend the day in camp, resting. It's going to be difficult for us to do that, if I keep wondering if you would welcome me next to you under that blanket."

Victoria's face was on fire. "Don't wonder! You would most certainly *not* be welcome. In fact, I'd . . . I'd . . ."

She broke off, wishing she had a gun to threaten him with.

"Bludgeon me to death with your book?"

"Don't make a joke of this," she said, feeling the helpless sensation of building tears. She would not cry, she told herself. There was no reason to, other than that, when she became overtired, she seemed to become weepy. Why hadn't she noticed this distressing tendency before? "I will not be taken lightly."

"My guess is, you won't be taken at all."

"Curb your tongue!"

"The point is," he continued flatly, "I'm not sure I can trust myself around you. Before last night, I thought I could."

"It was because of the cold, because of the storm, that we ended up in each other's arms," she insisted.

"That might have been a part of it," he conceded. "But we've gone too far to pretend nothing happened."

"Surely, if we both put our minds to it, we can put the unfortunate incident behind us."

"It would take a better man than I to do that."

"Be a better man, then!"

"I know what you taste like, Victoria." His eyes narrowed. "I've had my tongue all over your breasts. I've come within inches of touching your very core."

She swayed. What a despicable cad he was, to boast of such shameful acts. A sense of foreboding washed over her. His shocking words brought with them a fierce inner melting of her resistance.

Perhaps she was one of those bad women, after all, the kind who didn't care about marriage, children and making a home, the kind who thought only to gratify their carnal urges.

She hung her head. "There's no need to humiliate me."

"I'd like nothing better than to drop the ax I'm holding, pry away the book you're clutching so tightly that your knuckles have turned white, and raise your stubborn chin so you're forced to look at me. But if I do, I'm going to want to feel your mouth under mine, and we're going to be right back where we started."

"And there probably won't be another miracle to save us."

"Victoria."

At his gruff pronouncement, she raised her head. "What?"

His dark eyes burned. "Don't do that."

"Do what?"

"Babble about things that don't make a bit of sense."

"I do not babble!"

"Yes, you do," he corrected with surprising tenderness. "And I don't know why, but it excites me."

"Don't blame me for your perverted mind."

"You should know there are unlimited kinds of perversions," he told her with skin-prickling silkiness.

She marveled at his talent for setting her nerves on edge with the tone of his voice. He made his words sound as if they were being delivered courtesy of a velvet whip.

"I have no interest in your depravities."

"That's it, Victoria. Stoke the heat." Gone was his former even tone. The edge was back, sharper than ever. "You've got to know what you're doing, standing there with your wet dress plastered to you, using your tongue to whittle me down to size. Every thrust makes me think about doing some thrusting of my own."

Even though he seemed to think his argument had merit, she thought it obscure. The only thrusting with which she was familiar was that which she'd read about in books, which involved brilliantly executed swordplay. She didn't know what that had to do with their discussion, though they did frequently fence with the barbed words they exchanged. Perhaps the ax he gripped put him in mind of swords engaged in warfare.

"This craziness you inspire in me is the kind that tempts a man to do a little converting."

"Converting?" she asked, totally baffled. "What has religion got to do with this?"

"You were the one who brought up the subject of miracles."

"But I was referring to how the oxen appeared in the nick of time to stop us from doing anything we shouldn't."

"You consider that divine intervention?"

"Whatever it was, it worked. Since I don't plan to come that close to disaster again, this conversation is unnecessary."

"Not if one of us would *convert*."

"I already offered to reform you, and you turned me down. Other than transforming you into a respectable, God-fearing man, there's no way a good woman is going to want to have anything to do with you."

Logan's eyebrows converged. "Are you speaking for yourself, or how you think other women view me?"

Speaking for herself? A horrible suspicion began to grow within Victoria. Was it possible Logan actually believed she would allow him to court her if he *was* to forsake his loathsome ways? She had no wish to hurt him, to insult him more than she already had, but it had to be made unalterably clear that she wasn't harboring any thoughts of becoming involved with him.

Was that what he meant by "converting"—that he would change and thereby become acceptable to her? Surely not. It could not have escaped his notice that they were from entirely different worlds. They had absolutely nothing in common, other than a regrettable attraction for each other. They were from completely different social strata. And, well... The unvarnished truth of the matter was that he was much too earthy, indeed much too much a male on the loose, so to speak, to have any place in her life.

Goodness, she could just imagine what Mr. Pritchert and his employer would think, should she show up in Trinity

Falls to take over her impressionable ward's instruction with Logan Youngblood in tow. And there was the little matter of her turning him over to the authorities when they arrived in town. The likelihood that he would be imprisoned was definitely a deterrent to any lasting association between them. Surely he recognized that.

"It's taking you a long time to answer my question, Victoria."

There was a harshness to the set of his features that hadn't been there several seconds before.

"Uh, I forgot what it was," she admitted, flustered by the bizarre turn the conversation had taken.

"I asked if you think all women hold me in the same obvious contempt you do."

"Uh, well, I suppose if you were to pay your debt to society and refrain from any additional criminal acts, there would be several women who might allow you to... court them."

It was all she could do to get the words out. The thought of this rough-and-tumble man courting any woman was beyond her ability to imagine. He seemed more the type to unleash one of those Western lariats she'd read about and lasso himself a mate.

"But what if it was the other way around?" he inquired.

"I don't understand."

"What if *you* were the one to convert?"

"From what?" she asked bewildered. "To what?"

"From being so tightly laced that you've lost all feeling in your limbs."

"That's ridiculous. I haven't worn a corset since my first day on the wagon train."

"You're not paying attention, Victoria. I'm saying that you could discover what it's like to live in my world."

There was no way she could mask the horror his suggestion stirred. "You mean become a common criminal?"

His expression became shuttered. "That idea doesn't appeal to you?"

"Definitely not!"

"All right, then. I wouldn't expect you to take part in any...robberies. I would handle that aspect of our partnership."

She stared at him in absolute fascination. At last, when she no longer wished to hear it, came his confession. He was a thief. She experienced a crushing wave of disappointment.

"What is it that you steal, Logan?"

He rolled his eyes, and she thought perhaps it might be bad form to question a robber about such things.

"Cattle, horses, gold, strongboxes, whiskey, rifles, jewelry, mining claims, offerings from the collection box, family Bibles, pet dogs, unattended children...virgins' maidenheads. All the usual things."

Victoria felt light-headed. No wonder they'd locked him up and thrown away the key. Of course, there hadn't been a key. Just a thick iron bar secured between two anchoring posts.

"I see."

"Naturally, I wouldn't expect you to take part in those thefts if it offended your sensibilities. But you could tag along the rest of the time."

"It doesn't sound as if you would have much free time."

"Victoria..." he said in clear exasperation.

What did he have to be annoyed about? *She* was the one who was stuck with a virtual one-man gang.

"Yes, Logan?"

"Do you actually believe what I just told you?"

Feeling as weighed down as the heavy book she gripped, she nodded sadly. "I have no choice but to believe you."

His expression was watchful. "Of course you do."

His comment scarcely registered. "So, what you're asking is for me to become one of the bad women," she said slowly, finally making sense of his obscure trail of remarks. Indignation grew apace with her comprehension. "You want me to give myself to you without the benefit of marriage, and—"

"Now, be fair, Victoria. You consider yourself so far above me you would never consider marrying me. I wouldn't want to insult you by proposing."

"So you're asking me to do... *that thing* with you, just for the... fun of it?"

Incredulous, horrified and incensed all at once, she wondered how she could have ever let the blackguard touch her.

He nodded. She thought she saw a smile quirking at the corners of his mouth, but surely she was mistaken. This was no laughing matter.

"I have too much respect to offend you with an offer of marriage when I'm so clearly unworthy of you," he reiterated. "And it would be more than fun. It would be... earthshaking for us to come together."

She shook her head. Just a few minutes ago, Logan had said they needed to stay apart. She realized it had been after she casually mentioned that no good woman would want to associate with him that his manner abruptly changed. Clearly, his solution to the problem was to turn her into a... bad woman. The man's gall was astounding.

"I've never been so insulted in all my life."

"I'd say that just about makes us even then, Victoria."

"What?"

But he wasn't looking at her now. His unfathomable gaze had been jerked to something behind her right shoulder. Every muscle and line of his face seemed frozen. She began to turn to see what held his attention.

"Don't move."

With stomach-clenching dread, she watched him raise the ax. He paused, suspending it above him, as if waiting for a signal of some kind. Before she could ask for an explanation, he hurled the lethal weapon end over end past her.

It passed so closely by her ear that she heard its sizzling passage. Instinctively she whipped around, dropping the book from her nerveless fingers. She was in time to see the razorsharp blade strike a mountain cat in midjump. There was the sickening sound of impact, ax biting into furred mammal. A feral scream rent the clearing as the attacking beast dropped practically at her feet.

Everything happened so quickly, Victoria didn't have time to cry out. She wanted to close her eyes, but couldn't tear her gaze from the cruel sight of the felled creature with the blade protruding from its neck.

Logan strode past her. "I have to make sure it's dead," he said starkly. "Do us both a favor, and don't watch. I don't want you fainting."

"I shall endeavor to 'pass out,' then," she muttered, trying to count the colorful dots swimming in front of her. Her knees buckled, and she sank to the earth.

She shut her eyes and put her hands over her ears to block out the sounds of what Logan was forced to do to the animal.

It was a shame that such a beautiful creature had to die before its time. But, clearly, there was no way for wild beasts and people to inhabit the same space.

That thought saddened her. In the space of a few seconds, Logan had demonstrated that he had much of the wild beast within him.

The frightening thought surfaced that perhaps she wouldn't like him quite so much if he was not exactly as he was. A remorseless thief who, by his own account, was capable of stealing anything not rooted to the ground.

He'd just saved her life, she realized.

Now they were even.

Chapter Twelve

"We've got to get out of these wet clothes, Victoria."

Out of respect for her sensibilities, Logan had already dragged away the dead animal's carcass. He knew she was still dazed by the unexpectedness of the mountain cat's lunging attack, and by the expedient manner with which he'd disposed of it.

That she hadn't retrieved her fallen book showed how shaken she was. Before the attack, throughout their debate, she hadn't shown any apparent awareness of her wet hair and clothing. Now she stood with her arms wrapped around herself, shivering.

"Victoria." He said her name sharply.

She looked up, her gaze clouded. "Yes?"

"You need to get out of those wet clothes."

A spark ignited in those haunting green eyes of hers. Good.

"You have a one-track mind, Logan."

Her habit of thinking the worst of him caused another crack in the control he was trying to exert over his temper. Without answering, he stalked to the back of the wagon and leaned inside, searching for dry blankets. When he located a couple, he returned to her.

"Here." He tossed one to her. "Use this to maintain your precious privacy."

She caught the blanket and glared at him. "As I'm practically dry now, there's no reason to undress."

He bit back an oath. Since she had more clothes in the wagon, her reason from not wanting to change was probably an overabundance of modesty. Firmly gripping her shoulders, he turned her to face the wagon and gave her a firm nudge. "Find yourself something dry to wear. I'll build a fire."

She glanced over her shoulder, the one with the torn sleeve. He flatly refused to be enticed by the utterly feminine and innocently seductive gesture. Oh, hell, he *was* enticed. Her comment about his having a one-track mind rankled. The careless insult made him feel as if he were a lewd-minded lowlife. To his way of thinking, she had the part of Little Red Riding Hood down pat. He had no interest, however, in being the Big Bad Wolf, which was how she seemed to regard him.

"You won't be able to."

"Won't be able to what?"

"Build a fire."

His temper climbed. She was determined to view him as a thief, a reprobate, *and* inept. Of the three unflattering appraisals, he most disliked being judged incompetent.

"I damn well can build a fire, and you know it."

"Everything is too wet. There's no way the wood will burn."

"Just watch me, lady," he muttered under his breath.

Feeling as if his manhood had been challenged, Logan set about building a raging inferno that would make the doubting Easterner eat her words.

He started by pulling handfuls of grass and piling several inches of it across the burned-out shell of the campfire they'd used the night before. A slight breeze had already dried the wispy blades of greenery. Next, he snapped dead twigs off fallen branches that littered the forest floor. Using the ax, he hacked a dozen or so small limbs from those same branches. Finally, he propped several thick logs against each other over the bed of kindling, creating a three-foot-high tepeelike structure.

He looked up and watched Victoria circle the wagon. Obviously she intended to use the conveyance to block his view of her. What she hadn't taken into consideration was that with him kneeling, he had an excellent view of her bare legs as she stripped away her sodden garments. Since she had the entire wagon between herself and him, he didn't think he'd see anything particularly private.

But those wheels were large in comparison to her. When she stooped down to pick up something, he caught a flash of her lithe body. The unexpected view of her feminine assets lasted only seconds, but everything worth seeing was branded onto Logan's brain. His breath jammed in his throat. Other predictable physical reactions followed. His blood ignited, just as the tender shoots of dry grass caught the spark from the two flintlike rocks he'd struck together.

He glanced away. He hadn't meant to spy on her. Against his will, he returned his gaze to the wagon. She'd straightened. All he could see were her shapely calves. Her skin was pale and smooth. From this distance, he couldn't determine whether those winsome freckles extended to her slender limbs.

Unable to pry his renegade stare from the glimpses of Victoria's body, Logan watched her use the blanket to dry her legs, which meant she was bending down again. Her waist was trim, and her hips were gently flared. Her breasts were sweetly lush and delicately crowned with strawberry-hued tips. She was so damnably beautiful, she took his breath away. So damnably soft and feminine. So damnably...brave and stubborn, he thought, unable to regard her as merely a desirable female body, when she was so much more.

When he emerged from the forest and saw her with that thick book in her hands, his heart had taken a peculiar lurch. She'd looked for all the world like a drowned cat, clearly frightened but determined to face any potential threat. He'd wanted to take her into his arms, to kiss her until the fog rolled away and the sun came out—until nightfall, for that matter.

He prided himself on curbing the impulse. Then she'd started in again on her favorite subject—his base nature and its urgent need to be reformed. If he'd just had one sign that she'd elevated her opinion of him, he might have told her who he was.

Of course, she wouldn't believe him, not in a million years. And there was the rub. He refused to beg her to believe he wasn't on the same level as Jesse James. There were some things a man's pride wouldn't let him do.

Logan watched Victoria's feet step into a pair of white drawers. The feminine underpinnings were pulled over slender legs. Next a ruffled petticoat descended, followed by the falling hem of dark gray skirts. His gaze returned to the fire. Orange-and-crimson flames wound their way around the larger logs.

It had been when she said that no respectable woman would have him that he spun his lies about being a thief, lies she'd eaten up as greedily as a bear cub tasting its first dollop of honey. It was obvious she delighted in thinking the worst of him. He hadn't intended, however, to let his deception go so far as inviting her to become his partner in crime, or his lover.

That rash offer had been provoked by her prissy regard of him as the world's most reprehensible felon. He shook his head. Before now, he hadn't believed he had a rash bone in his body. He didn't understand what made him make such ridiculous statements. He only understood that Victoria had a knack for pushing him past the limits of reasonable behavior.

Victoria came around the wagon. Logan noticed that every button was in place and they ran from the bottom of her chin to her waist. Her sleeves were long and her cuffs securely fastened. Her hair was a damp thicket of confusion, but the hairbrush she held would soon take care of that splendid red chaos.

He tried to comprehend what it was about her that hit him on such a basic level. She wasn't a stunning beauty. He'd seen a couple in his lifetime. Robeena had been one. But Victoria had something more valuable than flash. There was a lively intelligence in those slanting green eyes of hers, as well as a sassy kind of courage that knocked him on his butt.

Considering the abundance of overly sentimental volumes he'd noted in her traveling library, she would certainly take grave offense at his unromantic outlook.

"You're staring," she told him in that cultured tone of hers that was no doubt supposed to put him in his place.

"You're worth staring at."

He was hunkered by the fire, absently watching it spit and hiss as it warmed him. It didn't take a leap of imagination to compare the flames with how Victoria affected him.

"I suppose I should admit I was wrong, Logan."

Her statement caught him by surprise. Had she been thinking about how impossibly outlandish his account of his misdeeds had been? Was she finally ready to concede that he wasn't the most dastardly outlaw between Boise City and St. Louis?

She picked up the thick book she'd dropped when the mountain cat appeared from nowhere. Her slender fingers gently brushed the dust from the leather cover. "It's obvious you were able to build a fire from wet wood."

"I told you I could," he said flatly.

"And I should have believed you," she returned softly.

He wished the conversation was about something more significant. He supposed he'd take what scant praise she offered when he could. "Are you hungry?"

"Starving," she admitted, returning the thick volume she'd been fussing with to the wagon. The gray skirts of her simply styled dress swayed provocatively with each graceful step.

He jerked his gaze away from the appealing view and stood. "I'll see about getting us some fish."

"And I'll cook us up some buckwheat biscuits," she called back to him.

Buckwheat biscuits... His thoughts shot back to their first meeting. It seemed incredible that that event had occurred only three days ago. They still had almost two weeks ahead of them on the trail. That was a long time to keep his thoughts and his hands off the bewitching woman. When she bent into the back of the wagon, her backside was displayed fetchingly as she foraged through her belongings. No man should have to live through this kind of mental and physical torture. Come hell or high water, though, he would resist her the rest of the trip.

The irony of Logan's goal didn't escape him. He should be completely unattracted to Victoria. She was the kind of woman he no longer wanted, the antithesis of the good-time gals he'd enjoyed with reckless pleasure before Maddy had become his responsibility.

He watched Victoria return to the fire, juggling a thick frying pan, an almost empty sack of flour, a tin of lard and her cooking fork. Her hair still danced freely around her gamine face. She must have decided to tame it later, as she'd left her hairbrush in the wagon, along with the book.

He leaped to his feet. "Here, let me help you with those."

Hearing his own gentlemanly offer, Logan winced. Lord, he was acting like a lovesick dolt in the throes of his first adolescent crush. "If you're not careful, you'll drop something."

She shot him a disgruntled look, but allowed him to take the frying pan and the container of grease. He'd rather have run his hands through her silky auburn hair. Determinedly he kept his hands and his compliments to himself.

Compliments like *Victoria, you have the most beautiful red hair of any woman I've ever known. Victoria, your legs are so sweetly shaped, I'd like very much to run my hands*

*over them. Victoria, do you realize how lovely your breasts
are?*

"Thank you."

It took a moment for him to realize why she was thanking him.

"I'll see about spearing us some fish," he managed to say
hoarsely.

Toying with danger, he absorbed everything about her
that made his heart hammer. Her splendid red hair, her
bright green eyes, her luscious mouth, her soft breasts,
concealed by her god-awful gray gown, her trim waist, the
gentle flare of her hips, the shapely limbs concealed by her
full skirts. Her light sprinkling of golden freckles, her unpredictable and wholly fascinating mind...

Her very sharp tongue.

He sighed, and felt foolish for doing so. It occurred to
him that Victoria Amory had well and truly ruined him. He
no longer felt coldly in charge of his destiny. Instead, he
sensed he was in imminent danger of succumbing to unrestrained outbursts of warm and mushy sentimentality.

What a revolting development. He should have been disgusted. He wasn't. He felt strangely optimistic. Which had
to be an aberration caused by their time on the trail. For he
was a cool-headed cynic who looked at the world through
eyes of stark objectivity. Which was how he damned well
liked it!

Until now, pointed out the part of his mind that insisted
on telling him the truth at the most inconvenient moments.
He sighed again. *Until now*, he acknowledged grimly. But
the battle wasn't over, he assured himself.

"Won't you need my cooking fork, Logan?"

He looked at her in confusion—he, who'd never known
a moment of confusion, except for the time he'd caught his
nearly nude fiancée in his brother's bedchamber.

"To harpoon the fish..." she prompted, her green eyes
watching him as if he'd suddenly sprouted blue spots.

"I'll sharpen a stick."

With that, Logan strode from the fire he'd impressed Victoria with by starting from wet branches and twigs. The man had hidden talents, she thought. It was unfortunate that he couldn't use those God-given abilities to live an honorable life.

She watched him disappear into the woods. The fog had lifted, and Logan became an undetectable part of the densely treed landscape. Lord help her, she liked it better when he was near, rather than far. Which just proved how addled she was becoming. For, after hearing from his own lips—those narrow, astonishingly kissable lips—what a miserable rogue he was, she should want as much distance between them as possible.

By the time Logan returned to camp, Victoria was turning the golden biscuits when he stepped into the clearing.

"That smells like heaven," he said appreciatively as he held out three cleaned trout for her inspection at the end of the sharpened stick.

She accepted the offering. "I'll fry the fish when the biscuits are done. They're about finished now."

She resented being self-conscious around him and wished there was some way to make the strange awkwardness she felt disappear. Yet a sense of self-protectiveness made her realize it was better that she not become too comfortable around Logan. It was safer to maintain a formal atmosphere between them. He was, after all, a very temporary part of her life.

Logan nodded. "I'll use the time to check the oxen. I meant what I said earlier about us resting today. Both we and the animals need a break from the fast pace we've set. Now that we're in Night Wolf's territory, we can ease up."

Victoria stared at Logan's neutral expression. It was as if the passion that had almost burned out of control between them had never happened. Almost as if he'd never invited her to embrace his wayward way of life. It was all for the best, she decided, that he obviously had no intention of pressing her to become his cohort in crime. And it demonstrated a shocking lacking moral fortitude on her part to regret for even an instant that he hadn't been serious about his indecent offer.

While Logan checked the oxen, she placed the biscuits on a plate to cool. The trout were almost fried to a succulent crispiness when an ominous buzzing caught her attention.

She glanced from the pan of sizzling fish and encountered the biggest, furriest bee she'd ever seen. It was the size of a hummingbird and boasted yellow stripes as wide as her pinkie.

"It's only a bee, Victoria. Ignore it."

At the sound of Logan's voice, her gaze momentarily left the hovering insect, which was flying back and forth over the skillet. She hadn't realized he'd returned to the clearing until he spoke. She found she didn't like his habit of sneaking up on her. It made for a disquieting lack of predictability.

"That's easy for you to say, but bees and I don't get along."

"You've been stung before?"

"Once, when I was a little girl." She returned her gaze to the hovering bee. "It was Easter Sunday. Annalee and I were in the flower garden, picking blooms to match our new dresses."

"Annalee is..."

"My younger sister. We weren't supposed to be in the garden. I don't remember which of us instigated the act of misbehavior. It was probably Annalee. I was always very well behaved."

"Of course," Logan said dryly.

She took exception to the note of skepticism she detected in his voice. It seemed remarkably arrogant of him to harbor any doubts about her conduct, when his own was so appallingly unsuitable.

"What happened?" he asked.

Victoria's attention was still focused on the restless drone of the menacing bee as it now stalked the plate of biscuits.

"I got stung, but not before I tried to outrun it. My escape attempt landed me in a sharp-thorned rosebush that our gardener had watered only that morning. You have to remember I was very young, Logan," she explained, lest he think her a total nitwit. "My father overheard my wails and came out to investigate the ruckus."

"It was a good thing he was close by."

"Not really," Victoria said, vividly remembering the painful childhood memory. "I'd ruined my dress—it was torn and muddy, you see. Father was furious. The carriage was ready, and it was time for us to attend church. My mishap was going to cause everyone to be late. And, of course, being late for Easter services simply couldn't be tolerated."

"What happened?"

"The family went without me. It was the only thing they could do."

"What about your sting?"

"The pain was hardly noticeable the next morning."

"And that's why you're afraid of bees?"

"I'm not actually afraid of them. I just respect them," she muttered. "There was another incident with one where I definitely came out the loser. Look, I say we let the bee have the biscuits. You and I can eat the fish for breakfast."

"I'm not sharing my food with any damned bee, Victoria."

"It won't actually eat them," she pointed out, gingerly reaching for the cooking fork, lest she draw the creature's notice. She removed a trout from the frying pan and put it on another plate. She kept careful track of their unwelcome guest.

Logan strode forward. "All we have to do it shoo it away."

"Don't!" she squealed, jumping back from the impending confrontation between the intrusive insect and Logan. "Some bees simply won't be shooed."

Her protest failed to deflect Logan from his course. She watched him swat at the circling intruder with his bare hand.

She didn't think she'd ever witnessed such a display of raw courage—or foolhardiness. The fuzzy creature's stinger was the size of a paring knife, or so it seemed.

"Be careful, Logan," she warned, stepping back.

The bee returned three times to the plate of biscuits before finally departing. During the contest of opposing wills, Victoria forced herself to remove the other two trout from the skillet. For, even though her heart was in her throat, she refused to let Logan's catch burn while he fought so bravely to protect them from the obviously savage bee.

Of course, she was reminded of Horace Threadgill and the debacle in her bedchamber that had precipitated her accepting Martin Pritchert's offer of employment and coming west. She couldn't help contrasting Horace's cowardly reaction with Logan's stalwart defense.

But then, to be fair, the bee didn't fly up Logan's pant leg. Still, she imagined that if it did, and she tried to assist him, he wouldn't stand feebly by, screaming for help, while she did all the work. And it would be obvious to anyone who happened to walk in on such an episode that she had not divested Logan of his britches against his will.

Clearly, the man was capable of getting out of his trousers.

Chapter Thirteen

Victoria walked alongside the wagon as it wound around another curve in the trail. For almost two weeks, she and Logan had made their way through the seemingly limitless forest that had become their world. They advanced five to seven miles each day, depending upon whether they were going uphill or downhill.

Living with Logan had become a way of life, she thought as she stepped around a white-blossomed thistle blocking her path. Every sunrise she awoke upon their pallet under the wagon, locked within his protective embrace. Outwardly, they ignored the intimacy, never speaking of it. There were many things of which they never spoke. It was safer that way, Victoria acknowledged to herself, and she was sure Logan had reached the same conclusion.

They were . . . careful with each other, discussing only the immediate circumstances of their forced togetherness. Conversation was limited to where they would camp, what they would eat and how much ground they expected to cover that day.

Where words could not, Victoria had learned, silence wove its own dangerous spell of intimacy. Her thoughts went their own merry way where Logan was concerned. They dwelled upon his remarkable capacity to provide for them in the wilderness, upon his hard, masculine body, and upon the occasional burning hunger she saw reflected in his brooding gaze.

Since the episode with the bee, they had not participated in one spontaneous burst of dialogue. The guarded, polite exchanges spun out between them until Victoria wished their seemingly endless journey was completed. Then she would realize that their arrival in Trinity Falls would end forever her contact with the man guiding the oxen over the next rise, and quiet despair would fill her heart.

No more Logan Youngblood. No more snuggling against his strong, virile body during the cool Idaho nights. No more watching his beard grow each day. No more waiting for the moment when he might take her into his arms again and cover her mouth with his. No more possibility of experiencing that fierce, close heat he stoked within her.

According to Logan's clipped remarks when they broke camp that morning, they'd already spent their last night on the trail, which meant she had spent her last night in his embrace. He'd informed her that sometime late this afternoon they would leave the mountains and descend into the valley. By nightfall, they would reach their destination. She struggled to suppress any useless pangs of regret, but it wasn't easy to dispel the feeling that she'd missed an opportunity to truly know Logan, an opportunity that would not come her way again.

There was so much about him that she didn't understand. Why did he lead a life on the wrong side of the law? What had his childhood been like? The thought of him not having loving parents made her heart twist. Her own father might be overly stern. But deep in her soul she believed he loved her and always acted in what he regarded as her best interests. Likewise, her mother might be preoccupied with her circle of friends and a hectic social schedule, but Victoria was certain the sometimes distracted woman loved her. Was there no one who had cherished and watched over Logan as a boy?

The wagon halted. The sun was high overhead. Breakfast that morning had consisted of a few wild berries and a rabbit Logan had snared. Victoria's stomach rolled. She knew it was foolish, but it had been difficult for her to choke down more than a couple of bites of the roasted meat.

During their wilderness odyssey, Logan had provided other game—squirrel, raccoon, and even a young elk. Since she was used to eating chicken, beef and pork, he'd pointed out, her squeamishness about eating the meat from the animals he successfully hunted was illogical. In theory, Victoria agreed with him. But in practice, she found it difficult to wolf down a creature that had been scampering through the woods minutes before it appeared in her cooking skillet.

She watched Logan jump from the wagon. He now moved with an easy male gait that seemed natural to him and indicated that his ribs no longer pained him. Nor did his face boast any signs of the beating he'd suffered at the fort. It was still impossible, though, to clearly discern the specific angles of his sharply defined features, because a thick black beard covered his jaw.

What with his prominent dark eyebrows and his blade of a nose, he definitely looked the part of a villain. A pirate, she thought. If he'd lived in an earlier century, he probably would have become a buccaneer, sailing the seven seas in search of adventure and treasures of gold. All he required was a loop earring and an eyepatch to complete the image.

"Are you hungry, Victoria?"

His question returned her thoughts to the present.

"What did you have in mind?" she asked uneasily, wondering what adorable woodland creature he meant to slay.

"I could spear us some more fish," he said, his dark eyes studying her closely. "You seem to like trout."

She had liked trout once upon a time, before Logan had provided it at every meal. It was after she innocently remarked that she was sick of fish that he'd begun decimating the forest population of small, cuddly animals.

Considering her choices, trout didn't sound so bad at the moment.

"Fish would be fine."

He nodded in satisfaction. "Good. There's something I want to show you before we leave here."

She couldn't imagine what, unless he'd hidden the loot from one of his robberies in the vicinity. Was that why he knew this part of the forest so well—because he'd used it to hide himself and his booty from the law?

Since this had all the appearances of being a brief stop, Victoria stole a moment of privacy to take care of her need to relieve herself. She'd discovered along the trail that it was easier for a man to accommodate such bodily functions than for a woman. A major complication, she reflected, lay in her bulky skirts and petticoats.

When Victoria completed her mission, she took her customary stroll around their temporary resting place. She'd almost reached her starting point when she found what she'd been searching for. Four books from the wagon. She picked up the neatly stacked volumes. Brushing away the dust, she noted that they were *Jane Eyre, Sense and Sensibility, Tess* and *A Tale of Two Cities.*

Since she'd already recovered these particular books on previous occasions, she suspected this was a silent game she and Logan played. Unless, of course, he couldn't read and had no idea that he kept discarding the same few books over and over again.

Frowning, Victoria glanced around and, seeing no sign of him, made her way to the wagon to tuck the volumes inside. She hadn't considered before the possibility that Logan didn't know how to read. It wasn't that she doubted his ability to learn if properly instructed. No, she reflected, if he hadn't mastered the accomplishment, it was because he'd never been taught.

She'd given up trying to fight the compassion and sympathy Logan stirred so effortlessly within her. If a woman wasn't careful, Victoria could see quite clearly how she could lose her heart to Logan Youngblood. He was at times bold, clever, rakish and . . . and quite splendidly reckless. And yet there was a solidness to him that invited fantasies of bearing his children and growing old with him. It was as if he were larger than life, Victoria mused. In fact, now that she thought about it, he *was* very much like a hero from one of her books.

But, above all things, Logan was also a thief. A woman would be a fool to surrender her heart to a man whose uncertain future might involve a prison sentence or harsh justice dispensed at the end of a rope. She knew they did that in the West—hanged men. And among the other commodities Logan had admitted to stealing he'd listed horses and cattle. Stealing either was a capital offense.

Yes, it would be lunacy for a prudent woman to waste her heart on such a man, no matter how accomplished a woodsman, or how passionate a lover, or how magnificently physically proportioned. Victoria feared she'd become that lunatic, for she couldn't seem to help her growing feelings of attachment to Logan. She found herself thinking about him all the time, even now, as she began gathering pieces of wood to make a fire to cook the fish.

Face it, Victoria. You've grown to care for him beyond anything that's sane. The man is trouble with a capital T.

She nudged a branch with the toe of her shoe. She very much feared that, despite her determination not to, she'd already lost her heart to . . . trouble.

"I wondered when I would see you again, my friend."

At the distinctive tone of Night Wolf's deep voice, Logan looked up from the stick he was sharpening.

The Shoshone stood less than three feet away. As usual, Logan was impressed with the man's ability to move silently. Bare-chested, wearing buckskin leggings and moccasins, the Indian was well suited to his environment.

"Since I've been wandering around your territory for almost two weeks, I'd guess you had more important things on your mind than catching up with me."

The corners of Night Wolf's mouth twitched. "I would not say you have been 'wandering,' Logan Youngblood. You have charted as direct a path as possible through this land. Not once have you deviated from your course, though it would have not added many days to your journey to visit our village."

Logan stared into the Indian's bold features. It wasn't his custom to notice another man's handsomeness, but Night Wolf cut such a striking figure, it was impossible to ignore the chief's compelling visage. Logan hated to stoop to Colonel Windham's pathetic level of jealousy, but the truth was, Logan had not particularly wanted Victoria to meet the Shoshone chief. She already had a hopelessly romantic view of life among the primitives. She would probably take one look at Night Wolf and…and be hopelessly ensnared by the man's exotic appearance.

Logan figured he'd learned his lesson about such matters with his fickle fiancée, Robeena Stockard. It would have been better had the woman never met his brother, Burke. Evidently, to the female of the species, vows of love and devotion meant little when measured against an unexpected attraction for another man.

Logan had always believed it was Burke who had seduced Robeena. Enough time had passed, however, for Logan's thoughts to clear, and he was no longer so certain about his conclusion.

Logan acknowledged that he and Victoria were *not* engaged. Still, he would be damned if he dangled her under Night Wolf's nose. His sense of possessiveness might not be logical, but he'd given up fighting the need to protect Victoria the second day he'd known her. He had come close to telling her more than once that he was her employer and that Madison was his ward. Only the conviction that such an effort would be wasted had checked the impulse. A man had his pride, and Logan's had been savaged enough by the exasperatingly naive Bostonian woman.

One thing was certain—when they reached Trinity Falls, he was going to demand his pound of flesh. Afterward, he would be magnanimous and accept her apology for thinking the worst of him. The glow of that imagined scene warmed him as much as the thought of seeing her on a daily basis once she assumed Maddy's instruction.

As much as he might want to deny it, he was reconsidering his vow never to marry.

"What thoughts do you think, Logan, to make your expression so grave?"

At Night Wolf's question, Logan started. He glanced self-consciously at the Indian. "I guess my mind wandered."

"Usually it is old men, women and children who let their thoughts drift like smoke from a poorly lit fire."

Logan chuckled. "That's what I like about you, friend. You have such a colorful way of talking."

"A young brave in love," Night Wolf continued, "also allows his thoughts to float in no particular direction."

"Like a poorly paddled canoe caught in a whirlpool?" Logan asked, unoffended by the Indian's attempt to bait him.

Night Wolf broke into a full-fledged grin. "You are learning the People's way of speaking, Logan."

"It's probably the time I've been spending with a certain redhead that has me expressing myself so poetically."

"Your woman is poetic?"

"She's a dreamer," Logan explained.

"Ah, she is a seer, then." Night Wolf nodded sagely. "She has the power to know of what is to come."

"Not exactly." Logan thought about how wrong Victoria was about him. If she was a seer, she was a poor one. "It's more that she has her head in the clouds. She's got her wagon packed with books and her mind stuffed with all kinds of nonsense."

"She is not an ordinary woman," Night Wolf remarked. "She has the protection of powerful spirits watching over her."

Victoria wasn't ordinary, but Logan wasn't convinced she had the protection of the Indian gods to whom Night Wolf referred.

Logan had no intention of ridiculing Shoshone beliefs. "She's lucky she's alive."

"Fort Brockton no longer stands," Night Wolf announced starkly.

Logan wasn't surprised by the news. Still, a shiver teased the back of his neck. "What happened?"

"What I warned. The longknives built their walls upon sacred ground." The Shoshone considered Logan somberly. "Why did you remain after the soldiers left?"

"I didn't have much of a choice." Logan didn't bother keeping the bitterness from his voice. "Colonel Windham rode out with me locked in the stockade."

The Indian's eyebrows climbed. "You were left to die?"

Logan nodded. "He had some crazy notion I'd been keeping company with his wife."

"And for that he sentenced you to death?"

"That and the fact I wouldn't lead him to your village."

"To save his life, another man—one with less courage—might have shown the bluecoats the way."

"I wasn't being brave. I didn't know Windham was going to have me beaten and thrown into the stockade."

"Knowing would have made no difference to you, my friend. It is not in you to betray a trust."

Logan shifted uncomfortably. After spending the past twelve days with Victoria, he wasn't prepared for such unvarnished praise. "Windham was acting so crazy, I doubt he would have let me live even if I had shown him the way to your village."

A knowing look flashed in Night Wolf's eyes. "Logan, no man, even a white one, wants to share his woman with another."

"I didn't sleep with his wife!"

"You share your blanket with many women, is that not true?"

At the barely veiled censure in the Indian's words, Logan flushed. He couldn't believe the strange collection of people with whom he'd lately discussed his love life. Windham, Victoria, and now Night Wolf. Folks ought to recognize there were some things a man preferred keeping private.

"The white man's ways are different from the red man's. In Trinity Falls, there's certain women who..." Logan scowled when he saw Night Wolf's downright fascinated gaze.

"Certain women who what?" the Indian asked encouragingly.

"Who are willing to frolic in a man's bed with no strings attached. They just want to have a good time."

"But you must pay for your good time?" came the shrewd question.

"Yeah, I pay for it. And it's a lot cheaper and less complicated than having to marry to get it."

"I see." Night Wolf paused, as if to consider the ramifications of Logan's explanation. "And they 'frolic' with many men? None of these paid-for women belongs to only you?"

"That's the whole idea. I don't want one woman." Maybe if he kept saying it, he might believe it.

"Not even the fire-haired one who journeys with you?"

Logan opened his mouth. Nothing came out.

"This fire-haired woman whom the spirits protect and who shares your blanket, Logan—do you pay her in the white man's paper or the People's gold?"

It was obvious that the Indian had no idea how insulting his question was. Still, Logan felt his temper rise. "I don't pay Victoria anything."

"Ah, she 'frolics' because she truly desires to?"

"She doesn't frolic!" Logan fairly snarled. "She's different."

"She is a dreamer," Night Wolf concurred, imbuing the word with far more substance than Logan had intended. "And she has great courage."

"Why do you say that?"

"When, for some reason, the other wagons went on without her, she continued alone."

"She didn't have a choice."

"Did she not, Logan?"

"She refused to lighten her wagon by leaving her books. When she couldn't keep up, she was left behind."

"That was her choice, then. To keep what she valued most."

"She should have valued her skin!"

"Dreamers do not always act in ways the rest of us understand. They follow a voice we do not hear."

Logan wished he'd never called her by that ridiculous name. Night Wolf was reading far too much into the casual reference.

"She's from Boston," Logan said, as if that somehow explained Victoria's behavior.

"I have heard of this Boston place. Is that not your home village?"

Thinking of the thriving seaport as a village took some doing. "It's where I grew up."

"Then you already knew this woman? Was she your friend?"

"Boston is a crowded city. We never met."

"It is strange that you would both travel to this place to find each other. The spirits must have willed it."

"No divine force brought us together, Night Wolf. Martin Pritchert hired her to tutor Madison. Meeting her before she arrived in Trinity Falls was a coincidence."

"I see."

It was plain from Night's Wolf's skeptical expression that he didn't see at all.

"It was just a case of bad luck, like me being thrown into the stockade because I gave Windham your warning about the fort being attacked." Logan rubbed the back of his neck. "From now on, though, I intend to mind my own business. No more risking my skin to save someone else's hide."

"You are wrong, my friend."

"If you have any more warnings about Indian attacks, keep them to yourself."

"There will be no more warnings." A look of sadness tinged the tall warrior's eyes. "I am taking my tribe north."

Logan was shocked. "You're leaving the territory?"

"There is not room for my people and yours to live here."

Logan didn't know what to say. Since he was a white man and did a brisk business with the miners who panned for Indian gold, he was as much an invader as the others of his kind.

"Do not feel guilty, my friend. I have known other white men. None are as honorable as you. Remember, you have not brought this trouble to us, and you cannot make it go away."

"I'm sorry." The words were pathetically inadequate, but Logan couldn't think of anything else to say.

"We will not see each other many more times, Logan Youngblood."

Logan experienced a sense of loss. Except for the brother who'd betrayed him, Logan hadn't shared another friendship as strong as the one he had with the solemn-eyed warrior.

"The longknives are close," the Indian informed him. "They water their horses downstream from where you left your woman."

Logan stiffened. "I better get back to Victoria."

"She is in no danger from them, but they might want to punish you for not leading them to our village."

"They'll want revenge for the fort being burned, and they won't be particular about which tribe they blame," Logan agreed.

"All Indians are the same to the bluecoats," Night Wolf observed.

"No matter what happens, I won't guide them to your village."

The Shoshone chief's gaze flashed with amusement. Logan couldn't imagine what the man found humorous.

"But what about your 'skin'? I thought you were going to guard it most carefully."

Logan frowned. "I can do both—stay alive *and* protect your people."

"My friend, you are the one with your head in the clouds if you believe the things you have told me this day."

"What do you mean?"

"You say the spirits have nothing to do with watching over your woman. But she is alive when she should be dead. Had you not been locked in the fort, and had she not freed you, both of you would have perished. And, if you do not 'frolic' with her, you are a fool. The spirits have given her to you, just as they gave you to her."

Logan's skin grew clammy at the thought of Victoria being killed. Yet he knew a woman traveling alone in this wild country was doomed to almost certain death. If he ever caught up with the wagon master who'd abandoned her, he was going to make the man pay for leaving her behind.

"Have you nothing to say, my friend?"

"Yeah. For all your talk about finding one woman to belong to you, I notice you share your blanket with no one. From what I've seen, there are several pretty Indian maidens who flutter their eyelashes in your direction."

Notwithstanding the warrior's dark coloring, a splash of crimson stained his sharply defined cheekbones.

"I have not found her yet, the one I will call wife."

"Maybe I haven't, either."

"Why do you tell yourself such lies?"

Logan glared at the chief. "You haven't even met Victoria. Why do you think so much of her?"

"I have seen her from a distance."

"And?"

"And the sun smiles upon this woman who walks boldly through the People's land. That she still lives proves the spirits also smile upon her. A man must respect and admire such a woman. She has . . . merit."

Logan felt a definite tug of jealously. "I'm surprised you would think any white woman has merit."

"My mother was white," the Indian reminded him.

Logan's gaze fell to the sharpened stick he still gripped. "She thinks I'm . . . unworthy of her."

"Ah."

Logan's head snapped up. "Ah, what?"

"Your pride is great, my friend."

"What the hell is that supposed to mean?"

"You told me once why you left your village. I do not think it wounded your heart when the woman from your past chose your brother instead of you. I think it pierced your pride."

"I should have never told you that story," Logan grumbled. Nor would he have shared that private humiliation, had he not been drunk on the cheap whiskey he'd been given to fight off the pain of a gunshot he'd received when tracking those damned renegades.

"You do not accept my counsel?"

"Let's just say that, when you have a wife of your own, I'll be more inclined to listen to your advice."

A faraway look filled the Indian's gaze. "I seek no such woman. For now, it is my people who claim my heart."

Logan had learned some things about the Indian way of life when he lived among them while recuperating from his wound, but there were elements of it that were still shrouded in mystery. He wondered, for example, whether there was a way in the Shoshone culture for Night Wolf to satisfy his physical urges without the sanction of marriage. He had no intention of asking. Unlike some people, he respected a man's privacy.

"There's a chance I might need to borrow one of your horses," Logan said, turning to a new subject.

"Just one?"

Logan nodded. He'd put together the beginnings of a plan whereby he and Victoria could be alone when she finally discovered who he was. Or, more importantly, who he wasn't. He didn't want to cause her public embarrassment. Besides, if they were alone, he would be able to accept her apology in a setting conducive to a passionate demonstration of her heartfelt repentance for thinking the worst of him.

It would be better for her reputation if she drove the wagon into town by herself. People would be impressed by her fortitude, and there would be no taint of scandal from their being together for almost two weeks.

"You have the look of a man with a plot, Logan Youngblood."

"You're right about that." Logan was confident that his hastily contrived scheme would benefit both him and Victoria.

All he had to do was avoid the cavalry and speak with Martin Pritchert before Victoria arrived in town.

"And it is a plan that will protect your pride?"

Logan smiled. "Of course."

"I fear you are headed for trouble, my friend."

Chapter Fourteen

From her position on the densely treed rise overlooking the riverbank below, Victoria stared in dismay at the dozen or so soldiers who had halted their mounts beside the strip of water.

It had been the muted sounds of their passage that drew her from the campsite. The sight of the uniformed men who stood clustered in small groups, conversing with one another while their horses drank from the stream, sent a bolt of dread through her. Victoria didn't delude herself as to why the sight of the soldiers panicked her instead of comforted her.

These men were part of the same army responsible for beating Logan and leaving him in that squalid stockade to die. A burning sense of outrage swelled within her. She wanted to charge down the riverbank and berate them for their savagery. Only the knowledge that she would place Logan in jeopardy stopped her.

She left the hilltop and retraced her steps to the clearing, realizing that, by not making herself and Logan's presence known to the soldiers, she had become his accomplice. Surely duty demanded she turn Logan over to the army. She swallowed the sharp-edged lump in her throat. She, who had been raised on duty, had just violated every precept she'd ever been taught.

Her father was a federal judge. He dispensed cold justice to men who broke the law. If he were in her place, he wouldn't suffer any qualms about turning Logan over to those soldiers.

She remembered the horrible beating Logan had suffered. Not even the rigid code of conduct upon which she'd been reared would make her return him to that vile authority.

"There you are," Logan said. "I wondered where you were."

Victoria came to a halt. So hurried had her pace been that she reached their camp without realizing it.

"Hush! Keep your voice down!"

His expression stilled. "What's wrong?"

"Nothing." *Everything! Not far away are soldiers I should turn you over to, but I can't because I'm afraid I've gone and done something so stupid as to fall in love with you.*

She drew a calming breath. "I see you caught more fish."

"Why are you whispering?"

"I have a headache. It soothes the pain if I lower my voice." Good grief, she was becoming a consummate liar.

He looked as if he didn't believe her brilliant fib. She supposed it was to be expected that a man who lived his life by deception recognized dissembling when he heard it.

"Then I'll keep my voice down. Maybe eating will make your headache go away."

"That depends."

"On what?"

"How far do smells travel?"

"What?"

"Well, we're supposed to be avoiding any unwelcome company, you know—like bears and Indians," she improvised. "I was just wondering if the smell of cooking food traveled far."

"We've been on the trail for almost two weeks. Why are you concerned about this now?"

"What about our run-in with that cougar?"

"We weren't cooking anything when that happened."

"I know." If she told him about the soldiers, she would have to explain why she hadn't delivered him into their hands. She refused to confess her feelings toward Logan when she couldn't admit them to herself.

As soon as they reached Trinity Falls, he would no longer be a part of her life. That would be soon enough to deal with her confusing emotions. It would be safer to come to terms with her attachment when he wasn't standing in front of her.

"I suppose I'm thinking we've been lucky avoiding any unwelcome company, except for the mountain lion and the bee."

He shook his head. "You're lumping a mountain lion and a bee together?"

She bristled at his mocking tone. "I'm concerned about our welfare. Now that we've almost made it to safety, it would be foolish to draw any unwelcome attention." She glanced around meaningfully at the lodgepole pines that marched up to their tiny camp. "I'll bet this forest is brimming with Indians looking for an opportunity to collect a few new scalps."

"We're in friendly territory now, Victoria."

"Well, there might be soldiers—" She broke off in disgust at where her words had taken her. The last thing she'd wanted to bring up was the presence of the United States Army.

"Night Wolf said there was a troop nearby."

His announcement stunned her. "You spoke to Night Wolf?"

He nodded. "A few minutes ago."

She looked past him in consternation. "But I wanted to meet your Indian friend. Why didn't you bring him to camp?"

Logan shrugged. "I didn't see the point."

"Didn't see the point?" Victoria demanded, incensed. She still remembered to keep her voice lowered. "I've been looking forward to meeting an American primitive. Night Wolf would have been perfect."

"Why is that?"

"Because he isn't hostile." Really, Logan could be quite dense at times. "I wanted to meet a real Indian chief. You can't deny you called him a brave and noble warrior."

"I'm not sure I used those exact words. Besides, I was trying to save you from being disappointed."

"What do you mean?"

"Your expectations of Night Wolf are too high. The truth is, he's..."

"What?"

"Old. Really old. He's lost all his teeth and most of his hair."

"I didn't realize Indians went bald," she mused, not caring that the Shoshone warrior was past his prime.

"Well, they do. And one more thing about Night Wolf— he really stinks. You never want to stand downwind of him. Nor do you want to eat with him. It's disgusting how he gums his food."

"Thank you for the warning, but it appears I shall never meet him."

"I'll introduce you to another Indian someday."

There would never be a "someday," Victoria thought, blinking away the sudden moisture that filmed her eyes. She busied herself with putting the skillet on the low-burning fire.

Logan watched Victoria cook the fish he'd caught. He wasn't surprised she was disappointed about missing Night Wolf. She'd obviously built up the Shoshone chief to be a great warrior.

Logan scowled. Since he, too, admired the Indian, Logan didn't dispute her estimation. What he did take issue with was her gazing at the man with admiration shining in the verdant depths of her green eyes. Since he, himself, had never sparked that reaction from her, he'd be damned if he watched her shower someone else with the gift of her feminine adoration.

That was something he wanted only for himself, just as he wanted her soft female heat for himself alone. But the only way he could receive those treasures would be to tell her who he was. And have her believe him. Of course, after they reached Trinity Falls, the matter would be moot. It would be proved irrefutably that he wasn't running from the law but was instead a respected citizen.

Victoria slid the fish onto a flower-patterned plate. "Lunch is ready."

She hadn't turned him over to the soldiers....

Logan had stood behind her on the bank as she looked down upon the troop of uniformed men. He'd held his breath, waiting to see what she would do. He really wasn't in that much danger, though, because Windham wasn't with the party. It was unlikely a warrant had been issued for Logan's arrest. He doubted the colonel wanted many people knowing how he'd left Logan to die at the fort for a matter so personal as the officer's offended honor over a supposedly adulterous wife. No, that was something a man liked to keep to himself.

As he helped himself to a couple of the fried trout, Logan studied Victoria. She had settled herself on a blanket and was listlessly using her fork to poke a piece of fish. Most people who spent any time on the trail would gobble down any morsel of food set before them. Not Victoria. She was one of the fussiest eaters he'd ever met. Her finicky attitude was probably a result of her refined upbringing, he decided. Just like her cultured way of speaking and her obsession with books.

She looked up. "Why are you staring at me?"

Why didn't you turn me over to the soldiers, Victoria? Have you begun to trust me, after all?

"I'm waiting for you to stop chasing that fish around your plate and eat."

She jabbed a chunk of the flaky trout, plopped it between her teeth and held his stare while chewing with dainty vigor.

There was no reason for him to find her rebellious gesture at all sensual. Yet he did. But then, he found most of the things she did disturbing to his senses. Like the way she walked—briskly, as if in a hurry, yet with an unmistakable sway to her hips. Or the way she blinked when she was caught off guard and tried to get her bearings. Or the way she tilted her head when she was amused by something. Even the way she breathed caused his pulse to beat in double time.

For a moment, he teased himself with the brief glimpses he'd caught of her body after the rainstorm, as she changed into dry clothing. He hardened at the memory and cursed himself for being stupid enough to invite the image into his mind in broad daylight with Victoria sitting less than five feet from him. He would have liked nothing better than to lower her onto that blanket and—

"Logan, you're being awfully quiet."

"I thought that was what you wanted." Somehow he got the words past his dry throat, just as he got the fish down that same tight passage. For all of Victoria's surprisingly good cooking, he might as well have been eating dirt. He tasted nothing.

She cocked her head, as if listening for something. A delicate furrow lined her smooth brow. "I think, as long as we talk quietly, there's no harm in engaging in a simple conversation."

Logan translated that to mean that she thought the soldiers had left and it was safe to resume normal activity.

He took a swallow of water from the dainty china cup Victoria handed him at each meal. "Was there anything in particular you wanted to discuss?"

"You mentioned earlier that you wanted to show me something."

A surge of anticipation shot through him. "As soon as we're done eating, we're going to take a short hike. There's a couple of things close by that you might find interesting."

"Such as?"

"I thought you might like to see the waterfalls."

Barely contained excitement shimmered in her upturned gaze. "Oh, Logan, I would love to see them."

Excitement shimmered in Logan, also. He tamped it down as best he could. "There are some hot pools nearby, too."

"Hot pools?"

He nodded, trying to keep his expression neutral. "They're deep, and just the right temperature for a bath. I thought you might enjoy one." He cleared his throat. "It would give you a chance to clean up before your arrival in town tonight."

A look of caution crept into Victoria's formally beaming countenance. "And where will you be while I'm taking my bath?"

He really shouldn't be insulted at her misgivings about his intentions, Logan reflected. After all, he'd almost ravished her twice. Because of her innocence, she didn't realize he'd made love to her a hundred times. In his mind.

"I'll be in my own hot pool, washing off several pounds of Idaho trail dust."

She raised a winged, auburn eyebrow. "How close will your pool be to mine?"

Damned if she wasn't catching on to how his mind worked.

"Pretty close."

She nibbled her lower lip. He could almost see her mind working as she weighed the pros and cons of accepting his invitation to use the warm springs.

"A hot bath sounds splendid," she observed thoughtfully. Her expression lightened. "And it's not as if I can't trust you to...respect my privacy. After all, we've been together for almost two weeks now, and except for...uh...our rather bumpy beginning, you've been a perfect gentleman." She beamed at him. "Let's take advantage of the pools. It would be wonderful to arrive in town refreshed."

Logan got to his feet. "I'll put out the fire."

She uncurled from the blanket and smiled. "Let me get a few things. I want to savor this experience."

So do I....

If his goal hadn't been strictly honorable, Logan might have felt guilty over Victoria's misplaced confidence, but his only aim today was to forge a bond of intimacy that she'd never experienced with another man. Her virginity would be safe.

His specific goal was to break down her inhibitions with him. Only *him.* He wanted her to understand that the fierce desire riding him also rode her, that they could make a fire hot enough to melt any walls or obstacles that might arise between them. He wanted to awaken her to the passion locked inside her. After experiencing that passionate awakening, she wouldn't be able to walk away from him, as Robeena had done. He'd learned his lesson from the past. He needed to possess Victoria so completely that there would be no room in her mind, her heart or her body for another man.

As he made that decision, Logan knew he would find no release with Victoria until he made her his wife. For, if he yielded to his own hungers, he would take something he sensed she was incapable of surrendering without a wedding ceremony. He wanted her love, her warmth and her laughter—not guilt, not remorse, not shame.

Soon they would leave these hills, taking a trail that angled downward to the main road leading to town. Tomorrow everything would change between them. She would discover he was her employer. While under the watchful eyes of the good people of Trinity Falls, they would have to display a strictly professional manner toward each other. It was essential that they set a good example for Madison. The girl was extremely impressionable, and in dire need of refinement if she was to successfully escape her rough upbringing and find a place in polite society, a place that would provide her with a husband and family someday.

"I'm ready."

Victoria's voice broke through Logan's thoughts. She had gathered a couple of towels, a change of clothes and a bar of pink soap, which rested atop the small stack of items.

"Good." He moved to the edge of the clearing. "We don't have far to go. It won't be much of a hike."

He glanced over his shoulder to make sure she followed. The path was steep, so he reached out and relieved her of the bundle.

"Thank you."

Her voice was breathless, and her eyes were alive with anticipation. Logan smothered a groan. "Just stay close."

"Don't worry," came her cheerful assurance. "I wouldn't want to miss this."

Despite the current of sizzling heat that snaked through Logan's groin, he managed to set a brisk pace through the trees. There were some pleasures a man hated to delay.

Once they arrived in town, he had every intention of courting Victoria properly. It had come to that, he admitted. Since he had no intention of sharing her with another man and had every intention of sampling each delectable inch of her sweetly curved body, he was going to have to make the supreme sacrifice and surrender his bachelorhood.

There would be rewards other than those of the marital bed, he knew. There would be the satisfaction of waking up each morning with her in his arms, of watching her incredible eyes light with excitement over some incomprehensible bit of drama from her books and hearing her voice, with its distinctive Boston accent, daintily assault his composure.

He could make her love him. He was convinced of that. Hell, it would be easy, once she knew he wasn't Logan the larcenous marauder of the West. Of course, there was bound to be a rough patch when she realized he'd withheld his true identity from her. But he was convinced he could sweet-talk her out of that little snit.

Everything considered, he was sure that, once they reached civilization, she would bend to his superior will. He would bring her flowers. Women liked that. He would get Martin to write her a poem or two, which Logan would then recite to her. He'd escort her to the hotel dining room for a dozen dinners and woo her with Pierre's outstanding French cuisine. Hell, with her finicky appetite, that act alone would earn her undying love.

He'd buy her jewelry, too. Robeena had always responded well to the diamond-studded trinkets he lavished upon her.

The thought struck him that it might be worthwhile to borrow Nate Bushletter's guitar and serenade Victoria under her window. Nate had done that with the young widow Harding, and the woman had been so overcome she climbed down her own trellis and, wearing nothing more than a cotton nightie, threw herself into Nate's arms. Reverend Donally had pronounced their vows the next morning.

Evidently, guitars were effective with females. Of course, Nate did have an outstanding singing voice. . . .

Logan shrugged away the thought. His courtship of Victoria was going to have to be circumspect. He wasn't going to do anything to jeopardize her reputation or endanger Madison's chances of living in a respectable household.

That meant no guitar and no…no anticipating their vows. At least not flagrantly. Nor would there would be visits to Dancing Belle's or The Golden Spur to work off his frustrations. Victoria wasn't the kind of woman to tolerate unfaithfulness in a would-be beau. That suited Logan just fine. He found no temptation in the good-time women who'd formerly satisfied his appetites. They were a part of his past.

Not that he hadn't enjoyed the benefits of his reputation as a womanizer. Accompanying some of the town's fancy women to the Prairie Rose Hotel was just the thing to discourage the town's doting mamas from peddling their virginal daughters as prospective brides. Nor had his reputation interfered with his business activities. Actually, it was just the opposite. Men tended to admire his casual approach where women were concerned.

The town council had picked him as the temporary mayor until the next election. To his way of thinking, that proved his reputation hadn't hurt him. Anyway, his past involvements with other women weren't any concern of Victoria's. He just hoped she would never hear anyone refer to him by the ridiculous name Windham had used, "Passion's Pirate."

The scent of the bar of soap he carried teased Logan's nostrils. He glanced behind him. Pink-faced, Victoria was right behind him.

He stopped and rearranged the things he carried under one arm, extending his other hand to help her over a couple of boulders. "We're here."

Chapter Fifteen

Victoria accepted Logan's tug, allowing herself to be lifted over the rounded bellies of several exposed boulders. The sound of falling water rumbled through the formerly quiet forest. When she reached his side, she looked across the cliff to the other side of the gorge, where three magnificent columns of cascading water plummeted from uneven precipices of several hundred feet. The frothy sheets of tumbling white liquid resembled gracefully shimmering wedding veils worn by brides of differing heights.

"They're so beautiful," Victoria said softly.

She turned to share her awe with Logan and received a terrible shock. He'd draped his arm around her waist, and his face was turned toward her. Her heart rammed up hard against her ribs.

I love him...

The horrible realization swelled inside her chest until she found it impossible to breathe. How could she have sunk so low?

"It's from these falls that the town gets its name."

Dry-mouthed, Victoria nodded at the obvious explanation. She knew she should pull away, but she couldn't. Instead, she stared at his lean, hard lips, now framed by a black mustache and beard. Goodness, if she was to stand on tiptoe and wind her arms about his neck, she would be able to plant a kiss squarely upon his unyielding but strangely beckoning mouth.

She ought to tear her gaze from his beloved countenance and experience the wild splendor of the falls presently roaring in her ears. She rationalized, however, that in his own way, Logan, too, was a natural, wild splendor. Besides, when he was gone, she surely would have ample opportunity to return to this place to enjoy the view.

"Why aren't you looking at the falls? You're not afraid of heights, are you?"

Only the heights where I suspect you can take me ...

She shook her head. "Looking down from high places has never overset me."

"Good."

With a mighty burst of will, she removed her gaze from his mouth. Before she could return her attention to the falls, however, his darkly penetrating eyes trapped her in their unfathomable depths.

His head lowered, so slowly that at first she thought she imagined the descent. Then his mouth touched hers. She sighed once, quickly balanced herself on tiptoe and twined her hands behind his neck. Everything was just as she'd visualized it.

And more.

His lips molded against hers. His tongue was bold and possessive. It invaded her mouth and stroked deeply. Beneath her skin, rivulets of excitement raced willy-nilly in a mad dash to nowhere.

She shook with such intensity that she felt the way a tuning fork must when slammed against a hard surface. Within her, a fierce vibration commenced. She couldn't find the strength to draw free from Logan's sensual aggression and end the rioting sensations flooding through her. The internal commotion he stirred was too powerful to resist.

Logan broke off the kiss with a groan. "Victoria..."

"Yes?" It was not a question, but an answer. She wondered whether he understood that.

Her breasts ached to feel his hands upon them. His mouth, too, she thought dizzily. Suddenly her clothing was a burden.

"Come on, I'll show you the hot springs."

She forced herself to loosen her grip around his neck. How embarrassing for him to have to pry himself from her impassioned grasp. Dazed by her strong reaction, she stepped back.

"Watch out!"

Logan's shout hurt her eardrums. His hands clamped around her waist and jerked her away from the airy void that yawned below.

"Did you forget we're standing on a cliff?"

"I must have."

A scowl gripped his set features. "Well, pay attention."

The man must be wrought from the same stone as the boulders they'd just traversed. How else could he think of such inconsequential matters as hot pools and mountain ledges?

"I'll be more careful." It was difficult to get the humbling words past her tingling lips.

If anyone deserved an apology, it was she. Logan should beg her to excuse his trespass upon her mouth. Then he should apologize for ending the interlude before she was satisfied.

His timing was dreadful. She wanted to be held in his arms far more than she wanted a bath. He should know that without her telling him so. As a gently bred woman, she wasn't permitted to issue such an invitation herself. Propriety demanded that the man take the initiative in situations like this. It was then up to the woman to decline or accept his advances.

Propriety? Victoria hated admitting it, but she feared she'd left such virtues somewhere between here and the fort. Perhaps it would have been better to sacrifice a book or two, rather than her integrity.

She supposed she ought to be grateful to Logan for having caught her before she tumbled into the river that flowed beneath the falls. He'd saved her life. But she wouldn't have lost her balance if he hadn't kissed her senseless. When one pondered the point, the blame was his for advancing and then retreating with nary a thought for her bursting lungs and overwrought inner tickings.

He continued to stare at her with a mean look in his eyes. Two could play that game. She raised her chin. If he insisted on acting as if the kiss they'd just shared were a normal part of their daily dealings, and unworthy of comment, so be it. She could be as blasé as the next person.

"Well, where are these hot springs?" she inquired briskly.

"I'll show you." Keeping one arm securely around her waist, he turned from the falls. He used his free hand to scoop up the bundle he'd laid on a nearby boulder. "They're just beyond that stand of cedars."

Victoria noticed that on this high mountain plateau the trees grew sparsely. There seemed to be an abundance of dead limbs and fallen pines. A faint whiff of sulfur reached her.

When they stepped through the cedars, they entered a small clearing washed in sunlight. The sulfurous smell was stronger, and the ground was dotted with a few resilient clumps of yellowish mountain grass and moss-covered rocks. There was a steamy density to the air that made it cling to her skin and hair.

The first hot pool they came to looked deep and inviting.

Logan set the towels and Victoria's change of clothes on a flattened slab of granite. "These pools are great for bathing."

Victoria looked around uncertainly. She spied four more nearby depressions filled with water, above which steamy vapors rose. The area was so open and unprotected, however, that it made her hesitate to peel to her bare skin. And there was the matter of Logan standing beside her.

Surely the toe-curling kiss they'd just shared was at odds with his assurances that he would behave as a gentleman. Perhaps the gentlemanly aspect of the unexpected liberty he'd taken when kissing her, she mused, came to bear in the way he'd abruptly terminated the intimate contact.

Victoria made the disheartening discovery that she wished Logan would act like the person he well and truly was—a man with no scruples, a man who would boldly take her into his arms and share the forbidden secrets he seemed to know about her body, secrets that were well kept from herself.

And if those marvelous sensations were rained upon her by his aggression and not her own surrender, then she couldn't be held responsible for what happened.

You're a coward, Victoria Amory... and a hypocrite.

The truth hurt, but did nothing to ease the dull throbbing centered in her female core.

"Don't tell me." Amusement laced Logan's voice. "Modesty prevents you from taking off your clothes and jumping in."

"A man of your nature may mock my modesty, but..."

But what? Are you going to lie and tell him you want him to leave?

Victoria closed her eyes and struggled for control, as well as with the gall to convince him that her thoughts were as pure as they'd been before he entered her life. "I admit I'm not the kind of woman who would permit a man who's not my husband to gaze upon my nude person in broad daylight."

There—she'd stated her position clearly, if not altogether honestly.

"What about in the dark?"

"There would be little point if it was dark."

Logan's dark eyes seemed to grow hot. Victoria ran her finger around her suddenly too-tight collar. Goodness, it was amazingly warm, standing so close to the hot pools.

"But you would let your *husband* look his fill at you? Without any clothes on? In broad daylight?"

Victoria swayed. She was in the midst of another highly improper conversation with Logan Youngblood that should be stopped before it went any further. And yet, as shocking as the words they exchanged were, they filled her with a surge of excitement. That excitement proved too seductive to resist. And, after all, when one got right down to it, they were only *talking*.

"I haven't given the manner much consideration, but I suppose, if my husband had a valid reason for wanting to…see me in an unclothed state, I would accommodate his wishes."

Logan's gaze turned speculative. "What you would call a valid reason?"

"I imagine that if I were ill or injured and he needed to ascertain my degree of unwellness…" She shrugged with affected negligence. "Under those circumstances, it would be reasonable to make such a request."

In one bold movement, Logan's smoldering eyes seemed to sweep over her. "Suppose you weren't ill or injured."

"Well, I, uh—"

"Suppose he just wanted to look at your soft body without your clothes getting in the way." Logan's voice lowered to a husky murmur that both caressed and scraped her nerve endings.

Her heart thumped against her ribs. "To my husband, I would grant such a liberty."

"Lucky man."

She flushed. "But what I would do with my husband, if there were such a person, is neither here nor there."

Logan's expression became shuttered. "So it appears."

"Then our discussion is utterly meaningless."

His lips curved into an infuriatingly cheerful grin. She was sorely tempted to push him into the nearest pool, clothes and all. Just to wipe that smug expression off his face.

"I'll turn my back while you strip," he announced with brazen directness.

"I'm not sure I trust you."

She swallowed. *Or myself.*

"You did back at the clearing," he reminded her. "You said that I've been a gentleman up to this point, and agreed there would be no risk in us taking advantage of the pools."

How convenient that he failed to mention the two occasions when his body had covered hers and he'd aroused a storm of unfulfilled longing within her.

"That was before."

"Before what?"

"Before you kissed me again." She drew herself to her full height. "You're not going to stand there and deny that less than five minutes ago you kissed me senseless."

His gaze sharpened. "Senseless, huh?"

The temptation grew stronger to shove him into a puddle of steaming water. "I exaggerated. Your kiss was merely..."

What? her brain demanded. Merely a raging conflagration that seared her entire being, merely a wild tempest that swept her into its swirling vortex, merely a thousand suns bursting in her soul...

"Merely... unexpected." *Like stepping off a cliff and having nothing beneath me save a thousand-foot drop to oblivion.*

He cocked his head. "You do like to challenge a man, Victoria. But then, I suppose it's natural for a woman of your temperament to race recklessly into danger."

A woman of her temperament? Race into danger? What was he talking about? "Obviously, you don't know me very well. I'm nothing like that."

"I see. You're just a shy, retiring miss who wouldn't say boo to her own shadow."

"There's no point in trying to frighten one's shadow," she observed repressively, hoping to put him in his place.

"You're just a simple little homebody," he continued, undaunted, "who doesn't live on the edge, place herself in reckless situations and risk life and limb in careless abandon?"

"That's correct," she agreed. "I am none of those things."

He laughed at her.

With no premeditation whatsoever, she raised her palms and shoved against his wide chest. A look of astonishment crossed his rugged features. But darned if he didn't catch his balance and sidestep the pool located so conveniently behind him.

His hands came up, and he gripped her wrists. "Honey, sometimes you just don't know when to quit."

"I'm not your honey!" Nor was there any sense in mourning the fact that she never would be. Clearly, the man was destined to end his brash life by a hangman's rope.

"But you could be, if you weren't so dead set on believing the worst of me."

She glanced at her trapped hands. "Release me."

"Say please."

She tugged instead.

Nothing happened.

She debated kicking him. She had on her nice sturdy walking shoes, the ones she'd purchased especially for her Western adventure at Mr. Hempstead's Shoe and Bootery.

She scowled. "Why are you acting so contrarily?"

"Maybe I'm tired of you not trusting me."

"Not trusting you! In case you forgot, I found you in a—"

"Stockade. I'm hardly likely to forget it, since you remind me of it every chance you get. But you've been around me long enough to form your own conclusions about my character."

"I have formed my own conclusions!"

"Based on a dismal first impression," he shot back.

She looked at him helplessly. What did he want from her? She was already closer than he could possibly know to becoming the reckless woman he'd mistakenly accused her of being.

"I've already told you—just a few minutes ago, if you'll recall—that I do trust you. After a fashion."

His thumbs gently rubbed the inside skin of her wrists. "That's pretty vague."

She tried to ignore the delicious sensations caused by his callused caress moving back and forth across the sensitive area.

"Then I'll make it simple for you. My confidence does not extend to bathing naked in full view of your roving eyes! Is that clear?"

If she said it loud enough, surely it would be true.

"Well, why didn't you say so?"

She snapped her teeth together. The man was deliberately trying to flay her patience. She had no idea what he hoped to gain by goading her, but she'd had enough.

"Are you going to let go of my hands?"

"I'm not sure. Are you going to try and push me into another hot pool?"

The question was framed with a lazy kind of amusement that made her cheeks flame.

"If you'll just leave me alone to enjoy my bath in private, I promise to refrain from any further attacks upon your person."

His head bent, and he placed a kiss on both of her white-knuckled fists.

Having Logan's black pelt of hair under the tip of her nose was disconcerting. She wanted to know how it would feel to thread her fingers through his thick, wavy locks.

He released his grip, and her hands hovered for a moment with no sure place to go. Before she did something so utterly devoid of morality as flinging them around his neck, she lowered the fisted palms to her sides.

"I really can't leave you here unattended, Victoria. It wouldn't be the responsible thing to do."

He was lecturing her about responsibility?

"I'm hardly in any danger of drowning."

"A bear could come along, or a wolf, or another mountain cat—all with the intent of feasting upon your delectable hide. We wouldn't want that to happen. Nor would we want a wandering Indian, should one venture by and catch a glimpse of you, having to fight off the temptation of making you his captive. It's as basic as *ABC* that I should stay close to you."

A signifying *Abandonment*. *B* for *Base Urges*. And *C* for *Carnal Intentions,* she thought dourly.

"I'm not taking off this dress with you watching me!"

"I'll turn my back like this," he said, suiting his actions to his words. "You can peel down and slip into the water. Then I'll shuck off my clothes and get into another pool."

"I have no intention of seeing you naked!"

"Then close your eyes," he told her, his back facing her.

She opened her mouth. Nothing came out. If this was his brilliant solution to the dilemma of her modesty, then . . . Then it should work well enough, she reflected glumly. As long as he didn't kiss her, touch her or look at her, she should be relatively safe. Or as safe as she wanted to be.

Her fingers went to her top button, then paused. "I'll give you fair warning, Logan Youngblood. I'm going to remove my clothing and avail myself of this hot water. If you turn around before I tell you to, if you make so much as one attempt to share this pool with me, or if you violate a single principal of gentlemanly conduct, I will . . ."

Oh, drat. She should have thought of what threat she would hold over his head before the actual moment arrived when she voiced it.

"What will you do, Victoria?"

The timbre of his voice was deep and husky. She shivered and released another button.

"I shall be very disappointed in you."

"And?"

She finished unfastening her gown and slipped it off. "I know how to hold a grudge."

"Do you now?"

The taunting drawl raised goose bumps on her arms and elsewhere.

She removed her shoes and stockings, then quickly shed her undergarments. And stood utterly nude, with Logan Youngblood scarcely a foot away. Feeling the sunshine and a soft breeze against her naked flesh while surrounded in bright sunlight seemed the height of wantonness. She kept her gaze locked on him, as if that would somehow prevent him turning around, and dipped her big toe in the water.

The temperature was perfect. With more haste than gracefulness, she lowered her left leg as far as it would stretch into the pool's clear depths. She couldn't feel the bottom, and it was difficult to judge just how deep the water was.

"Are you in yet?"

"No! Don't turn around!"

Awkwardly she maneuvered herself so that she stepped into the pool backward. She balanced herself on the side and then let go. There was a splash, and a fast descent, and then the soles of her feet came into contact with the smooth rock bottom. She was standing in hot water that ended just below her bosom.

"Can I turn around?"

She encountered the scandalous sight of her bared breasts.

"No!"

"I thought I heard you get in."

"Well, I'm not all the way in." Bending her knees, she watched the tips of her breasts sink below the steamy surface.

Unfortunately, the pool was as clear as glass, and it scarcely mattered that her bosom was below the water's rim.

"Uh, Logan . . ."

"What?"

"Could you walk a few more feet away and use the hot spring to your left?"

"I suppose so."

"Well, do it. Then you can turn around."

Surprisingly, he obeyed her request and approached the farthest pool before stopping and turning. Somehow, however, the additional few feet weren't reassuring. Logan stood less than five yards away. Unsure of just how keen his vision was, she crossed her arms across her chest.

"It looks like you forgot something, honey."

There was that endearment again. She decided to ignore his use of it, this once. "What?"

"Your dainty little bar of pink soap." He smiled innocently. "Do you want it?"

"Of course I want it."

"Then I better bring it to you." He scratched his whiskered jaw. "That is, unless you want to climb out and get it."

"Just shut up and hand it to me."

He chuckled softly. "Anything you say."

In several strides, he'd picked up the soap and stood at the pool's edge, looking down at her. Her arms shielded her breasts, but there wasn't much she could do about the rest of her.

"Now this is interesting," he drawled wickedly.

"Just give me the damned soap."

"For me to do that, you're going to have to reach for it."

She glared at him. He was right. Gingerly she slipped one arm free. Immediately her left breast slid into full view. A hot blush stung her cheeks. She refused to meet Logan's gaze. Instead, she raised her hand, holding it above her, waiting for him to drop the cake of soap into her palm. Time stood still. It seemed to take forever for her to feel the weight of the scented bar in her hand. When she finally did, she curled her fingers around it and lowered her arm until it again cradled her.

The silence was as thick as the humid air that pressed against them.

"Victoria."

She forced herself to raise her bowed head. Logan stood above her. His intense stare slammed into her composure like a runaway locomotive bent on destroying anything in its path.

"I've never seen anything as beautiful as you."

Breathing became a chore.

With his lean fingers, he began unbuttoning his shirt. She wanted to protest that he was standing much too close and he needed to retreat to the far hot spring. But her tongue proved useless, and she watched mutely as the edges of the blue military shirt parted and his darkly furred chest came into view.

He tugged his shirttail free from the waistband of his black trousers and shrugged off the garment, dropping it to the ground beside her discarded clothing.

His hands were on his belt buckle. She knew he was watching her watch him, but that knowledge wasn't sufficient to make her look away. There was something so rawly mesmerizing about Logan's unselfconscious actions that she was held spellbound.

The belt came off with a faint rasping sound.

His fingers moved to his trouser's front closure.

"I should warn you, Victoria." His voice was a thick growl.

"Okay."

"When a man wants a woman, he can't hide it."

She saw the outline of the bulge that heralded his desire and knew he spoke the truth. Curiosity and a flood of burgeoning desire made it impossible to lower her eyelids.

The masculine striptease changed course for a moment as Logan balanced on his right foot and pulled off his boot, the remaining one followed in quick succession.

"The fact is," he continued, his voice rushing over her like sweet honey that had been set ablaze, "men are built pretty basically. We see a woman who heats our blood, and we get hard."

As he lowered the pants over his muscular flanks, she saw that he spoke the blunt truth. His male member sprang free, as bold and brash as the man himself. She shut her eyes. It was too late, of course, much too late, to erase the primitive beauty of Logan Youngblood's virile body from her mind. It occurred to her that he had behaved with far more discretion than had she. At least he'd turned his back while she undressed. She, on the other hand, had acted the part of one of those bad women Logan had described in such detail.

What was wrong with her? Why did she feel this strange lethargy that made her act so shamelessly? It was as if a stranger possessed her body, a stranger unable to resist Logan's stark masculine appeal.

"Did I shock you, Victoria?"

No, I shocked myself!

From the retreating sound of his voice, she could tell he'd moved away. She heard a splash and knew he'd entered another pool. Her lashes raised slightly, then jerked upward. He'd availed himself of the hot spring right next to hers!

She snagged her lower lip between her teeth. After witnessing him remove his garments, she could scarcely assume the role of an outraged innocent.

She watched Logan lean back in his pool and tip his face toward the sun. He looked as if he hadn't a care in the world. Didn't it matter to him that their imminent return to civilization signaled an end to their time together, or that he was most likely facing a prison sentence?

Perhaps it was second nature for him to remain untroubled by what the future held. Maybe it was that attitude of unconcern that had led to his life of criminal activities.

Sighing, she worked the soap into a lather and scrubbed. It felt so good to be completely clean. She washed her hair three times, to make certain she'd dislodged every last bit of Idaho grime, before she set the scented bar on the ground next to her. Then she eased herself into a position similar to Logan's, so that she rested the back of her head against the rock ledge.

The naturally heated water gradually relaxed her muscles to a state of boneless languor. Her eyelids drifted closed. If she hadn't feared drowning as a consequence, she would have succumbed to her growing lethargy and fallen asleep.

"How you doing over there?"

Logan's rich voice nudged her to heightened alertness. She moved her hands through the water, savoring the feel of it against her skin. "I'm in heaven."

"There's nothing like a hot bath to improve a person's mood," he observed, sounding thoroughly content. "Are you willing to share that bar of soap with me?"

She smiled. "You'll smell like a bouquet of roses."

"I don't mind. Toss it this way."

She obliged him, and the pink bar sailed through the air. He caught it without mishap, and was soon up to his bearded jaw in pink lather.

Her smile became bittersweet. She would never understand him, this wild, reckless man who'd barreled into her life with such shattering force and who seemed content to live with no thought of the morrow.

They drifted into another companionable silence. Again Victoria found herself dozing. She had no idea how much time had elapsed before she heard the sounds of Logan emerging from his hot pool. One moment she was drifting in a sea of warmth, and the next her attention was captured by the unmistakable sounds of him rising from the hot pool. Instinctively she turned her head. Rivulets of water sluiced down him, leaving gleaming trails across his hair-roughened, muscular body.

Immediately she averted her gaze. It didn't help her peace of mind to hear his husky chuckle.

"It's a little late to turn shy, honey."

She felt his shadow cover her and knew he was standing in front of her. "Now that I've satisfied my curiosity, there's no need for me to view you further."

Oh, Lord, she was in deep trouble. Why had she given in to the temptation to gaze upon his nude form?

"Give me your hand, Victoria."

"Why would I want to do that?" she asked, striving for calm. Belatedly it occurred to her that she was in a delicate situation. Just how did she plan on getting out of the steep edged pool? She doubted she had the strength to haul herself directly upward and out of the five-foot hole, as Logan had done.

"It should be obvious to you, honey, that you're going to need my help getting out of there."

She raised her lashes. Planted squarely before her were two overly large male feet, supporting twin columns of wet hairy legs.

"I can see that. Now," she muttered, vexed by her own lack of foresight, "may I suggest that you get dressed before assisting me from the pool?"

Surely it would be better if at least one of them was clothed. That way her naked skin wouldn't brush against his, and a modicum of decency would be preserved.

"Yeah, you can suggest it," he told her, with the satisfaction of a man who was in a superior bargaining position.

Odious creature. Odious, magnificently formed, breath-stoppingly virile creature.

"Stop tormenting me," she said firmly, striving for an air of authority, which wasn't easy, as he was dripping puddles of water within scant inches of her. Not to mention the fact that from his vantage point he had a clear view of her. Naturally, her crossed arms shielded her bosom, but she suspected his gaze might be focussed elsewhere. And *elsewhere* was pulsing with disheartening enthusiasm. "Put your pants on!"

He hunkered down instead. Valiantly she exercised the resolve necessary to keep her gaze from drifting to that manly part of him which he apparently suffered no compunctions about displaying. Clearly, modesty and Logan Youngblood were strangers.

"I want to look at you. All of you. And I want you to look at me. All of me."

"You know it wouldn't stop at looking," she said around the fullness that constricted her throat.

"I want to touch you, too. Wouldn't you like to touch me?"

Why not ask whether she wanted to take her next breath? The answer would be the same.

The alarming pictures Logan was firing in her fevered thoughts frightened Victoria. She sensed she was on the edge of a precipice that would forever change her life. She was a good woman. Despite the innocent mishap that had destroyed her reputation and sent her halfway across the country.

But she was a good woman who yearned for a bad man.

"We won't do anything you don't want to," he said softly.

Well, goodness, she *wanted* to do everything, and therein was the dilemma. If she did...everything with Logan, she would be unfit to assume a trusted position tutoring an innocent girl. That was how society worked, and despite her woeful desire to lie with Logan Youngblood, Victoria believed firmly in following society's strictures. It was those strictures that kept the world running as it should.

"I fear you have the power to make me want to do things I shouldn't. The truth is, you're a terrible influence on me."

"Am I?"

"And I had such high hopes for our association," she said, with a pitiful whine that grated on her own ears.

"What hopes were those?"

"That I could rehabilitate you, of course."

"And you think you've failed?"

"If I allow you to pull me from this water, with you as naked as the day you were born, I most certainly have failed. I hate to say it, but I'm afraid you're a lost cause. There doesn't seem to be a thing I can do to prick your conscience. And you, on the other hand, have me contemplating a disastrous fate."

"If I have to sacrifice morality and honor for the chance to have you in my arms, I'm willing to make the trade."

"But it shouldn't be that way!"

"Give me your hand, Victoria."

She looked into his darkly compelling eyes and, as if hypnotized, raised her arm. Within seconds, her dripping body was lifted from the pool and engulfed in Logan's hot embrace. None of her imaginings could have prepared her for the sensation of her wet flesh rubbing against his lightly furred skin.

She braced her palms against his chest to protest against his drawing her any closer, but the texture of the black, springy hair dusting his muscular torso proved her undoing. There was no way she could prevent herself from running her fingertips across the lush pelt.

He lowered her onto the disheveled heap of their clothing. "Oh, honey. I didn't plan on feeling this way. I thought I could look at you, hold you and...and not take it any further."

She stared at his roughly bearded, leanly sculptured features. The dark hunger radiating from his possessive gaze banished resolve and reason.

"I—I didn't plan on feeling this way, either," she confessed tightly. "I suppose we must resign ourselves to the inevitable."

A savage grin slashed his harshly stamped features, making him look for all the world like the fierce pirate she'd silently called him. "Such a brave little soldier."

"Kiss me, Logan." Her boldness astonished her, but she was desperate to feel his mouth against hers.

"In a minute," he said. "Before we go any further, there's some things we have to settle."

She knew for a fact that it was his rigid manhood, not a pinecone, that was pressed against her hip. Since it was perfectly obvious that he was as aroused as she was, she didn't understand why he would pick now to have a chat. Besides, she needed him to sweep her up into a maelstrom of physical ardor, so that she wouldn't have time to think about what she was about to do.

She wanted passion, not debate.

She ran her fingertips across his powerful shoulders. "We can talk later, Logan."

"I like your spirit, honey. But there's some things you need to know about me before—"

She moved her fingertip to his mouth, to forestall any confessions. "There's nothing more I need to know about you."

Other than that I've foolishly lost my heart to you, and I'm going to steal this moment from fate and let you love me the only way you're probably capable of loving. And it's going to be enough for me.

A barrier seemed to go up behind his eyes. "I see."

She smiled encouragingly at him. "It's very noble of you to remind me of your tarnished past. I—I know we have no future together. But we have now, Logan. This minute."

His gaze remained ominously brooding, yet a mocking smile curved his mouth. "And here I thought you'd already insulted me all the ways a man could be insulted."

She looked at him in bewilderment. "What do you mean?"

He leaned forward and brushed his lips across her shoulder. The unexpected contact sent a sizzling current of fire rushing through her. "It's going to take me a lot longer than a minute to make love to you."

More delicious heat gathered within her. She felt as if he were setting a hundred fires beneath her skin. She recalled that he was very skilled at getting a spark to catch.

"Lord, you're beautiful."

The husky compliment was more dry grass laid upon the blaze.

"You're beautiful, also." It was the truth, she thought dazed. Logan Youngblood was a beautifully created man.

"I was right about your freckles."

His head bent over her breasts. Abruptly Victoria glanced down to what seemed to hold Logan's hot gaze enthralled. The sight of her bare bosom right under his nose seemed the most scandalous thing she'd ever witnessed.

In the passion of the moment, she'd forgotten about her freckles. She knew men preferred women with creamy, unblemished complexions, and here she was, virtually covered in spots. She stiffened beneath him. If her appearance displeased him, then it was time to call a halt to this lovemaking business.

"So beautiful..." The tip of his tongue flicked over a nipple. A hundred...nay, a thousand pinpricks of tingling energy swept through her. She trembled, of course. And kept her attention avidly focused on the thrilling sight of Logan's mouth moving across her breasts.

"It's as if your skin has been sprinkled with gold dust," he breathed, raining more sultry kisses across her flesh.

A thief would be attracted to gold dust....

"Your nipples are exactly the same shade of pink as the roses in my family's garden." He suckled lightly. "Every bit of you is perfect, Victoria."

He raised himself and moved the callused palm of his big hand to the part of her that had turned to bubbling honey. His fingers probed gently, then deeply.

She couldn't speak. Instead, she turned her head into his shoulder and closed her eyes. Logan's clean, musky scent, laced lightly with the fragrance of roses, filled her senses. She'd never felt anything like the sensations tugging and pulling at her.

"Have I told you how much I love your red hair? When I first met you, you reminded me of a little red-feathered bird." As his deep voice washed over her, his fingertips continued to work their mysterious magic.

Victoria yielded to the growing forces that gathered within her. She knew instinctively that something quite extraordinary was about to happen and made no effort to control the way her hips moved beneath Logan's caress.

"I've found your nest, little red bird. It's soft and silky and shelters something very special." He changed the rhythm of his strokes. Victoria arched toward him.

"That's it, honey. Spread your wings and fly."

She nipped his shoulder and wondered whether she was losing her mind. Then, without warning, a pulsing convulsion seemed to grip her within its spinning center. It was as if one moment she hovered on the brink of some delicious torment and the next she was sliding into paradise.

"Logan!"

"Yeah, sweetheart, let it take you..." His gritty voice became a part of the wild splendor burning out of control within her. She shuddered against his embrace, savoring the cast-off embers of the tumultuous blaze that had just swept through her.

Caught up in a wondrous glow, Victoria was dimly aware of Logan shifting his position above her so that she cradled him between her upraised thighs.

"I thought I could take you this far and stop without—" He pinned her with a tortured stare. "I thought I could bind you to me, but I'm the one who's been captured, honey. I. I can't keep from loving you."

She looked into Logan's harshly sculpted features and was struck by an incredible feeling of inevitability, as if this moment between them had been destined to happen, and nothing that she or he could have done would have prevented fate from having its way.

She reached up and ran her fingertips across the bunched muscles of his strong forearms, gazing at him with all the unspoken love that filled her heart. "I think you've waited long enough, Logan."

"Oh, honey..."

With that, Logan Youngblood surged into her with one possessive stroke that took her breath away. There was pain...brief and soon forgotten. There was rapture...

hot, sweet and pulsing... brought to shattering fulfillment
by the wild cadence of Logan's deep, powerful thrusts.

And there was regret....

Chapter Sixteen

All at once, it was as if time had sped up. One moment Victoria was sharing Logan's fevered embrace, and the next they were dressed, back at the clearing and standing beside the wagon.

Logan looked toward the sun. "There's enough sunlight left in the day to see you to Trinity Falls."

A sense of bereftness cut through her fragile defenses. She felt so exposed that she had to remind herself she was fully clothed. Confused, she studied Logan's profile. In the aftermath of his powerful possession, there had been no further expressions of tenderness, no endearments, no whispers of affection—not even a measly "honey" to assuage her shattered sensibilities.

There had only been his determined rush to see them both dressed and on their way. She sensed a barely checked anger on his part, but was unable to guess what had caused it. A hot flush stung her cheeks. From his exultant shout of satisfaction when he convulsed on top of her, she'd assumed she'd pleased him well enough during the blissful throes of mindless release.

But now that the fury of the storm was spent, Logan seemed a stranger. A grumpy one, at that.

"Victoria!"

At his sharp tone, her head snapped up. *A damned ungrateful stranger!*

"What?"

"It will be better if you ride in the wagon for this part of the trip."

She ignored the closed expression that discouraged debate on the matter. "Why?"

His scowl indicated that she'd been right. He wasn't in a talkative mood. She frowned back at him. That was just too bad. Clearly, not only was this man a reprehensible blackguard, he was also a lackluster lover. Oh, not when the actual moment of coupling occurred, she conceded. It was after the deed was dispatched that he fell far short of her expectations.

Victoria sighed. For the time being, he was *her* blackguard, and she supposed it was up to her to tell him what a woman yearned for after his fiery brand of lovemaking. On the heels of that thought followed the realization that she would be a fool to instruct him in the ways of making other women happy.

"In just a couple of miles, this trail will take a steep downward drop onto the main road into town. After that, the oxen will be moving at a brisk pace."

She'd believe that when she saw it. By her observation, oxen had only one rate of speed. Sluggish.

She allowed Logan to assist her into the wagon, assuming he'd forgotten the other times she'd managed satisfactorily on her own. When one's heart was bleeding from a mortal wound, one hardly quibbled over small issues.

Victoria knew what she had to do. And she would have to do it soon. It struck her that in the space of a single day she would violate the central core of everything she'd ever believed.

"Uh, Logan..."

He'd already gathered the bullwhip with one hand and taken the reins in the other. "Hold on, honey. It's going to be a rough ride."

Now, when it was too late to soothe her ragged nerves, the endearment flowed from his mouth with a smoothness that made her want to cry, or gnash her teeth, or strike him over the head with a thick book.

The oxen lurched forward. One of Logan's arms curved around her, and he anchored her to his side. For the next half hour, Victoria thought she'd been tossed back in time. Pine branches tore at the wagon's canopy as Logan guided the team through a wild stretch of hilly terrain that left her feeling battered. Then, mercifully, they came to a stop, poised on a bend that overlooked the flat valley below. Clearly visible was a jumble of tents and buildings that seemed to have sprung up from the sagebrush.

"There it is," Logan announced.

Victoria stared in dismay at the sprawling conglomeration of wood edifices and haphazardly placed rows of dingy tents.

"Trinity Falls?"

He shot her an amused glance. "Don't tell me, you're disappointed."

Victoria noticed that whenever Logan began a sentence with "Don't tell me," he seemed, annoyingly, to have guessed her thoughts.

"It's different than I expected." She wondered if he had any idea how much of an understatement her observation was. "Bigger, too."

"Trinity Falls boasts twenty-two saloons, four general stores, a doctor's office, a newspaper, four hotels, three churches, a school and a branch of Western Banks United. Recent gold strikes have made it a bona fide boomtown."

One would have thought, from Logan's obvious pride in the fledgling community, that he was selling town lots. "And does it have a jail?"

His expression clouded. "Naturally."

"Logan, there's something I have to tell you before we go any farther."

"Go ahead, Victoria."

He looked if he were prepared to hear something significant. A painful possibility occurred to her. Did Logan believe that, because she'd given herself so completely to him, he could play upon her sympathy and induce her not to turn him over to the authorities? Was that why he'd unleashed his wildly splendid ardor upon her? Were the kisses, the caresses, the visit to the hot pools, all an effort on his part to make her forget her duty?

Reason suggested that it would have been easier for him to push her off a cliff to rid himself of her. But would it have been as enjoyable for him? She gazed into his eyes and wished she could read his thoughts, wished she could see beyond his shuttered expression, wished her doubts didn't inflict such pain upon her.

"When you were talking to Night Wolf, I—I saw a troop of cavalry soldiers. There were watering their horses at the river."

"Were they?"

She nodded. "I...I know I should have called out to them."

Belatedly it occurred to her that if she'd done so, she wouldn't have been seduced by Logan.

"Why didn't you?"

"I was afraid of what they might do to you," she replied honestly. "I just couldn't turn you over to them."

A hard smile edged his lips. "If I'm such a despicable felon, you should have."

"I realize that," she said morosely. "There's something else you should know."

"Yes?"

"When we arrive in Trinity Falls, I won't be able to bring myself to turn you in to the sheriff."

"You won't?"

She shook her head miserably. "So, if you made love to me so I wouldn't—"

His strong hands came from nowhere and closed around her shoulders. A scowl as menacing as a mountain thunderstorm contorted his face. "Don't push me too far, Victoria."

The rawly palpable anger simmering in his eyes convinced her, as nothing else could have, that he'd had no ulterior motive in claiming her.

"I was just wondering," she whispered. "I mean, it did seem possible that a man on the run would do just about anything to escape punishment."

His ominous gaze blistered the thin veneer of her brittle composure. "It always comes back to that, doesn't it?"

"Well, your being a criminal is bound to be a significant factor in your dealings with other people, Logan."

"I'm not."

His tight, almost gutturally voiced denial touched Victoria profoundly. She smiled sadly. "That's the spirit. All great journeys begin with a single step."

"What the hell are you talking about?"

"Think about it, Logan. You were left in that stockade to die. Night Wolf told you that the Indians burned the fort to the ground. That means, to the army and everyone else, Logan Youngblood is dead. You can start over. You can choose a new name, a new life and a new place to live."

He loosened his grip. Disbelief and frustration seemed to move across his features, along with residual traces of anger.

"So you're going to let me . . . escape?"

"I *do* believe in you, Logan," she said thickly, "I know that if you try hard enough you can mend your wayward ways. You must remember, though, not to yield to temptation." She hesitated. "This love you seem to have for gold needn't be a bad thing—as long as you're willing to put in an honest day's labor to earn it."

He stared off into the distance for a moment, then leveled another sharp stare at her.

"Then this is goodbye?"

"I'm afraid so." She blinked rapidly, trying to stave off a deluge of useless tears. "I—I want you to know that I shall remember you always with great . . . affection, Logan."

"Suppose I told you this isn't goodbye, that I've been a law-abiding citizen of Trinity Falls for almost six years. I own the town bank—I own all of Western Banks United. And the city council appointed me mayor when—"

"Stop!" Victoria couldn't bear to hear any more of Logan's outrageous lies. "If you're truly going to start a new life, you must be scrupulous in telling the truth."

"Hell."

"And excessive profanity is not conducive to forming associations with respectable people, either."

"Well, my little doubting Thomas, you've left me no choice but to let you discover the hard way that first appearances can be deceiving, and everything isn't always as it seems."

Logan's words struck a sympathetic chord within Victoria. On the one hand, she knew that his exaggerated claims of who he was were patently false; on the other, she understood that someone like Logan probably felt he had to lie to receive any praise.

"I know that appearances can be misleading," she said carefully, reluctant to share her past, but suspecting that her experience could help him. "You asked me once why I came west. Well, I was *forced* to make the fresh kind of start I know you're capable of achieving."

"What happened?"

"I was caught in a . . . compromising situation."

"What kind of compromising situation?" The words were evenly paced, like gunshots fired in a precise order.

"An innocent, completely harmless incident that could have been easily explained, had anyone been interested in discovering what had transpired," she informed him. "The point I'm trying to make is that I know what it's like to be misjudged. A person cannot use that unpleasant circumstance, however, as an excuse to justify subsequent misbehavior."

"You have an answer for everything, don't you?"

She shook her head sadly. "Not everything. I fear we did not use our time together wisely, Logan. And I must bear much of the blame for that. We wasted so many days not speaking to each other, when they could have been put to a better purpose."

His eyes gleamed faintly. "Hmm... I wonder what better purpose that could have been."

With his free hand, he brushed his fingertips across her cheek. The gentle gesture was almost her undoing.

"I could have taught you how to read and write."

Abruptly he dropped his hand. "So now, among all the villainies of which I stand accused, you've decided I'm illiterate, too."

"Logan, I don't speak to wound your pride," she assured him. "But I've been finding the books you've tried to throw away."

He arched an eyebrow. "Have you?"

"They've been the same few volumes over and over again."

"And from that you concluded I wasn't able to read the titles?"

"What else could I have thought?"

"That I *do* know how to read and we were playing a game?"

The wry, faintly ironic question caught her by surprise. She concluded Logan was telling the truth. He'd discarded the books and tossed them in easy-to-find locations, as part of a game.

"I can see I've rendered you speechless."

He handed the reins to her. She looked at them stupidly. With a casual ease she had yet to achieve, he climbed from the wagon's high bench scat.

She stared down at him in dismay. "What are you doing?"

"Leaving."

"But... but..."

"But what? You said you were setting me free. You haven't changed your mind, have you?"

An oppressive chill squeezed her heart. This was it. Logan was well and truly going. "I suppose it's better this way." She regarded him gravely. "But how are you going to survive out here alone?"

"I'll manage."

He turned.

"Wait! Don't go yet. I have something to give you."

She laid aside the reins and clambered into the wagon. She tossed aside various items, searching for the one thing she could offer him that might help him begin a new life. Her frantic search ended when her fingers closed around the small pouch she'd secreted in a remote cubbyhole.

She was breathless when she emerged into the sunlight. Logan remained exactly as she'd left him, looking impatient to be on his way. His easy acceptance of their imminent parting stung deeply. It would have eased her own burgeoning anguish if he'd evidenced the slightest trace of regret. Unfortunately, he appeared to be a man with nothing more pressing on his mind than an afternoon stroll.

Suppressing the urge to berate him, she climbed from the wagon and thrust out her hand. "Here, take this."

He eyed the extended pouch with a flicker of curiosity, but didn't reach for it. "What is it?"

"Some gold coins to help you begin your new life."

"And here I was expecting you to offer me a book as a parting gift."

"That would hardly be practical."

He shrugged. "You must have a copy of the Holy Bible among your collection. I figured you were going to give it to me as part of your quest to improve my character."

"I do have such a volume, but I fear it's too heavy to carry on your travels." She jiggled the small drawstring bag. "I'm sure the money will prove far more practical."

He crossed his arms. "I don't want your damned gold."

A thief who didn't want gold? She would have liked to interpret Logan's actions as an indication that he truly was turning over a new leaf, but she feared the truth lay in another direction. He was simply too proud to accept money from a woman.

"Don't think of this as charity. Consider it a loan until you can repay me."

His gaze narrowed. "From the future you have mapped out, the odds are we won't see each other again."

Her eyes filmed with hot moisture. A jagged lump rose in her throat. "You could always mail me the funds."

"Then you plan to remain in Trinity Falls?"

"I...I don't know," she confessed softly. "I'm not certain that as things stand I'll be able to honor my contract with Mr. Pritchert."

"What the devil are you talking about?"

"Well, after what we did..." She found she could no longer meet Logan's glare. "I mean, I'm not exactly the same person Mr. Pritchert hired to tutor his employer's ward, am I?"

Victoria took a deep breath and raced onward with her jumbled thoughts. "I'm sure that part of the reason he secured my services was because of his acquaintance with my father and the reputation of our family. He chose to ignore an unfortunate rumor being circulated about me, because he assumed I would be a proper influence on the young woman he represented. I fear I'm no longer worthy of his trust and, in all good conscience, I should inform him of that fact."

"Don't be a fool, Victoria. Tell no one about what happened at the hot pools."

"But, surely—"

"I mean it. You'll bring nothing but heartache on yourself if you do. You're the same woman you were before I lost control and took things further than I had any right or intention to do."

"I . . . I was the one who permitted the liberties," she reminded him gently. "I have to accept responsibility for my actions." Her gaze dropped to the pouch Logan had failed to accept. "Please take this."

"Under one condition."

"What's that?"

"Promise you'll tell no one about what transpired between us these past two weeks."

Understanding made her stomach twist. "I see, you're afraid I'll mention you by name and the authorities will discover you weren't killed at the fort."

"Honey, at this point there's not a damned thing to be gained by talking to you." He snatched the gold from her in clear exasperation. "Just promise that you'll keep your guilty conscience to yourself for the time being. There's no need to ride into town with a scarlet *A* embroidered on your collar."

She took exception to his droll tone. Again she wondered how he could jest at a time like this, a time when her heart was in peril of crumbling.

"I had planned on being discreet and only speaking of the matter with Mr. Pritchert."

Logan thrust his bearded face into hers. "You won't tell Mart—Mr. Pritchert—a damned thing about us. Is that clear?"

"I'm not certain I care for your tone, Logan. Besides, what difference could it possibly make to you? You'll be miles away, and I've already told you I won't identify you by name."

"Victoria, I want your promise, and I want it now."

She stared at him in mounting fury. What gave him the mistaken notion that he had any authority over how she conducted her life? Theirs was clearly a fleeting association, doomed by events and circumstance to end when she got back into the wagon and drove her team into town.

And yet . . . Clearly, this matter meant a great deal to Logan. Was his demand for silence his small way of attempting to look after her future, as she was trying to look after his? The possibility touched her, and her anger softened.

"All right, Logan," she finally conceded. "I shall say nothing to Mr. Pritchert."

The taut lines of his body relaxed perceptibly.

"See that you don't change your mind."

Suddenly self-conscious again, Victoria stepped back. This really was goodbye. She could think of no other reason to detain him. She'd given him her best counsel, eighty dollars in gold coins, and her promise to keep their illicit liaison a secret. Any business between them was well and truly completed.

"Goodbye, Victoria."

Hot tears rose. She tried to blink them away, but wasn't wholly successful.

He turned. Without realizing that she was going to do so, she reached out and grasped his arm. "Don't go yet. I—I have something else for you."

If she hadn't known better, she would have thought she saw tenderness shining from Logan's gaze.

"I don't need any more money."

"It's not that. Wait here, I'll be right back."

And then she was in the wagon again, foraging through her beloved collection of books, seeking one special volume. When she found what she was searching for, she dashed outside, fearful that Logan might already be gone.

He was, however, exactly where she'd left him.

Her hands trembled as she presented him with a slim leatherbound book. "I want you to have this."

Demonstrating none of the reservations he'd shown about accepting the gold coins, Logan immediately reached for the gift.

"What is it?"

"A book."

He rolled his eyes. "I can see that."

"Well, now that I know you can read, I want to give it to you. It's a volume of poetry by Keats. And . . . it's very special."

Again something akin to tenderness shone from Logan's gaze. "I'll treasure it."

"Whenever you read it—" her voice broke, and she took a deep breath "—I hope you'll remember me."

"Oh, hell."

His expletive took her aback.

"Don't you want to remember me?"

"Honey, there's no way on this good earth that I could ever forget you. You're getting worked up over nothing. I promise, this isn't goodbye."

She took a fierce swipe at her burning eyes. "But this must be our final farewell. It would be much too dangerous for you to show your face in Trinity Falls. People there must know you. If the military finds out you're still alive, they'll finish the task of killing you."

He stared deeply into her eyes; she had the feeling he was branding her in his memory. "Stubborn."

"What?"

"You might call it strength of character or determination, honey. But the truth is, you're the most stubborn woman I've ever met."

"What does *that* have to do with anything?"

"Only everything." He slipped the slim volume she'd given him into his shirt. "Goodbye for now, Victoria."

She couldn't call him back a third time. Yet she couldn't let him walk out of her life without sharing her deepest feelings. Within her heart, she knew that, despite his reassurances to the contrary, she would never see him again.

"I love you, Logan Youngblood."

Her soft declaration was made to his broad back. He stood stockstill, then turned slowly. His bearded features held a look of wary optimism. "Promise you'll remember those words the next time you see me."

She refused to cry, but the emotions churning inside her were so powerful she couldn't speak. She nodded instead.

Take me in your arms, Logan. Kiss me goodbye.

But he didn't.

He just turned again and walked out of her life.

As she watched him through the watery mist of her tears, it was as if he were returning to the otherworldly fog he'd stepped through the morning after the storm. Instinctively she moved toward him, but then she stopped. They'd said their goodbyes.

It was finished.

Chapter Seventeen

Victoria inspected her image in the hotel room's cheval mirror. She saw a serious-faced woman with sunburned skin wearing a dark plaid jacket over a white blouse tucked into a gray skirt.

She ran her fingertips across the dove-gray pleats, smoothing away any wrinkles the hotel laundry might have left unattended. It was only her nervousness, she told herself, that compelled her to reexamine her appearance every few minutes.

She continued to study her reflection, fussing with the lapels of the fitted jacket and adjusting her ruffled cravat. The feeling grew that she was gazing at a stranger. Could the outwardly composed woman in the mirror really be her?

She'd fashioned her hair in a neat twist, and she wore a small black straw hat perched above it. Hopefully, the cameo brooch pinned to the ruffles at her throat softened her outfit's stark simplicity. She didn't want to appear too severe for her interview with her new employer.

She drew a calming breath, but the constraining tightness of her corset made it difficult to breath deeply. After months of traipsing across the Western trail, it was difficult to reaccustom herself to wearing the rigid garment. But then, it also seemed unnatural to be surrounded by polished paneled walls, instead of gently swaying lodgepole pines, and to have a white plaster ceiling overhead instead of wide-open blue skies. Instead of the fresh smells of wild mint and evergreen, she detected the subtle scent of cotton-seed furniture polish and traces of kerosene oil.

Victoria turned from the mirror. The hotel suite Martin Pritchert had shown her to the night before was as elegantly appointed as any Boston drawing room. Clearly, the Prairie Rose Hotel was an establishment of superior quality. The Oriental rugs, maroon velvet draperies and plushly padded settee and armchairs attested to that.

She glanced at the high poster bed. To stretch out between crisp cotton sheets covering a downy soft mattress had seemed the height of luxury. She couldn't remember when she'd enjoyed an evening's sleep more. Except when she'd laid upon the hard ground, with Logan Youngblood's powerful arms enveloping her.

That errant thought brought with it a flash of pain. *You aren't going to think about Logan.* She steeled herself against the sense of bereavement she experienced when she remembered their abrupt parting. Everything had happened for the best. There was no way she and a man like Logan Youngblood could have had any future together. They were as different as fire and ice.

She had no illusions about which of them was the source of the flame and which of them had been reduced to an unseemly puddle during the elemental contest that had raged between them.

Logan had thawed every vestige of her frozen innocence, until all that remained was the shameless longing to again warm herself in the blaze of his shattering passion.

The clock on the mantel chimed. Victoria started. Martin Pritchert would be arriving any moment to take her to his employer's office. She reflected upon how, if they knew what had happened to her on the trail, neither Martin Pritchert nor the man he worked for would deem her fit to instruct their charge. Her stomach clenched. Despite the censure that had been heaped upon her when Horace Threadgill was discovered in her bedchamber, Victoria wasn't used to feeling unworthy.

She'd heeded Logan's counsel, though, and not disclosed to Mr. Pritchert anything about Logan's companionship during the past two weeks. Her brow knit. It would have been excruciatingly humiliating to introduce such an unseemly topic with the amiable man and his wife while they supped last night in the hotel restaurant. Yet, in the face of his kindness, she felt like a fraud. Surely, after her wanton behavior with Logan, she had forfeited the right to mingle with chaste people.

Despair seemed to permeate the very air she breathed. She missed Logan so terribly! It was as if a part of her had been torn asunder when he disappeared into the forest. She had the dismal feeling that she'd made a ghastly mistake. She should have followed Logan to the ends of the earth and endured a life of uncertainty and hardship rather than lose the man she loved.

He never said he loved you....

There was that, she mused dejectedly. If only she could have been a different sort of woman. If only she could have been as bold and reckless as Logan had called her. But the truth was, she was quite cowardly when it came to taking risks. Until this point in her life, the most dangerous thing she'd ever done was to come west, and hundreds of people did that every week.

An awful feeling of desolation continued to weigh down her spirits. Her mind knew she'd made the right choice. But her heart was a hollow shell of quiet despair. If she could have gone back and changed the past, she would have. Even if the wrong choice could never provide lasting happiness, it would have given her more time with Logan.

A knock sounded at the door. Victoria immediately opened it. Martin Pritchert, looking slightly rumpled and pudgy in a dark blue suit, greeted her with a friendly smile on his ruddy face. He'd applied a liberal amount of tonic to his thick, frizzy gray hair. Both it and the great whiskers framing his pink jowls were meticulously combed.

The man's blue eyes sparkled with vitality and good humor. "Well, now, I see you're ready for your appointment, Miss Amory."

"Yes, I am."

There was no reason for Mr. Pritchert's jovial presence to make her feel shy, yet Victoria found herself struggling to subdue a bout of timidity. She wondered if her time alone in the wilderness had withered her ability to engage in small talk. Then she remembered her final day with Logan Youngblood. She hadn't had any difficulty thinking of things to say to him. If anything, her tongue had run away with her, and she'd uttered several remarks that should have gone unspoken.

I love you...

"Then I suggest we be on our way. My employer isn't a man who appreciates being kept waiting."

"Of course." Victoria gathered her drawstring purse from the brilliantly polished mahogany surface of a nearby table. "Will I require a coat?"

Mr. Pritchert shook his head. "It's a fine day. The wind's not blowing, and the streets are dry."

Victoria allowed him to take her arm as they progressed down the hotel corridor. "Do you get much rain here?"

"Not as much as in the mountains," her companion observed cheerfully. "How was breakfast this morning? Did you get plenty to eat?"

"It was a feast." Victoria recalled the heavily laden tray delivered to her room. Ordinarily, she would have enjoyed the eggs, biscuits and ham. This morning, however, her appetite had been nonexistent. She wondered what Logan would have made of that unlikely circumstance. "It was considerate of you to have it sent to my chamber, but I wouldn't have minded eating in the hotel dining room."

They came to a wide oval staircase. Mr. Pritchert patted her arm. "Trinity Falls is a town overflowing with miners, Miss Amory. It wouldn't do for you to go about on your own. There are rough and wild men roaming the streets."

She'd just spent two weeks with her very own rough and wild man, Victoria reflected. How she ached to hear his voice and feel his arms around her. She even missed his provocative comments.

"Surely a woman can eat unaccosted in the hotel," she said, forcing her thoughts to the conversation at hand.

"A lone woman, especially one as lovely as you, Miss Amory, if you'll allow me to say so, must be escorted at all times. Remember, you're no longer in Boston."

As they left the hotel and stepped onto the boardwalk, Victoria concurred with Mr. Pritchert's statement. This definitely wasn't Boston. A wide dirt road ran through the middle of town. Upon its dusty, rutted surface rolled wagons drawn by teams of six and eight. A variety of oxen, mules and horses did the pulling. There were several carriages, and dozens of men on horseback riding to and fro. Dust boiled up in the wake of their swift passage.

Pedestrians in the form of roughly dressed men filled the sidewalks. Hundreds of them, some tall, some slight, some dressed in fine clothing, most in baggy trousers and plaid shirts, milled about the street. They were going into and coming out of saloons, hailing each other in loud voices, laughing, swearing, singing, shouting.... It was absolute mayhem.

Here and there, she did notice an occasional skirt passing among the male population. She noticed, also, that the scant number of women were accompanied by masculine escorts.

Her most vivid impression of the place was that of unrestrained noise. The constant onslaught of sound seemed especially jarring after her time in the nearly silent mountains. Here on this Western street, harness leather jingled, men whistled, and she was certain she detected the jaunty rhythms of at least three different pianos being played.

Two gunshots were fired in rapid succession. Victoria jumped.

"Don't be alarmed, Miss Amory. Gunfire in town rarely indicates serious trouble. It was probably just a minor skirmish over a card game."

Victoria swallowed. "Is it always like this?"

"Today might be busier than usual. Several supply wagons arrived yesterday, and there was news of a new gold strike." Mr. Pritchert took a firmer grip on her arm. "The Western Banks United building is across the street. When I say, 'Go,' I want you to run for it, and don't stop until we get to the other side."

Victoria nodded, trying to spot a break in the almost endless stream of traffic flowing in front of them.

"I must say, Miss Amory, I'm very impressed that you traveled through the mountains without mishap and made it safely to town. You're a remarkable woman."

Since there was no way she could have made the trip without Logan's help, Victoria felt guilty about accepting the falsely inspired praise. "It was certainly fortuitous that you happened to be out on the road yesterday."

Had she not met the man, it definitely would have been a challenge to search through town at dusk to find him. She was grateful to have been spared that inconvenience. During the final leg of her ride into town, she had not encountered another traveler on the roadway. Though there had been that lone rider streaking past her as twilight hovered on the horizon. It had surprised her that the man didn't stop his galloping mount to exchange a word with her on the lonely road.

Something about the rider's bearing had reminded her of Logan, which illustrated how deeply the man had infiltrated her thoughts. Last night, when she and Mr. Pritchert dined in the hotel dining room with his wife, Victoria had thought she heard the husky timbre of Logan's deep voice several times. On three occasions, she'd glimpsed broad-shouldered men with dark hair who made her turn and try to look into their faces, thinking she would see Logan's beloved countenance.

Foolish woman, she thought. Yet she was unable to keep from scanning the crowd of moving men for the heart-stoppingly familiar sight of Logan Youngblood's bold figure. Nor did it help to remind herself that he was miles from Trinity Falls. A part of her wanted to believe, against all reason, that he might have decided to see her one more time before leaving the area.

Foolish woman, indeed.

"There it is! Go!"

It took a second for Mr. Pritchert's words to make sense. Then she was galloping across the wide street, holding on to her hat with one hand and being pulled along by the other.

"Whoa!" A rider drew back on the reins, and his horse pawed the sky.

Victoria looked over her shoulder. The horseman had his mount under control, but a wagon drawn by a team of black mules was bearing down on her and Mr. Pritchert. She surged forward, which was no easy feat, considering the constraints of her corset.

They reached the boardwalk together, both of them flushed and panting.

"My goodness, do you go through that every time you want to cross the street?" she gasped, holding her hand over her heart.

"It does enliven one's senses, doesn't it?" Mr. Pritchert asked, his eyes twinkling with irrepressible humor.

"Good grief, if we'd been a minute slower, that wagon would have run us down."

"In a second," Pritchert agreed cheerfully.

Victoria surprised herself by laughing at the man's unfailing goodwill.

"Is that why you hired me, because I looked like a fast runner?"

Before Mr. Pritchert could respond, one of the men jamming the crowded sidewalk evidently misjudged the space needed to weave through the milling masses and bumped into Victoria. It was only a glancing blow, yet it was delivered with sufficient force to send her flying toward Mr.

Pritchert. Startled by the unexpected impact, she braced herself against the older man's flabby chest.

Before she could disentangle herself, two beefy paws closed around her arms and set her back on her feet. "I'm sorry, miss. I didn't see you standing there."

Victoria pushed back the straw hat that had fallen over her eyes. Before her stood a huge, grizzled man twisting a battered, dirt-stained hat between his broad hands. His deeply set brown eyes were filled with contrition, and he resembled nothing so much as a hulking Saint Bernard that had offended its master and sought forgiveness.

Someone else rushed by, jostling Victoria's other shoulder. She glanced around the chaotic melee of moving men. With herself, Mr. Pritchert and this massive stranger blocking a significant portion of the roughly planked walkway, it felt as if they were a bit of flotsam caught in a surging river.

"Watch what you're doing!" the giant yelled after the man who'd brushed too closely to them, before returning his attention to Victoria. "Are you all right, miss?"

"I—I'm fine," she said, a bit breathlessly.

"Here, then, stand clear!" came Goliath's mighty roar.

Almost magically, a pocket of space cleared around them. Victoria smiled at the man. "Thank you, sir."

"Hell..." A look of chagrin swept his rough features, turning his swarthy complexion crimson. "Pardon my language, miss. I'm right sorry about that. Nobody calls me sir, though. My name's Newt. Newt Timothy White."

"Well, Newt," she said, deciding to forgo formalities and address him by his Christian name, "no harm was done. As you can see, I'm perfectly fine."

Newt bobbed his head. "I can see that, miss. You sure are mighty fine, and I'm mighty pleased to meet you." The man shot a surprisingly fulminating glance at Mr. Pritchert. "You need to take better care of the young lady."

Mr. Pritchert looked significantly at the crush of humanity sweeping past them. "With the sidewalks filled like they are today, my good man, that's not an easy task."

Newt nodded gravely. "Where are you headed?"

"Miss Amory and I are on our way to Western Banks United."

"If it's okay with you, I'll walk beside the lady and make sure nobody else bumps into her."

Considering what she'd survived over the past few weeks, the man's concern would have been ludicrous, had his intentions not been so obviously sincere.

"Thank you, Newt," she said, taken aback by the stranger's unusually friendly manner.

The giant beamed. Mr. Pritchert coughed. And Victoria found herself accompanied by two gentlemen instead of one. They had only advanced a few more steps before they were stopped.

"Who's your lady friend, Newt?"

The short, bandy-legged man asking the question had just emerged through the swinging doors of a saloon. He was framed by several companions. They all stared at her as if she were the missing nugget of gold for which they'd been searching. Their avid interest made Victoria feel self-conscious. She wasn't used to generating this much attention.

"This here is Miss Amory. I'm walking her to the bank to make sure she gets there safely," Newt announced importantly.

The men crowded closer.

"Say, your Miss Amory's a right pretty woman."

"She's a real lady, sure enough."

"She smells good, too."

"What's she doing in Trinity Falls?"

Newt beamed. "I don't know, but she sure is fine."

"A fine lady."

"Don't that beat all...."

None of the complimentary observations that swirled around Victoria were addressed directly to her. It was a curious sensation, being talked around, as if she were a statue to be gawked at instead of a real person.

"We'll walk with you, Newt."

"That's right." The shorter man nodded enthusiastically. "You can't be too safe."

"You're right about that," Newt said. "Is that okay with you, Miss Amory?"

Somewhat dazed, Victoria nodded. She glanced at Mr. Pritchert. He didn't look the least bit surprised by what Victoria thought was a remarkable turn of events.

Thus, their numbers grew. It wasn't long before they were stopped again. As before, the only introduction made was that she was Miss Amory and on her way to the bank. By the time they reached their destination, no fewer than thirty men had joined in the short exodus. As she and Mr. Pritchert stepped through the front door, dozens of male voices called out good-days, assorted good wishes and gratitude for having been allowed to walk her down the sidewalk.

When the bank's door closed, their hearty farewells only dimmed in volume. She looked at Mr. Pritchert in stupefaction. "Goodness, what was that all about?"

"There aren't that many young, pretty women in Trinity Falls," he informed her blithely. "You're going to find that you'll draw a crowd wherever you go in town, until the men get accustomed to your presence. Most of them are decent sorts who are lonely for the sight of a refined woman."

Victoria thought of her shocking involvement with Logan Youngblood and didn't feel the least bit refined. She felt like an impostor

"Uh, this is going to take some getting used to." She tugged at her gray gloves while she considered what life was going to be like in the West.

It was a bit daunting to think of herself as some kind of...beauty. She had grown up with a truly beautiful younger sister and had no illusions about her own unremarkable appearance. There was the matter of her red hair and her freckles. In Boston, those were not considered attributes.

"Well, come along."

Victoria allowed herself to be guided past four tellers' cages, where she noticed several neatly attired young men.

All stopped conducting various transactions and gawked at her.

She and Mr. Pritchert stopped in front of a sturdy oak door with gold lettering. She was unable to read what was written, however, because his portly frame blocked her view.

The older man knocked twice, then turned the brass knob and pushed open the door. "Go on in. Your employer is waiting for you."

Before Victoria could thank Mr. Pritchert for his assistance, he left, closing the carved oak portal behind him.

Caught off guard by his sudden departure, she glanced about the apparently empty office into which she'd been shown. She realized abruptly that Pritchert had neglected to provide her employer's name or introduce her to the man, which meant that the forthcoming meeting was going to begin awkwardly.

The room in which she found herself was as meticulously appointed as her hotel suite. There was a wide, relentlessly polished mahogany desk that filled most of the elegant chamber. Two ornately carved chairs faced it, while a large high-backed dark green brocade chair was presently turned toward a bookcase on the other side of the massive desk.

Absently she noted several brass lamps with green shades, assorted small tables and a richly patterned Oriental rug. There was also a small settee upholstered in a tapestry fabric composed of shades of chestnut and amber. The office bespoke money and refinement and smelled faintly of cigar smoke and lemon wax.

She took several steps into the room. The green brocade chair suddenly swiveled around. The unexpected movement, for Victoria had thought she was alone, elicited a startled gasp.

Filling most of the chair was an impeccably dressed, wide-shouldered man in his late twenties or early thirties. His hair was dark brown, perhaps even black, and closely trimmed. His intelligent, watchful eyes were a deep shade of sienna. She found his unwavering gaze subtly disconcerting. He boasted a cleanly shaved, square jaw and lean, sharply chiseled cheekbones.

She knew she was staring, but couldn't help herself. The individual presently inspecting her with his starkly riveting gaze was one of the most singularly handsome men she'd ever seen. The distinct cleft in his strong chin only added to the raw masculine vitality he radiated.

Victoria found her unexpected feminine approval of the stranger immensely depressing. For, only the morning before, she'd surrendered herself to another man whom she'd believed so completely filled her senses that she would never again experience any awareness or attraction toward another member of the male sex.

What a deplorable, wayward character she possessed!

Realizing the silence had drawn out well past the stage of awkwardness, Victoria forced a polite smile to her lips. Since he was her employer and had been the one to arrange this meeting, surely it was he who should speak first.

"Don't you have anything to say?" he inquired at length, rising from his chair with lazy male grace.

His husky voice jarred her. Her mind was obviously playing tricks on her, because this incredibly striking man sounded very much like her Logan. In an attempt to gain control of her flagging spirits and the clumsily proceeding interview, Victoria extended her gloved hand briskly to her new employer.

"How do you do, sir? I'm Victoria Amory, and I'm pleased to finally be able to meet you."

A look of undisguised incredulity swept the man's gaze.

She wondered if he was confused about his day's schedule and had been expecting someone else. Or perhaps there was something about her appearance that he found surprising. It was possible, she supposed, that he'd anticipated someone older filling the position of tutor for his ward.

"Victoria."

For some reason, the way he said her name raised tiny goose bumps on her arms. Again, his voice reminded her of Logan's.

"Yes, that's right," she confirmed.

The man continued to stare, as if waiting for her to say or do something significant.

Victoria was completely at a loss as to how to proceed. It occurred to her that, despite his sophisticated appearance, her new employer could do with a bit of tutoring himself, on how to conduct an interview.

There was another full minute of excruciating silence. The man had yet to accept her extended hand, and she began to wonder if perhaps he considered the gesture too forward upon her part. It was at this wholly inopportune juncture that her memory chose to fill her mind with the shocking image of Logan Youngblood's magnificently nude body claiming her in one bold thrust.

She felt her ears turn hot and knew she was blushing. She started to lower her hand, but then, without warning, her employer caught it in his powerful grasp. A startling frisson of tingling energy penetrated the flimsy layer of fabric from which her gloves were made and singed her fingertips. Nor was the pulsating current contained there. Instead, it traveled with alarming rapidness up her arm, fanning outward until it reached some inappropriate and definitely vulnerable places.

Instinctively she tried to yank her palm free from his disturbingly personal grip. For the space of a heartbeat, she wasn't certain he was going to release her. Something possessive hovered in his hooded gaze. She had a startling sense of déjà vu that left her disoriented.

"Please be seated, Miss Amory."

Since her knees had become woefully inadequate for the task of supporting herself, she accepted his suggestion with alacrity and plopped down upon one of the chairs that faced his wide desk. She couldn't help but wince at her inelegant collapse, knowing that, had her mother been present, she would have been distressed by her elder daughter's lack of grace.

An irreverent bubble of laughter threatened to break free as Victoria realized there were other, much more grievous aspects of her daughter's recent behavior that would have distressed her mother far more than a momentary bout of clumsiness.

Like bathing outdoors with a man who wasn't her husband, and letting him have his evil way with her. Only, of course, at the time, nothing about Logan Youngblood's irresistible seduction had seemed the least bit evil.

Get hold of yourself, Victoria.

"Well, as you can see, I've finally arrived," she observed with dogged brightness, wanting to get the interview back on track. After all, she'd already been hired by Martin Pritchert, and she had a signed contract in her possession to seal the arrangement. This meeting with her employer was really nothing more than a formality.

In a smoothly fluid movement, the impeccably dressed man reclaimed the large chair behind his desk. "I imagine your trip west was a difficult one...."

The husky observation was left hanging, as if to encourage her to elaborate upon any hardships she might have endured. Yet, as casually voiced as the remark seemed, it was accompanied by a piercing stare that made her shift uncomfortably. Again his voice sounded identical to Logan's. Would there ever come a time when he wasn't on her mind? "For the most part, my journey was...uneventful."

In a gesture hauntingly reminiscent of Logan, her employer's left eyebrow rose. "I was led to believe from my assistant, Mr. Pritchert, that you somehow became separated from the wagon train and were forced to travel the last part of the way alone."

"Well, yes. That's true."

"Through hostile Indian territory?"

"I never actually saw any Indians," she pointed out, in the interest of accuracy.

He leaned forward and steepled his fingertips. "Forgive me, Miss Amory, but I find it difficult to believe a woman alone could have driven a team of oxen all the way from Fort Brockton to Trinity Falls during an Indian uprising and not encountered any hostile opposition."

"I came by way of the mountains."

That left eyebrow rose again. "Did you?"

She nodded. "It seemed the best way to avoid trouble."

"Allow me to compliment you on your keenly developed sense of direction, Miss Amory."

"Uh, well, thank you," she replied, with what she hoped was believable conviction, all the while assuring herself that it was only her guilty conscience that made him seem so similar to Logan. "I was very fortunate."

"My thoughts exactly," came his rough rejoinder.

Another pool of silence widened between them. Victoria was confused by the small inner voice that warned her to be careful of the man across the desk. It was as if she sensed upon a primary level that defied logic that her new employer harbored a residue of antagonism toward her and was deeply suspicious of everything she told him. And yet, at the same time, she felt herself drawn to him.

Unsettled by the conflicting feelings churning inside her, Victoria cleared her throat. "I'm very much looking forward to meeting Madison. From what Mr. Pritchert told me last night at dinner, I understand she's a bright and enthusiastic young woman."

"Madison is very special." His lean fingers plucked a sheet of paper from a neat stack of documents on the desk. "For that reason, I intend to be extremely demanding of her tutor."

A warning alarm sounded in Victoria's head. "What precisely do you mean by 'demanding'?"

For the first time during their interview, the corners of the man's mouth curved upward. For some reason, Victoria's sense of disquiet grew.

"I made my specifications emphatically clear to Mr. Pritchert. I want Madison to be instructed by a woman of rare breeding. It goes without saying that she must have a spotless reputation and set a strong example of moral integrity for my ward. Of course, she must also be intelligent and capable of bridging the unfortunate circumstances of Madison's early history."

The queasy distress in Victoria's stomach grew. If her employer was to discover that she had surrendered her virginity to a common criminal like Logan Youngblood, the self-righteous man would boot her out of his elegant office in a heartbeat.

"I have other requirements, as well," came the deeply modulated voice that scraped the last fragments of Victoria's composure. "Tell me, do you wear spectacles, Miss Amory?"

The unexpected inquiry had her raising her eyebrows. "I beg your pardon?"

"Pay attention," he chided softly. "My time is valuable, and I dislike having to repeat myself."

Victoria flushed. She resented his arrogance, his high-handed manner and, most of all, his smug, condescending attitude. She wondered how long *he* would be able to survive on his own in the rugged mountain country through which Logan had safely guided her.

Victoria raised her chin. "I do not wear spectacles, sir."

She bit her tongue to keep from pointing out that whether she did or didn't wear eyeglasses had nothing to do with her competence to instruct a young woman.

"Then you consider your eyesight to fall within normal abilities?"

Victoria nodded.

Again, something about the man's measured tone put her senses on alert.

Several times in her life, she had been allowed to watch her father preside as a judge over legal disputes. Her new employer's confrontational manner bore an alarming resemblance to the attorneys who had figuratively waged war upon the witnesses they questioned.

"And your memory?" he probed deliberately. "I assume you're capable of remembering facts and dates of historic significance."

"Of course."

"In what year did the Norman Conquest begin?"

She blinked at the irrelevant question, but answered anyway. "Most people would say 1066, but I believe 1055 is the more accurate response."

"And the year Lincoln became president?"

"1861."

Gradually, the inescapable conclusion swept through Victoria that there was something gravely amiss with the man presently grilling her on historic milestones. Clearly, he was not in full possession of his faculties. She wondered if this mental malady was a recent development, so recent that even Mr. Pritchert had no inkling of his employer's descent from sanity to lunacy. Though, in this particular man's case, Victoria had the feeling the trip had been a short one.

"Very good, Miss Amory," he said in a tone that was obviously dissatisfied.

When he rose to his feet, Victoria also stood. She had no wish to deal with a madman, no matter how virile or handsome, from a sitting position.

Bleakly she questioned why lately her life seemed fraught with so many disasters—from the incident with the crazed bee in her bedchamber and its vicious attack upon Horace Threadgill, to an unsympathetic wagon master who couldn't understand the importance of her books, then her discovery of an abandoned felon locked in a military stockade, and now a bizarrely eccentric employer. It seemed her existence comprised one ignominious mishap after another.

"I'm relieved to know that both your eyesight and your memory are in good working condition."

Victoria forced an amiable smile to her mouth while inching toward the door. Her situation was precarious, she realized. There was no way she could remain in this lunatic's employ. She'd given all her immediate cash to Logan Youngblood to start a new life. That meant another disaster loomed. How on earth was she going to acquire the funds she needed to return to Boston?

And, even if she managed to reach home, she was not anticipating a cheerful reunion with her father. Oh, dear, things were rapidly going downhill. She wondered with a flash of desperation whether she might be able to find work in Trinity Falls. Perhaps Newt, the miner of gargantuan proportions, needed an apprentice?

"Where are you going, Miss Amory? Our interview isn't completed."

"Uh . . ." With her back to the door, she groped for the doorknob. "I'm feeling a bit unwell, sir. I think a breath of fresh air would—"

He rounded the desk. "You're not going anywhere, Victoria."

Before she could open the door, two large hands closed around her arms.

Stunned as she was by the man's bold assault, it took a second for her to think to scream. When she did open her mouth to cry for help, it was summarily crushed beneath the hotly urgent trespass of her employer's hard kiss.

Several moments of panicked resistance followed. Then the strangest thing happened. Her body slowly yielded to the inexorable mastery of the man who'd swept her into his embrace. The surrender, she supposed, began in her mind and in her swimming senses. She tasted Logan, she smelled Logan, she felt Logan.

Swamped by the wild confusion racing through her, Victoria kept her eyes open. The male tongue that had gained entry to her mouth leisurely sampled its interior. She was put in mind of a sleek panther padding into its secret lair. His broad hands cupped her buttocks and held her close to his hard heat. His breathing was harsh and shallow. His taste was darkly inviting.

She stared at him through trembling eyelashes. And in his sensually glowing eyes she discovered the unassailable truth.

Logan Youngblood held her.

Chapter Eighteen

For an instant, Victoria thought it was she who'd lost her mind. How could the impossible be possible? How could this handsome, sophisticated man be her Logan? Her untamed, lawless lover, dressed in a suit? Now *that* was the stuff of madness.

Their kiss continued, sensuously intimate, hotly contested. And, for a few moments, being in his arms was enough. To feel his hands cupping her to him, to feel his tongue rhythmically stroking her, to feel his male heat embracing her... To know it truly was him and that he'd somehow contrived to meet her...

It was more than enough.

Gradually, however, as much as Victoria tried to resist them, doubts began to plague her. What was Logan doing here? Surely he'd risked his freedom—if not his life—by returning to Trinity Falls. Why was he in her employer's office, an office that just happened to be located in a...*bank?*

Suddenly Victoria stopped yielding and started resisting. She wrested her lips from his tender possession. "Logan, you shouldn't be here."

His seeking mouth moved to the sensitive column of her throat. "Why is that?"

His casual manner exasperated her. "Will you stop kissing me, and tell me what you're doing here?"

He raised his head and regarded her with laughing eyes. "Kissing you."

She struggled to free herself from his hold, which was difficult, considering that she was exactly where she wanted to be. It didn't help the situation to feel his bold hands gently massaging her bottom.

"Logan, this is no laughing matter. It was very foolish of you to risk seeing me." Even as she chastised him, she wondered whether he'd come to the bank because of her or because of the money locked inside its safe. Several more concerns emerged. "What have you done with my employer? How did you reach town before I did? Whose clothes are you wearing?"

A horrible vision surfaced in her mind, that of the man who'd hired her being tied up and reduced to his long johns. At any moment she expected the hue and cry of outraged bank tellers charging into the office, with the law not far behind.

"Victoria, relax. You're as white as a ghost."

"You're going to know firsthand what a ghost looks like if you don't tell me what's going on!"

From the smile that softened the hard line of his mouth, she realized he didn't take his precarious situation seriously. Clearly the man didn't learn from past mistakes. He'd probably been laughing his fool head off when they marched him into that stockade.

"Honey, settle down. There's nothing to worry about. Everything is under control."

"Logan, *nothing* is under control," she said sharply. "You've got to get out of here before somebody discovers you've snuck into this office. And please tell me what you've done with my poor employer. You haven't hurt him, have you? I mean, other than stealing his clothes?"

Logan's features sobered, making Victoria fear the worst. Surely, he hadn't…killed anyone. She refused to believe that of him. Or maybe she just didn't want to believe she could have fallen in love with a murderer.

Logan reached out and gripped her shoulders, giving her a slight shake. "Victoria, I swear, if you accuse me of one more crime, I'm going to turn you over my knee and paddle you."

She stiffened. "Don't think you can bully me by threats of physical mistreatment. Unlike my employer, who is probably frail and old, I am quite capable of defending myself."

"Oh, hell."

"It's not that you don't look very fine in the suit, Logan," she continued earnestly. "Why, with your hair trimmed and your beard shaved, I hardly recognized you."

"*Hardly* recognized," he repeated, his tone inexplicably irate. "Lady, I made love to you yesterday, and today you didn't even know who I was!"

It occurred to her that Logan was angry at her for failing to identify him at once in his fancy clothes. She flushed. She supposed it didn't say much for her powers of observation not to have known immediately it was Logan.

In her own defense, however, she'd never really had a clear look at his face. Initially, when they met, his features had been horribly swollen and disfigured. Later, his countenance had been obscured by a thick black beard and mustache.

"Pardon me, but you were the *last* man I anticipated encountering in this office." She stared at his remarkably splendid visage and swallowed. "Allow me to say that you clean up very nicely, Logan."

His scowl softened. "So do you."

Under his warm and approving gaze, Victoria's heartbeat quickened. "I am glad to see you, but you took a dreadful risk coming here."

"Victoria, if you'll just listen, you'll find out that everything is okay."

She wanted to believe him, but feared the worst. It was possible, she supposed, that he'd used the money she'd given him to purchase his suit of clothing. She clung to that hope. "How did you get to town so quickly?"

"I borrowed a horse."

"I see." She interpreted that to mean he'd stolen one. Her heart sank. "Were you the rider that passed me on the road about dusk?"

"I was."

"And you didn't stop because..."

"I wanted to get to town before you. I was the one who sent Martin Pritchert out to meet you."

Nothing he said made any sense. "I don't understand."

He gently squeezed her arms. "I wanted Martin to escort you to make sure you were safely settled your first night in Trinity Falls."

"But how did you know where to find him? Trinity Falls is a big place."

"And getting bigger every day," Logan observed. "Honey, I know Martin because he works for me. I told you the truth when I said I was wrongly locked up in that stockade and left to die. I did bring the warning to the fort. I am the owner and president of this bank. I'm also acting mayor. Madison is my ward. And I'm your new employer."

Logan's manner was very convincing. For the first time since they'd met, Victoria wondered if she'd been mistaken in her assumptions about him. There was a curious humming in her ears. She felt as if the earth were shifting on its axis and gravity suddenly had ceased to have any effect upon physical objects.

"When I told you to begin a new life..." She took a deep breath. "You already had one?"

He nodded. "So you see, honey, everything is all right."

All right? Oh, no, not by any stretch of the imagination was everything all right!

A hot anger began to boil in Victoria's blood. She had been duped and deceived by this conniving man. All the while they'd been together, all the while she'd tried to reform him, all the while she'd been falling in love with him, he'd been secretly laughing at her. It didn't help her temper for her to realize that her naiveté had been grandly worthy of his amusement.

The plain and simple truth was that she'd been an absolute ninny, an idiot of the first magnitude, with this man, her new...employer. The title made her cringe. Under no circumstance did she intend to work for Logan Youngblood. He might not be a thief or a murderer, but he was bad enough. He was a rogue and a scoundrel.

"Well, haven't you anything to say?"

His question lit the fuse on her rapidly climbing fury. "Why, yes, Logan, I do have something to say."

It was all she could do to get the words past her clenched teeth.

Looking self-satisfied, he smiled at her. "I'm thinking a two-week courtship should be ample. Of course, I realize two or three months probably would be more acceptable to the town gossips, but there's no way I'll tolerate delaying our wedding that long."

Victoria stepped back, breaking the contact of his hands upon her arms. She wasn't sure she could trust herself to utter a single word, when all she wanted to do was scream.

"Naturally, we'll sleep together each night of those two weeks," he continued. "There's no way I'm going to deny myself the incredible feeling of you climaxing with me deep inside you. We'll just have to be careful, so we don't get caught. It's going to help matters considerably that your hotel room is next to mine. After Madison is tucked into bed at night, I'll slip into your chamber. As I said, everything will work out quite nicely."

She strolled to his desk and stared at the items covering its surface with detached interest. There was a stack of neatly arranged papers, a silver letter opener, a pen resting in an inkwell, and a chunk of shiny pink crystals he probably used as a paperweight.

"Victoria?"

Her palm closed around the blunt object. Even though she was furious with Logan, she really couldn't see herself attacking him with a letter opener. Blood was so difficult to get out of one's clothes, and this was her best outfit. She'd surely be needing it to find another post.

"Hmm?"

"You're being awfully quiet."

Crystal in hand, she turned to face him. "Am I?"

He eyed her warily, as if anticipating an explosion of some kind. Smart man.

"I expected you would be a little upset when you finally learned that I wasn't the rascally outlaw you seemed determined to view me as. But you've got to admit, you weren't willing to believe anything I tried to tell you to the contrary."

She hated it when he was right. Regretfully she laid the crystal paperweight back down on his desk. She wasn't a violent woman, one prone to outbursts of temper, shouting tantrums or stamping her foot in frustration. More the pity, she thought.

"Loathe as I am to admit it, I wasn't willing to accept that you were falsely imprisoned," she conceded. "My father's a judge. I was raised to respect the law and all it stands for."

The cautious look in Logan's eyes faded. "I'm more than willing to accept your apology, honey."

Victoria's hands clenched. "I haven't offered it."

He moved toward her. "That's all right. You don't have to come right out and say the words. I don't like admitting when I'm wrong, either. We'll just pick things up from here."

He extended his arms to gather her to him. Victoria dodged his grasp.

"Don't you dare touch me!"

Even as Logan's arms fell to his side, something elementally primal flickered in his dark eyes. "Calm down, Victoria."

"I don't want to be calm. I don't want to be reasonable. You made a fool of me, Logan Youngblood! And...and you had no right to...to make love to me without me knowing who you really were. That was vastly unprincipled of you. So...so even if you aren't a robber or a murderer, you most certainly are no gentleman, either!"

"I didn't mean to make love to you," he growled bleakly.

Victoria felt as if she'd been dropped into an icy river. "That's a despicable thing to say."

"It's the truth, and from here on that's the only thing we're going to have between us—the truth."

"Are you saying that *I* seduced *you?*" she demanded angrily.

"Of course not. I had to work like hell to get you to take your clothes off at the hot springs. Luckily for me, you happen to be a woman who can't resist a bath."

His sarcasm brought a hot flush to her cheeks. "Then how can you stand there and brazenly state you didn't intend to make love to me?"

"I only meant to warm you up, honey." He strode forward and swept her into his embrace before she could stop him. "I knew that when we finally reached Trinity Falls, you would likely be upset, and I decided I needed an edge that would help me . . . tame you."

Victoria's spine became rigid. She knew intuitively that she wasn't going to like Logan's explanation, but she was morbidly curious to discover the dark workings of his masculine mind.

"So you made love to me in the mountains in order to . . . *tame* me?" It was all she could do to get the reprehensible words past her stiff lips.

"I made love to you because there was no way I could feel your soft, naked body against me without being inside you."

His potent words brought with them the recollection of how it had felt to feel herself pressed against Logan's hot, muscular flesh. Victoria quivered at the sweet, sensual memory.

"I wanted to make you feel connected to me, Victoria," he went on to say, his voice a husky rasp. "I wanted to caress you, to stroke you, to cherish you in ways you'd never experienced. I wanted to taste your hard little nipples, and I wanted to touch your wet, trembling heat and show you how it feels to shatter into a million pieces.

"I wanted you to experience all that and know I was the one who was making it happen. What I hadn't planned on was how sweetly passionate you would be and how feeling you climax beneath my fingertips would drive me out of mind. I intended to show you how good it could be between us, so that you wouldn't be able to walk away from me. But I didn't know that watching your golden little body come apart in my hands would push me over the edge.

"There's no way I could resist you, even though I knew it was wrong. So I guess, in a way, it was you who ultimately seduced me. And the only thing I regret is that we didn't have hours instead of minutes to experience that blaze of passion. But, come tonight, I intend to make up for our hurried lovemaking. We'll have a soft bed, and the whole evening to explore each other, to drive ourselves crazy with desire."

Victoria sagged in Logan's arms. She bit her lip and commanded her sinful nature to behave itself. There was no way she would let Logan's sultry words woo her into another disastrous surrender of the flesh. Surely she had the strength of character to resist his shameless attempt to seduce her.

It didn't escape her attention that he hadn't mentioned one particular word, however. *Love.* Clearly, he suffered from no such noble emotion. It was evident from his justification of the passionate interlude they'd shared that Logan Youngblood's entire range of sentimental inclinations resided below his belt. While it astonished her that she'd somehow managed to arouse this virile man's lust, she wasn't obligated to satisfy it.

As for his talk of marriage, she considered it just that. Talk. It was obvious he wanted two hedonistic weeks of unrestricted lovemaking from her, and then he would probably dismiss her. Good grief, it was possible she was one in a long line of Eastern tutors he'd tricked into coming west so that he could have his wicked way with them.

Slowly Victoria eased herself from Logan's embrace. "Uh, well, I . . ."

Say something, you ninny! Something that will get you out of this office and out of this man's frightening sphere of power.

"Yes, honey?"

She cleared her throat. The problem, she surmised, was that deep inside her, she really didn't wish to escape Logan's evil clutches. If truth be told, the man possessed the most remarkably alluring clutches.

"Are you serious about wanting to marry me?"

It was best to get that salient point in the open, she decided.

He smiled. "Allow me, Miss Amory, to express my tender regards. Would you do me the singular honor of becoming my wife?"

Her traitorous heart melted, even though she clearly detected his mocking usage of the nearly archaic phrasing. For a moment, she wondered whether he was laughing at himself and not at her. For even though laughter lurked in his eyes, there appeared to be genuine affection hovering there, also.

She sighed. At this juncture, it really didn't matter whether or not Logan was sincere. She had to be true to herself. The irony of her situation didn't elude her. She remembered very clearly, planning to go to the outrageous lengths of making up a false fiancé for her sister's benefit, so that Annalee would be able to marry one of her many suitors. Yet, when the opportunity of having a real flesh-and-blood man propose did occur, Victoria found she could not accept his offer, at least not before she was convinced Logan's feelings went deeper than mere physical desire.

It was a startling revelation to realize that she would not settle for less than love. From any man, even one as deplorably appealing as Logan Youngblood.

"I'm afraid I cannot accept your proposal."

Her words seemed very small in the confines of the office, yet she took comfort from their firmness. Still, she couldn't quite meet Logan's gaze.

The pregnant silence that filled the chamber was as oppressive as any Victoria had endured. When she could bear the tomblike atmosphere no longer, she hazarded a peek at him through her lashes. An air of absolute determination sharpened Logan's rugged features. She sensed that an argument of major magnitude was about to erupt, for Logan's stubborn expression didn't resemble the look of a man to be graciously dismissed.

"You're still upset with me for not being able to convince you I wasn't the most notorious outlaw since Jesse James."

Victoria scowled. Logan made her sound like the gullible fool she felt. "It would be foolish for either of us to entertain thoughts of marriage."

"And why is that?"

The soft question drifted through the office on wings of steel.

"We are strangers and share no common ground."

"Wrong."

Her chin came up. "I didn't even know who you were until ten minutes ago."

"A day ago, under the wide-open sky, you spread your soft thighs and invited me inside you. I'd say that makes us much more than strangers."

Victoria recoiled at his bluntness. "I gave myself to a man who doesn't exist!"

Logan thumped his chest. "I'm standing right in front of you. How can you say I don't exist?"

"But I don't know you! I fell in love with a no-account drifter with a penchant for being locked up in stockades. You're not him. You're a...a *banker*."

Exasperation filled Logan's eyes. "That has to be the stupidest thing you've ever said."

Victoria's eyes swam with tears. "Well, I guess I am stupid. Stupid for letting myself be seduced by a man who was sneaky and devious and...downright weasely."

"Now, honey, don't start crying."

"I'll cry if I want to."

"You have to marry me," he said gruffly. "You love me."

"No, I don't!"

"But you just said—"

"I fell in love with another man."

"But *I'm* the other man!" Logan roared.

"Yelling at me isn't going to do any good. I've made up my mind. I'm not going to marry you. And I'm not going to work for you, either. I'm going home."

Even as she said the words, they held no appeal. But she was so confused by the recent turn of events she couldn't think straight. She suspected she might need another good cry before she was able to sort things out. She held Logan responsible for her uncustomary weepiness.

"Victoria, you can't go back to Boston."

Her head jerked up. "Why not?"

"You gave me all your money."

His reminder further inflamed her temper. "Return it to me at once." She thought of something else. "And I want my book back, too."

"I'm not giving you back the book, Victoria. I consider it one of my most treasured possessions and refuse to part with it."

"Do you also refuse to part with the money I gave you?" She looked around at her plush surroundings significantly. "Such a paltry sum must be insignificant to you."

"On the contrary, those gold coins represent an invaluable investment, one I intend to hold on to for as long as I live."

Since Victoria had discovered which of them truly was the fool, she supposed she shouldn't be surprised by his unhelpful attitude. "I'll sell my wagon and oxen."

"Then how will you travel?"

"I'll sell my...books." Just making the statement was enough to break her heart, as if it hadn't already been shattered into a hundred little bitty pieces. "That should generate enough cash to get me back home."

"Yeah, I'll bet there's just hundreds of miners ready to stand in line to buy *The Decline and Fall of the Roman Em-*

pire. You'll probably have a riot on your hands trying to control the mob of men wanting to improve their minds."

His sarcasm had her eyeing the letter opener on his desk and rethinking her reservations against unleashing it upon his arrogant hide. "It's none of your concern. I'll think of a way."

"You're forgetting something."

"What's that?" she asked suspiciously.

"You signed a contract to work for me and tutor Madison. You came west on the funds Martin advanced you. You have no choice but to honor that contract."

Victoria's head pounded. She missed her image of Logan as an illiterate common thief. "You can't expect me to fulfill that agreement. Not after everything that's happened between us."

He smiled that confident smile she'd grown to resent and strolled toward his office door. Once there, he leaned negligently against the frame. His obvious blocking of the only exit from the room jarred her. She had the feeling that any attempt to wage war with Logan would leave her outgunned and outmaneuvered.

"I *expect* you to accompany me to the hotel. I *expect* to introduce you to Madison. I *expect* you to honor the terms of your contract and spend the next two years teaching her how to read and write, as well as instructing her in history, arithmetic and literature. You will also edify her upon the subtle nuances of becoming a lady."

Pushed to the extreme, Victoria decided to fight back with the only means left to her. "I'm surprised that you would allow someone of my tarnished virtue within a hundred feet of the girl. I'm hardly what you'd call a . . . lady."

Logan's eyes narrowed to pinpoint fury. He straightened from his casual stance and looked as menacing as she'd ever seen him. "To the rest of the world, you're very much a lady, Victoria. I'm the only one you've allowed to experience your sweet fire. I'll treasure that memory for as long as I live, and I won't let you make something ugly of it."

Shamed but not cowed by his rebuke, she cast about for some other way of extricating herself from the wretched bog she was mired in. But the dismal truth was, she could see no way out. Even more disheartening was the admission that two years of being legally bound to Logan Youngblood wasn't exactly a horrible fate.

She wouldn't marry him in haste. Nor would she permit him entry to her bedchamber. But perhaps, in time, if he was extremely contrite and conducted a long and proper courtship, she just might agree to become his wife. Of course, he would have to fall as deeply in love with her as she was with him.

Victoria squared her shoulders. "It appears you do have me somewhat over a barrel. I will teach Madison."

"How very wise of you."

"But I wish to make it clear that ours is to be strictly a business relationship. I will be in your employ, and I shall expect you to conduct yourself in a circumspect manner. There will be no late-night visits to my bedchamber. There will be no untoward embraces or kisses. We shall conduct ourselves as respectable adults."

"I understand."

She looked at him in surprise. "You do?"

He nodded grimly. "You're going to make me suffer before allowing me into your bed."

"It's exactly comments like that which must cease," she said dourly. It made her uncomfortable to realize Logan had divined her intentions. She *did* wish for him to suffer before she accepted his proposal.

"How long is it going to take, Victoria?"

She bristled. It was extremely rude of Logan to put things so baldly. "A lot longer than two weeks!"

"I suppose you expect me to bring you flowers."

"Flowers would be nice." She remembered Annalee's suitors had always had their house brimming with fragrant bouquets.

"Candy, too," he reflected glumly.

"Well, yes, I do have a bit of a sweet tooth." Actually, she didn't, but surely she could develop one.

"You'll be expecting me to take you to dinner, no doubt."

"The Prairie Rose has an elegant dining room."

"All right, then."

His quick capitulation caught her off guard. "Then you agree to...uh..."

"I think the word you're looking for is 'court' you."

She knew she was blushing. Goodness, the thought of this virile man actually courting her was surprisingly heady. She was certain she loved him, but he was, nevertheless, very intimidating.

"And, hell, yes," he continued roughly, "I'll let you put me through my paces in order to legally bind you to me, Victoria."

His cold-blooded pronouncement alarmed her. She hadn't meant for things to be so cut-and-dried. In truth, she'd been hoping for a little romance. But there was nothing at all romantic in Logan's fierce gaze. He looked uncomfortably like a man about to ride into battle.

Her trepidation grew. She had the feeling that she'd somehow challenged the darkest, most frightening part of Logan to claim her. Still, while vaguely daunted by his bold demeanor, she experienced a sharp thrill of excitement.

All of which meant she was probably destined for a life of unparalleled adventure. Her heart tripped over itself. When she'd come west in search of her great adventure, she'd hardly envisioned it in the rugged form of Logan Youngblood.

Surely she was woman enough to rise to the occasion. In fact, the more she reflected upon it, she was probably the only woman in Trinity Falls capable of making Logan toe the line.

She would certainly give it her best effort.

Chapter Nineteen

Martin Pritchert poured himself a drink from the brandy decanter on Logan's desk. "At least there weren't any shots."

Logan stretched his legs in front of him on the settee in his hotel suite. "That's only because Victoria didn't have a gun."

"I'd say she took the news that you were her employer remarkably well. I wasn't able to detect any sounds of shattering bric-a-brac, either." Martin carried his glass to a high-backed chair, where he settled himself. "Victoria Amory seems to be a level-headed young woman."

"You might not think so if you had seen her eyeing the letter opener on my office desk," Logan muttered.

Also vividly etched in his memory was the militant look in her eyes when she'd picked up the crystal paperweight. There had been a point in their heated discussion when he was sure she would hurl the heavy object at him.

"Nonsense, I would say that Miss Amory is a perfect model of propriety and decorum."

Logan shifted uncomfortably at the realization that she had boasted those attributes until she became involved with him. He frowned thoughtfully at his boots. She still was a lady, dammit, even if she didn't think so. She was *his* lady, and she was going to become his wife.

And he wasn't going to let her call the shots between them. He had no intention of letting the date of the wedding drift on the whim of her offended feminine pride. They would be married at the end of two weeks. And they would share a bed tonight. He had let Victoria think she could make him dance to her tune in order to soothe her outraged sensibilities. Tonight, when he came to her chamber, she would discover that the passion that existed between them was too strong to be doled out in miserly dribs and drabs.

What he'd accomplished in his office this morning was to buy time. She would have the rest of the day to accustom herself to the fact that he wasn't a felon on the run from the law. Her anger would subside by nightfall, he assured himself.

Victoria had been wrong when she said that they were strangers. During their journey to Trinity Falls, Logan had learned a great deal about her. And one of her most endearing qualities, he reflected, was her fundamentally kind nature. Even though she'd been furious when she learned how wrong she'd been about him, she hadn't resorted to profanity or violence.

Lord, she might have had murder in those magnificent green eyes of hers, but she'd gained control of her anger. Tonight, he told himself, she would be more than ready to warm herself in the smoldering embers of the fire that momentarily lay banked between them.

"I am curious, however, about what did transpire between you and Miss Amory during the two weeks you were gone."

Logan looked up from his contemplation of his boots. "You may assume I developed an appreciation of Miss Amory's sterling character," he remarked significantly. "And that appreciation had grown to remarkable fondness. I intend to marry her."

"You'll pardon my shock, but I recall upon occasions too numerous to count statements to the effect that you would rather be drawn and quartered than married. What is it about Miss Amory's character that's made you change your opinion?"

Logan found his friend's question as irritating as the amused sparkle in the older man's gaze.

"Some things are hard to explain. What was it, for example, about your wife's character that made you want to marry her?"

"It's really quite simple. I fell head over heels in love with her. She was gay and beautiful and had a willowy form that quite took my breath away. I admit I was a bit misled about her temperament. I saw her more as a vivacious girl than a strong-minded woman, but over the years I've found myself relieved she has a serious side to her nature."

Logan nodded thoughtfully. Victoria was no vapid young miss prone to giggles. Though, he mused, she did tend to blush frequently. Of course, since he knew he was guilty of saying some downright provocative things to bring the color to her cheeks, he didn't hold that against her. Actually, he admitted to himself, he liked the fact that he could fluster her sufficiently to make her flush. It did something to a man's confidence to know he had the power to unsettle his woman.

"I have no doubts Victoria will make me a good wife, and she will also be a positive influence upon Madison."

"Congratulations, friend. After your disastrous experience with Robeena Stockard, I'd begun to doubt you would permit yourself to fall in love again."

"Who said anything about love?"

"I just assumed... I mean, I..." Martin's words ground to a halt, and he regarded Logan in clear disappointment.

"If your matchmaking efforts were an attempt to ensnare me in a love union, you failed, Martin."

"My 'matchmaking efforts'?" the man blustered.

"I specifically remember telling you I wanted an older woman to tutor Madison. You know me well enough to understand the last place I'd want that woman to come from is Boston. I can only assume that you ignored my preferences and hired a young and beautiful *Bostonian* because you envisioned more than a professional relationship developing between us."

"Confound it, I'm not a damned fortune-teller, Logan. I had no way of knowing that Colonel Windham would imprison and then abandon you at the fort, and that Miss Amory would arrive there alone to rescue you. Nor could I have foreseen that you would spend two weeks with the woman, traveling through the mountains to reach Trinity Falls. The last letter I received from her indicated she was going to be delayed leaving Independence."

"But you knew that when she did arrive, she and I would be practically living together, day in and day out, at the hotel. Did it escape your memory she was supposed to board with you and Constance?"

A rash of heightened color brightened the older man's already ruddy complexion. "Er, I... Well, dammit, man, you do need to get on with your life."

"Why Victoria Amory, Martin? What made you choose her for your scheme to end my bachelorhood?" Logan asked curiously, not angry at the turn of events, but determined to unravel the chain of incidents that had led to Victoria's arrival at the fort.

"Her father and I have been friends since we were boys. Even though Miss Amory doesn't recall the encounter, we met several years ago. I was impressed by her poise and her intelligence. When Judge Amory mentioned in a letter that she'd become embroiled in a bit of scandal, which he strongly stated was wholly innocent upon her part, and I knew you were seeking a woman to instruct Madison, it occurred to me that... Well, that it was possible Victoria Amory might be just the woman to help you forget that scheming bitch Robeena."

"I can't imagine any hint of scandal attaching itself to Victoria."

"I'm certain it was, as the judge explained, a misunderstanding."

"And was it just a simple misunderstanding that made you neglect mentioning my name to Judge Amory or his daughter?"

"You're well aware that there is an unfortunate stigma attached to your name in certain circles since the rather infamous afternoon you failed to appear at your own wedding. Besides, Benjamin Amory and I have the kind of respect for each other that doesn't depend on unimportant details."

"Was my brother in accord with your decision to keep my name a secret?" Logan inquired softly.

In the process of taking another swallow of his drink, Martin was seized by a paroxysm of coughing. "What makes you think Burke knows anything about this?"

"I've never been a believer in coincidences. When you happened to show up in Trinity Falls within months after I arrived, I had to ask why a prosperous and successful businessman like yourself would leave Boston. I seemed to remember that you were well acquainted with my brother. In fact, you were business associates, as I recall."

"Do you realize this is the first time you've brought his name up between us?"

Logan nodded gravely. He wasn't sure what was driving him to discover Burke's role in Victoria's selection as Madison's tutor. Perhaps it was simply that enough years had passed for some of Logan's bitterness toward his brother to fade.

Martin cleared his throat. "I did write to Burke to see if he felt Miss Amory would be a suitable candidate."

"To tutor Madison?" Logan prompted.

The older man shook his head. "Actually, our goal was to introduce a decent woman into your life, someone who might make you forget your unfortunate experience with Miss Stockard."

"Did Burke marry Robeena?" Logan asked with a curious sense of detachment.

Again Martin shook his head. "No doubt that's what Miss Stockard hoped for when she arranged for you to discover her in your brother's bedchamber. But Burke was no more interested in making her his wife than he was in making her his paramour."

His friend's words seemed to hang in the hotel suite with a tantalizing promise of healing the long estrangement between Logan and Burke. It was possible, Logan admitted, that being young and hotheaded, he'd jumped to the wrong conclusion about what he saw that night in his brother's room. Had Robeena been responsible for the illicit tryst Logan had blundered into?

"Why did you come to Trinity Falls five years ago, Martin?"

"Burke knew that I'd been toying with the idea of coming west for a long time. He suggested Trinity Falls."

"Why?"

"Why do you think?" Martin snapped with uncustomary asperity.

"He wanted you to keep an eye on me," Logan guessed, remembering that, when they were growing up, his older brother had had an annoying tendency to be overprotective.

"I haven't had an easy time of it, you know." Martin finished the last swallow of his brandy. "When I showed up, you were living with the damned Indians, if you'll remember. Lord, what a sight you were. You'd gone native, for God's sake."

"Reflecting back on it, I remember it was your suggestion that I consider establishing a bank in Trinity."

"You come from a family of bankers, Logan. What could have been more natural than for you to draw on the funds you'd left in Boston and begin your own financial institution in the West?"

"Another one of Burke's ideas, I suppose."

"He...uh...might have made reference to approving such a venture."

"Lord, is he the silent partner we bought out last year?"

"What do you think?" Martin asked, his normally guileless blue eyes shining with disconcerting shrewdness.

"I think I've had a damned watchdog looking after me ever since I left Boston!"

"He didn't have an easy time of it when you volunteered for the military."

"I'm surprised he didn't conspire to have me discharged."

"I'm sure he thought about it."

A memory surfaced. During his war experience, Logan had had the dubious pleasure of becoming close friends with one Bartholomew Bridger. The burly man, a former Boston dockworker, had accompanied Logan into every battle. On several occasions, Bridger had gone out of his way to place himself between Logan and danger. When the war ended, the hearty stevedore had received a cash windfall and bought his own damned ship. It was more than likely that Bridger had been another of his brother's guardian angels.

"Burke never lost track of you, Logan."

"Well, hell."

Martin raised a bushy gray eyebrow. "Somehow I expected a greater display of anger if you ever discovered Burke was interfering in your life."

"I guess enough time has gone by for my anger to cool."

"Six years of silence between you and your brother is too long, Logan. You need to let go of the bitterness."

Logan wondered whether the time had come for him to visit Boston and hear Burke's side of the story.

"I have more news."

"About my brother?" He was suddenly curious to hear what else Burke had been up to all these years.

"No, this is about someone a little closer to home." Martin rose and set his empty glass on a silver tray. "When I was in the hotel lobby earlier, I saw Colonel Windham. I overheard him telling a concerned citizen that reinforcements have arrived, and he intends on riding against the Indians."

Logan swore succinctly. "The man's a menace to himself and everyone else. He's incapable of admitting that the band of Indians who burned the fort are probably long gone from the area. The fool will end up attacking Night Wolf and his tribe."

"I gather that the colonel doesn't distinguish between different tribes. All Indians are the same to him."

"I'll have to warn Night Wolf."

"If Windham catches you attempting to do so, he won't waste time arresting you—he'll stand you before a firing squad."

"I'd like to see him try."

"Logan, be reasonable. You're not going to find a single ally in the territory who will support you if you side with the Indians."

Logan thought about Victoria and her sympathetic attitude toward Night Wolf's people. "Not all whites hate Indians."

"Maybe not, but most are afraid of them. And most people are greedy. They want the Indians' land, and their gold. Face it, Logan, you would be risking your life for a lost cause."

"I have to warn Night Wolf," Logan said stubbornly. "Is Madison still with Constance?"

Martin withdrew his pocket watch from his vest. "I would say that right about now Madison is in her room, putting the finishing touches on the dress she bought this morning to impress Miss Amory. We are to lunch with the ladies in the hotel dining room."

A new thought struck Logan. "Was Constance involved in your plot to unite me and Victoria?"

"Good Lord, no." A look of chagrin crossed the older man's features. "As much as I love my wife, I'm forced to admit the woman couldn't keep a secret to save her life."

What Martin didn't say but was probably true was that Constance, a stickler for proper behavior, would have objected to someone of his own jaded reputation associating with a blue-blooded innocent like Victoria.

"Did you have Victoria's books delivered to her suite, as I instructed?"

"As you can imagine, there were any number of volunteers willing to cart the collection to her room. I've already sold her team and wagon."

"You didn't give her the money from the sale, did you?" Logan asked sharply.

"The proceeds from the transaction are in my coat pocket, though it's not ethical for us to retain those funds."

"Don't worry about it, Martin. She'll get the money. Eventually."

After she's married to me.

Logan got to his feet. "Shall we join the ladies for lunch?"

When Victoria heard the knock at her hotel room door, she was happily lost in the task of organizing her books into neat stacks. Straightening, she brushed the accumulated dust from her hands and wound her way through the marginally organized chaos.

On the other side of the large oak portal stood Martin Pritchert's wife. She'd briefly made the older woman's acquaintance the night before.

"Mrs. Pritchert . . . Hello."

The friendly-faced matron smiled. "You were going to call me Constance, remember?"

Victoria returned the woman's smile. "Thank you. Please come in. You'll have to excuse the mess. You caught me in the midst of unpacking."

"Goodness. It looks as if you plan on starting a library. Are all these volumes yours?"

Well used to peoples' startled reaction to her book collection, Victoria didn't take offense at the woman's clearly astonished question. "Once I get them into bookcases, it won't seem as if there are so many."

"I suppose not," Constance agreed. "Are you ready? We need to collect Madison and meet Martin and Logan downstairs."

Victoria was eager to meet her student. "Just give me a minute to wash my hands and tidy up."

Constance picked up a book that Victoria had left on a table. "*Little Women*. I've heard of that. It's supposed to be very entertaining."

Victoria poured some water from a gaily painted pitcher into a washbowl. "I haven't gotten very far into it yet, but the characters are delightful."

"It's about four sisters, isn't it?"

Victoria dried her hands on a towel. "I'm hoping it's a story Madison might enjoy."

"You'll have to teach her to read first."

"That's right, Logan mentioned she hasn't had any schooling."

Realizing she shouldn't have referred to Logan by his first name, Victoria winced. She hoped Mrs. Pritchert hadn't noticed the slip, which indicated just how well acquainted Victoria was with her new employer.

Constance smiled ruefully, apparently oblivious of Victoria's indiscreet use of Logan's Christian name. "You should know, Madison has been raised like a barbarian."

"A barbarian?"

The older woman nodded. "I suppose it's not my place to tell you this, but I haven't always admired the man with whom my husband works. Logan Youngblood has lived his life with no regard to the social niceties the rest of us adhere to. But, when he accepted the responsibility of seeing to Madison's welfare, I was forced to revise my opinion of him.

"I can see by your expression that you don't approve of my criticism," Constance said, her manner strained. "But I feel it is my duty to warn you that your employer has a terrible reputation when it comes to his association with women."

Victoria found it difficult to meet the woman's genuinely concerned gaze. It would be too easy to betray by a blush that she knew firsthand that Logan didn't always behave like a gentleman, and that she herself didn't always act like a lady.

"They call him 'Passion's Pirate,' you know."

"*What?*" There was no way for Victoria to mask her amazement at the lurid turn of phrase.

"It's a shocking but appropriate title," Constance said. "He has certainly worked hard to earn it."

How did one go about earning such a name? Victoria wondered, but dared not ask.

"He has made it a habit to consort with the town's most notorious women," Constance went on to elaborate, her eyebrows drawn together in clear disapproval. "He has escorted these . . . fancy women to public gatherings, treating them as if they were respectable, instead of females of easy virtue."

Victoria refrained from criticizing Logan's scandalous behavior. How could she, when she was clearly one of those women of "easy virtue" to whom Constance referred with such disdain?

"I see that I've shocked you with my direct manner of speaking, but I consider it my Christian duty to forewarn you about the character of your employer." She glanced around the hotel suite, her countenance darkening even further. "You must be especially careful to maintain a demeanor of propriety, since you will be residing in such intimate proximity to him. Do you comprehend what I am saying, Victoria?"

"Uh . . . I think so."

"Do not give Logan Youngblood an inch, or he shall surely take a mile," the woman stated with clear conviction.

On the heels of that cliché, another drifted through Victoria's thoughts, the one about closing the barn door *after* the cow had wandered off.

"I suppose his descent into moral depravity began the afternoon he abandoned poor Miss Stockard at the wedding altar," Constance observed. "That sorry debacle demonstrated quite clearly Logan Youngblood's contempt for the gentler sex. It's no wonder he got himself into trouble with Colonel Windham."

The sudden shift of subject distracted Victoria from her grim thoughts about the man who'd seduced her so com-

pletely during their brief time together. "Colonel Windham acted with despicable cruelty toward Logan!"

"Well, my dear, when a man confronts his wife's lover,
he's bound to be a trifle miffed," the woman said with a
shrug. "I know my dear Martin would shoot the man who
dared take liberties with me."

The clock on the mantel chimed as Victoria mulled over
Constance Pritchert's disheartening revelations about Logan.

The woman started visibly, and her gaze went to the clock.
"My goodness, we need to fetch Madison and be on our
way."

Victoria was still trying to come to terms with what she'd
learned about Logan when she and Constance stopped in
the hotel corridor before another room on the same floor.

Constance didn't bother knocking, but instead walked
directly into the suite. The tableau that greeted them momentarily pushed all thoughts of Logan from Victoria's
mind.

A slim young woman dressed in a bright pink dress with
rows upon rows of white ruffles cascading from its neck,
sleeves and bunched-up skirts sat on the floor, clutching a
wad of paper bills in one hand while tossing two dice with
the other. A gaunt older gentleman dressed in the hotel's
black livery knelt next to her.

"Well, Lordy, Miss Farley, you done rolled another
seven," he groaned in disappointment. "I swear you've
cleaned me out."

"Madison! What is the meaning of this?" Constance
Pritchert bellowed with astonishing vigor.

The man in the hotel uniform jumped to his feet as if he'd
been jerked to attention by unseen strings.

"Uh, I beg your pardon, ma'am. I was just..." He
glanced around the suite frantically, as if trying to come up
with an explanation that would soothe the enraged matron
glaring holy fire at him. Evidently he realized the hopeless-
ness of justifying his purpose for being in the room.

The girl, on the other hand, was amazingly composed as she uncurled from her position on the floor. Victoria noticed that she even had the forethought to fold the cash she held before tucking it unobtrusively into the pocket concealed amid the profusion of ruffles.

"Calm down, Herbie, or you'll have another one of your seizures," the girl admonished calmly.

"He'll have more to worry about than some seizure," Constance Pritchert threatened, her face mottled a shade of pink remarkably similar in hue to the incredibly fussy gown worn by the slender young woman. "I vow that you will be dismissed before the day's end. When my husband and Mr. Youngblood inform the proprietor what you've been up to, you'll be out on the street!"

Apparently untroubled by the older woman's thunderous disapproval, the girl Victoria assumed was her new charge smiled reassuringly at the trembling, white-faced man. "Don't worry, Herbie, I'll explain that none of this was your fault. You won't lose your job, I promise."

Herbie looked as if he were going to break into tears. It made no sense under the circumstances, but Victoria felt sorry for the man. He didn't appear to have the stamina to secure employment that required any degree of strength.

"You are in no position to make any promises, young lady!"

The girl smiled with an impish charm that Victoria realized would, in a few years, blossom into irresistible feminine beauty.

"Now, Mrs. Pritchert, there's no call to be upset with poor Herbie. He was just showing me how to add up those numbers you keep telling me I need to learn."

Which, of course, in no way explained the money that had been tucked out of sight, Victoria reflected.

Constance didn't look totally convinced by the far-fetched explanation; however, her complexion was no longer an alarming shade of pink. "You are excused, sir," she intoned with ominous gravity. The hapless man took his leave on stumbling feet, and the older woman turned to Victoria.

"As you can see, Miss Amory, your services are in severe demand. Allow me to introduce your charge, Madison Earley."

Aware of the girl's close scrutiny, Victoria extended her hand. "How do you do, Madison?"

"I reckon I've done better." Her vivid blue eyes narrowed speculatively as she accepted the proffered hand in a vigorous, pumping handshake. "So you're the fancy woman Logan sent for to make a lady out of me?"

"Madison!" Mrs. Pritchert sputtered. "Miss Amory is most certainly not a fancy woman!"

Unrepentant amusement flickered in the girl's direct gaze. Victoria found it impossible to take offense. Even though it was obvious that Madison Earley was a lively, free-spirited young woman who would prove a challenge to educate, Victoria knew intuitively that she would enjoy her association with the vixen. The girl's eyes reflected a good-natured sparkle that was uncannily similar to her sister Annalee's enthusiastic approach to life. Oh, yes, Madison was going to be a challenge, but she was also going to be a delight.

Chapter Twenty

Lunch in the hotel dining room with Logan, Madison, Martin and Constance proved an enlivening experience for Victoria. The conversation rarely lagged as the perfectly prepared food was expeditiously dispatched.

Victoria noticed, however, that Logan remained largely silent as the various courses were served and removed from their table. She, too, was content to let Madison and the Pritcherts assume control of the various topics of discussion.

Logan sat directly across from Victoria, and she was fiercely aware of his possessive gaze as it repeatedly fell upon her. Even though she appreciated the grandness of the repast laid before her, she scarcely tasted it.

For a significant portion of the meal, she found herself transfixed by Logan's strong, tanned hands as he wielded his eating utensils with a casual efficiency that reminded her of how it felt to have those very hands upon her naked flesh. The searing memory of his bold caresses made her tremble. She shifted on her chair and wondered what the others at the table would think if they knew she'd fallen victim to such shocking thoughts. No doubt they would consider her as tarnished as the other women Logan had apparently escorted about town.

"Oh-oh . . . Logan, don't look now, but Colonel Windham and his wife just walked into the dining room."

As nothing else other than a shout of "Fire!" could have done, Martin Pritchert's observation freed Victoria's thoughts from their improper course. She glanced in the direction the others were looking.

A slight man dressed in a bright blue uniform conspicuously decorated with gold braiding, along with a demurely dressed but unarguably beautiful woman wearing a lavender gown, entered the room. The attractive blonde stood a couple of inches taller than her husband.

Victoria tensed as she stared at the vile beast responsible for almost killing Logan. It required all the inner discipline she possessed to subdue the urge to charge across the room to berate him for his wretched treatment of the man she loved.

"Of all the nerve," Madison snarled. "How dare he show his ferret face in public after what he did to you!" The girl leaped to her feet. "Even if you did sleep with his wife, he had no call to—"

"Sit down, Madison," Logan stated, with sufficient force to ensure the girl plopped back to her chair. "For the record—" Logan's ruthlessly intense gaze washed over Victoria "—*nothing* of a personal nature has transpired between Athena Windham and myself."

In the silence that followed Logan's announcement, the hard-faced military man and his wife crossed the room. When the couple were within a foot of the table, both Martin Pritchert and Logan stood.

The ensuing tension was volatile enough to catch fire without the benefit of a spark.

"Well, I see your luck held out, Youngblood, and you made it back to town alive."

From the short, mustached man's clipped observation, one wouldn't have guessed the officer had left Logan behind at the fort to face certain death.

"No thanks to you," Logan observed mockingly.

A look of hatred radiated from the colonel's eyes. "What do you mean? I left orders that you were to be released from the stockade and provided with a mount for your return to

Trinity Falls." A nasty smile twisted one corner of his mouth. "Naturally, during the last-minute confusion of evacuating the fort, I was unable to personally bid you a safe trip."

His obvious skepticism about Windham's words was reflected in Logan's chilling gaze, yet he said nothing.

"You realize, Youngblood, our business isn't finished," the officer went on to say. "I'm dispatching several of my men to escort you to the temporary office I've set up at the Methodist church so we'll be able to finish the discussion we began at the fort."

Victoria's gaze went to the woman, who hadn't once spoken or looked up from the lace handkerchief she twisted between white-knuckled fingers. Surely the colonel wouldn't voice in so public a setting his ugly suspicions about his wife and Logan.

"I consider that subject closed," Logan stated with numbing coldness.

Victoria didn't understand how Windham could bait Logan, when it was obvious he wanted nothing more than to tear the officer apart limb from limb.

"The murdering savages who burned down the fort are still at large. You will lead my men to their stronghold so that we can exterminate them."

Victoria looked around the large dining room, suddenly aware that Windham and Logan's confrontation had attracted a large audience. It occurred to her that most of those present would undoubtedly agree with the colonel that all Indians should either be killed or be driven from the territory.

"I'm always happy to oblige the military," Logan said, with a lethal mildness that made Victoria's mouth go dry.

She was terrified that if Logan was to ride into the mountains with Windham, the colonel would make certain he wouldn't return alive. Yet, even though every line of his rugged body had tautened with barely checked fury, Victoria discerned that Logan was not the least bit afraid of the military man. Did Logan truly intend on betraying his friend

Night Wolf, or was the offer an attempt to postpone the hour of reckoning?

She marveled at Logan's control and realized that he'd spoken the truth in the mountains. He did not suffer from ordinary human fears. She didn't consider his courage a positive attribute, however. Surely he would be in less danger if he respected the colonel's hatred.

"My men will arrive shortly to make sure you reach my office without any unforeseen complications," Windham informed Logan with barely veiled contempt. "Come along, Athena. We've delayed our meal long enough."

As one, the couple continued on their way. Victoria noted that before being led away by her husband, Mrs. Windham allowed herself one hurried glance at Logan. In that single brief look, Victoria thought she detected a flash of poignant longing in the woman's overly bright eyes.

"Well, my goodness, that was quite a scene." Constance Pritchert fanned herself with a napkin as she stared at Logan. "That man has taken a strong aversion to you."

"You ought to rip off his privates and use 'em for target practice," Madison suggested spiritedly, her blue eyes shooting sparks.

"Madison!" both Martin and Constance Pritchert chided in unison.

Though she did not say so, Victoria viewed the girl's proposal as sound.

Logan laughed harshly as he returned to his chair. "I suspect his wife already does that on a regular basis."

No one bothered to chastise Logan for the crude remark.

"What are you going to do?" A marked concern etched Martin's normally benign features as he, too, sat down. "It's obvious Windham hates you and would rather see you dead than have you come back alive from the mountains."

"I don't have a choice. Even though I'm a civilian, Windham has the authority to order me to lead him to Night Wolf."

From Logan's casual statement, one would never have surmised his life hung in the balance.

"But you can't do that!" Madison protested. "Night Wolf saved my life after Pa was killed by those claim jumpers. Why, my bones would have been picked clean by the buzzards if he hadn't shown up when he did."

"Don't worry about Night Wolf, Maddy." Logan smiled reassuringly at the distraught girl. "The last time I talked to him, he told me he was moving the tribe northward."

"If you lead Windham to an abandoned Shoshone village, he'll probably shoot you on the spot," Martin pointed out grimly.

"But you just spoke with Night Wolf yesterday," Victoria felt compelled to say. "How much distance can an old man travel in that short period of time, especially if he's trying to move an entire tribe?"

Four pairs of surprised eyes regarded Victoria. She couldn't imagine what she'd said to provoke such a reaction from them.

"Where'd you get the idea that Night Wolf was an old man?" Madison asked in a loud voice as she absently blew a couple of drooping ringlets from her eyes. "Why, I expect he's younger than Logan, and you can't rightly call Logan old."

Victoria looked at Logan in confusion. "But you said he was a very elderly, frail man."

A dark flush stained Logan's high cheekbones. "I was probably referring to Night . . . *Wind* at the time."

"Who the blazes is Night Wind?" Madison asked. "I never heard tell of him before, and I thought I'd met everyone in Night Wolf's tribe."

"He's an old, toothless Indian chief," Victoria filled in helpfully, wondering how on earth Logan could say he'd been describing someone other than Night Wolf.

"Well, that's neither here nor there," Martin interjected. "If you ride out of town with Windham, I don't think you'll be returning, especially if you fail to deliver Night Wolf."

As the statement's validity registered on them, an oppressive silence hung over the table. The abrupt arrival of four somber-faced men dressed in bright blue military gear only heightened the escalating tension.

"Mr. Logan Youngblood?" one of them inquired respectfully.

Logan rose. "Yes?"

"You're to come with us."

"Don't go with them, Logan." Victoria and Madison both voiced the same plea as they pushed back their chairs and jumped to their feet.

Logan looked from one to the other with unexpected tenderness. "Ladies, I appreciate your concern, but I have no choice other than to accept these gentlemen's invitation to join their commanding officer."

"But Windham's sitting right over there with his wife, feeding his weasely face," Madison blurted out.

Logan rolled his eyes. The soldiers, however, looked anything but amused at Madison's insulting reference to their commanding officer.

"Maddy, behave yourself."

The young woman's chin rose mutinously as she jammed her fist into the folds of her prolifically ruffled gown. "I got me a gun here, and I'm fixin' to shoot daylight into the first one of you mangy varmints who makes a move toward Logan."

"Oh, my God!" Constance Pritchert cried.

Victoria was marginally calmer than the older woman, because Madison had stuck her hand into the same pocket where she'd tucked the wad of bills she'd won gambling with Herbie. Still, neither the soldiers nor Logan knew that the unseen bulge outlined beneath the pink fabric of her frilled dress was not a pistol.

"Maddy, stop your theatrics and sit down," Logan commanded succinctly.

Victoria held her breath. She honestly didn't know what the unpredictable rebel would do. Inwardly, though, she applauded the girl's courage.

At last Madison yielded to Logan's rigid glare and returned in a dejected slump to her chair.

Victoria, however, remained standing.

Logan flicked a significant glance from her to the empty chair beside her. "You may also be seated, Victoria."

"I . . ." She licked her suddenly dry lips. "I should like to go with you and these nice soldiers to the Colonel's office."

"And why is that?" Logan inquired softly. "Do you have a gun with which you'd like to ventilate the 'nice' soldiers?"

Victoria flushed. Leave it to Logan to resort to his particular brand of dark humor at a time like this. "Of course not. I have some important information to provide Colonel Windham."

"It's probably best if you remain here, ma'am," one of the men said, not unkindly. "If the colonel needs to speak with you, he'll send for you."

Aware that she'd drawn the attention of all present in the dining room, Victoria forced herself to appear utterly unmoved by the anxiety she suffered.

"I have no wish to argue with you, sir," she said smoothly. "It's just that I know the Indian you're seeking—I believe he's called Night Wolf—has left the Idaho Territory. When Mr. Youngblood accompanied me to Trinity Falls from the fort, we encountered the...savage. He had his entire tribe with him and they were headed . . . west. As this encounter happened more than a week ago, there's no way Mr. Youngblood will be able to guide you to him. The plain and simple truth is that Night Wolf could be anywhere."

Of course, there was nothing plain or simple—or truthful—about what she'd just said. Victoria waited for either a bolt of lightning or a bullet to strike her down for voicing such an outrageous falsehood. She knew that everyone at their table was aware of her lie. After all, until a few minutes ago she hadn't even known that the Shoshone wasn't an old man. And, she'd publicly announced her association to Logan to all present.

Despite her inner turmoil, she was conscious of Madison's admiring gaze. Oddly, earning the plucky girl's approval eased some of Victoria's tension. As long as she didn't let her glance stray to Logan's glowering countenance, she thought she would be able to pull off her incredible bluff.

"Maybe you should come with us, ma'am."

"What the hell do you think you're doing?"

Logan's gritty question slammed into Victoria's diminishing confidence with the force of a powerful fist. From the Prairie Rose, the soldiers had taken them to, of all unlikely places, a Methodist church to wait for Colonel Windham to arrive.

"It should be obvious," she replied in a shaking, low-pitched voice, having no wish to draw the attention of the uniformed men who left her and Logan to their own devices in the back of the high-beamed chapel. "I'm saving your life. Again."

Logan's black eyebrows formed an angry vee. His tightly reined features radiated bleak fury. "Honey, you don't know what you're getting into. Windham isn't exactly rational where I'm concerned. The best thing you can do is to stay out of his way. I'll handle things on my own."

"The last time you 'handled' things, you ended up in a stockade," she reminded him.

"Victoria, the matter isn't up for debate. I'm telling you I don't want you involved. There's no telling what Windham might do. I've got the feeling he's close to the edge. If he's pushed too far, I don't think he'd balk at hanging a woman."

Logan's words struck Victoria with the force she knew he'd intended. Her knees might be trembling, but nothing he could say would make her leave him. She'd let him walk out of her life once, believing they could never have a future together. She'd been terribly wrong, and not because she'd discovered Logan wasn't on the run. She'd been wrong because she'd let something come between her and the man who'd stolen her heart. She refused to make that mistake again.

And even if Logan didn't love her, even if his stated intent to marry her was based on nothing more than arrogant desire, she would not forsake him. His pride might not want to let him admit it, but she was his best chance of staying alive. She thought briefly about the heroines who peopled her treasured books and realized they shared one common trait. Courage.

She was about to demonstrate to Logan and herself that she possessed that same noble quality. If she didn't pass out first, she thought, trying to manage a deep breath despite the constraints of her corset.

"I assume Windham's seemingly unreasonable animosity has been kindled because of your, er...association with his wife," Victoria returned primly. "Through the ages it's been well documented that a husband tends to be possessive of his wife's faithfulness. Good grief, until quite recently duels have been fought over such incidents."

"I never slept with the woman," Logan said with even-paced savagery.

Victoria knew her face was crimson. "You're certain of that?"

"Lord, just when I thought you'd condemned me for every conceivable flaw a man could possess, you've come up with a new crime to lay at my door."

"Well, she's quite beautiful, and she does seem to... uh...be greatly attracted to you."

Logan flushed. "What makes you say that?"

"She gazed at you most longingly."

"That's it? A woman looks at me and I stand condemned of seducing her?" Outrage coated the question.

She was tempted to tell him that if his reputation with women in general wasn't in such shambles, the bizarre situation would never have arisen, but she refrained from assaulting that weak point. She wasn't about to berate Logan for his past when his future hung in such desperate uncertainty.

"Not by me, Logan," she whispered sincerely. "I believe you when you say that nothing amiss occurred between you and Athena Windham. But, clearly, the woman's husband has grave doubts about the matter, and those doubts are clouding what is probably a usually clear-thinking military mind. Still, I'm convinced I can appeal to his practical side."

"Victoria, I swear to God, if you don't leave now, while you have the chance, I'm going to turn your over my knee and administer some sweet justice to your backside."

"I don't think those soldiers will let you," she pointed out with strained patience. Apparently it was asking too much for Logan to believe in her. "You know, it's extremely annoying of you to keep threatening to punish me as if I were an unruly child. You ought to be thanking me, instead."

"Victoria—"

"It wouldn't hurt you to have some confidence in me," she said, cutting him off before he could issue any more threats. "If you didn't suffer from an overabundance of manly arrogance, you would be able to admit I'm in the perfect position to extricate you from the snare in which Colonel Windham has trapped you."

"I don't know what the hell you're talking about, but—"

"Of course you don't," she said, interrupting him again. "Because you're a man who thinks women are useful for only one thing."

A sudden gleam flickered in Logan's dark eyes. There was no doubt in her mind as to what he thought that *one* thing was.

"Don't stop now," he said huskily. "You've got my full attention."

"Pray pull your thoughts from . . . er . . . ah . . ."

"Yes?" he prompted softly.

"Logan, a man standing on the brink of disaster should have his mind set on lofty matters," she intoned repressively. "You issued an ultimatum that I was to marry you, and—"

A tinge of uncertainty entered Logan's usually confident gaze. "I admit my proposal was a bit rushed, and not overly romantic, but I'd hardly call it an ultimatum."

"Women have probably been dispatched to prison with more sentiment than you demonstrated in your office," she observed with asperity.

"Honey, you weren't exactly in the mood to listen to any sentimental blatherings about love."

Victoria's heart took the hit dead center. Was that how Logan thought about love? *Sentimental blatherings?* Of course, she reflected dejectedly, men who abandoned brides at the altar probably were not, in general, a romantic lot.

"Be that as it may, I...I've decided that I owe you a great deal for getting me safely to Trinity Falls. Marrying you, however, as a repayment of your services, seems unreasonably excessive. Helping you escape Colonel Windham's malevolent grasp will be a much more fair exchange."

She interpreted Logan's thunderous glare as an indication that he wasn't in full accord with her decision. Before either of them could continue the discussion, the door to the church swung open and Colonel Windham swaggered into the chapel.

A charged silence gripped the room. For a moment, everything stood stock-still; then movement seemed to spiral around them as the soldiers appeared at her and Logan's side and ushered them to the front area, where Windham stood waiting, like a poisonous spider decked out in military regalia.

"Lieutenant Lawson told me you had some information you wanted to provide, Miss Amory."

She could see in the man's cold blue eyes that he'd already made up his mind that anything she said would have no effect on the decision he'd already reached to have Logan guide him into the mountains.

She surmised her best way of dealing with the officer was with a direct frontal attack, something he probably wouldn't be anticipating from a woman.

"When Mr. Youngblood and I were traveling to Trinity Falls, we encountered an Indian named Night Wolf and his tribe."

"You mean Logan took you to their village," Windham suggested harshly.

Victoria shook her head. "No, we were on the move, and so was Night Wolf."

"Heading west, as I believe you told one of my men?"

Victoria realized the story she'd told in the hotel dining room had already been repeated to the officer.

"That's right. So you see, Mr. Youngblood's presence won't be of any assistance to you. He won't be able to take you to Night Wolf."

Colonel Windham studied her with such unveiled disgust that Victoria suddenly had grave doubts about trying to reason with the man. Maybe Logan had been right. Maybe the officer was incapable of altering the brutal fate he seemed determined to inflict.

"You have my congratulations, Youngblood."

She felt Logan stiffen beside her at the mocking words.

"Congratulations for what?" he asked, his tone guarded.

"For finding yet another victim for your lustful games." His sneering gaze swept over Victoria with enough calculated contempt to make her feel unclean. "She's a cut above the usual doxies you get to spread their legs for you."

Logan gave no warning before he attacked. One moment he stood beside her, and the next he lunged at Colonel Windham's throat. The uniformed men around her sprang into action, trying futilely to pull him off Windham.

They wrestled on the floor, crashing over chairs, slamming against a desk and knocking down the soldiers attempting to jerk Logan from their commanding officer.

The savage melee was unlike anything Victoria had ever witnessed. The unleashed violence of flying fists, harsh grunts and coarse oaths made her recoil, even as she sought a way to end the horribly unfair fight. She noticed that, despite being outnumbered, Logan appeared to be on the verge of pounding the life from Windham.

It was by accident that her desperate gaze fell upon the wicked-looking pistol that had been left unattended on the desk. Instinctively she reached for the weapon. Their wagon master had provided rudimentary instructions on using firearms before they left Independence. Her knowledge was sufficient for her to cock the gun and wave it threateningly.

"Stop, or I'll shoot!"

The command had no effect upon the thrashing men.

She held her arm high, closed her eyes and pulled the trigger. The subsequent explosion inside four walls brought about an immediate cessation of falling blows.

The men jumped to their feet and drew their own weapons. Too late, Victoria realized she was hopelessly outgunned. Logan staggered to his feet, absently using the back of his hand to wipe the blood from his split lip. The sight of his beloved face once more battered by an unjust beating fueled her anger to white-hot fury.

"Put down the gun, Miss Amory."

As one would have assumed the command came from Colonel Windham. She derived a savage shaft of pleasure at how many blows Logan had managed to land upon the officer's bruised and bleeding visage.

"What will you do if I don't—shoot me?"

"Victoria..." the cautionary use of her name came from Logan.

"Yes, darling?"

At the high-pitched endearment, Logan raised an eyebrow. She couldn't imagine what he was thinking, but suddenly she felt quite fearless. Holding a loaded gun no doubt contributed to the heady feeling.

"It would probably be a good idea to do as Colonel Windham says."

"I don't think we need to be too concerned about his opinions any longer."

"And why is that, Miss Amory?" the officer inquired with ominous blandness.

"It's just occurred to me that you do not realize with whom you're dealing. I am not, as you so crudely phrased it a moment ago, one of Logan's 'doxies.' It just so happens that my father is a federal judge who has many friends in high places, the kind of friends who would not take kindly to seeing his daughter publicly or privately abused by a member of the military."

Windham wiped his bloodied mouth with his sleeve. "Am I supposed to accept your word that you're who you say you are?"

Despite his scorn, Victoria stood taller. "I'm not in the habit of having my word doubted."

"When you lie down with dogs, you shouldn't be surprised to get up with fleas, Miss Amory."

She met his contemptuous stare head-on. "What a quaint expression. It puts me in mind of something Senator Wilson is fond of saying—something about it's not what you know in life, but who." She smiled thinly. "Father had the senator and his wife over for dinner shortly before I left Boston. It was quite a festive gathering, what with General Bradshaw and his wife in attendance, also. It's hard for me to remember if the general was more excited at the news of his impending fatherhood or his transfer to the capital."

Windham's eyes glittered briefly, but then a look of resignation settled over his mauled face. "You are free to leave, Miss Amory."

"I'm free to leave only if Logan accompanies me," she returned unflinchingly.

"Mr. Youngblood hasn't completed his duty as a citizen of the United States by providing his assistance in locating hostile Indians."

"I don't think my father would share that opinion," she mused with deliberate emphasis. "Mr. Youngblood and I are engaged to be married. As you can see, I am not exactly fresh from the schoolroom. My father has been waiting for some time for me to provide him with a son-in-law. In fact, I daresay that the continued good state of Logan's health is of paramount importance to my father."

A look of bitter surrender flashed in Windham's gaze, and Victoria sensed she had won this battle. Her feeling of euphoria grew. She had done it! She had saved Logan's life!

She shot him a quick, victorious glance. Instead of looking properly grateful or admiring, Logan wore an inexplicably shuttered expression.

"Naturally, I'm inclined to respect the wishes of a federal court judge," the colonel told her.

She graced him with a conciliatory smile. "I'm relieved to hear that."

"So much so, in fact, that I've decided to see his daughter securely married to the man he appears to think so highly of."

"What?"

"You heard me, Miss Amory. Since you claim this man is your fiancé, what possible objection could you have to a speedy marriage that will place him even more securely under your father's protection? While I admit I could not in clear conscience ask a married civilian to risk his life for his country, I would have few qualms about making such a request of a bachelor."

Victoria was aware of Windham's expectant scrutiny. Did he think she would back down in the face of his direct challenge?

She glanced around the empty church. "You mean here and now?"

"Lieutenant, tell Reverend Donally that we require his services."

Victoria swallowed. She dared not look at Logan, for fear of the rage she thought she might see. He *had* asked her to marry him, she reminded herself. In fact, he'd been quite bullish about the matter. But he could have hardly anticipated being forced at gunpoint to exchange his vows. And it was possible he hadn't been sincere in the offer, she reminded herself. Perhaps he'd just wanted to... have her compliant body at his disposal while he conducted another of his scandalous affairs.

"Is there a problem, Miss Amory?"

She forced herself to smile. "No, of course not. I just assumed I'd be married in something a little more elaborate than a day dress."

"Tsk, tsk, madame. Surely those are small considerations when undertaking a holy union of this magnitude."

I really hate this man, Victoria thought.

"There's something else you need to attend to, Colonel Windham."

The officer's gaze narrowed. "And what is that, Miss Amory? Did you wish for my men to pick flowers to decorate the church?"

She *wished* she were a man and could direct a few blows of her own at the wretched creature. "When Logan was put in the stockade, one of your soldiers stole his timepiece. I want it returned to him."

Windham turned to Logan. "You're accusing one of my men of being a thief?"

Logan's expression was coldly composed. "Forget about it. I can always buy a new watch. Get Donally."

Victoria wondered what Logan was thinking as the soldier left to collect the reverend. She decided she wasn't in a hurry to find out. The important thing was that she'd saved his life. Again. Too bad she hadn't been able to recover his timepiece for him, also.

Chapter Twenty-One

"You knew exactly what weakness of Windham's to threaten. You attacked his career in the military."

Those were the first words Logan had spoken since he'd become her husband. The soldiers who escorted them to the Prairie Rose had done so in silence. The men were gone now, and she and Logan stood outside her hotel room.

"Something about the way he strutted in his precisely pressed uniform, with all its glittering braid and dangling medals, made me think that, next to the love of his wife, being an officer was the most important thing in his life."

"And you quite ruthlessly exploited that weak spot in his character," Logan continued reflectively, gently crowding her against the closed door. "I had no idea you were such a...masterful woman."

She stared into Logan's newly battered face, wondering at his enigmatic tone of voice. Did he not approve of how she'd taken charge of the tense situation inside the chapel to save his life? Or was he upset that her threats to Colonel Windham had resulted in a hasty marriage to a woman he hardly knew? She recalled the furtive glances she'd slanted toward him while Reverend Donally conducted the brief wedding ceremony.

Did Logan resent the manner in which he'd been forced at gunpoint to become her husband?

But just that morning he'd proposed of his own volition, she reminded herself with desperate hope. In fact, he'd practically ordered her to marry him. She searched his indecipherable expression, yearning to see a hint of satisfaction at the unexpected outcome of her interference.

"Logan," she breathed uncertainly. "You're not upset about... about us, are you?"

He brushed his bruised knuckles across her cheek. Seeing the kindling warmth in his steady gaze, she thought that, had his bottom lip not been swollen, he might have smiled. "Go inside. We'll talk later."

She stiffened. "What is there to talk about?"

"All kinds of things."

"Can't we discuss them now?"

"I want to wash off the remnants of my scuffle with Windham's men."

"It was hardly a scuffle," she protested. "Your clothes are torn and streaked with blood!"

"Brings back memories of how we met, doesn't it?" he drawled.

Her thoughts spun back to how he'd looked that first morning, when he stumbled from the stockade. He'd resembled a magnificent, untamed beast. She considered him now and swallowed. Nothing had changed. She'd lost her heart to a passionate, possessive being who'd laid waste to the barriers she erected against him.

And he was her husband.

"Logan, come inside. I'll tend your wounds," she offered, finding it difficult to speak past the thickness in her throat.

He shook his head. "For once, my managing lady, we'll do things my way."

He leaned forward. She thought he was going to kiss her, but he reached around her instead and opened the door. With a firm shove, he sent her into the chamber.

Before she could object to his high-handed tactics, the door closed, and she was alone in her room.

"Well, what happened?"

Victoria jumped. She wasn't alone, after all. Madison Earley, ruffles and springing ringlets in motion, crossed the suite.

"Where's Logan?" the girl demanded.

"In his room."

"What's he doing there?"

"Taking a bath, I think," Victoria answered absently, wondering how he had the gall to say he wanted to do things *his* way, when all along he'd dominated the events between them.

"He looked clean to me. Why's he washing up in the middle of the day?" Genuine curiosity filled the girl's blue eyes.

"Because he's a man." Victoria sighed. "And men are really very odd creatures."

"But Windham let him go," Madison said, fiddling with one of her ringlets. "I'd say that's downright amazin', considering he was mad as hops."

Victoria found herself studying the pulchritudinous ruffles and ringlets engulfing the young woman speaking so earnestly. "Uh, Madison, who picked out your dress and styled your hair?"

"I did," the girl boasted with heart-tugging pride. "Logan said he was sending for a real lady to teach me. Even if I don't know how to read or write or talk fancy, I wanted to look nice." She shook the swirling skirt's flounces. "How'd I do?"

A wellspring of tenderness rose within Victoria. Not for all the first editions in the world would she hurt the vulnerable girl's feelings.

"I'd say you did fine."

Whistling under his breath, Logan rose from his bath. The movement sent soapy water sluicing over the sides of the tub. He disregarded the small puddles he padded through to grab a towel. He was too happy with the world to find fault with anything.

He had her. There wasn't going be to a long-drawn-out battle to claim Miss Victoria Amory as his lawfully wedded wife, after all. Her own clever machinations had brought about the union he'd feared he would have to wage war to accomplish.

He needn't concern himself with how he was going to lure her into his bed tonight. She was damned well going to be there because she belonged to him, before the eyes of man and God.

Absently he slung the towel over his shoulder. He was reaching for the trousers he'd laid across a chair when the sound of the door to his suite opening caught his attention. He broke off in midwhistle and wrapped the towel around his waist. There wasn't a doubt in the world as to who'd just entered the room.

Victoria hadn't been pleased at having to postpone, even briefly, the matters they needed to settle between them. Out of respect for her sensibilities, he would cover himself for the first few minutes of their discussion. Then, he thought, smiling confidently as he strode from his bedchamber, tonight was going to come sooner than he'd dared hope.

He stepped into the sitting room and halted. His visitor most emphatically was not his new bride.

"Mrs. Windham," he growled, "what the hell are you doing here?"

Dressed in a flawlessly designed light blue silk gown, the woman smiled with startling composure. "I really tried to stay away, but I couldn't. Don't worry, my husband has no idea where I am. Don't be angry with me, Logan," she entreated him, her mouth curving ruefully. "I know I've caused you a great deal of trouble, but I'm ready to make that up to you."

"That's not necessary," Logan hastily assured her, gripping his towel more firmly. The openly hungry expression in the woman's bold gaze made him nervous. He was reluctant to employ force against her, but male instinct warned him it might be the only means by which he could evict her from his room. Hell, just the thought of the scene that would cause made his blood grow cold. "Why don't you do us both a favor and leave? We'll forget you were ever here."

"But I don't want to forget," she said lightly. "Come now, Logan, we're both adults. I've heard about your exploits with women. You're Trinity Falls's very own Casanova." Her fingers strayed to the top button of her gown. "It's not as if I'm asking you to do what you haven't done with countless others. I won't make any social demands on you." She laughed softly. "I have a husband, after all."

"Then go to him and let him—"

"He rides a horse better than he rides a woman," she countered bluntly, moving to the next button. "Don't you understand? I want to be made love to by a man who's dark and mysterious and who'll know how to please me. My husband has received transfer orders. This is the last chance for us to be together."

She glided toward him.

"Stop! Don't come any closer!"

Logan felt like an ass for uttering the melodramatic words, but he'd never been in a situation like this before, that of being stalked by a married woman.

"Don't fight it," she cooed silkily. "I promise to please you. There's certain acts I've heard that women can perform for men. Unfortunately, my husband finds such things distasteful, but I'm sure you won't."

Logan realized he'd been backing up as Athena Windham drew closer. Her gown was fully unbuttoned now, and she'd contrived to dress herself so her that nude bosom was exposed above her corset. He didn't experience one twinge of desire. Panic was the overriding prod that had him reaching for her shoulders to push her away.

The woman was stronger than she looked, Logan discovered as she launched herself at him. He felt the towel drop to the floor and swore.

At that perilous juncture, he heard the door to his suite open again. With his luck, he expected to see Windham standing in the doorway with a drawn gun.

It was Victoria, though, not the enraged colonel, who stood before him.

Logan swore again, crudely and succinctly. There wasn't a woman alive who would believe he was an innocent victim of Athena Windham's unwelcome advances. For the first time in years, he'd held happiness in his hands; now it was about to be snatched from him.

He opened his mouth to defend himself. Dammit, none of this was his fault, and no matter what it took, he was going to convince Victoria of that.

"Mrs. Windham, you really must leave Logan alone. He's a married man now, and he belongs to me. I have no intention of sharing him with anyone else."

Dumbfounded by Victoria's calm manner, Logan freed himself from Athena's grip. Realizing he was buck naked, he plucked the towel from the floor and wrapped it around his waist.

Athena Windham also exhibited an amazing degree of composure, Logan thought as the woman methodically rebuttoned her dress. "I'm very disappointed in you, Miss Amory."

"It's Mrs. Youngblood." But curiosity obviously got the better of her. "Why are you disappointed in *me?*"

"You've married 'Passion's Pirate'!"

Logan's skin burned at the offensive title. He'd hoped Victoria would never hear it.

"And that's really not fair," Athena continued, drifting toward the doorway before pausing. "Men like Logan Youngblood aren't meant to be ordinary husbands," she said chidingly. "They're supposed to run free, like wild stallions who know no master. They're a dream all women share in the darkest hours before dawn. And once in a lifetime, if a woman is fortunate, she has a chance for him to make love to her."

Athena Windham shut the door quietly behind her.

"Victoria, you've got to let me explain."

"I would very much like to hear your explanation."

"That woman came into my room without an invitation! She . . . she threw herself at me."

"I see."

"And I was naked because I'd just taken a bath."

"That makes sense."

"Then you believe me?"

"Absolutely."

Logan's eyes narrowed. From the first moment he heard Victoria's voice, when he was locked in the stockade, it had been one pitched battle after another between them.

It was inconceivable that she would so easily accept his flimsy explanation of why she'd caught him in his bedchamber, stark naked, with a half-dressed woman in his arms.

"Why?"

"Why what?"

"Why do you believe me?" Logan held his breath. Would she tell him it was because she loved and trusted him? Or was the real truth that she didn't care that deeply about him and, therefore, was indifferent to whatever he did.

"I believe you because the very same thing happened to me."

"*What?*"

"Well, it wasn't exactly the same. My disaster was hardly on the scale of 'Passion's Pirate' being seduced by Athena, the Greek goddess of warfare."

"Damn it, Victoria. I never wanted you to hear that name!"

"'Passion's Pirate'?"

"For your own protection, honey, never say it within my hearing again."

A look of bone-melting softness filled her eyes. "Even before Constance Pritchert told me of it, I'd begun to think of you as my very own personal pirate."

Logan found redeeming merit in the formerly offensive title. Anything that pleased his new wife was fine with him.

"You were telling me about a compromising scene from your past," he prompted, moving toward her. It occurred to him that his sweet rescuer had on too many layers of clothing. He needed to do something about that.

"Now that I reflect upon it, there are a couple of similarities between my experience and yours. I was in my bedchamber, and I was wearing only my chemise and drawers. And when Mother and her friends entered my room in response to Mr. Threadgill's cries for help, he was minus his britches."

Logan stopped in his tracks. From Victoria's amused features, he sensed the incident had not been what it appeared—a young woman and her lover being caught in an illicit tryst. Still, he was enraged that a man had evidently tried to take advantage of her.

"You better tell me exactly what happened."

"It was all a misunderstanding. Mr. Horace Threadgill had climbed the trellis outside my chamber, bearing a rose for my sister. It was afternoon, and I'm certain he merely intended to leave it on her pillow as a token of his esteem."

"He sounds like a fool."

"An infatuated fool," Victoria said, in a wistful tone that Logan found strangely irritating. "He entered my room by mistake. As I said, it was a simple misunderstanding."

"And he lost his pants because . . ."

"I removed them."

Logan squeezed Victoria's shoulders. "Stop torturing me, honey. Tell me what happened."

She sighed, allowing him to draw her close. With her cheek resting against his chest, her words drifted up to him. "There was this really savage bee. It had been hiding inside the rose, waiting for an opportunity to attack an innocent person. Well, it proceeded to choose poor Horace Threadgill as its target by flying up his pant leg and assaulting him."

"Don't tell me," Logan said, his shoulders shaking. "You tried to help by removing the man's trousers so you could get to the bee."

"Are you laughing at me?"

He stared down at the auburn crown of her hair and smiled. "Never, honey. Never."

Some of Logan's light-heartedness faded as he recalled a scene from his past, when he'd walked into his brother's room and discovered Robeena. That situation had been hauntingly similar to the one Victoria had interrupted with Athena Windham.

The subtle doubts he'd experienced lately as to what he'd really seen that hideous night intensified. As if sensing his disquiet, Victoria tugged herself from his embrace and regarded him solemnly.

"Is something wrong?"

"I'm remembering an episode from my past, one regarding my older brother and my fiancée."

Her interested expression encouraged him to continue. "I caught them together, very much as you discovered me with Athena."

"That must have hurt you," she said, her tone filled with compassion. "Was your brother able to explain her presence in his room?"

"She was in his bed. I didn't stay for explanations."

"And now you're beginning to wonder if you should have?" she asked with uncanny intuitiveness.

"Yeah, honey. That's exactly what I'm wondering."

"This woman, your fiancée...was she the one you abandoned at the altar?"

Logan flinched. "Good Lord, how on earth did you find out about that?"

"Constance Pritchert enlightened me."

"Damn. I know she's Martin's wife and he loves her to distraction, but she's a real busybody."

"She was just warning me about your reckless reputation with women," Victoria observed charitably. "She didn't know it was too late for any warnings."

A cold place in Logan's heart began to thaw. It seemed the most natural thing in the world to wrap his hand around the back of Victoria's neck and pull her to him for a hot kiss.

Her soft palms stroked his chest. He knew he was moments away from disgracing himself with his new bride if he didn't gain control of the heat she stirred within him. Her sweet tongue agilely caressed the inside of his mouth. He groaned and deepened the already burning kiss.

When he lifted his mouth from hers, his heart was pounding. He was already fully aroused and aching to be inside her. With a frustrating groan, he shoved her gently from him.

Her green eyes were wide with feminine yearning and confusion. "What's wrong? Why did you stop?"

"Honey, I'm going to lock the damned door before anyone else comes charging into this suite."

A look of startled comprehension flashed across her features. His explanation surprised a giggle from her and, as if embarrassed, she put her hand over her mouth.

In that moment, seeing her in her prim and proper plaid jacket with the double rows of gray braiding at her cuffs and along the hem, her face flushed, her eyes huge and her hand trembling, Logan Youngblood knew he'd fallen hopelessly and irrevocably in love.

Before him was the woman who had not only saved his life twice—once at the stockade and this afternoon with her wily scheming—but had also saved him from the haunting loneliness that had infiltrated his soul without his even realizing it.

"I love you, Victoria Amory Youngblood."

A look of surprise crossed her features. Logan cursed his timing. He should have confessed his love the afternoon at the hot pools, when he seduced her.

Her nimble fingers went to her jacket. She wasted no time in discarding it. "And I love you, too, my fierce pirate."

It amazed him that he could be touched by her use of the name he loathed.

"Do you know how much power you hold over me?" he asked in bemusement.

She shook her head. "How can you say I have any power, when you make me feel as if I'm a fragile leaf caught in a wild windstorm?"

Her hands went to the front of her blouse, and she freed the buttons one by one. Whereas the identical act performed by Windham's wife had left him cold, Victoria's actions caused a raging conflagration to sweep through him.

"Oh, honey, the storm is inside me, and it's about to break."

He couldn't wait for her to remove her clothes. Instead, he strode forward and captured her in his arms. She squeaked delightfully as he carried her to his bed. In moments, he had her where he wanted her, completely, softly, deliciously nude, and writhing helplessly beneath his intimate caresses.

His fingers sought and found the sleek, wet channel that had been fashioned just for him. Her nails dug into his shoulders. He kissed her again and again. He couldn't get enough of her, couldn't get enough of feeling her smooth, silky skin brushing against him. Her nipples were pretty pink pebbles, and he savored their taste and texture as if he were a man who'd gone too long without sustenance.

She whimpered. "Oh, Logan, I don't know how much more of this I can take."

Her soft, womanly thighs parted. He wanted to wait, to draw her desire and his to their fullest, sharpest limits, but he couldn't. This woman owned him—heart, body and soul. There was no way he could delay for even a heartbeat returning to the tight, wet heat that had been seared into his memory.

When he entered her, he did so in one smooth stroke. She cried out his name again. It was impossible to think. This woman, his woman, had taken him to a reckless place of mindless ecstasy. He could only surrender to the primitive need within him to drive himself and her to the outer limits of their control.

He heard her frantic cry as she hovered on the brink of fulfillment, inhaled the smell of her unique feminine scent, felt the beginning tremors of her ultimate release. Sheathed completely within her, he experienced his own harshly demanding ascent to paradise.

He shouted her name and his love in one urgent, mangled breath.

Almost immediately, Logan regretted the nearly savage taking of his bride. He withdrew from her perspiration-slickened body with the guilty knowledge that he'd rutted with his wife in a carnal manner he'd never used with another woman. Hell, he thought grimly, he'd shown more consideration for the females he paid for than he had toward Victoria.

With a pang of remorse, he studied his companion's achingly fragile, beautifully formed body. He wanted to reach out to her, to draw her to him, but he was afraid of her reaction. Her dark red lashes rested against her pale cheeks, and her arms lay weakly at her sides. Her thighs were still parted, and damned if he didn't feel another rush of hot desire. The little red nest of curls held his unwavering regard. He wanted nothing more than to lean forward and use his mouth and his tongue to bring her to another shattering climax.

Lord, he was hopeless.

"You're not planning on going anywhere, are you?"

Her drowsy voice wafted over him like a warm morning breeze.

"I hadn't planned on it," he said neutrally, waiting for the outburst that was sure to come.

"That's good, because you know I really didn't like it the first time you made love to me, and—"

"Honey," he interjected, wanting desperately to forestall her entirely justified complaint. "I don't know what came over me, but I promise the next time will be different."

"The next time?" she asked in that same lazy voice.

Lord, she wasn't going to tell him that he'd so disgusted her that she wasn't going to give him another chance to prove he could be a considerate lover. Logan's jaw clenched in determination. Just because they'd gotten off to a rocky start, that didn't mean he intended to be shut out of his wife's bed.

"There definitely is going to be a next time," he said harshly.

She opened her eyes and regarded him with obvious bewilderment. "But, that's just the point. I don't want *this* time to be over yet. I want you to come back into my arms. I want us to kiss some more. I want to...touch you all over, and I want you to..."

"Yes?" he asked, his lungs fairly bursting and his skin strung hot and tight across his rapidly hardening body.

"I want you to touch me. Everywhere."

A feral joy erupted in Logan. Something very basic and very male inside him was pleased to know he'd satisfied his woman and she wanted more of him.

"I want to kiss you all over," he told her huskily.

Her legs shifted against the bed coverings. "You do?"

He nodded. "Your skin is such a beautiful golden color. I want to taste every bit of it."

A lovely pink blush spread to the tips of her breasts and climbed up her throat. "I know you're my husband, but it's very...unsettling when you look at me like that and say such things to me."

He ran a fingertip across the satiny flesh that beckoned.

"I like unsettling you, Victoria."

"And you should know," she continued, in a breathless voice that bit into the tattered fragments of the control he'd barely managed to resurrect, "that my skin isn't truly golden. If the light were better, you would see I'm covered in freckles!"

Her definitely unhappy wail made Logan smile. "And I saw every one of them when we made love at the hot pools."

"I've heard that lemon juice can bleach them, but I haven't tried it."

He leaned forward and planted a kiss on her stomach.

"Logan!"

"Yes, sweet?" He began to use his hands with sensual intent, and his lips, too.

"Oh!"

"Do you like that?" He breathed the question against her passion-scented curls. "I've been wanting to do it for a long time."

"Oh, my goodness!"

And, for the next little while, Logan Youngblood found himself serenaded by his lovely bride's lilting cries.

He felt as if he truly had captured a little red bird and taught her to sing her own special song just for him. He knew his years of feeling like an outcast were over. She'd freed him from a prison darker than men could build. She'd taught his heart to take flight. And together, with Madison, they would live in the sunlight of love and happiness.

Logan's future hung before him like a glimmering, newly minted gold coin. Even the idea of his healing his estrangement with his brother no longer seemed impossible.

"Logan..."

He trailed his fingertips down her spine as she lay pressed up close to him. "Hmm?"

"You're going to have to build us a house, you know."

He cupped her bottom and squeezed lightly. "Am I?"

Her soft moan made his heart expand.

"A hotel, even one as nice as this one, is no place to raise Madison."

"I suppose I'll have to build a mansion to hold all those books of yours."

Victoria's cheek rested against his chest, and when she spoke he felt the whisper of her breath upon his skin. "It doesn't have to be a mansion. I want a home to hold our love, a home where Madison can grow up surrounded by that love. A home where, in time, our own children can be nurtured and cherished."

Logan closed his eyes, embarrassed by the thickness in his throat that his wife's words caused. "There will be room for your books, too, honey. I'll build you a library big enough to hold every single volume you carted here, plus space for a thousand more. I can afford the best for us."

It pleased him that he spoke the truth; his wife would lack no material luxury.

She twisted from his side and leaned over him, regarding him with an earnest intensity that made his heart tremble.

"Darling, I would be content to live in a tent with you, if that was all you had to offer."

"When you thought I was a drifter on the wrong side of the law, you sent me packing," he pointed out. "I want to make sure you understand I have the means to take care of you. For a lifetime."

He'd always wondered if a part of the reason Robeena turned to Burke had been that he was the older and more established Youngblood brother.

She pressed a kiss to his lips, then raised her head. "You'll never know how much I regretted doing that."

"Did you?"

She nodded. "I changed my mind, but there was no way for me to find you." The sheen of unshed tears touched her green eyes. "I knew I'd made the worst mistake of my life when I let you go, but I didn't know how to fix it. I thought I'd lost you forever."

A tear splashed on his chest. Logan hugged her to him. "Hush, darling, don't cry."

"I can't help myself," Victoria whispered thickly, thinking how close she'd come to never seeing Logan again. "I was such a self-righteous prig where you were concerned."

"We both made our share of mistakes." His hands caressed her back.

"And then I was furious with you when I realized that you'd made a fool of me by going along with my false assumptions about your character."

"Or lack thereof."

She lightly pinched his chest. "I'm trying to be serious."

"Ouch. All right, we'll be serious, then. There just came a point, honey, when I gave up trying to convince you I wasn't a wild desperado."

"I apologize."

Logan was silent for a moment. "Is that it? I was expecting something a little more elaborate."

She placed a moist kiss on his chest. "I'm willing to humor you."

"Well, now..."

Logan rolled over. Victoria found herself on her back gazing up at his bruised, mildly predatory features.

"Yes?"

"Say you're sorry for thinking I was a half-wit."

"I'm sorry."

His wide palm stroked her breast. "And for thinking I was an outlaw."

"Yes..."

He teased her hardening nipple. "For thinking I was going to steal Night Wolf's gold."

"Yes."

He lowered his head and used the tip of his tongue to caress her. "For assuming I couldn't read..."

"Yes!"

He suckled gently. "For thinking I'd come to the bank to rob it."

"Oh Logan..." He'd set another of his masterful blazes. "Forgive me for ever doubting you."

He stared at her with open, undisguised hunger. "And?"

"And..." And *what?* she thought, utterly swept up in his possessive brand of lovemaking.

"You trust me completely."

"I proved that when I didn't find a gun and shoot you when I caught Mrs. Windham in your room!"

"But I didn't know if that was because you trusted me, or because I didn't matter to you."

Victoria's heart expanded wider to accept Logan's unexpected vulnerability. "Oh, you matter, darling...."

"Thank God."

His arms closed around her. Victoria turned this new knowledge over in her mind, the knowledge that a man could be strong, fearless *and* uncertain. She sensed he wouldn't like acknowledging such a weakness, but to her it wasn't weakness. She thought of her aloof father and realized that being married to a man capable of strong emotion and strong passion was a special blessing.

"And, if it'd make you happy, darling, I promise to shoot you if I ever find another woman in your arms."

She felt Logan's deep chuckle in a dozen interesting places.

"It makes me happy to know you belong to me."

"When did you know you loved me?"

It was a question that begged to be asked.

"Well, I *wanted* you from the start."

"Oh, Logan, you hated me on sight!"

He squeezed her. "Now pay attention, honey. We've got to get this right for our children. When I stepped out of that cell and laid eyes on you, I noticed right off that you were a fine-looking woman."

"You certainly didn't act as if you liked me. In fact, I remember most clearly that you were disappointed I wasn't the 'kid' who fed you those biscuits."

"Well, I took a liking to the 'kid.' I was visualizing a spunky tadpole with a lot of grit. What I found when I walked into the sunlight was a sassy female with a Boston accent and a wagon full of books."

"What's wrong with being from Boston? You're from there."

"I had a grudge against the place, but that's in the past now."

"It is?"

A smile touched his soul. "It's your birthplace, honey. As far as I'm concerned, that makes it Paradise."

"Oh..."

Victoria's little sighs and moans were demolishing Logan's ability to think.

"A-about that library?"

"What library?" he mumbled, losing himself in her scent and her texture.

"The one you want to build me..."

"What about it?"

"Well..." She did a little serious kissing of her own. "I was thinking that it's probably selfish of me to keep all those books to myself. A town like Trinity Falls should have a public library, don't you think?''

Think? Logan wasn't sure he could breathe, let alone think.

"Sure, honey, anything you say."

They were words she'd demanded when she so earnestly tried to initiate her "chain of command." But her days of trying to outmaneuver and reform Logan were past. As his caresses became bolder, Victoria Amory Youngblood abandoned herself completely to her beloved outcast's tender possession.

And a Western adventure wilder and more spectacular than any she'd ever envisioned.

* * * * *

Harlequin® Historical

Another spectacular medieval tale from
popular, award-winning author

SUZANNE BARCLAY

The next book in her ongoing
Sommerville Brothers series:

Knight's Ransom

Watch for this passionate story
of a French knight who captures
the daughter of his enemy for revenge,
but finds love with his captive instead!

**Coming this October
from Harlequin Historicals**

BIGB96-8

Merry Christmas, Baby!

A romantic collection filled with the magic of Christmas and the joy of children.

SUSAN WIGGS, Karen Young and Bobby Hutchinson bring you Christmas wishes, weddings and romance, in a charming trio of stories that will warm up your holiday season.

MERRY CHRISTMAS, BABY! also contains Harlequin's special gift to you—a set of FREE GIFT TAGS included in every book.

Brighten up your holiday season with *MERRY CHRISTMAS, BABY!*

Available in November at your favorite retail store.

HARLEQUIN ®

Look us up on-line at: http://www.romance.net

MCB

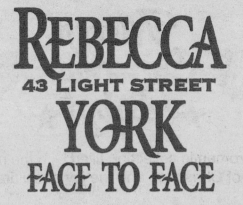

REBECCA
43 LIGHT STREET
YORK
FACE TO FACE

Bestselling author Rebecca York returns to "43 Light Street"
for an original story of past secrets, deadly deceptions—and
the most intimate betrayal.

She woke in a hospital—with amnesia...and with child.
According to her rescuer, whose striking face is the last
image she remembers, she's Justine Hollingsworth. But
nothing about her life seems to fit, except for the baby
inside her and Mike Lancer's arms around her. Consumed
by forbidden passion and racked by nameless fear, she
must discover if she is Justine...or the victim of some mind
game. Her life—and her unborn child's—depends on it....

Don't miss *Face To Face*—Available in October, wherever
Harlequin books are sold.

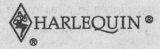

HARLEQUIN ®

You are cordially invited to a

HOMETOWN REUNION

September 1996—August 1997

Bad boys, cowboys, feuding families, arson, babies, mistaken identity, a mom on the run... Where can you find romance and adventure? Tyler, Wisconsin, that's where!

So join us in this not-so-sleepy little town and experience the love, the laughter and the tears of those who call it home.

WELCOME TO A
HOMETOWN REUNION

They're still talking about the last stranger who came to Tyler, and now there's another. He's an arson investigator with a job to do. But...his prime suspect's daughter and her kids make it increasingly hard for him to do what he must.

***The Reluctant Daddy* by Helen Conrad**

Available in October 1996 at your favorite retail outlet.

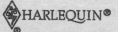

HARLEQUIN®

HTR2